Prepare to be dazzled by the
breathtaking beauty of India and
melt in the arms of a gorgeous tycoon!

Enjoy our new 2-in-1 editions of stories
by your favourite authors—

for double the romance!

with

A TRIP WITH THE TYCOON
by Nicola Marsh

INVITATION TO THE BOSS'S BALL
by Fiona Harper

Dear Reader

We hope you like our new look and format!

We want to give you more value for your mon[ey] and the same great stories from your favou[rite] authors! Now, each month, we're offering you [two] Mills & Boon® Romance volumes. Each volume [will] include two stories. This month:

A trip to India and an invitation to an oh-so-delicious boss's ball are on the itinerary

A TRIP WITH THE TYCOON
by Nicola Marsh
&
INVITATION TO THE BOSS'S BALL
by Fiona Harper

* * *

And follow the first steps and first smiles of these bouncing babies and their proud parents in…

CLAIMED: SECRET ROYAL SON
by Marion Lennox
&
EXPECTING MIRACLE TWINS
by Barbara Hannay

For more information on our makeover, and to buy other Romance stories that are exclusive to the website and the Mills & Boon Bookclub, please visit: www.millsandboon/makeover.co.uk.

The other titles available this month are: **KEEPING HER BABY'S SECRET** by Raye Morgan and **MEMO: THE BILLIONAIRE'S PROPOSAL** by Melissa McClone.

Best wishes

Kimberley Young

Senior Editor, Mills & Boon® Romance

A TRIP WITH
THE TYCOON

BY
NICOLA MARSH

MILLS & BOON

First published in Great Britain 2009
Harlequin Mills & Boon Limited,
Eton House, 18-24 Paradise Road, Richmond, Surrey TW9 1SR

© Nicola Marsh 2009

ISBN: 978 0 263 86965 1

Set in Times Roman 13 on 14½ pt
02-0909-49809

Harlequin Mills & Boon policy is to use papers that are natural, renewable and recyclable products and made from wood grown in sustainable forests. The logging and manufacturing process conform to the legal environmental regulations of the country of origin.

Printed and bound in Spain
by Litografia Rosés, S.A., Barcelona

Dear Reader

Travel is in my blood. I first flew at two months of age, and haven't stopped since! I love the different cultures, the food, the sights and the people of our big, wide world, and I have been lucky enough to visit many places.

For me, India evokes images of spices, saris, sun and sand. The people are as diverse as the delicious cuisine, their monuments steeped in tradition centuries old. It is a land of contrast, of mystique, and what better place to set a romance novel?

Such a spectacular setting is the perfect backdrop for Tamara and Ethan's story. Tamara, of Indian descent, is on a journey of self-discovery. Travelling on the majestic 'Palace on Wheels' train through Rajasthan, and later Goa, she never expects to find romance. Suave, sexy Ethan has other ideas, and the corporate pirate sweeps Tamara off her feet.

There's nothing like a holiday romance—but what happens when these two return to Melbourne? Turn the pages to find out!

I hope you enjoy this magical journey through India.

Happy reading!

Nicola

Visit Nicola's website at www.nicolamarsh.com for the latest news of her books.

For Uncle Ian and Rayner,
who kindly shared their recent memories of the
'Palace on Wheels' as I wrote this.
Thanks for the photos, the anecdotes, the laughs—
and for bringing the trip alive.

CHAPTER ONE

TAMARA RAYNE's high heels clacked impatiently against the cobblestones as she strode towards Ambrosia, Melbourne's hippest restaurant, a gourmet's delight and the place where she was trying to get her life back on track.

Her favourite butterscotch boots, patent leather with a towering heel—impractical yet gorgeous—never failed to invoke the stuff of her surname as plump drops splashed down from the heavens and lashed her in a stinging sheet.

With her laden arms and no umbrella, she needed a mythical knight in shining armour. She'd thought she'd had him once in Richard. How wrong she'd been.

Blinking back futile tears—wasted tears, angry tears—she pushed on Ambrosia's door with her behind, staggering with her load, almost slamming into her knight.

More of a pirate, really, a corporate pirate in a

designer suit with rain-slicked dark hair, roguish blue eyes and a devilish smile.

'Need a hand?'

Definitely devilish, and used to great effect if the constant parade of women traipsing through Ethan Brooks's life was any indication.

'You're back.'

'Miss me?'

'Hardly.'

She hadn't meant to sound so frosty but then, what was he doing? Flirting? She barely knew him, had seen him three times in the last year out of necessity, so why the familiarity?

'Too bad.' He shrugged, his roguish smile widening as he pointed to the bundle in her arms. 'Do you want help with that?'

Quashing the urge to take her load and run, she nodded. 'Thanks.'

He grunted as she offloaded the bag perched precariously on top of the rest. 'What's in here? Bricks for the new tandoori oven I've ordered?'

'Almost as heavy.'

Her voice wobbled, just a tad, and she swallowed, twice. It was the mention of the tandoori oven that did it.

Her mum had loved tandoori chicken, had scored the chicken to let the spices and yoghurt marinate into it, had painstakingly threaded the pieces onto skewers before grilling, while lamenting the loss of her real oven back in Goa.

Her mother had missed her homeland so much, despite living in Melbourne for the last thirty years of her life. It had been the reason they'd planned their special trip together: a trip back in time for her mum, a trip to open Tamara's eyes to a culture she'd never known even though Indian blood ran in her veins.

Thanks to Richard, the trip never happened and, while her mum had died three years ago and she'd come to terms with her grief, she'd never forgiven him for robbing her of that precious experience.

Now, more than ever, she needed her mum, missed her terribly. Khushi would've been her only ally, would've been the only one she trusted with the truth about Richard, and would've helped her reclaim her identity, her life.

Hot, bitter tears of regret stung her eyes and she deliberately glanced over Ethan's shoulder, focusing on anything other than the curiosity in his eyes.

'Can you take the rest? My arms are killing me.'

She knew he wouldn't push, wouldn't ask her what was wrong.

He hadn't pushed when she'd been detached and withdrawn following Richard's death while they'd sorted through the legal rigmarole of the restaurant.

He hadn't pushed when she'd approached him to use Ambrosia six months ago to kick-start her career.

Instead, he'd taken an extended business trip, had been aloof as always. There was a time she'd thought he disliked her, such was his distant demeanour whenever she entered a room.

But she hadn't wasted time figuring it out. He was Richard's mate and that was all the reason she needed to keep her distance. Ethan, like the rest of the planet, thought Richard was great: top chef, top entertainer, top bloke.

If they only knew.

'Sure.' He took the bulk of her load, making it look easy as he held the door open. 'Coming in?'

She didn't need to be asked twice as she stepped into the only place she called home these days.

Ambrosia: food of the gods. More like food for her soul.

It had become her refuge, her safe haven the last few months. Crazy, considering Richard had owned part of it, had been head chef since its inception, and they'd met here when she'd come to critique Melbourne's latest culinary hot spot.

For that alone she should hate the place.

But the welcoming warmth of Ambrosia, with its polished honey oak boards, brick fireplace and comfy cushioned chairs that had drawn her here every Monday for the last six months was hard to resist and what better place for a food critic determined to return to the workforce to practise her trade?

Throw in the best hot chocolate this side of the Yarra and she couldn't stay away.

As she dumped her remaining load on a nearby table and stretched her aching arms, her gaze drifted to the enigmatic man lighting a match to kindling in the fireplace.

What was he doing here?

From all accounts, Ethan was unpredictable, blew hotter and colder than a Melbourne spring breeze. His employees enjoyed working here but never knew when the imperturbable, ruthless businessman would appear.

She'd been happy to have the place to herself the last six months, other than the skilled staff and eager patrons who poured through the door of course, had been strangely uncomfortable the few times she and Ethan met.

There was something about him…an underlying steeliness, a hard streak, an almost palpable electricity that buzzed and crackled, indicative of a man in command, a man on top of his game and intent on staying there.

He straightened and she quickly averted her

gaze, surprised to find it had been lingering on a piece of his anatomy she had no right noticing.

She'd never done that—noticed him as a man. He was Richard's business partner, someone who'd always been distantly polite to her the few times their paths had crossed, but that was it.

So why the quick flush of heat, the flicker of guilt?

It had been a year since Richard's death, two since she'd been touched by a man, which went a long way to explaining her wandering gaze. She may be numb on the inside, emotionally anaesthetised, but she wasn't dead and any woman with a pulse would've checked out Ethan's rather impressive rear end.

'If I get you a drink, will you tell me what's in the bags?'

Slipping out of her camel trench coat, she slung it onto the back of a chair. She didn't want to tell him, didn't want to show him the culmination of half a year's work.

She'd come here for privacy, for inspiration, and having him here intruded on that. Ridiculous, considering he owned the place and could come and go as he pleased, but something about his greeting had rankled, something about that damn smile.

'I'd kill for a hot chocolate, thanks.'

'Coming right up.'

His gaze lingered on the bags before meeting hers, challenging. 'I won't give up until I know what's in there so why don't you just tell me?'

He stared at her, unflinching, direct, his persistence indicative of a guy used to getting his own way, a guy who demanded nothing less.

She fingered the hessian holding her future, *mind your own business* hovering on her lips. His authority niggled, grated, but he'd given her the opportunity to relaunch her career by using this place and she should be civil if nothing else.

'If you throw in a side of marshmallows, I'll show you.'

'You're on.'

With a half salute and a twinkle in his eyes, he strode towards the bar.

Ah…the pirate was in top form today. Full of swagger, cheek and suave bravado. She was immune to his charm, of course, but for a split second it felt good, great, in fact, to be on the receiving end of some of that legendary charm.

While he headed for the espresso machine behind the bar she plopped onto a chair, stretched her legs and wiggled her toes. She loved these boots, she really did, but they were nothing but trouble for the weather, her feet and her back, which gave a protesting twinge as she sat up.

Though that could be more to do with the ten-ton load she'd hefted up the street, but she'd had no choice. She held her future in her hands—literally—and, despite the gut feeling she was ready for this, it wouldn't hurt to get Ethan's opinion on it. If anyone knew this business inside out, he did.

'Here you go. One hot chocolate with a double side of marshmallows.'

He placed the towering glass in front of her, a strong Americano in front of him, and slid into the chair opposite, fixing her with a half-amused, half-laconic tilt of his lips.

'I've kept my side of the bargain, so come on, what's in there?'

'A girl can't think without a sip of chocolate first.'

She cradled the mug, inhaled the rich chocolate-fragrant steam, savoured the warmth seeping into her palms and, closing her eyes, took a deep sip, letting the sweet lusciousness glide over her taste buds and slide down her throat.

Ethan made a strange sound and her eyes flew open, confused by the flicker of something darker, mysterious in his eyes before he quickly masked it.

'Right. One sip, you said.' He tapped the nearest bag. 'Now, let's have it.'

'You hotshot businessmen are all the same. Way too impatient.'

She placed her mug on the table, unzipping the first bag and hauling out a folder.

He tilted his head on an angle to read the spine. 'What's that?'

'A list of every restaurant in Melbourne. The new list I've been compiling over the last six months.'

Her tummy quivered as she glanced at the folder, at what it meant for her future.

'I'm ready.'

His eyes sparked with understanding and she wondered how he could do that. He'd read her mind, whereas Richard hadn't a clue what she'd been thinking after three years of marriage. Then again, considering what he'd been up to, he probably hadn't cared.

'You're going back to work?'

'Uh-huh. Thanks to your chef whipping up those amazing meals and letting me get my hand back into critiquing, I reckon I'm finally ready.'

She gnawed on her bottom lip, worrying it till she tasted the gloss she'd swiped on this morning.

'Think I'm crazy?'

His eyebrows shot up. 'Crazy? I think it's brilliant. Just what you need, something to focus on, get your mind off losing Rich.'

She hated the pity in his eyes, hated the fact she still had to fake grief, still had to pretend she cared.

She didn't.

Not since that first incident four months into her marriage when the man she'd married had given her a frightening glimpse into her future.

She'd thought Richard was the type of guy to never let her down, the type of guy to keep her safe, to give her what she'd always wanted: stability, security—something she'd never had since her dad had died when she was ten.

But Richard hadn't been that guy and, from the accolades of his adoring public and coworkers, she was the only one who knew the truth.

That Richard Downey, Australia's premier celebrity chef, had been an out-and-out bastard. And it was times like this, when she had to pretend in front of one of his mates, that an all-consuming latent fury swept through her.

If he hadn't upped and died of a heart attack, she would've been tempted to kill him herself for what he'd put her through, and what she'd discovered after his death.

'This has nothing to do with Richard. I'm doing it for me.'

Her bitterness spilled out in a torrent and she clamped her lips shut. He didn't deserve to bear the brunt of her resentment towards Richard. She'd wasted enough time analysing and self-flagellating and fuelling her anger. That was all she'd been doing for the last year since he'd died—speculating, brooding over a whole lot of pointless 'what-ifs'.

What if she'd known about the affair?

What if she'd stood up to him and for herself, rather than keeping up appearances for the sake of his business?

What if she'd travelled to India with her mum when Khushi had first asked her years ago? Would any of that have changed her life for the better?

'I didn't mean to rehash any painful stuff for you.'

Shaking her head, she wished the simple action could wipe away her awful memories.

'Not your fault. It's not like I don't think about it every day anyway.'

He searched her face for—what? Confirmation she wasn't still grieving, wasn't so heartbroken she couldn't return to the workforce after wasting the last few years playing society hostess to a man who hadn't given a damn about her?

What he saw in her expression had his eyes narrowing in speculation.

'You should get away. A break, before you get sucked back into the full-time rat race. Take it from me, a certified workaholic, once you hit the ground running you won't have a minute to yourself.'

She opened her mouth to protest, to tell him that as a virtual stranger he could stick his advice, but he held a finger to her lips to silence her, the impact of his simple action slugging her all the way to her toes. It had to be the impulse to tell him to shut up rather than the brush of his finger against her lips causing her belly to twist like a pretzel.

'A piece of advice. Seeing you six months ago, seeing you now, you've held together remarkably well considering what you've been through, but it's time.'

He dropped his finger, thank goodness.

'For what?'

'Time for *you*. Time to put aside your grief. Move on.'

He gestured to the stack of folders on the table between them. 'From what I've heard, you're a damn good food critic, one of Melbourne's best. But honestly? The way you are right now, the tears I saw when I made a simple flyaway comment about an oven, what you just said about thinking about Rich every day, holding down a regular job would be tough. You'd end up not being able to tell the difference between steak tartare and well-done Wagyu beef, let alone write about it.'

She should hate him for what he'd just said. It hurt, all of it. But then, the truth often did.

'You finished?'

She knew it was the wrong thing to say to a guy like him the instant the words left her mouth, for it sounded like a challenge, something he would never back away from.

'Not by a long shot.'

Before she could blink, his mouth swooped, capturing hers in a heartbeat—a soul-reviving, soul-destroying, terrifying kiss that stirred her dormant body to life, setting it alight in a way she'd never dreamed possible.

She burned, swayed, as he changed the pressure, his lips coaxing a response—a response she couldn't give in her right mind.

But she wasn't in her right mind, hadn't been from the second his lips touched hers and, before she could think, rationalise, overanalyse, she kissed him back, an outpouring of pent-up passion from a shattered ego starving for an ounce of attention.

Her heart sang with the joy of it, before stalling as the implication of what she'd just done crashed over her in a sickening wave.

Ethan, the practised playboy, Richard's friend, a guy she barely knew, had kissed her.

And she'd let him.

Slivers of ice chilled her to the bone as she tore her mouth from his, staring at him in wide-eyed horror.

She couldn't speak, couldn't form the words to express how furious she was with him.

Though her anger was misplaced and she knew

it. She was furious with herself for responding; worse, for enjoying it.

'Don't expect me to apologise for that.'

His eyes glittered with desire and she shivered, petrified yet exhilarated to be the focus of all that passion for a passing moment in time.

'That should show you you're a vibrant woman who needs to start living again. You should start by doing one thing you've always wanted to do before you return to work.'

He made sense, damn him, prove-a-point kiss and all. And while her body still trembled from the impact of that alarming kiss and her astounding response, at least it had served a purpose. If she'd been prevaricating about taking a trip before, he'd blasted her doubts sky-high now.

She had to go, had to leave Ambrosia, for facing him in the future would be beyond mortifying.

Mustering a haughty glare that only served to make his eyes gleam more, she shook her head.

'I can't believe you just did that.'

Shrugging, he sat back and crossed his ankles, the supremely confident male and proud of it. 'Many people can't believe a lot of the stuff I do, so don't sweat it. Let's talk about this trip of yours.'

'Let's not,' she snapped, annoyed by his persistence, more annoyed by the glimmer of anticipation racing through her.

She'd already been thinking about a trip herself. Specifically, the trip she'd booked with her mum. The itinerary they'd planned was tucked away in her old music box at home, the one her dad had given her when she'd been three, the one with the haunting tune that never failed to make her cry when she thought of all she'd lost.

She'd contemplated taking the trip on her own for all of two seconds before slamming the idea. The trip would've been emotional enough with her mum by her side but without her?

Her eyelids prickled just thinking about it and she blinked, wishing Ethan would put that devilish smile to good use elsewhere and butt out of her business.

'Think sun, sand and surf. Somewhere hot, tropical, the opposite of blustery Melbourne at the moment.'

Considering her toes were icy within her boots and she couldn't feel her fingers, the thought of all that heat was tempting.

India would be perfect, would fit the bill in every way. Buoyed by an urge to escape, she rummaged through the top folder, wondering if a brochure was still there. She'd had hundreds of the things when they'd been planning the trip, immersing herself in India, from the stone-walled city of Jodhpur—home of the Mehrangarh Fort and the grand palaces of Moti Mahal, Sheesh Mahal, Phool Mahal, Sileh Khana and Daulat Khana—to Ranthambhore National Park, India's best wildlife sanctuary, to see the majestic tigers, eager to see as much of the intriguing country as possible.

She'd kept them everywhere, hiding them from Richard when he'd first expressed his displeasure at letting her out of his sight, tucking them into books and magazines and her work stuff.

Suddenly, she really wanted to find one, wanted to see if the tiny flame of excitement flickering to life could be fanned into her actually doing this.

Flicking to the front of the folder, she dug her fingers into the plastic pocket and almost yelled for joy when she pulled out a glossy brochure featuring the Taj Mahal and the legendary Palace on Wheels train on the front.

'You're one of those incredibly annoying, painfully persistent guys who won't give up, so here. Take a look.'

She handed him the brochure.

His eyes widened. 'India?'

'I planned to visit a few years ago but it never happened.' She stared at the brochure, captivated by the exoticism of it all.

She should've thrown this out ages ago, but as long as she hung onto it, as long as the promise of her mum's dream trip was still a reality, albeit a distant one, it was as if she were keeping alive her mum's spirit.

Every time she found a brochure tucked away somewhere she felt connected to her mum, remembering the day she'd picked them up as a sixtieth birthday surprise and they'd pored over them during an Indian feast of spicy, palate-searing beef vindaloo, masala prawns, parathas and biryani, her favourite spiced rice, rich in flavoursome lamb.

They'd laughed, they'd cried, they'd hugged each other and jumped up and down like a couple of excited kids heading away on their first camping trip.

She'd wanted to explore the part of her history she knew little about, wanted to take the special journey with her mum.

Richard may have put paid to that dream and, while she'd love to take the trip now, it just wouldn't be the same without Khushi.

'Guess I should explore all my options first.'

She fiddled with the brochure, folding the ends into tiny triangles, absentmindedly smoothing out the creases again.

'Uh-uh.' He snapped his fingers. 'You're going to take the trip.'

Her eyes flew to his, startled by his absolute conviction, as a lump of sorrow lodged in her throat and she cleared it. 'I can't.'

She'd find another destination, somewhere she wouldn't have a deluge of memories drowning her, missing her mum every step of the way.

He stabbed at the brochure. 'You can. Clear your head, make a fresh start.'

She shook her head, using her hair to shield her face. 'I can't do this trip alone. I'd planned to take it with my mum. This was her trip—'

Her voice cracked and she slid off her chair and headed for the fireplace, holding her hands out to the crackling warmth, wishing it could seep deep inside to the coldest, loneliest parts of her soul.

'You won't be alone.'

He came up behind her, the heat from the fire nothing on the warmth radiating from him—a solid, welcoming warmth she wished she could lean into before giving herself a swift mental slap.

Stepping around in front of her, he stared at her, direct, intense, the indigo flecks in his blue eyes gleaming in the reflected firelight.

'You won't be alone because I'm coming with you.'

'But—'

'No buts.'

He held up a hand. 'I'm going to India anyway, to lure Delhi's best chef to work here.'

One finger bent as he counted off his first point.

'You need company.'

The second finger went down.

'And, lastly, I've always wanted to do the Palace on Wheels trip and never got around to it so, this way, you're doing me a favour.'

Her eyes narrowed. 'How's that?'

'I hear it's an amazing journey, best shared with a beautiful companion.'

His smile could've lit the Arts Centre spire, damn pirate, and in that second she snapped to her senses.

What was she doing? He'd be the last person she'd take a trip with, the last guy to accompany her anywhere considering he'd just kissed her and turned some of that legendary charm onto her. Beautiful companion, indeed.

'Your mum would've wanted you to go.'

Oh, he was good.

Worse, he was right.

Khushi would've wanted her to go, to visit Goa and the beach where she'd met her father, to take a magical train journey through India's heartland, to visit the Taj Mahal, something her mum had craved her entire life.

She wanted to rediscover her identity. Maybe a link to her past was the best way to do it?

Staggered by her second impulse in as many minutes—she determinedly ignored the first, foolishly responding to that kiss—she slapped the brochure against her opposite palm, mind made up.

'You're right, I'm taking the trip.'

She fixed him with a glare that lost its impact when her lower lip wobbled at the enormity of what she was contemplating.

'That's great. We'll—'

'I'm taking the trip. *Alone.*'

'But—'

'I don't even know you,' she said, wishing she hadn't stayed, terrified how that incredible kiss had made her feel for a fleeting moment.

It had obviously given him the wrong idea. What sort of a guy went from a cool acquaintance to kissing her to thinking she'd go away with him?

Maybe she was overreacting, reading more into the sudden twinkle in his sea-blue eyes and his scarily sexy smile?

Leaning forward a fraction, invading her personal space with a potent masculinity she found disconcerting, he lowered his voice. 'That's what the trip is for. Loads of time to get to know one another.'

She wasn't overreacting. He was chatting her up!

Sending him a withering glance that would've extinguished the fire at her back, she headed for the table and slipped her trench coat on.

'Thanks for the offer but I like being on my own.'

When he opened his mouth to respond, she held up a hand. 'I like it that way.'

Before he could protest any further, she slung her bag over her shoulder and pointed to the stack of folders. 'I'll come back for these tomorrow.'

His knowing gaze followed her towards the door and she knew he'd get the last word in.

'Going solo is highly overrated.'

Halting with her hand on the door, she glanced over her shoulder, startled by the ravenous hunger in his greedy gaze.

'Someone like you would think that.'

Rather than annoying him, a triumphant grin lit his face, as if she'd just paid him a compliment.

'Next to business, dating is what I do best so I guess that makes me qualified to pass judgement.'

'Overqualified, from what I hear.'

His grin widened and she mentally clapped a hand over her mouth.

What was she doing, discussing his personal life? It had nothing to do with her and, while she valued the opportunity he'd given her in using Ambrosia as a base to relaunch her career, what he did in his spare time meant diddly-squat to her.

Propped against the bar, he appeared more like a pirate than ever: all he needed was a bandanna and eye patch to complete the over-confident look.

'You sure you wouldn't like me to tag along?'

'Positive.'

She walked out, somewhat satisfied by the slamming door.

Take a trip with a playboy pirate like Ethan Brooks?

She'd rather walk the plank.

CHAPTER TWO

'WHAT the hell are you doing here?'

Ethan grinned at Tamara's shell-shocked expression as he strolled towards her on the platform at Safdarjung Station.

'You mean here as in New Delhi or here as in this station?'

Her eyes narrowed, spitting emerald fire. 'Don't play smart with me. Why are you here?'

'Business. I told you I'm a workaholic. The Delhi chef wasn't interested so there's a chef in Udaipur I'd like to lure to Ambrosia. Rather than commute by boring planes I thought I'd take the scenic route, so here I am.'

By her folded arms, compressed lips and frown, she wasn't giving an inch.

'And this *business trip* just happened to coincide when I'm taking the trip. How convenient.'

'Pure coincidence.'

He couldn't keep the grin off his face, which

only served to rile her further. That smile may well have seduced every socialite in Melbourne, but she wasn't about to succumb to its practised charm. He laid a hand on her arm; she stiffened and deliberately stepped away.

'If it makes you feel any better, it's a big train and the trip only lasts a week.'

'It doesn't make me feel better.'

If the Tamara he'd seen all too infrequently over the last few years was beautiful, a furious Tamara was stunning—and vindicated why he'd booked this trip in the first place.

It was time.

He was through waiting.

'Why don't we stop quibbling and enjoy this fanfare?'

He thought she'd never relent but, after shooting him another exasperated glare, she turned towards their welcoming committee.

'Pretty impressive, huh?'

She nodded, maintaining a silence he found disconcerting. He preferred her annoyed and fiery rather than quiet and brooding.

Only one way to get her out of this huff. Turn on the charm.

'Just think, all this for you. Talented musicians playing tabla as you board the train, young Indian girls placing flower garlands around your neck, being greeted by your own personal bearer for your carriage. Nothing like a proper welcome?'

The beginnings of a smile softened her lips as a bearer placed a fancy red turban on his head as a gift.

'Looks like I'm not the only one getting welcomed.'

He wobbled his head, doing a precarious balancing act with the turban and she finally laughed.

'Okay, you can stay.'

He executed a fancy little bow and she held up a hand.

'But remember I like being on my own.'

He didn't. Being alone was highly overrated and something he'd set about compensating for the moment he'd had his first pay cheque or two.

He liked being surrounded by people, enjoyed the bustle of a restaurant, thrived on the hub of the business world and relished dating beautiful women. Most of all, he liked being in control. And, finally, this was his chance to take control of his desire for Tamara.

He'd kept his distance while Rich was alive, had respected his friend's marriage. But Rich was gone and his pull towards this incredible woman was stronger than ever.

He wanted her, had wanted her from the first moment they'd met and had avoided her because of it.

Not any more.

That impulsive kiss had changed everything.

He'd forfeited control by giving in to his driving compulsion for her, hated the powerlessness she'd managed to wreak with her startling response, and he'd be damned if he sat back and did nothing.

Having her walk away had left her firmly in charge and that was unacceptable. He was here to reclaim control, to prove he couldn't lose it over a woman, beautiful as she may be.

Seduction was one thing, but finding himself floundering by the power of a kiss quite another.

Clawing his way to the top had taught him persistence, determination and diligence. When he wanted something in the business world, he made it happen by dogged perseverance and a healthy dose of charm.

Now, he wanted Tamara.

She didn't stand a chance.

Tapping his temple, he said, 'I'll try to remember. But, you know, this heat can play havoc with one's memory and—'

'Come on, let's board. Once you're safely ensconced in the lap of luxury, maybe that memory will return.'

'You make me sound like a snob.'

'Aren't you? Being Australia's top restaurateur and all.' She snapped her fingers. 'Oh, that's right.

You're just the average run-of-the-mill billionaire who happens to rival Wolfgang Puck and Nobu for top restaurants around the world. Nothing snobby about you.'

'Come on, funny girl. Time to board.'

She smiled and, as he picked up their hand luggage and followed the porter, he could hardly believe the change in Tam.

Sure, there was still a hint of fragility about her, the glimpse of sorrow clinging to her like the humidity here, but it looked as if India agreed with her. After she'd finished berating him, she'd smiled more in the last few minutes than she had in the odd times he'd seen her.

'You know I have my own compartment?'

She rolled her eyes. 'Of course.'

'I wouldn't want you compromising my reputation.'

She smiled again and something twanged in the vicinity of his heart. She'd had the ability to do that to him from the very beginning, from the first time he'd met her—an hour after she'd met Richard, worse luck.

She'd been smitten by then, with eyes only for the loud, larger-than-life chef, and he'd subdued his controlling instincts to sweep her away.

Neither of them had ever known of his desire for the woman he couldn't have; he'd made sure of it. But keeping his distance was a thing of the past and the next seven days loomed as intriguing.

'Your reputation is safe with me. I'm sure all those society heiresses and vapid, thin models you date on a revolving-door basis are well aware this boring old widow is no competition.'

'You're not boring and you're certainly not old.'

As for the women he dated, there was a reason he chose the no-commitment, out-for-a-good-time-not-a-long-time type. A damn good one.

The smile hovering about her lips faded as fast as his hopes to keep it there.

'But I am a widow.'

And, while he'd hated the pain she must've gone through after Rich died, the struggle to get her life back on an even keel, he couldn't help but be glad she was now single.

Did that make him heartless? Maybe, but his past had taught him to be a realist and he never wasted time lying to himself or others. Discounting the way he'd kept his attraction for Tam a secret all these years, of course.

'Maybe it's time you came out of mourning?'

He expected her to recoil, to send him the contemptuous stare she'd given him after he'd kissed her. Instead, she cocked her head to one side, studying him.

'Are you always this blunt?'

'Always.'

'So you'll ignore me if I tell you to butt out, just like you did by gatecrashing my trip?'

He feigned hurt, smothering his grin with difficulty. 'Gatecrashing's a bit harsh. I told you, I'm here on business.'

He only just caught her muttered, 'Monkey business.'

She fidgeted with her handbag, her fingers plucking at the leather strap as she rocked her weight from foot to foot, and he almost took pity on her before banishing that uncharacteristic emotion in a second.

He had to have her, was driven by a primal urge he had no control over and, to do that, he needed to get her to look at him as a man rather than a bug in her soup.

With a bit of luck and loads of charm, he intended to make good on the unspoken promise of their first kiss—a promise of so much more.

'You're not still hung up over that kiss, are you? Because, if you are—'

'I'm not. It's forgotten.'

Her gorgeous blush belied her quick negation and had him itching to push the boundaries. But he'd gained ground by having her accept his presence so quickly and he'd be a fool to take things too far on the first day.

'Forgotten, huh? Must be losing my touch.'

'There's nothing wrong with—'

He smothered a triumphant grin. He may have lost his mind and kissed her to prove she needed to start living again but her eager response had blown him away. And fuelled his need for her, driving him to crazy things like taking time off work, something he rarely did, to pursue her.

'Let's put it down to a distant memory and move on, shall we?'

To his horror, her eyes filled with pain, which hit him hard, like a slug to the guts, and he tugged her close without thinking, enveloping her in his arms.

'Hell, Tam, I'm sorry. I shouldn't have mentioned memories.'

She braced herself against his chest, her palms splayed, and his body reacted in an instant, heat searing his veins as he cradled a soft armful of woman.

She sniffled and he tightened his hold, rather than his first instinct to release her in the hope of putting an instant dampener on his errant libido.

His hand skimmed her hair, thick and dark like molten molasses, soothing strokes designed to comfort. But, hot on the heels of his thoughts of how much he wanted her, his fingers itched to delve into the shiny, dark mass and get caught up in it. He could hold her like this all night long.

'You okay?'

Ethan pulled away, needing to establish some distance between them, not liking her power over him. He didn't do comfort. He never had a hankie in his pocket or a host of placating platitudes or a shoulder to cry on. He didn't do consoling hugs; he did passionate embraces.

So what had happened in the last few minutes? What was it about this woman that undermined him?

'Uh-huh.'

She managed a watery smile before straightening her shoulders and lifting her head in the classic coping pose he'd seen her exhibit at Rich's funeral and his admiration shot up another few notches.

How she'd handled her grief after the initial shock of Rich's heart attack, burying herself in the business side of things, sorting through legalities with him, only to approach him several months later for the use of Ambrosia to get her career back on track, had all served to fuel his respect for this amazing woman.

Quite simply, she was incredible and he wanted her with a staggering fierceness that clawed at him even now, when he was left analysing how he'd let his control slip again in her intoxicating presence.

'I can see you're still hurting but if you ever want to talk about Rich, remember the good times, I'm here for you, okay?'

Maybe, if she opened up to him, he could encourage her to get it all out of her system and move on. Highly altruistic but then, when was he anything but?

To his surprise, she wrinkled her nose and he knew it had little to do with the pungent odours of diesel fumes, spices and human sweat swirling around them.

'Honestly? I don't want to talk about Richard. I'm done grieving.'

A spark of defiance lit her eyes, turning them from soft moss-green to sizzling emerald in a second. 'I want to enjoy this trip, then concentrate on my future.'

He'd never seen her like this: resolute, determined, a woman reborn.

He'd seen Tam the society wife, the perfect hostess, the astute businesswoman, the grieving widow, but never like this and a part of him was glad. Releasing the past was cathartic, would help her to move on and he really wanted her to do that on this trip. With him.

'Sounds like a plan.'

Her answering smile sent another sizzle of heat through him and he clenched his hands to stop himself from reaching out and pulling her close.

Plenty of time for that.

* * *

Tamara lay down on the bed, stretched her arms over her head and smiled.

The rocking motion of the train, the clickety-clack as it bounced its way out of Delhi, the aroma of marigolds and masala chai—the delicious tea, fragrant with cardamons—overloaded her senses, lulled her while making her want to jump up and twirl around from the sheer rush of it.

For the first time in years, she felt free. Free to do whatever she wanted, be whoever she chose. And it felt great. In fact, it felt downright fantastic.

While she'd once loved Richard, had desperately craved the type of marriage her folks had had, nothing came close to this exhilarating freedom.

She'd spent months playing the grieving widow after Richard had suffered that fatal heart attack, had submerged her humiliation, her bitterness, her pain.

Yet behind her serene, tear-stained face she'd seethed: at him for making a mockery of their marriage, at herself for being a gullible fool and for caring what people thought even after he was gone.

She hadn't given two hoots about social propriety until she'd married him, had laughed at his obsession with appearances. But she'd soon learned he was serious and, with his face plastered over every newspaper, magazine and TV channel on a regular basis, she'd slipped into the routine of being the perfect little wife he'd wanted.

While his perfect little mistress had been stashed away in a luxurious beach house at Cape Schanck, just over an hour's drive from Melbourne's CBD where they'd lived.

Damn him.

She sat bolt upright, annoyed she'd let bitter memories tarnish the beginning of this incredible journey, her gaze falling on the single bed next to hers. The single bed her mum should've been occupying while regaling her with exotic tales of Goa and its beaches, Colva beach where she'd met her dad, her love at first sight for a scruffy Aussie backpacker with a twinkle in his eyes and a ready smile.

Tales of the Taj Mahal, the monument she'd always wanted to see but never had the chance. Tales of an India filled with hospitable people and mouth-watering food, imparting recipes in that lilting sing-song accent that had soothed her as a young girl when the nightmares of losing her dad would wake her screaming and sweat-drenched.

Khushi should've been here. This was her trip.

Instead, Tamara swiped an angry hand across her eyes, dashing her tears away.

She wasn't going to cry any more. She'd made herself that promise back in Melbourne when she'd decided to take this trip.

And while she knew her heart would break at

every turn on the track, at every fabulous place she visited, wishing her mum was here to share it with her, she should be thankful she'd taken another positive step in getting her life in order.

She was through cringing with shame and humiliation at what Richard had put her through, done feeling sorry for herself.

This was *her* time.

Time for a new life, a new beginning.

So what the heck was Ethan Brooks doing here, muscling in on her new start?

Ethan, with his smiling eyes and that deadly smile. Where was the famed hard-ass, hard-nosed businessman? Instead, Ethan the pirate, the player, the playboy, had swaggered along on this trip and while every self-preservation instinct screamed for her to stay away, she couldn't be that rude.

He'd helped her with the legalities surrounding Ambrosia after Richard's death, had smoothed the way for her to re-enter the workforce by allowing her to use Ambrosia as a base. She owed him.

But he had her rattled.

She preferred him business-oriented, juggling a briefcase, a laptop and barking instructions on a mobile phone at the same time, barely acknowledging her presence with an absentminded nod as he strutted into Ambrosia.

He'd practically ignored her when their paths

had crossed while Richard had been around, his head always buried in financial statements and yearly projections, and that had been fine with her.

He made her uncomfortable and it had nothing to do with the fact that they didn't really know each other. The shift had happened when they'd met to sort out Ambrosia's ownership, those two times when she'd noticed things: like the way he cracked pistachio nuts way too loudly, flipping them in the air and catching them in his open mouth, how much he loved Shiraz Grenache and sticky date pudding and the North Melbourne Football Club.

Trivial things, inconsequential things that meant little, but the fact that she'd noticed and re-membered them annoyed her.

As for that kiss…she picked up a pillow and smothered a groan, hating how it haunted her, hating how she'd dreamed of it, hating how the dream had developed and morphed into so much more than a kiss, leaving her writhing and panting and sweat-drenched on waking.

She didn't want to remember any of it, didn't want to remember his expertise, his spontaneity, his ability to dredge a response from her deepest, darkest soul, better left untouched.

But she did remember, every breathtaking moment, and while her head had slammed the door on the memory of her temporary insanity, her body was clamouring for more.

Now this.

Him being here, all suave and charming and too gorgeous for his own good, was making her nervous. Very nervous.

She didn't need anyone in her new life, least of all a smooth tycoon like Ethan Brooks.

As for her wayward thoughts lately in the wee small hours of the morning when she lay sleepless, staring up at the ceiling and trying to regain focus to her meandering life, she'd banish them along with her anger at Richard.

Wondering what would've happened if she'd gone for Ethan rather than Richard that fateful night she'd entered Ambrosia four years earlier was a waste of time.

Now was her chance to put the past to rest and concentrate on her future.

CHAPTER THREE

'TELL me you're not working.'

Ethan pointed at the small blue notebook tucked discreetly under her linen serviette—obviously not discreetly enough.

Ignoring him, Tamara sliced a vegetable pakora in two and dipped it in the tamarind sauce, her taste buds hankering for that first delicious taste of crispy vegetables battered in chickpea flour and dunked in the sour, piquant sauce.

'Fine, I won't tell you.'

He shook his head, laughed, before helping himself to a meat samosa from the entrée platter between them.

'You're supposed to be on holiday.'

'I'm supposed to be getting back to work soon and I need the practice.'

Resting his knife and fork on his plate, he focused his too-blue gaze on her.

'You're an expert critic. One of Australia's best.

Skills like that don't disappear because you've had a year or so off.'

'Two years,' she said, quelling the surge of resentment at what she'd given up for Richard. 'Despite the last six months at Ambrosia, I'm still rusty. The sooner I get back into it, the easier it'll be.'

She bit down on the pakora, chewed thoughtfully, knowing there was another reason she had her trusty notebook within jotting reach.

The minute she'd opened her compartment door to find Ethan on the other side in charcoal casual pants and open-necked white shirt, his gaze appreciative and his smile as piratical as always, she'd had to clamp down on the irrational urge to slam the door in his face and duck for cover.

It had been her stupid thoughts earlier of *what if* that had done it, that had made her aware of him as a man—a gorgeous, charming man—rather than just her…what was he? A business acquaintance? A travelling companion? A friend?

She didn't like the last two options: they implied a closeness she didn't want. But they'd moved past the acquaintance stage the moment he'd kissed her and there was no going back.

She didn't want to have these thoughts, didn't want to acknowledge the sexy crease in his left cheek, the tiny lines at the corners of his eyes that added character to his face, the endearingly ruffled dark hair that curled over his collar.

She'd never noticed those things before or, if she had, hadn't experienced this…this…*buzz* or whatever the strange feeling coursing through her body was that made her want to bury her nose in her notebook for the duration of dinner and not look up.

That might take care of day one, but what about the rest of the week as the Palace on Wheels took them on an amazing journey through Rajasthan?

Ethan was Richard's friend, reason enough she couldn't trust him, no matter how much he poured on the charm.

She'd fallen for Richard because he'd been safe and look at the devastation he'd wreaked. What would letting her guard down around a powerful, compelling guy like Ethan do?

Inwardly shuddering at the thought, she reached for the notebook at the same instant that he stilled her hand. Her gaze flew to his, her heart beating uncharacteristically fast.

He'd touched her again. First that hug on the station and now this. Though this time her pulse tripped and her skin prickled as determination flared in his eyes, while fear crept through her.

Fear they'd somehow changed the boundaries of their nebulous relationship without realising, fear they could never go back, fear she could lose focus of what she wanted out of this trip and why if she was crazy enough to acknowledge the shift between them, let alone do anything about it.

'This is the first holiday you've taken in years. Don't be so hard on yourself.'

He squeezed her hand, released it and she exhaled, unaware she'd been holding her breath.

'You'll get back into the swing of things soon enough. Once I coerce the super-talented Indian chef to leave the Lake Palace and work at Ambrosia, critiquing his meals will keep you busy for months.'

'You're too kind.'

She meant it. He'd never been anything other than kind to her, helping her with Richard's business stuff, arranging a special table for her at Ambrosia away from the ravenous crowd so she could sample the food and write her critiques in peace.

But kind didn't come close to describing the hungry gleam in his eyes or the subtle shift that had taken place between them a few moments ago—dangerous, more like it. Dangerous and exciting and terrifying.

He screwed up his nose, stabbing a seekh kebab from the entrée platter and moving it across to his plate. 'You know, *kind* ranks right up there with *nice* for guys. Something we don't want to hear.'

'Fine. You're a cold, heartless businessman who takes no prisoners. Better?'

'Much.'

His bold smile had her scrambling for her notebook, flipping it open to a crisp new blank page, pen poised. 'Now, take a bite of that kebab and tell me what you think.'

He cut the kebab—spiced lamb moulded into a sausage shape around a skewer and cooked to perfection in a tandoor oven—and chewed a piece, emitting a satisfied moan that had her focusing on his lips rather than her notebook.

'Fantastic.'

He screwed up his eyes, took another bite, chewed thoughtfully. 'I can taste ginger, a hint of garlic and cumin.'

He polished off the rest with a satisfied pat of his tummy, a very lean, taut tummy from what she could see of it outlined beneath his shirt.

Great, there she went again, noticing things she never normally would. This wasn't good—not good at all.

Pressing the pen to the page so hard it tore a hole through to the paper underneath, she focused on her scrawl rather than anywhere in the vicinity of Ethan's lips or fabulous tummy.

'Not bad, but that's why you're the guy who owns the restaurants and I'm lucky enough to eat in them and write about the food.'

He smiled, pointed at her notebook. 'Go

ahead, then. Tell me all about the wonders of the seekh kebab.'

She glanced at her notes, a thrill of excitement shooting through her. She loved her job, every amazing moment of it, from sampling food, savouring it, titillating her taste buds until she couldn't put pen to paper fast enough to expound its joys, to trying new concoctions and sharing hidden delights with fellow food addicts.

As for Indian food, she'd been raised on the stuff and there was nothing like it in the world.

'The keema—' he raised an eyebrow and she clarified '—lamb mince is subtly spiced with an exotic blend of garam masala, dried mango powder, carom seeds, raw papaya paste, with a healthy dose of onion, black pepper, ginger, garlic and a pinch of nutmeg.'

'You got all that from one bite?'

She bit her lip as she pushed the notebook away, unable to contain her laughter as he took another bite, trying to figure out how she did it.

'My mum used to make them. I memorised the ingredients when I was ten years old.'

Her laughter petered out as she remembered what else had happened when she was ten—her dad had dropped dead at work, a cerebral aneurysm, and the world as she'd known it had ceased to exist.

She'd loved listening to her parents chat over

dinner, their tales of adventure, the story of how they'd met. She'd always craved a once-in-a-lifetime romance like theirs. Richard hadn't been it. Now she'd never find it.

'Hey, you okay?'

She nodded, bit down hard on her bottom lip to stop it quivering. 'I still miss my mum.'

He hesitated before covering her hand with his. 'Tell me about her.'

Tell him what?

How her mum used to braid her waist-length hair into plaits every day for school, never once snagging the brush or rushing her?

How she'd concocted an Indian feast out of rice, lentils, a few spices and little else?

How she'd loved her, protected her, been there for her in every way after her dad had died?

She couldn't put half of what she was feeling into words let alone articulate the devastating sadness reaching down to her barren soul that she was here on this train and Khushi wasn't.

Besides, did she really want to discuss her private memories with him? Revealing her inner-most thoughts implied trust and that was one thing she had in short supply, especially with a guy hell-bent on charming her.

'Tell me one of the favourite things you used to do together.'

'Watch Bollywood films,' she said on a sigh, reluctant to talk but surprised by his deeper, caring side, a side too tempting to ignore.

The memory alleviated some of the sadness permeating her thoughts as she remembered many a Sunday afternoon curled up on the worn suede couch in the family room, a plate of jalebis, milk burfi and Mysore pak—delicious Indian sweets made with loads of sugar, milk and butter—between them, as they were riveted to the latest Shah Rukh Khan blockbuster—India's equivalent to Hollywood's top A-list celebrity.

They'd laugh at the over-the-top theatrics, sigh at the vivid romance and natter about the beautiful, vibrant saris.

Raised in Melbourne with an Aussie dad, she'd never felt a huge connection to India, even though her mum's Goan blood flowed in her veins. But for those precious Sunday afternoons she'd been transported to another world—a world filled with people and colour and magic.

'What else?'

'We loved going to the beach.'

His encouragement had her wanting to talk about memories she'd long submerged, memories she only resurrected in the privacy of her room at night when she'd occasionally cry herself to sleep.

Richard's sympathy had been short-lived. He'd told her to get over her grief and focus on more important things, like hosting yet another dinner party for his friends.

That had been three years ago, three long years as their marriage had continued its downward spiral, as her famous husband had slowly revealed a cruel side that, to this day, left her questioning her own judgement in marrying someone like that in the first place.

He'd never actually hit her but the verbal and psychological abuse had been as bruising, as painful, as devastating as if he had.

Ethan must've sensed her withdrawal, for he continued prodding. 'Any particular beach?'

She shook her head, the corners of her mouth curving upwards for the first time since she'd started reminiscing about her mum.

'It wasn't the location as such. Anywhere would do as long as there was sand and sun and ocean.'

They'd visited most of the beaches along the Great Ocean Road after her dad had died: Anglesea, Torquay, Lorne, Apollo Bay. She'd known why. The beach had reminded Khushi of meeting her dad for the first time, the story she'd heard so many times.

Her mum had been trying to hold on to precious memories, maybe recreate them in her head, but whatever the reason she'd been happy to go along for the ride. They'd made a great team and she would've given anything for her mum to pop into the dining car right now with a wide smile on her face and her hair perched in a plain bun on top of her head.

'Sounds great.'

'It's why I'm spending a week in Goa after the train. It was to be the highlight of our trip.'

She took a sip of water, cleared her throat of emotion. 'My folks met on Colva Beach. Dad was an Aussie backpacker taking a year off after med school. Mum was working for one of the hotels there.'

She sighed, swirled the water in her glass. 'Love at first sight, apparently. My dad used to call Mum his exotic princess from the Far East, Mum used to say Dad was full of it.'

'Why didn't she ever go back? After he passed away?'

Shrugging, she toyed with her cutlery, the familiar guilt gnawing at her. 'Because of me, I guess. She wanted me to have every opportunity education-wise, wanted to raise me as an Australian, as my dad would've wanted.'

'But you're half Indian too. This country is a part of who you are.'

'Honestly? I don't know who I am any more.'

The admission sounded as lost, as forlorn, as she felt almost every minute of every day.

She'd vocalised her greatest fear.

She didn't know who she was, had lost her identity when she'd married Richard. She'd been playing a role for ever: first the dutiful wife, then the grieving widow. But it was all an act. All of it.

She'd become like him, had cared about appearances even at the end when she'd been screaming inside at the injustice of being abused and lied to and cheated on for so long while shedding the appropriate tears at his funeral.

Ethan stood, came around to her side of the table and crouched down, sliding his arm around her waist while tilting her chin to make her look him in the eye with his other hand.

'I know who you are. You're an incredible woman with the world at her feet.' He brushed her cheek in a gentle caress that had tears seeping out of the corners of her eyes. 'Don't you ever, ever forget how truly amazing you are.'

With emotion clogging her throat and tears blinding her, she couldn't speak let alone see what was coming next so when his lips brushed hers in a soft, tender kiss she didn't have time to think, didn't have time to react.

Instead, her eyelids fluttered shut, her aching

heart healed just a little as her soul blossomed with wonder at having a man like Ethan Brooks on her side.

His kiss lingered long after he pulled away, long after he stared at her for an interminable moment with shock in the indigo depths of his eyes, long after he murmured the words, 'You're special, that's who you are.'

A small part of her wanted to believe him.

A larger part wanted to recreate the magic of that all-too-brief kiss, as for the second time in a week she felt like a woman.

The largest part of her recoiled in horror as she realised she'd just been kissed—again—by the last man she could get close to, ever.

Ethan sprang to his feet and catapulted back to his chair on the opposite side of the table, desperate for space.

She'd done it again.

Left him reeling with her power to undermine his control.

Those damn tears had done it, tugging at non-existent heartstrings, urging him to kiss her, to comfort her, making him *feel*, damn it.

He'd been a fool, urging her to talk about her mum. He should've known she'd get emotional, should've figured he'd want to play the hero and help slay her demons.

'You're good at that.'

His gaze snapped to hers, expecting wariness, thrown by her curiosity, as if she couldn't quite figure him out.

'At what?'

'Knowing when to say the right thing, knowing how to make a girl feel good about herself.'

'Practice, I guess.'

If his offhand shrug hadn't made her recoil, his callous comment did the trick.

He'd just lumped her in with the rest of his conquests—something she'd hate, something he hated.

But it had to be done.

He needed distance right now, needed to slam his emotional barriers back in place and muster the control troops to the battlefront.

'Lucky me.'

Her sarcasm didn't sock him half as much as her expression, a potent mix of disappointment and derision.

He had to take control of this situation before it got out of hand and he ended up alienating her completely, and all because he was furious at himself for getting too close.

'Before I put you off your food with any more of my renowned comforting techniques, why don't we finish off this entrée? I've heard the lentil curry to come is something special.'

She nodded, her disappointment slugging him anew as she toyed with the food on her plate.

Establishing emotional distance was paramount. He'd come close to losing sight of his seduction goal moments before but steeling his heart was one thing, carrying it through with a disillusioned Tam sitting opposite another.

'What do you think of the potato bondas?'

An innocuous question, a question designed to distract her from his abrupt turnaround and get them back on the road of comfortable small talk.

However, as she raised her gaze from her plate and met his, the accusatory hurt reached down to his soul, as if he were the worst kind of louse.

For a moment he thought she'd call him on his brusque switch from comforting to cool. Instead, she searched his face, her mouth tightening as if what she saw confirmed her worst opinion of him.

'They're good.'

Hating feeling out of his depth, he pushed the platter towards her. 'Another?'

'No, thanks.'

They lapsed into silence, an awkward silence fraught with unspoken words—words he couldn't bring himself to say for fear of the growing intimacy between them.

Being here with her wasn't about establishing an

emotional connection, it was about seducing the one woman he'd wanted for years and couldn't have.

He needed to keep it that way, for the other option scared the life out of him.

CHAPTER FOUR

ETHAN focused on the tour guide as he droned on about Hawa Mahal, the Palace of the Winds.

Structurally, the place was amazing, like a giant candyfloss beehive with its tiers of windows staggered in red and pink sandstone.

Architecture usually fascinated him—every restaurant he purchased around the world was chosen for position as well as aesthetics—but, while the guide pointed out the white borders and motifs of Jaipur's multi-layered palace, he sneaked glances at the woman standing next to him, apparently engrossed in what the guy had to say. While he, Ethan, was engrossed in her.

As the train had wound its way from New Delhi to the 'Pink City' of Jaipur overnight, he'd lain awake, hands clasped behind his head, staring at the ceiling.

For hours. Long, endless hours, replaying that

comfy scene over dinner and cursing himself for being a fool.

He'd overstepped with the cosy chat about her mum, had panicked and back-pedalled as a result.

The upshot? Tam's barriers had slammed down, shutting him out, obliterating what little ground he'd made since she'd forgiven him for crashing her trip.

Stupid, stupid, stupid.

Ever since he'd boarded the train he'd been edgy, unfocused, displaced. And he hated feeling like that, as if he had no control.

Everyone said he was a control freak and, to some degree, he was. Control gave him power and impenetrability and confidence that things would work out exactly as he planned them, at total odds with his childhood, where no amount of forethought could give him the stability he'd so desperately craved.

When he'd first landed in this cosmopolitan, jam-packed country, he'd had a clear goal: to seduce Tam.

He wanted her—had always wanted her—but had stayed away for business reasons. Richard had been the best chef in the country and he'd needed him to cement Ambrosia's reputation.

Nothing got in his way when his most prized possession was at stake, not even a beautiful, intelligent woman. He hadn't needed the distraction at the time, had been hell-bent on making Ambrosia Melbourne's premier dining experience.

He'd succeeded, thanks to Richard's flamboyance in the kitchen and a healthy dose of business acumen on his part. Now, nothing stood in his way. Discounting his stupid over-eagerness, that was.

He sneaked another sideways glance at Tam, wondering if her intent focus was genuine or another way to give him the cold shoulder.

She wasn't like the other women he'd dated: everything, from her reluctance to respond to his flirting to the lingering sadness in her eyes, told him she wouldn't take kindly to being wooed.

He hoped to change all that.

'Some structure, huh?'

She finally turned towards him, her expression cool, her eyes wary.

'Yeah, it's impressive.' She pointed at one of the windows. 'Don't you think it's amazing all those royal women of the palace used to sit behind those windows and watch the ceremonial processions without being seen?'

He squinted, saw a pink window like a hundred others and shook his head.

'Sad, more like it. Having to stay behind closed doors while the kings got to strut their stuff. Don't think many women would put up with that these days.'

She stiffened, hurt flickering in the rich green depths of her eyes.

'Maybe some women find it's easier to give in to the whims of their husbands than live with callous coldness every day.'

Realisation dawned and he thrust his hands in his pockets to stop from slapping himself in the head. Had she just inadvertently given him a glimpse into her marriage to Richard?

He'd seen Rich like that at work. All smiles and jovial conviviality but if things didn't go his way or someone dared to have a different opinion to King Dick, he'd freeze them out better than his Bombe Alaska.

Would he have ever treated his wife the same way?

He hated thinking that this warm, vibrant woman had been subjected to that, had possibly tiptoed around in order to stay on his good side, had put a happy face on a marriage that would've been trying at best.

She didn't deserve that, no woman did, and the least he could do now was distract her long enough so she forgot his unintentional faux pas and enjoyed the rest of their day in Jaipur.

'I've seen enough palaces for one day. How about you and I hit some of those handicraft shops the guide mentioned earlier?' He bent towards her ear, spoke in an exaggerated conspiratorial whisper. 'By your different footwear for breakfast, lunch and dinner, I'd say you collect shoes on a weekly basis so I'm sure the odd bargain or two wouldn't go astray.'

She straightened her shoulders, flashed him a superior smirk while her eyes sparkled. 'I'll have you know I only buy a few pairs of shoes a year, mainly boots. Melbourne's winters can be a killer on a girl's feet.'

'I'll take your word for it.'

He smiled, thrilled that his distraction technique had worked when she returned it. 'So, you up for some shopping?'

'I'm up for anything.'

Their gazes locked and for a long, loaded moment he could've sworn he saw a flicker of something other than her usual reticence.

'Come on then, let's go.'

As she fell in step beside him, his mind mulled over her revelation. He had no idea what sort of a marriage Rich and Tam had shared; he'd barely seen them together, preferring to make himself scarce whenever she'd appeared.

He'd cited interstate or overseas business whenever she'd hosted a party and had avoided all contact if she dropped into Ambrosia to see Rich on the odd occasion.

In fact, he'd rarely seen the two interact, such had been his blinding need to avoid her at all costs.

Maybe he was reading too much into her comment about tolerant wives and their private battle to keep the peace? Probably a passing comment, nothing more.

Then why the persistent nagging that maybe there was more behind her fragility than ongoing grief for a dead husband?

Jamming his hands into his pockets, he picked up the pace. The sooner they hit the shops, the sooner she'd be distracted and the sooner he'd lose the urge to bundle her in his arms, cradle her close and murmur soothing words again. Last night had been bad enough and he had no intention of treading down that road again.

He shouldn't get involved.

Her marriage was her business and the less he thought about it the better. Remembering she had once loved another man enough to marry him didn't sit real well considering how much he wanted her.

Besides, it would be dangerous—very dangerous—for Tam to become emotionally attached to him and that was exactly what would happen if he started delving into issues that didn't concern him and offering comfort.

He didn't do emotions, hated the wild, careening, out-of-control feelings they produced, which was why he dated widely and frequently and never got involved.

Never.

Better off sticking to what he knew best: work. He understood work. He could control work. He could become the man he'd always wanted to be through work. That suited him just fine.

As for Tam, he'd concentrate on keeping things light and sticking to his original plan.

These days, what he wanted he got and he had his sights firmly fixed on her.

She was no good at this.

Her plan to freeze Ethan out had hit a snag. A big one, in the shape of one super-smooth, super-charming, super-likeable pain in the butt.

She wanted to maintain a polite distance between them to ensure he didn't get the wrong idea—that she was actually starting to enjoy his flirting.

A long camel ride across the sand dunes of Jaiselmar had been perfect for her plan. Little opportunity for conversation, lots of concentration required to stay on the loping dromedaries.

But she hadn't counted on arriving at this romantic haven in the middle of the desert for an early dinner, nor had she counted on the persistent attention of one determined guy.

She'd been so close to seriously liking him last night, when he'd encouraged her to talk about her mum. To trust him enough to do that alarmed her, for it meant she was falling under his legendary spell.

Thankfully, he'd retreated quicker than she had at the sound of Richard's footfall after work and, while she'd been hurt at the time, she was now grateful.

Smooth, charming Ethan she could handle—just.

Caring, compassionate Ethan had the power to undo her completely.

So she'd retreated too, limiting their time spent together by taking breakfast in her carriage rather than the dining car, making boring, polite small talk at lunch.

Now, forced to be in his company on this tour, she'd maintained her freeze but, despite her monosyllabic responses, her deliberate long silences and her focused attention on the horizon, he persisted.

For some reason, Ethan was determined to get her to respond to him as a man. Why? Why here, why now?

They'd crossed paths infrequently over the last year and he'd been nothing but super-professional, almost aloof. So what was with the charming act?

He'd gone from teasing to full-on flirting and,

try as she might, she couldn't maintain her freeze much longer. Under the scorching Indian sun, there was a serious thaw coming.

'Pretty spectacular, huh?'

With a weary sigh, she turned to face him, instantly wishing she hadn't when that piercing blue-eyed gaze fixed on her with purpose.

'Sure is.'

Her gaze drifted back to the beautiful tent city silhouetted against a setting sun, the sky an entrancing combination of indigo streaked with mauve and magenta where it dipped to the horizon, a sweep of golden sands as far as she could see.

A tingle rippled through her and she shivered, captivated by the beauty of a land she felt more for with each passing day.

This was why she'd come—to reconnect with herself, with her past. When she'd first booked this trip she'd envisioned shedding tears, letting go of some of her anger and discovering that missing part of herself tied up in this mystical country.

Never in her wildest dreams had she anticipated feeling like this. Not that she could verbalise what *this* was.

But every time Ethan had glanced at her she felt overwhelmed, dizzy, off-kilter, *alive*.

It was more than his inherent ability to coax a smile to her face, to make her laugh despite the unrelenting bitterness weaving a constricting net around her heart

No, there was more—much more than she could handle. An off-guard glance, a loaded stare, a little current of something arcing between them like the faintest invisible thread—intangible, insubstantial, yet there all the same.

And it terrified her.

This journey had been about self-discovery. Well, she'd certainly discovered more about herself than she'd anticipated in the startling, frightening fact that she was attracted to a man totally wrong for her.

'Let's get something to eat.'

She forced herself to relax as Ethan helped her down from the camel by holding her hand and placing his other in the small of her back, a small gesture which meant nothing.

So why the heat from his palm through her thin cotton sundress, the little tingle skittering along her skin, making her wish he'd linger?

She could blame this new awareness on India, its wild, untamed edge bringing out the same in her. But she'd be lying, and if there was one thing she'd learned through her fiasco of a marriage it was never to lie to herself again.

As he held open a tent flap for her and gestured for her to enter, his enquiring gaze locked onto hers and she swallowed at the desire she glimpsed.

He knew she was trying to avoid him and he didn't care.

So much passed in that one loaded stare: challenge, intent and heat—loads of heat that sizzled and zapped and had her diving into the tent for a reprieve.

She was crazy. Playing it cool with Ethan had been a monumental error in judgement. A guy like him would now see her as a challenge and she'd be darned if she sat back and watched him try to charm his way into her good graces. She wasn't interested in anything remotely romantic and, even if she was, he'd be the last guy she'd turn to.

'You can't keep up the silent treatment for ever.'

The amusement in his voice only served to irk more.

'Watch me.'

She swivelled on her heel and he grabbed her arm, leaving her no option but to face him while trying to ignore the erratic leap of her pulse at his innocuous touch.

'So I kissed you again? It was nothing. Surely we can get past it?'

Ouch, that hurt.

Of course a kiss would mean nothing to a playboy like him and, while she should be glad he was brushing it off, a small part of her hurt. She'd done her best to forget it, but she couldn't.

The kiss last night had been different from the

impulsive, passionate kiss in Ambrosia the day he'd returned.

This kiss had been filled with tenderness and compassion and understanding, his gentle consideration in stark contrast to the powerful man she knew him to be and thus so much more appealing.

This kiss had unlocked something deep inside, the touch of his lips bringing to life a part of her assumed long dead.

That something was hope.

'Come on, Tam. What do you say we put it behind us and enjoy this lovely spread?'

He waved towards the linen-covered tables covered in a staggering array of mouth-watering dishes she normally would've pounced on if her stomach wasn't tied in knots, the hint of that pirate smile tugging at his mouth.

How could a woman resist?

'Okay. But, just so you know, I'm not interested in anything…er…what I mean to say is…'

'It was just a kiss.' He ducked down to murmur in her ear and she gritted her teeth as a surge of renewed lust burst through her at his warm breath fanning her cheek. 'An all too short one at that.'

'I've heard that one before.'

'About it being just a kiss? Or me not apologising for it?'

'Yeah, that. It's a catchphrase of yours.'

He laughed, released her arm, and headed for the table, leaving her torn between wanting to shake him and admiring him for not backing down.

She sank into the chair he held out for her as a waiter bearing several silver-domed platters bore down on their table, deposited their meal, whipped off the domes and retreated with a small bow.

The fragrant aromas of spicy curries never failed to set her salivating but tonight her stomach clenched as she realized, no matter what she said to him, he'd continue to do exactly what he liked—and that was flirt with her.

'I'd like to propose a toast.'

He picked up his champagne flute, waited for her to do the same.

'To new beginnings and new experiences. May this journey bring us everything we could possibly wish for.'

Tam stared into her flute, watching the effervescent bubbles float lazily to the surface.

New beginnings, new experiences…hadn't she wanted all that and more on this trip? So why was she getting hot and bothered over a little harmless flirtation?

She knew Ethan's reputation, that flirting would come as easily as his millions. It meant nothing to him, he'd said so. She was so out of practice dealing with a charming man she'd lost perspective. Time to chill out.

'To new beginnings.'

She lifted her glass, tapped his, before raising it to her lips, wondering if the slight buzz was from the bubbles sliding down her throat or his mischievous smile.

'Let's eat.'

Silence reigned as they tucked into Jaipuri Mewa Pulao, a spiced rice packed with dried fruit, Rajasthani Lal Maas, a deliciously spiced lamb and Aloo Bharta, potato with a chilli kick, with relish.

As each new flavour burst on her tongue the words to describe them flashed through her mind in the way they'd always done when she'd worked full-time, vindication that the time was right to get back to the workforce on her return. Rather than being nervous, she couldn't wait.

As Ethan licked his lips and moaned with pleasure, she laughed. 'I take it you're enjoying Rajasthani cuisine.'

'Can't get enough of it.'

Popping another ladle of potato onto his plate, he nodded. 'Want to hear a fascinating fact I heard from our tour leader?'

'Uh-huh.'

'Rajasthan is an ancient princely state and it gave rise to a royal cuisine. The Rajas would go on hunting expeditions and eat the meat or fowl they brought back, which is why their feasts flaunt meat.'

'It all sounds very cavemanish.'

He glanced around, as if searching for something. 'Where's my club?' Accompanied by a ludicrous wiggle of his eyebrows. 'Fancy checking out my cave?'

She chuckled, glad she'd made the decision to lighten up. Sharing a meal with a charismatic dinner companion was enjoyable and definitely more fun than dining alone, something she'd honed to a fine art in the last year.

Though, in reality, she'd been alone a lot longer than that, Richard's long absences put down to work or media appearances or travelling to promote his latest book. Oh, not forgetting the time he'd spent holed away with his mistress.

Before she could mull further, he shot her a concerned glance and pushed the platter of potato towards her. 'More?'

Grateful for his distracting ploy, she nodded and ladled more food onto her plate.

'How did you get your start as a food critic?'

Another distraction and she silently applauded his ability to read her moods. Though it wouldn't take a genius to figure out her expression must've soured at the thought of Richard and his girlfriend.

'I've always been passionate about food and I

loved telling a good story at school. So I worked in a professional kitchen for a while, cultivated my palate outside of it, immersed myself in all things food, then spent a year as a hostess at Pulse.'

'You must've learned a lot there. That place was big—before Ambrosia opened, of course.'

She smiled. 'Of course.'

She'd loved her experience in the industry: being able to give an in-depth description of an entire meal, the restaurant, its décor, how the service contributed to the dining experience. Work had never been a chore for her and, thanks to Ethan and the opportunity he'd given her at Ambrosia for the last six months, she now had the confidence to get back to it.

'Can I ask you a stupid question?'

'Sure.'

'Does all that writing spoil the fun of eating for you?'

She shook her head. 'Uh-uh. I love to eat, I love what I do. It's as simple as that.'

And as they made desultory small talk over dessert, Churma Laddoos—sweet balls made from flour, ghee, sugar, almonds and carda-moms—she pondered her words.

As simple as that.

Were things simple and she was complicat-ing them?

She'd wanted to expand her mindset on this trip, wanted to explore a side of her long quashed, away from the sour memories dogging her, away from Richard's malevolent presence still hanging over her.

While she had no interest in romance, maybe she could explore the side of her long ignored?

She was a woman—a woman who'd had her self-esteem battered severely, to the point where she didn't trust her judgement any more.

Maybe Ethan could help reaffirm the woman she'd once been—a woman who'd loved to smile and laugh and flirt right back.

She longed to be that woman again.

But would she have the courage to try?

CHAPTER FIVE

'It's beautiful.'

They stood inside Udaipur's Jag Niwas, the stunning Lake Palace that rose out of the blue waters of Lake Pichhola like an incredible apparition, looking out over the rippling, murmuring waves lapping the foreshore.

When Tamara had been planning this trip with her mum, she'd wanted to stay in this dreamlike marble palace with its ornately carved columns and tinkling fountains and clouds of chiffon drapes, now a grand heritage hotel.

Now, with Ethan by her side, she was glad she wasn't. The last thing she needed was to stay in some exquisitely romantic hotel with a man putting unwanted romantic ideas into her head.

She turned away from the picture-perfect view, gestured to the silver-laden table behind them. 'You ready to eat?'

He nodded, dropped his hand, and she clamped

down on the instant surge of disappointment. 'Business all done. The chef signed the contract in front of me.'

He pulled out her chair in a characteristic chivalrous act she loved. If Richard had ever done it, he'd plonked his own selfish ass in it before she could move.

'He's one of India's best. And, considering my other choice in Delhi wouldn't budge, it's a coup getting this guy on board. Can't wait for him to start at Ambrosia.'

She sat, smiled her thanks. 'If you can't wait, neither can I. Just think, I get to sample his Chicken Makhani and crab curry and sweet potato kheer for nothing, all in the name of work.'

He chuckled, sat opposite her and flicked out his pristine white linen napkin like a troubadour before laying it in his lap.

'It's a hard life but somebody's got to do it, right?'

'Right.'

Hope cradled her heart, warming it, melting the band of anguish circling it. This was one of those moments she'd grown to crave yet fear, a poignant moment filled with closeness and intimacy.

A moment that said she was a fool for thinking she could start testing her flirting prowess and come out unscathed—or, worse, wanting more.

He broke the spell by picking up the menu,

scanning it. 'Let me guess. You've already studied this in great depth and have your trusty notebook at the ready.'

She tossed her hair over her shoulder, sent him a snooty stare that lost some of its impact when her lips twitched.

'My trusty notebook is safe in my bag.'

He raised an eyebrow and sent a pointed look at her favourite patent black handbag hanging off the back of her chair.

'No notes today?'

'Not a one.'

The corners of his mouth kicked up into the deliciously gorgeous smile that had launched this crazy new awareness in the first place. 'Well, well, maybe you're starting to like my company after all.'

'Maybe.'

She picked up a menu, ducked behind it to hide a faint blush.

'Want to know what I think?'

He leaned forward, beckoned her with a crook of a finger, leaving her no option but to do it.

'You're going to tell me anyway, so go ahead.'

He murmured behind his hand, 'I think that notebook is like Bankie.'

'Bankie?'

'The security blanket I had when I was a toddler. I couldn't say blanket, so called it Bankie.

A frayed, worn, faded blue thing that went every-where I did.'

Her heart turned over, imagining how utterly adorable he would've looked as a wide-eyed two-year-old clinging to his blanket.

He'd never spoken of his family but she assumed he had one tucked away somewhere; probably parents who doted on their wonder-boy son and a proud sibling or two.

'Why do you think I need a security blanket?'

'Because of what's happening between us.'

Her belly plummeted. She didn't want to have this conversation, not here, not now, not ever.

Darn it, until now she could've dismissed the awareness between them as a figment of her imagination.

Now it was out there.

Between them.

Larger than life and more terrifying than anything she could've possibly imagined.

She could ignore it, try and bluff her way out of it. But this was Ethan. The guy who'd helped her with the legal rigmarole after Richard's funeral, the guy who'd given her a chance at getting her career back on track. She owed him her thanks if not the truth.

'Seeing as you keep kissing me, what do you think is happening between us?'

He paused, shifted his plate and cutlery around before intertwining his fingers and laying his hands on the table and leaning forward.

'Honestly? I like you.'

He leaned closer, lowered his voice, and she had no option but to lean closer too. 'I like that you've changed since we've arrived here.'

This she could handle. She could fob him off with the real reason behind her change: her journey of self-discovery, her awakening to being her own person, her enjoyment of answering to no one but herself. All perfectly legitimate reasons to satisfy his curiosity and hide the real reason behind her change.

She shrugged, aiming for nonchalance. 'India's in my blood. Maybe my inner self recognises it on some subconscious level.'

He shook his head. 'I think there's more to it.'

'Like?'

'Like you opening your mind. Like you contemplating maybe there could be a spark between us.'

'I'm not contemplating anything of the sort!'

It sounded like the big fat lie it was.

He merely smiled, a captivating, sexy smile that made her feel a woman and then some.

'Come on, Tam. Admit it. You're as attracted to me as I am to you.'

She pushed away from the table, stood abruptly. 'I'm going for a walk.'

He let her go but she knew it wouldn't be for long. While he'd been surprisingly relaxed and laid-back on this trip, she'd seen his underlying streak of steel that had taken him to the top of the restaurant game around the world.

He'd made every rich list the year before, had women clamouring after him. So what the heck was he doing harassing a boring, sad-case widow like her?

She headed for the lake, head down, sandals flapping against the ancient stone path, eager to be anywhere other than sitting opposite the man she *was* attracted to in a palace restaurant in one of the most romantic settings on earth.

'Hey, wait up.'

His shout had her wanting to pick up the pace and flee. Futile, really, because she'd be stuck on the train with him for another few nights regardless if she outran him now.

Slowing her steps, she reached the edge of the lake, staring into the endless depths, searching for some clue to her problem, the problem of opening her heart to trust again, only to find the guy she liked was the one most likely to break it.

She knew when he reached her, could sense his body heat behind her, and she turned slowly, no closer to answering him now than she had been a few moments earlier.

He reached for her, dropped his hands when she frowned.

'You know I'm blunt. I call it as I see it and, deny it all you like, but something's happening between us.'

'Nothing's happening.'

A sudden breeze snatched her defiant whisper, making a mockery of her feeble protestation.

'If that's what you want to believe…' He shrugged, turned away, stared out over the lake to the island in the middle housing an entertainment complex where they'd have afternoon tea later, giving her time to concoct more excuses, more repudiation.

As if time would help.

She could protest all she liked but it wouldn't change the fact that everything had shifted and she didn't have a clue what to do about it.

How could she tell him that acknowledging the attraction between them, let alone giving in to it, was beyond frightening? How could she make him understand what a big deal this was for her?

It came to her as she glanced at his profile: so rugged, so handsome, so strong. She needed his strength, needed someone in her corner.

She'd never felt so alone as this last year, the last few years, despite being married and the implicit promise of safety it provided. And, while

Ethan was the last guy she'd turn to for safety, having him here, every enigmatic, enthralling, enticing inch of him, being more honest than Richard had ever been, went a long way to soothing her fear that this crazy, burgeoning physical need for him was totally wrong.

She laid a hand on his arm, dropped it when he turned towards her.

'Want to know what I believe? I believe you're a good guy. You make me laugh when you tell those horrible corny jokes. You make me smile with your outrageous flirting. But, most of all, you've made me believe I can have a fresh start.'

Some nebulous emotion bordering on guilt shifted in his eyes before he blinked. 'Good guy? Far from it.'

He glanced away, rubbed the back of his neck. 'I think you're amazing and I'm attracted to you, but don't go thinking I'm some prince because I'm not.'

'I gave up expecting a prince to rescue me a long time ago,' she said, annoyed she'd let slip another indication that Richard had been anything other than the guy Ethan thought him to be.

He searched her face—for answers, for the truth?

'You want me to drop this? Pretend it doesn't exist?'

That was exactly what she wanted but, for one tiny moment, the faintest hope in her heart that there could ever be anything more between them snuffed out like a candle in the breeze.

'Yes,' she breathed on a sigh, wishing there could be another way, knowing there wasn't.

She'd lost her mother, her husband and her identity over the last few years and she'd be darned if she lost the chance at a new start.

Falling for Ethan would be beyond foolish, destined to shatter what little of her trust remained and there was no way she'd put herself through something like that ever again.

A new hardness turned his eyes to steely blue as he nodded. 'Fine, have it your way. But know this. Pretending something doesn't exist won't make it disappear.'

He turned on his heel and strode towards the palace, leaving her heart heaving and her soul reaching out an imaginary hand to him, grasping, desperate, before falling uselessly to her side.

He wouldn't give up.

It was a motto that had got him through a horror childhood, the nightmare of his teens, and had taken him to the top of the restaurateur game.

Right now, what was at stake was just as important as scavenging for the next food scrap to fill his howling belly or opening a new restaurant in New York.

Tam had blossomed, had become a woman who smiled and laughed and raised her face to a scorching Indian sun. She ran through ancient forts. She sampled the spiciest dishes and called for more chilli. She played with the little children who dogged their steps when the train stopped, bestowing smiles and hugs and her last rupees.

This was the woman he wanted with an unrelenting fierceness that constantly tore at him, an overwhelming need out of proportion to anything he'd remotely felt before.

Now she'd let down her guard, was attracted to him. He could see it in the newly sparkling eyes, the quick look-away when he captured her gaze, the smile never far from her lips, which had been constantly downturned until recently.

And, no matter how much she wanted to pretend, this attraction wasn't going away. Not if he had anything to do with it.

In the business arena, he was notorious for his ruthlessness, his take-charge and take-no-prisoners attitude. He didn't have much time left with Tam and, the way he saw it, he needed to make something happen—now.

He just hoped she'd still talk to him after she discovered what he'd done to help them along a little.

* * *

She stood at the bow of the boat, a vision in a white dress scattered with vivid pink and red flowers, her hair loose and flowing around her shoulders, fluttering in the breeze.

He'd never seen anything so beautiful, so vibrant, so stunning, and his desire for her slammed into him anew.

Yeah, he was through waiting. He'd waited years already and now there was nothing standing in his way.

She glanced up at that exact moment, sending him a tentative smile, and he strode towards her, needing little invitation to be right by her side.

'You sure we've got time to cruise the lake and check out the entertainment complex on the island?'

He glanced at his watch, noting the time with satisfaction.

'Plenty of time.'

The glib lie slid from his lips and he didn't regret it, not for a second.

Udaipur's Lake Palace was one of the most romantic hotels on earth and if he couldn't convince her to confront their attraction here, it wouldn't happen anywhere.

She smiled and he instantly quashed his yearning to slip a possessive arm around her waist as his heart slammed against his rib cage and his blood thickened with the drugging desire to make her his.

'You sure? We wouldn't want to miss the train and be stuck in this place.'

She waved towards the tranquil lake, the Palace on the far shore. 'I mean, staying in the hotel wouldn't be a hardship, but stuck with you? Now, that'd be tough.'

Ignoring the flicker of guilt that he was instigating just such an outcome, he propped his elbows on the railing and leaned back.

'Are you actually teasing me?'

She glanced at him from beneath lowered lashes and he could've punched the air with elation that she was lightening up enough to spar with him.

'Maybe.'

'Well, if this is the reaction I get for suggesting a simple boat ride, I'm going to do it more often.'

The light in her eyes faded as her gaze left his to sweep the horizon.

'I'll be busy relaunching my career when we get back to Melbourne and you'll be too busy being the hotshot businessman so I think any boat rides down the Yarra are wishful thinking.'

Was that her way of saying what happened in India stayed in India? That, even if she eventually capitulated and acknowledged their attraction or, as he was hoping, did something about it, things would come to an abrupt end when they got home?

'In that case, let's make the most of our time cruising here.'

'Okay.'

He didn't push the issue and it earned him a grateful glance, but he didn't want her gratitude, damn it. He wanted her to look at him with stars in her eyes and hope in her heart—hope that they could be more than friends.

'Speaking of Melbourne, can I ask you a question?'

She could ask him to take a flying leap and he'd ask how high. 'Sure, shoot.'

'You and Richard were mates. Why didn't I see you at the dinner parties he was so fond of? And, when we did cross paths, it was almost like you avoided me.'

Her question hit too close to home and dread settled like overcooked Beef Wellington in the pit of his stomach, solid and heavy with discomfort assured.

Since he'd started pursuing her he'd known they'd have this conversation one day, surprised it'd taken her this long to ask and wishing it wasn't here, now, when he was making serious headway in his quest to have her.

'I wasn't avoiding you.'

'No?'

What could he say?

That he'd wanted her so badly he'd kept his distance for fear it'd distract him from his job? Or, worse, cause a serious problem between him and Rich, thus affecting their business?

That he'd wanted her so badly he'd dated a few look-alikes?

That he'd been so envious of Rich he'd taken a month off from the restaurant when they'd married?

That he'd been unable to look at the two of them together without wanting to hit something in frustration?

'I guess we moved in the same social circles occasionally, but I was busy schmoozing or courting business deals at those events to make chit-chat. Business, you know how it is.'

He avoided her shrewd stare by looking over her shoulder at the Palace shimmering in the distance. 'Never enough hours in the day.'

'Yet, by all accounts, you have plenty of time to date. Hmm…'

She tapped her bottom lip, drawing his attention to its fullness; as if he needed reminding. 'I guess what the rumour mill says about you is true.'

'What's that?'

'You're a seasoned playboy and Melbourne's number one eligible bachelor.'

'Playboy, huh?'

Her teasing smile surprised him, warming him

better than the fiery vindaloo he'd sampled at lunch. 'Bet you're proud of it too.'

He pretended to ponder for all of a second before shrugging, feigning bashfulness.

'That's some title. Care to help me live up to my reputation?'

He expected her to leap overboard at what he was suggesting but once again she surprised him, merely quirking an eyebrow, her smile widening.

'What? And become yet another statistic?' She shook her head. 'Nope, sorry, no can do. But don't worry, I'm sure you'll have loads of dewy-eyed, stick insect bimbos lining up when your plane touches down at Tullamarine.'

He chuckled, only slightly disconcerted by the fact that she'd described his usual dates to a T.

'Are you implying I'm shallow, Miss Rayne?'

'I'm not implying anything. I'm stating a fact.'

She joined in his laughter and he marvelled at the transformation from reserved widow to relaxed woman. He'd always thought her beautiful but when she was like this—laughing, laissez-faire—she was simply stunning.

'Lucky for you, the boat's about to dock. I don't think my ego could take much more of your kid-glove treatment.'

'There's plenty more where that came from.'

'I stand duly warned.'

As they disembarked, Ethan didn't have a care in the world. The woman he wanted was definitely warming to him and they'd have several days together away from the train to get to know each other much better.

He was making things happen, was back in control—exactly where he wanted to be.

'What do you mean, we missed the train?'

Tamara stared at Ethan in open-mouthed shock, his calm expression only serving to wind her up. 'You said we had plenty of time.'

He shrugged, checked his watch again. 'I made a mistake. Sorry.'

'*Sorry?* Is that all you can say?'

As the concierge glanced their way, she lowered her voice with effort. 'This is ridiculous.'

'Look, it's no big deal. We get a couple of rooms for the night, make arrangements to catch the train at the next stop.'

'It's not that easy.'

She sank into the nearest chair, tired after their long day, annoyed he'd made them miss the train and afraid—terribly afraid—of spending the night in this romantic hotel with Ethan.

There was a difference between not acknowledging the simmering attraction between them, the newly awakened awareness that shimmered between them hotter than the Indian sun, and trying to ignore it in a place like this.

'We'll miss the next stop tomorrow and that leaves the last day, the most important of the whole trip.'

'Because of the Taj?'

She nodded, a tiny pinch of latent grief nipping her heart. 'And the birds. My mum was obsessed with birds. She collected figurines of anything from geese to cranes and she always wanted to visit Bharatpur's bird sanctuary.'

He must've caught the hint of wistfulness mingled with sadness in her tone, for he pulled his mobile out of his pocket and leapt to his feet.

'I'll handle this. We'll stay here tonight and tomorrow we'll head to Bharatpur, then Agra.'

Before she could respond, he was already punching numbers on his phone. 'Don't worry, you won't miss a thing.'

'But all my clothes are on board. I don't have—'

'I'll sort everything out. Trust me.'

He held up a finger as someone answered on the other end and she snuggled into the comfortable lobby sofa, grateful to be stuck with someone so commanding.

She was tired of making decisions over the last year: when to return to work, what to do with the house, with her stock in Ambrosia, to take this trip. Sure, she'd appreciated the independence, especially since she'd been robbed of it for so long, but here, now, with Ethan taking charge, she was happy to sit back and go with the flow.

Strangely, she did trust him—with their travel arrangements, at least. He'd make things happen, he was that kind of guy.

'Right, all taken care of.'

He snapped the phone shut, thrust it into his pocket and dusted off his hands, mission accomplished.

'With one phone call?'

He grinned and held out a hand to help her up from the sofa. 'My PA's handling all the arrangements. In the meantime, let's grab a room.'

Her heart stuttered, her pulse skipped and she broke out in a cold sweat before realising it was just a figure of speech. He meant two rooms; he'd said as much earlier.

'Or we could get the honeymoon suite if you're feeling particularly adventurous.'

Her shocked gaze flew to his, only to find his too-blue eyes twinkling adorably.

With a shake of her head, she waved him away. 'As tempting as that sounds, I've already told you I'm not another statistic.'

His mischievous grin had her wishing she could throw caution to the wind and become just that.

'Too bad, my bedpost needs a new notch.'

'You're—'

'Adorable? Endearing? Growing on you?'

Biting the inside of her cheek to stop herself from laughing out loud, she said, 'Pushing your luck. I'm beat. How about we get a *couple* of rooms?'

She only just caught his muttered, 'Spoilsport,' under his breath as he proceeded to charm the check-in staff as easily as he did everyone else.

Glancing around at the pristine marble floor, the majestic columns, the sweeping staircase and the glistening chandeliers, she couldn't help but be glad.

She was spending the night in a beautiful palace on a world famous lake with the most charming man she'd ever met.

And while she could vehemently deny her insane attraction to a guy so totally wrong for her, it didn't hurt to let some of the romance of this place soften the edges of her hard resolve. Right?

Oh, boy.

There was a difference between softening her resolve and it melting clean away, and right now, staring at Ethan in her doorway, with champagne in one hand and a glossy Taj brochure in the other, she knew her resolve wasn't softening, it was in tatters.

'Mind if I come in?'

Yeah, she minded, especially since she'd rinsed

her dress and underwear and was in a fluffy complimentary hotel robe.

If she felt vulnerable to him in her clothes, what hope did she have naked?

Oh, no, she couldn't think about being naked under her robe, not with him staring at her with those twinkling cobalt eyes, and the mere thought had a blush creeping into her cheeks.

'I come bearing gifts.'

He waved the champagne and brochure to tempt her. As if he wouldn't be enough to do that. The thought had her clutching the door, ready to close it.

'Actually, I'm pretty tired.'

And confused and drained and just a tad excited.

He'd showered too and, with his slicked-back wet hair, persuasive sexy smile and magnetic indigo eyes, he looked more like a pirate than ever.

Ethan was dangerous: too glib, too smooth, too gorgeous.

At that moment, she knew exactly why she found him so attractive. She'd married Richard because he'd made her feel safe. The older guy who loved her, took care of her, made her feel special, and while it may not have lasted, that hadn't stopped her from cherishing the feeling of security he'd temporarily brought to her life.

Which explained why she suddenly found

Ethan so appealing. That edge of danger, of unpredictability, was something she'd never experienced and, while she wouldn't want someone like him in her life, for someone who'd played it safe her entire life, she could understand the allure.

He held up the brochure, cleverly honing in on her weak spot. 'Share one drink with me, whet my appetite for the Taj Mahal and I'm out of here. Promise.'

Her instincts screamed to refuse but he'd been nothing but helpful in organising their rooms, transport for tomorrow and entry to the bird sanctuary and the Taj. The least she could do was appear grateful rather than churlish.

'Okay.'

Besides, it was only one drink. Barely enough time to make small talk, let alone anything else happening. Not that she wanted anything to happen.

Great, there went another blush. She quickly opened the door further and ushered him in.

'Room okay?'

'Are you kidding?'

When she'd wanted to stay here, she'd had no idea the rooms would be this gorgeous: the cusped archways, the carvings, the Bohemian crystal lights and the miniature paintings. It was like living in a fairy tale, being a princess for a night.

As long as there was no pea under the mattress, and no prince on top of it.

'It's fantastic.'

'Good. For a while there, I thought you'd behead me for making us miss the train.'

'Wasn't like you did it on purpose.'

Guilt tightened his features as he turned away to uncork the champagne and pour it into the exquisite crystal flutes which were standard room supplies, but it disappeared as he handed her a glass, joined her on the sofa; she must've imagined it.

'Here's to the rest of the trip being as eventful.'

He raised his glass to hers, tapped it and drank, his eyes never leaving hers for a second.

There was something in his stare—something resolute, unwavering and it sent a shiver through her. She had to look away, had to break the spell cast over her the moment he'd walked into the room.

Was she kidding? He'd cast a spell on her the moment he'd landed in India and railroaded her trip.

Lowering his glass, he placed it on a nearby table and did the same with hers before leaning forward, way too close.

'Tell me. Is my being here making you uncomfortable?'

'A little.'

She settled for the truth, hating how gauche and floundering and out of her depth he made her feel.

She hadn't asked for this, hadn't fostered this attraction or encouraged it but it was there all the same, buzzing between them, electrifying and alive, no matter how hard she tried to ignore it.

'Why?'

He didn't back away. If anything, he leaned closer and her skin tingled where his shirt cuff brushed her wrist.

'Because you're the type of guy any woman in her right mind should stay away from,' she blurted, silently cringing at her brusque outburst.

Rather than offending him, he laughed, the rich, deep chuckles as warm and seductive as the rest of him.

'You keep coming back to that playboy thing. Don't believe everything you hear.'

She raised an eyebrow. 'So you're not a ladies' man?'

'Let's just say my reputation may be embroidered somewhat.'

His laconic response drew a smile. While Ethan was trying to downplay his reputation, she had little doubt every word was true. She'd seen his passing parade of women, either in the tabloids or at the restaurant, and while she should be the last person to judge who he paired up with—look at the monumental mistake she'd made in marrying Richard—the vacuous women didn't seem his type.

'It really bothers you, doesn't it? My past?'

She shrugged. 'None of my business.'

'I'd like it to be.'

He was so close now, his breath feathered over her cheek and she held her breath, wanting to move away, powerless to do so with her muscles locked in shock.

If she turned her head a fraction, he'd kiss her. His intent was clear—his words, his closeness, his body language—and she exhaled softly, her body quivering with the need to be touched, her heart yelling *no, no, not him!*

Rivers of heat flowed from her fingertips to her toes, searing a path through parts of her she'd forgotten existed. Her body blazed with it, lit up from within and in that instant her resolve was in danger of going up in flames.

'Tell me what you want, Tam.'

The fire fizzed and spluttered and died a slow, reluctant death as reality hit.

She knew what she wanted: to build a new life, to move forward, without the encumbrance of a man.

Yet she was wavering, seriously contemplating giving in to her irrational attraction for a man— not just any man, a man totally wrong for her.

That thought was enough to snap her out of the erotic spell he'd wound around them and she leaned back, forcing a laugh to cover the relief mingled with regret that she'd come to her senses in time.

'I want to take a look at that gorgeous brochure. So hand it over.'

He let her get away with it, but not before she saw the glitter of promise in his eyes.

This wasn't the end of it—far from it.

Ethan waved the brochure at Tam, snatching it away as she reached for it, laughing at her outrage.

He'd wanted her to say those three magical words—*I want you*—three little words that would've given him the go-ahead to seduce her in this exquisite room, a memory to last her a lifetime.

He wasn't a romantic, far from it, but he wanted her first time with him to be special, something she'd remember when they parted back in Melbourne.

After what she'd been through, she deserved special. Hell, she deserved the world on a plate and then some.

'Give me that!'

He raised the brochure higher. 'Uh-uh. Not until you ask nicely.'

She made a grab for it, leaning over far enough that the front of her robe parted and gave him a glimpse at heaven, her breasts lush and free and begging to be touched.

He swallowed, the game he was playing taking on new meaning as she leaned closer, reaching further, his lust skyrocketing as her tantalising exposed skin came within licking reach…

'Hand it over.' Laughing, she added, 'Pretty pleeeease,' before making a frantic lunge at his arm stretched overhead.

That last grab was her undoing, and his, as she teetered on her knees, precariously balanced, before tumbling against him and knocking him flat on his back on the sofa.

'Oops, sorry.'

Staring up at her, propped over him, her palms splayed against his chest, her mouth inches from his, her eyes wide and luminous and darkening with desire, she didn't look sorry in the least.

The brochure fluttered to the floor, forgotten, as she poised over him, hovered for an endless tension-fraught moment before lowering her head and slamming her mouth on his, eager, hungry, desperate.

He didn't know what shocked him more: the sheer reckless abandon with which she kissed him or the yearning behind it as her lips skidded over his, craving purchase, demanding he respond.

He didn't need to be asked twice, opening his mouth, the thrill of her tongue plunging in and exploring him tearing a groan from deep within.

How many times had he fantasised about having her?

But never in his wildest dreams had he envisioned her like this: crazy with passion, commanding, on top and totally in control.

Realisation slammed into him as she eased the kiss, lifted her head to stare at him with adoration in her glistening green eyes.

He wasn't in control any more, had lost it the second she'd pinned him down and initiated the kiss, demanding a response he was all too willing to give, but at what cost?

If losing control wasn't bad enough, the clear message in her eyes was.

She cared.

Too much.

He should've known a woman like her wouldn't respond physically to him unless she made an emotional connection and, by his own foolishness in encouraging deeper conversations, she had, damn it.

He wanted her so badly his body throbbed with it but this was all wrong.

It had to be on his terms, with her fully aware of what she was getting into, without hope in her heart and stars in her eyes.

Placing his hands around her waist, he lifted her so he could sit up, releasing her when they sat side by side.

Confusion clouded her eyes, with just a hint of hurt, but he couldn't acknowledge that, otherwise he'd find himself right back where he'd started, offering comfort when he shouldn't, giving her the wrong idea.

'What's wrong?'

'Nothing.'

He stood and strode to the door, needing to retreat before she pushed for answers he wasn't willing to give.

'I thought that's what you wanted.'

Her voice trembled, giving him another kick in the guts and he clenched his hands, thrust them into his pockets to stop himself from heading back to the sofa, sweeping her into his arms, carrying her to that tempting king-size bed and showing her exactly what he wanted.

'What about what you want?'

'That's pretty obvious. At least, I thought it was. Maybe I've been out of practice too long.'

He jammed his fists further in his pockets, rocked by the relentless urge to go to her.

She sounded so sad, so confused, and it was his fault.

He needed to get out of here. Now.

Spinning to face her, he strode back to the sofa, picked up the brochure lying at her feet and placed it on her lap when she didn't make a move to take it.

'Here's what you want.' He stabbed a finger at the glossy image of the Taj Mahal. 'I'm just a pushy guy bustling in on your dream.'

Her accusatory glare cut deep and he hated himself for putting her—them—in this position.

'I don't understand.'

Unable to resist dropping one last swift kiss on her lips, he muttered, 'Neither do I,' as he headed for the door.

CHAPTER SIX

TAMARA still didn't understand the next day when they reached Bharatpur.

She'd spent a sleepless night, analysing the moment Ethan had pulled away, over and over, replaying it until she'd turned over and stuffed her face into the pillow to block out the memory.

She'd kissed him, he'd pulled away.

No matter how many times she went over it in her head, it all came back to that.

It didn't make any sense. The way he'd been flirting, the way he'd been charming her from the moment she'd walked into Ambrosia and found him there, the way he'd been kissing her, repeatedly…

Something wasn't right and, in the wee small hours of the morning, she'd come to a decision.

Forget the humiliation, forget the embarrassing kiss, forget she'd made a fool of herself.

This trip was too important to let one cringeworthy moment tarnish it. She'd waited too long to take it, was finally discovering her old self beneath layers of battered esteem.

And she liked what she was discovering: that she could feel again, that being with a man could be pleasurable rather than horrifying, that she liked feeling like a desirable woman rather than an ornamental wife brought out of her box to perform on cue at dinner parties and shelved the rest of the time.

If that scared Ethan, tough.

Maybe the guy was too used to getting his own way, was one of those strong guys who preferred to do all the chasing? Well, he could keep chasing, for that was the first and last time she showed him how amazing she found this irrational, incongruous attraction.

She should be glad he'd back-pedalled today, had made urbane small talk and eased off the flirting on their trip here, had made it perfectly clear he didn't want to discuss his about-face last night.

Instead, she found herself darting curious glances at him, trying to read his rigid expression—and failing—somewhat saddened by their long lapses into silence.

'Your chariot…'

Ethan gestured at the rickshaw he'd hired to take them around Keoladeo Ghana National Park, Bharatpur's famous bird sanctuary, and she smiled, relieved, when he responded with one of his own.

Buoyed by the first sign of anything other than irresolute self-control, she said, 'Chariot, huh? Does that make you Prince Charming?'

He shook his head, but not before she glimpsed his familiar rakish smile, her heart flip-flopping against her will in response.

'What is it with girls and princes?'

She could've elaborated on the whole 'being swept off their feet, rescued and living happily ever after' scenario girls loved from the moment they could walk. But considering her fantasy had evaporated quicker than Richard's love for her, she shrugged and stepped up into the tiny rickshaw. Her relief at being sheltered from the relentless sun instantly evaporated as he swung up beside her and she realised how small these rickshaws really were.

'Let's get moving. I don't want to spend too long here when we've got the Taj this afternoon.'

She agreed, though his brisk tone implied he couldn't wait to get to the end of this trip, couldn't get away from her quick enough.

She wasn't going to overanalyse this, remember? Wasn't going to waste time trying to read his mind or figure out his motivations.

'Can't wait.'

After instructing the driver to go, he leaned back, his thigh brushing hers, his arm wedged against hers as she wished her fickle body would stay with the programme.

This was a transient attraction, a natural reaction of her hormones considering she hadn't been with a man for almost two years. Richard hadn't touched her during that last year of their marriage, and she hadn't wanted him to. It made her skin crawl just thinking about where he'd been at the time, who he'd been with.

Silence stretched taut between them and she needed to say something—anything—to distract from her skin prickling with awareness where it touched his.

'My mum talked about the Taj constantly. About its inception, its history, but she never got to see it. This was going to be her first time…'

Her breath hitched on a part sob and she clamped her lips shut, wishing he'd sling an arm across her shoulders and cradle her close. He'd been nothing but comforting the last time she'd spoken about Khushi, had encouraged her to do so.

But, despite the momentary flicker of compassion in his eyes, the flash of understanding, he remained impassive, jaw clenched so hard the muscles bulged.

'You'll get to see it through her eyes, through her stories. You may be the one standing before it today but she'll be the one bringing it alive for you.'

She raised her gaze to his, emotion clogging her throat, tears stinging her eyes, but he glanced away, leaving her torn between wanting to hug him for saying something so perfect and throttle him for cheapening it by looking away.

'Thanks, I needed to hear that.'

'My pleasure.'

Empty words, considering there was nothing remotely pleasurable about the barrier he'd erected between them, the severing of an emotional connection no matter how tentative.

She'd been frozen inside for years, emotionally frigid as she'd shut down to cope with Richard's psychological abuse, numbing her feelings to stop the constant barrage of verbal put-downs and criticism.

She'd thought she was incapable of feeling anything again, yet Ethan had given her that gift.

Despite the urge to go running and screaming in the opposite direction, the more he charmed her, despite the fear that her body was responding to him and overthrowing her mind, despite the paralysing terror of feeling anything for a man ever again, she'd allowed him to get close enough to melt the icy kernel surrounding her heart and, for that, she was eternally grateful.

Her lower lip wobbled at the thought of how far she'd come and she blinked, inhaled sharply, her senses slammed by his sandalwood scent from the hotel's luxurious selection of complimentary toiletries, as she savoured the illicit pleasure of being this close to him.

With a small shake of her head, she pulled a guidebook from her bag and rattled open the pages, desperate for a diversion from her thoughts, her emotions and the uneasy silence.

'It says here this place is a bird paradise, with over three hundred and eighty species, including some rare Siberian cranes.'

He turned, leaned over her shoulder, peered at the book and she held her breath, unprepared for all that hard male chest to be wedged up against her.

'What else have they got?'

Forced to breathe in order to answer him, she inhaled another heady lungful of pure male tinged with sandalwood, momentarily light-headed. Her palms were clammy, her body on fire and her head spun with the implications of how she was reacting to him, despite all her self-talk that she shouldn't.

Peering at the guidebook as if it had all the answers to questions she shouldn't even be contemplating, she cleared her throat.

'Hawks, pelicans, geese, eagles among countless other species, and they also have golden jackals, jungle cats, striped hyenas, blackbuck and wild boar.'

'Great.'

Yeah, great. He'd hired the rickshaw driver for an hour and in that time she'd be stuck here, nice and tight, unable to breathe without his tantalising scent assailing her, unable to move without encountering way too much firm muscle, unable to think without rehashing reasons why this could be better if he opened up and she shed her inhibitions.

As a pelican flew at the rickshaw in an indignant rage, the driver swerved, throwing her flush against Ethan and all that glorious hard muscle.

Righting her, he smiled, a warm, toe-curling smile that reached down to her heart, the type of smile that made resistance futile, the first genuine smile he'd given her all day.

Desperate to prolong the moment now she'd finally seen a glimpse of the old Ethan, she said, 'No need to throw myself at you, huh?'

Her hands splayed against his chest, the rhythmic pounding of his heart proof that he was as affected by their proximity as her.

'You don't hear me complaining.'

He held her gaze and she couldn't speak, couldn't breathe, the distant screech of an eagle as hauntingly piercing and achingly poignant as the sudden yearning to stay like this, touching him, secure in his arms, for more than a brief moment.

She wanted to push him for answers, to ask why he'd gone cold on her but, as much as her foolhardy heart urged her, she couldn't do it.

She'd taken a risk on a man once before and her judgement had been way off. She'd thought Richard had been a safe bet, she'd trusted him and look how that had turned out. Trusting Ethan would be tantamount to handing him her heart on a serving platter complete with carving knives.

As she tried to muster a response, he straightened her, putting her away from him with strong yet gentle hands. 'You know what you look like?'

'What?'

'A worm surrounded by the entire population of this bird sanctuary.'

He tucked a strand of hair behind her ear, allowed his fingers to linger, brushing the soft skin of her neck. 'I'm not going to bite, Tam. So quit looking at me like I'm the big bad wolf.'

Before she could respond, he ducked his head, captured her mouth in a swift, urgent kiss that barely lasted a second, leaving her dazed and stunned and more baffled than ever.

'Though I have to say, you'd look great in red.'

With that, he turned to watch a gaggle of geese take flight as she sat there, bracing her feet to stop herself from rocking against him any more than necessary, absolutely speechless, thoroughly perplexed, and touching her trembling lips with a shaky hand.

He confounded, mystified and thoroughly bamboozled her, blowing hot and cold just like his employees said and, right now, she wanted to be like those geese. Free to take off, free to expand her wings, free to be whoever she wanted to be.

She wanted to feel carefree and light-hearted and unburdened for the first time in years, wanted to have the courage to explore outside her comfort zone, to let the winds of chance take her wherever.

Darting a quick glance at Ethan, still staring resolutely out the other side, she knew with the utmost certainty that he was a part of that yearning to explore the unknown, the craving to take a chance, no matter how much his behaviour bewildered her.

She was so used to repressing her true feelings, so used to playing a part, that she didn't know who she was any more, let alone how to be the carefree, happy woman she'd once been.

Ethan could help her.

He could help her rediscover her zing, could nurture their spark towards something exciting, something beyond her wildest dreams.

But she had to take a chance.

Was she willing to take a risk for a fleeting happiness that would dissolve when Ethan stepped on a plane bound for Melbourne?

Some choice and, as the rickshaw bumped and rocked and swayed through the sanctuary, she knew she'd have to make up her mind and fast. They had half a day and one night left together. Not a heck of a lot of time to make a decision.

Chance. Risk. Gamble. Venture.

Things she'd never done when married to Richard, content in the security he'd provided, when she'd been the dutiful wife so in love with her husband she'd been blinded to his faults until it was too late.

But that part of her life was over, her dreams of happily ever after shattered by a selfish egomaniac, and for the first time in years she could do as she damn well pleased.

Stakes were high.

Make a mistake and she'd lose the tentative friendship she'd developed with Ethan, something she'd grown to depend on over the last week.

Make it work and they could shoot to the moon and back.

With a heartfelt sigh she sat back, braced against the rocking, and watched the geese fly higher and higher, reaching for the stars.

Maybe she should too.

CHAPTER SEVEN

'YOU ready?'

Tamara nodded, took a deep breath and opened her eyes, the air whooshing out of her lungs as she caught her first unforgettable glimpse of the Taj Mahal.

The incredible monument shimmered in the early dusk, its white marble reflecting in the long moat in front of it, casting a ghostly glow over the magical gardens surrounding it.

'It's something else.'

She glanced at Ethan, too choked to speak, grateful he knew how much this moment meant to her.

Sliding an arm around her waist, he hugged her close. 'Your mum's here with you. She'd want you to enjoy this, to be happy.'

Gnawing on her bottom lip to keep from blubbering, she searched his eyes, wondering if he knew how much of an integral part he played in her happiness these days.

All she saw in those fathomless blue depths was caring, compassion and a tenderness that took her breath away.

Thankfully, they'd broken the ice following the rickshaw ride and, while he hadn't slipped back into full-on flirting just yet, she had hopes that their last kiss hadn't ruined their friendship for ever.

For no matter how many logical, sane reasons she'd pondered as to why they couldn't be anything more than friends, they all faded into oblivion the second she caught her first breathtaking glimpse of the Taj.

There was nowhere else she'd rather be this very moment than right here, with this man.

Placing a hand on his cheek, she caressed the stubble, enjoying the light prickle rasping against her palm.

'I hope you know that sharing this with you is beyond special.'

Surprise flickered in his eyes—surprise tinged with wariness.

'I'm a poor stand-in for your mum but I'm glad I can be here for you.'

He semi-turned, forcing her to drop her hand, and she followed his line of vision, blown away by the fact that she was standing in front of one of the new Seven Wonders of the World, the River Yamuna flowing tranquilly nearby, surrounded by fellow tourists yet feeling as if she were the only woman in the world to have ever felt this incredible in the face of such beauty.

'It's stood the test of time, hasn't it?'

She followed his line of vision, taking in the curved dome, the archways, the exquisite ornamentation. 'Considering it took twenty-two years to build, I guess they made it to last.'

He did a slow three-sixty, taking in the gardens, the fountains, before fixing his gaze on the Taj again. 'I knew it'd be impressive but I didn't expect anything like this.'

'I know,' she breathed on a sigh, closing her eyes for a second, savouring the moment, elated that when she opened them again she'd see the same incredible sight. 'Do you know the story behind it?'

He held up his hand; it wavered from side to side. 'A little. Shah Jahan, a Mughal Emperor, had it constructed in memory of his beloved wife Mumtaz Mahal. Took about twenty thousand workers, a thousand elephants to haul materials and used about twenty-eight precious and semi-precious stones to do the inlay work.'

She smiled. 'Someone's been reading their Lonely Planet guide.'

He raised an eyebrow. 'Okay, Miss Smarty Pants. Why don't you tell me what you know?'

'My version reads like a romance novel.'

'I'm a sensitive New Age guy. Go ahead. Try me.'

'Okay, but you'd better sit down. This could take a while.' She sank onto the ground, clasped her hands around her knees and rested her chin on her knees, waiting until he sat to begin.

'Shah Jahan was the son of the fourth Mughal emperor of India. He was fourteen when he met Arjumand Banu Begum, a Muslim Persian princess, who was fifteen. It was love at first sight.'

She sighed, wondering what it would be like to be swept away like that, to know in an instant you were destined to be with that person.

Richard had charmed and blustered and cajoled his way into her affections, offering her the safety of marriage, a safety she'd craved since her dad had died. Yes, it had been quick and, yes, she'd fallen hard but nothing like locking eyes with a person and knowing with the utmost certainty he was *the one*.

'But they were kids! That's not even legal.'

She waved away his protest. 'Different times. We're talking about the early sixteen hundreds. Do you want to hear the rest or not?'

'Go ahead. I can see you're busting to tell me.'

Sending him a mock frown, she continued.

'After meeting the princess, Shah Jahan went back to his father and declared he wanted to marry her. They married five years later. When he became emperor eleven years later, he entrusted her with the royal seal and gave her the title Mumtaz Mahal, which means "jewel of the palace". Though he had other wives—'

'That's not romance, that's bigamy.'

She rolled her eyes. 'That's allowed in his religion. Anywaaaay—'

He grinned at her obvious annoyance at his constant interruptions.

'She was his favourite, accompanied him everywhere, even on military campaigns. But when she was giving birth to their fourteenth child—' Ethan winced and she couldn't blame him '—there were complications and she died. Apparently, legend has it that she secured a promise from him with her last breath to build a beautiful monument in her memory.'

She gestured to the Taj Mahal. 'And he did.'

Her glance roved over the towering dome, the intricate archways, the cypress trees nearby, as she pondered the depth of that kind of love, captivated by the spellbinding romance of it all.

'That's some story.'

He stared at the monument, the sudden tension in his shoulders alerting her to the fact that something bothered him, before swiftly turning to her and fixing her with a probing stare.

'Do you believe in love at first sight?'

At that moment, with his intense blue eyes boring into hers, his forearm brushing hers, his heat radiant and palpable and real, she wished she did.

'My parents did. They took one look at each other on Colva beach and fell in love.'

He didn't let her off that easily. 'I didn't ask about them. I'm asking you.'

Here was her chance to tell him she'd been thinking about pushing the boundaries, possibly seeing where it could take them.

But the reservations of a lifetime dogged her. She'd always done the right thing, been the dutiful daughter, the good little wife. She didn't like rocking the boat, changing the status quo. She'd tried it once before, was still dealing with the consequences.

Drawing a harsh, shaky breath, she forced her fingers to relax rather than leave welts from digging into her hands.

'I don't know what I believe any more.'

He shook his head, disappointment clouding his eyes. 'That's a cop-out.'

'Pardon?'

'You heard me. You're a strong, resilient woman. You've coped with losing your husband.

You've made decisions to move forward with your life. Plans to return to work.' He jerked his head towards the Taj Mahal. 'Coming here.'

He laid a hand on her arm and she started. 'All major decisions—but see that? The way you just jumped when I touched you?' He shook his head, his mouth twisting with disappointment as he released her. 'You're selling yourself short there. You're not being honest.'

She leaped to her feet, needing space, a continent's worth to flee the truth of his words and the reckless pounding of her heart.

'This isn't about honesty. It's about taking a risk and I hate taking risks.'

When a passing couple stared, she ran a weary hand over her face, lowered her voice.

'I'm not like you. You're brave. Fearless. Take charge. Everything so clear in black and white. While I feel like I've been living in some alternate grey universe and I'm finally coming out the other side.'

He stood, reached for her but she held him away. 'No, let me finish. I need to say this. You're successful, accomplished, but you know what I envy the most? You know who you are. You know your place in the world and, right now, that's something I don't have a clue about…'

Her declaration petered out on a whisper, a

taut silence stretching between them until she wished he'd say something—anything—to fill the tense void.

Finally, he slid an arm around her waist, pulled her close, and she let him.

'I didn't know.'

'That I'm such a sad case?'

Her attempt at humour fell flat.

'That you felt like that. I'm sorry.'

'Don't be. It's something I have to work through.'

Something she was determined to do. Everything seemed much easier here, away from the memories of Richard, of discovering the truth.

'You've had a rough trot. You know you deserve to be happy, right?'

She'd spent years pretending she was happy when she was anything but: pretending Richard's passive-aggressive barbs didn't hurt, pretending his criticism was well-intended, pretending she still loved him when inside she'd died a little every day.

The pretence had extended following his death, playing the grieving widow for appearance's sake when deep down she'd felt like screaming at his treachery, at his selfishness in making her life miserable while he had a ball with another woman behind her back.

'I want to be happy…'

'Then let go.'

She knew what he was implying, could read it in every tense line of his body.

Meeting his unwavering stare, she suppressed her inner voice screaming, *no, no, don't do it*.

'With you?'

He nodded slowly, his eyes never leaving hers. 'Want to know why I came on this trip?'

'I thought it was all business?'

He smiled at her soft sarcasm, his expression inscrutable.

'Because of you.'

He gripped her arms, his fierceness so over-whelming she would've taken a step back if he wasn't hanging on to her.

'Then why do you keep pulling away? It's like you get too close and then—wham, nothing.'

He shook his head, his hands tightening their grip as he hauled her closer. 'I barely knew you before this trip and spending time with you changed everything. Yeah, I'm a red-blooded male and I want you. But now—'

He searched her eyes for—what? Approval? Some sign that she wanted to see this through until the end?

'What do you want from me now?'

'This.'

Before she could make sense of his words, before she could push him for an explanation, his mouth swooped and captured hers in a hungry, rash kiss, blindingly brilliant in its savage intensity.

Her senses reeled as he deepened the kiss, as she let him, stunned by the ferocity of her own response as she grabbed frantically at his T-shirt, clung to him, dragged him closer.

If he'd slowed down, been tender and gentle rather than commanding and masterful, she would've had time to think, time to dredge up every rational reason why she shouldn't be doing this after the way he'd rebuffed her last night.

Instead, she let go, became herself, not some mouse-like woman worried about what other people would think of her for staying in a loveless marriage with a heartless tyrant if they knew.

Her knees wobbled as he pulled her closer, his hands strumming her back, his lips playing delightful havoc with hers as he challenged her with every tantalising sweep of his tongue, with every searing brush of his lips.

It was the kiss of a lifetime.

A kiss filled with promise and excitement and wonder, without a shade of grey in sight.

A kiss memories were made of.

An eternity later, when the initial blistering heat subsided and their lips eased, lingered, before releasing, the reality of the situation rushed in, the old self-doubts swamping her in a crushing wave.

'Don't do that.'

He tipped her chin up, caressed her bottom lip with his thumb. 'Don't go second-guessing yourself or what just happened.'

'I'm not—'

His mouth kicked up into the roguish smile she loved so much. 'This is me you're talking to.'

'That's what I'm afraid of,' she murmured, smoothing his T-shirt where she'd gripped it so hard she'd wrinkled it to the point where it needed a shot of steam or two to de-crease.

'Just take that kiss at face value, as a first step.'

She was almost too afraid to ask. 'A first step to what?'

Brushing a soft, barely-there kiss across her lips, he said, 'That's something we're about to find out.'

CHAPTER EIGHT

As FAR as first dates went, Ethan couldn't fault this one. He leaned back on outstretched arms and looked up at the monstrous India Gate in the centre of New Delhi.

In reality, he could've been in a dingy alleyway in the back of Timbuktu and the date would've been amazing all the same, courtesy of the stunning woman by his side, looking happy and more relaxed than he'd ever seen her.

'What are you thinking?'

Tamara smiled up at him from her vantage point, stretched out on the grass on propped elbows.

'I'm thinking if I see one more monument or fort or palace I'll go cross-eyed.'

He laughed, reached out to pluck a blade of grass stuck to her hair. 'But this is the Arc de Triomphe of India. It commemorates the seventy thousand Indian soldiers who died fighting for the British Army in World War One and is inscribed with the names of over thirteen thousand British and Indian soldiers killed in the 1919 Afghan war.'

She shook her head. 'There you go again, swallowing another guidebook. You know, all those facts will give you indigestion.'

He winked, ducked his head for a quick kiss that left her blushing. 'Just trying to impress you.'

'You've done that already.'

Her praise, the easy way she admitted it, warmed his heart, before stabbing doubt daggers into it again.

He'd tried his best to back off, to subdue his panic, to alienate her.

It had worked for a while; he'd regained control but it hadn't eradicated the fear.

The fear that he was already feeling way too much, the fear that what was happening between them was beyond anything he'd ever felt before but, most of all, the fear that no matter what he did, how hard he tried to stay in command, his overwhelming need for this woman would engulf him anyway.

He wanted this—right? Then why the constant nagging deep in his gut that this was more than he could handle?

During his relentless pursuit, he hadn't actually spelled it out that he wasn't interested in a relationship. He hoped to date for a while, have some fun together, explore the underlying spark simmering between them.

But that was where things ended. Would Tam want more? He doubted it, considering she'd talked about new beginnings, a fresh start. Believing her only encouraged him to indulge their attraction, guilt-free.

If things got too heavy, he knew what he had to do: run, just like his mum.

He'd loved her, had been secure she returned the sentiment until his childish delusions had been ripped from under him, leaving him a homeless orphan with a mother who'd rather be on her own than stuck with a five-year-old.

'What's wrong?'

He blinked, wrenched back to the present by her tentative question, her hand on his arm, and he mentally dusted himself off.

Today wasn't a day for sour memories.

Today was a day for creating brilliant new ones.

'Just thinking about where we go from here.'

It wasn't a lie exactly. He'd been stewing over their future since they'd opened an emotional Pandora's Box at the Taj yesterday.

He wanted this, wanted more than friendship with this incredibly special woman. Then why couldn't he rid himself of the faintest mantra stuck on rewind in the back of his mind, the one that chanted *be careful what you wish for?*

He'd always been ambitious, driven to succeed, craving control to stave off the darkness that crept into his soul at the oddest of times—a darkness filled with depressing memories of physical abuse and living on the streets and starving to the point of desperation.

Being one hundred per cent focused on business had served him just fine. Until now, when his legendary control was smashed like a soup tureen by a temperamental chef by taking the next step with Tam.

He half expected her to balk at the question, to shirk it. Instead, she fixed him with those mesmerising green eyes, eyes he could happily get lost in for ever.

'Honestly? I have no idea. I'm in Goa for the next week. You're here on business.'

She idly plucked at the grass beneath her hands, picking blades and letting them fall. 'I guess we wait until we're back in Melbourne and see what happens.'

For some strange reason her answer filled him with relief when he should be pushing her, ensuring she wouldn't back off once their journey together ended today.

What the hell was happening to him?

Sure, he enjoyed the thrill of the chase as much as the next guy but usually didn't tire of something once possessed—until the woman in question wanted to possess him. So why was he feeling like this? So uncertain, so uneasy, so unhinged.

His goal had been to seduce her and he was almost there. Then why the unrelenting fear he'd got more than he'd bargained for?

'You're not happy about that?'

He forced a smile, tension sneaking up the back of his neck and bringing on one of the classic headaches reserved for day-long meetings.

'We've come a long way in a week. Maybe things will be different when we get home.'

A tiny frown puckered her brow as she pushed up to a sitting position. 'That's not like you. You're the optimistic one. I'm the confirmed pessimist.'

What could he say?

That he didn't want a full-blown relationship? That he didn't trust what they had? That he didn't trust easily, period?

Reaching out, she draped a hand over his, squeezed softly. 'There's more. Tell me.'

If he looked for excuses long enough he'd find them and at that moment a veritable smorgasbord flooded his mind, leaving him to choose the juiciest one.

'The press hounded you for weeks after

Richard's death. What do you think they'll do when they discover we're dating?'

Her frown intensified as her hand slid off his. 'They'll probably say I'm some kind of trumped up tart who waited until her dearly beloved husband was cold in the ground for a year before moving on from the chef to the billionaire restaurateur where he worked. So what? It's all nonsense. Who cares what they say?'

But she was worried. He saw it in the telltale flicker in her eyes, in the pinched mouth.

If Tam had put up with the constant publicity barrage being married to Rich entailed, she had to care about appearances and, no matter how much she protested now, he knew the first hint of scandal in the tabloids back home would send her scuttling for cover.

Where would that leave him? Content to sit back and watch from the sidelines? He'd be damned if he settled for that again.

'As long as you're sure—'

'Of course I'm not sure!'

She jumped to her feet, eyes flashing, hands clenched, more irritated than he'd ever seen her.

'But you wanted this—*you*. You pushed me. You chased and pulled back several times, confusing the heck out of me until I couldn't think straight but I'm still here.'

She stabbed a finger in his direction, glared at him, all bristling indignation and fiery righteousness, and he'd never seen anything so beautiful.

'Now I'm ready to take a chance on us, you start hedging. What's with that?' She ended on a half sob and he leaped to his feet and reached for her.

'Don't, just don't.'

She held up her hands to ward him off and he couldn't blame her.

He was still a screwup. No matter how far he'd come from that lonely, desperate, filthy street kid who'd scrounged food scraps to survive, no matter how rich or successful, he was still the same wary guy who wouldn't let anyone get too close, let alone a woman.

But he had to fix this, and fast, before he not only ruined any chance they had of dating but shot down their new friendship too.

'Tam, listen to me. I—'

'Why should I? Give me one good reason why I should listen to you?'

She folded her arms, glared, her stoic expression at odds with her trembling mouth, and it took every ounce of self-control not to bundle her into his arms.

He held his hands out to her, palms up, and shrugged. 'Because I care about you.'

She wrinkled her nose. 'Care, right. Well, you

know what? If you cared, you wouldn't say you want one thing, act another when you get it. I'm sick of it.'

Tears glistened in her eyes, turning them a luminous green and slugging him harder than his first shot of alcohol as a shivering fourteen-year-old squatting in a Melbourne hovel, desperate to stay warm.

Shaking her head, she swiped a hand over her eyes, sniffed. 'I don't need this. I didn't ask for it, I didn't want it, but at least I had the guts to take a chance, so I'll be damned if I stand here and let you play me for a fool.'

'I'm not—'

'You are.'

If she'd shouted, ranted, abused him, he might've stood a chance at convincing her otherwise but her soft, empty words, frigid with contempt, reached icy fingers down to his soul, freezing what little hope he had left.

'You've got a week to figure out what you want.'

He reached for her hand, briefly capturing her fingertips before she snatched it away.

'Tam, don't do this.'

She straightened, fixed him with a superior glare at odds with her shaky hands. 'Do what? Stand up for myself? Speak my mind?'

Her mouth twisted into a wry grimace. 'This is

my time now. Time I start looking after number one, and that's me.'

She shook her head, gathered her hair, piled it into a loose bun on top of her head before letting it tumble around her shoulders again. He loved watching her do it, an absentminded habit she did when thinking or uptight.

'I just want to make sure you know what you're getting yourself into. As far as I know, I'm the first guy you've dated since Rich and that's got to be a big step for you.'

'But it's my step to take!'

He'd never seen her so irate and for a moment he wondered if there was more behind her flare-up. Was she nervous and covering it with bluster? Or was she as crazy for him as he was for her and had no idea how to control it, just like him?

'You know, for the first time in forever, I felt safe yesterday. At first I thought it was the Taj, the overwhelming sense of calm that flowed through me when I stepped inside. But it wasn't just that.'

She raised her wide-eyed gaze to his, her un-guarded expression beseeching him to understand. And he did, all too well. Tam needed a man to make her feel secure, to cherish her, to spoil her, to do all the things Rich had done.

But he couldn't be that man.

He couldn't relinquish control of anything, let

alone lose it over a woman, no matter how special. However, now wasn't the time to get into all that. The way things were heading, it looked like their first date may also be their last.

'It was you, Ethan. You being there with me, sharing it, treating me like a woman…'

She trailed off, shrugged and took a step backwards. 'Maybe it was just the monument, after all.'

'Tam, look—'

She raised her hand—to ward him off? To say goodbye?

'I'll see you in Melbourne.'

While his heart urged him to follow her, to tell her the truth, to make her understand, his feet were rooted to the spot as he watched the woman who'd captured his heart without trying walk away.

CHAPTER NINE

TAMARA slid her sunglasses into place, tucked the latest crime novel under her arm, slung her towel over her shoulder and headed for the beach.

She'd been in Goa two days—two long days when she'd spent every waking moment touring around, filling the hours with sights and sounds of her mum's birthplace.

'Prawns today, missie?'

Smiling, she stopped at one of the many food vendors scattered along the roadside leading to Colva Beach. She'd been starving when she'd arrived here her first day and the tantalising aroma of seafood sizzling in garlic and turmeric had led her straight here.

'Two, please.'

She held up two fingers for reinforcement, knowing the wizened old man would give her four, just like he had the previous times she'd stopped here. Not that she was complaining but the waistbands of her skirts sure were.

His wide toothless grin warmed her heart as she handed over the rupees and juggled the hot prawns, waving the skewer around and blowing on them before biting into the delicious crispy flesh, savouring the freshness of the seafood drenched in spicy masala.

She devoured the first prawn in two bites, saliva pooling in her mouth at the anticipatory bite of the next as she strolled past another vendor selling a fiery fish vindaloo that smelled as good as the prawns.

'Tomorrow,' she mouthed to the hopeful guy whose face fell when she didn't stop.

Not that she wasn't tempted but at that moment her new friends caught sight of her and were busy hopping from one foot to the other in some bizarre welcoming dance that never failed to bring a smile to her face, and she had no option but to stop.

'You build?'

The eldest of the group of five kids, ranging from three to six, pointed to a makeshift bucket made from an old ghee tin while the rest dropped to their knees and started digging in the sand with their hands.

'Sure.'

She knelt, picked up the tin and started scooping, enjoying the hot sand beating down as she fell into a rhythm: scoop, pat, dump, scoop, pat, dump, listening to their excited chatter, unable to understand a word of the rapid Hindi but returning their blinding smiles as their castle grew.

Today, like the first day they'd beckoned her to join in their fun, she took simple pleasure in doing something associated with her childhood, the repetitive activity as soothing now as it had been then.

She'd built monstrous sandcastles after her dad had died, had poured all her energy into the task in an attempt to block out the pain. But, as the castles had grown, so had her resentment until she'd kicked them down, one crumbling turret at a time.

Yet she'd started building the moment her mum had taken her to the beach the next time, painstakingly erecting the towering castles, complete with shell windows and seaweed flags.

Until it hadn't hurt so much any more and she'd stopped kicking them down, happy to watch the sea gently wash away her creation.

It had taken time to release her resentment—at losing her dad, the unfairness of it—and now, with the sand trickling through her fingers, calmness stole over her, soothing the discontent gnawing at the edges of her consciousness since she'd arrived.

She'd tried ignoring it, had even tried meditating as darkness descended each evening and she sat in a comfy cane chair on her veranda looking out over peaceful Colva beach, her beach hut the perfect spot away from the madding crowds.

While the deliberate relaxation had gone a long way to soothing her weary soul, to banishing some of the anger and acrimony that had dogged her incessantly for the last year, it had also served to tear a new wound in her already bruised heart.

Thanks to Ethan.

Even now, she had no idea what had happened in the interim between their first kiss and her walking away from him in Delhi.

She'd often felt like that with Richard—lonely, as if floating on a sea of anonymity despite being constantly surrounded by his business acquaintances and friends. She'd been a part of his life, a fixture, like part of the furniture, smiling and chatting and playing the perfect hostess while inside she'd been screaming.

She hadn't told her mum about it. Khushi had lived through enough trauma of her own, had lost a husband, a country. Her mum had fussed over her enough when she was growing up, overprotective to the point of stifling at times. She'd understood it, her mum's need to hang on to the only family she had, and in her own way she'd wanted to return the favour.

She'd never spoken an ill word against Richard,

despite her growing despair that her husband had morphed from a strong, steady man to a controlling, spoiled tyrant with a penchant for wine and women.

Losing her mum had been devastating but, considering what she'd learned about Richard when he'd died, a small part of her had been glad her mum hadn't been around to see it.

Bitterness had plagued her for the last year, yet over the last week it had ceased seeping into her soul and sapping her energy.

Because of Ethan.

Ethan, who by encouraging her to open her heart to him, only to hand it straight back to her, had now left her unhappier than ever.

He'd been relentless in his pursuit of her ever since they'd started this trip—discounting the occasional withdrawal—yet when she'd finally given in he'd retreated faster than a lobster sighting a bubbling bisque.

And she'd overreacted. Boy, had she overreacted and the memory of how she'd berated him made her knock over a turret or two as her hands turned clumsy.

The kids frowned as one and she shrugged in apology, intent on smoothing her side of the castle, wishing she could smooth over her gaffe with Ethan as easily.

She'd picked a fine time to rediscover her assertiveness and, while it had felt great standing up for herself and verbalising exactly how she was feeling, she'd chosen the wrong place, the wrong time, the wrong man.

He hadn't deserved her outpouring of anger any more than she'd deserved any of Richard's callous put-downs.

Shame she wouldn't get the chance to tell him, for she was under no illusions that, once they returned to Melbourne, Ethan would move onto his next challenge, relegating her to what? Distant acquaintance again? Friend?

Considering they hadn't been anything remotely near friends before this trip, she should be grateful. Instead, she couldn't help but wish she'd had a chance to rediscover another part of her identity: that of a desirable woman with needs desperate to be fulfilled.

Dusting off her hands, she stood, surveying their creation. The kids imitated her and she pointed at the lopsided castle and applauded them, charmed by their guileless giggles and high-fiving.

Everything was so simple for these kids: they had little, lived by the sea in makeshift shanties, shared a room with many siblings, had few toys, yet were happier than any kid she'd ever seen rollerblading or skateboarding in Melbourne.

Another lesson to be learned: keep things

simple. She had once, content to curl up with a good romance novel, soft jazz in the background, a bowl of popcorn.

Living the high life, living a lie with Richard, had changed all that but it was time to get back to the basics. Her few days in Goa had taught her that if nothing else.

Waving goodbye to the kids, she set off for the shade of a nearby tree, throwing down her towel, smoothing it out and lying down, watching a couple stroll hand in hand down the beach.

She wanted to warn them that the first flush of love didn't last, that it soured and faded, no matter how committed the other person was to you.

She wanted to caution the beautiful young woman against giving too much of herself all in the name of love, wanted to alert her against loving too much to the point she risked losing herself.

She wanted to rant at the injustice of being a loyal, loving wife, only to have it all flung back in her face in the form of a six-foot Dutch ex-model with legs up to her neck and a dazzling smile.

But she didn't do any of that.

Instead, she slapped on her sun hat, flipped open her book and buried her nose in it. A much safer pastime than scaring young lovers and wasting time wishing she could change the past.

* * *

Ethan had enough business meetings to keep him busy for the next month.

This trip had been a success: he'd secured the chef he'd wanted and had put out feelers for a new flagship restaurant in Mumbai. He'd flown the length and breadth of India over the last two days, from Delhi to Mumbai to Chennai.

However, as he sat in the plush surrounds of the InterContinental Hotel in Chennai, he couldn't concentrate on business. Thoughts of Tam consumed him, as they had since she'd walked away from him in New Delhi.

He'd reached for his mobile phone numerous times, desperate to call her, to see how she was doing, to simply hear her voice. But he'd stopped each and every time, all too aware that ringing her would prove what he'd suspected for a while now—his legendary control was slipping.

Slipping? More like shot.

During their journey on the Palace of Wheels he'd dreamed of surprising her in Goa, of spending a leisurely week getting to know each other in every sense of the word.

So much for that dream.

'Ethan, my boy, good to see you.'

Dilip Kumar, his Indian representative in business matters, appeared out of nowhere, slapped him on the back as he stood. 'This is Sunil

Bachnan, the investor we discussed on the phone last week.'

'Pleased to meet you.' He shook Sunil's hand, a giant of a man with a rounded belly protruding over his trousers, testament to a lifetime's worth of chappatis and dosais, the crispy rice pancakes filled with spicy potato he'd become addicted to.

'Likewise. I hear you're looking to open a restaurant here?'

He nodded, resumed his seat along with the other men, grateful to be back doing what he knew best. Business.

This he could manage. Unlike the rest of his life, which had spiralled dangerously out of control since he'd landed in this mystical country.

'Actually, I was thinking Mumbai. The growth there is staggering.'

Sunil gestured to a waiter for menus, nodded. 'The entire country is an economic boom. Pick a city, any city and your famous Ambrosia will do big business.' Patting his ample gut, he chortled. 'We love our food here in India.'

'You and me both.'

Though his appetite had vanished the last few days, a shame considering the array of amazing food on offer everywhere he went. For a guy who made his life out of food, he'd landed smack bang in food paradise.

'Right. Let's talk business as we eat.' Sunil rattled off an order in rapid Hindi to the hovering waiter as Dilip raised his beer. 'Cheers, my friend. And how is your travelling companion?'

'Good.'

He sculled half his beer in two gulps, wishing he hadn't opened his big mouth and mentioned Tam, not wanting to discuss her. The less he said the better, considering the constant repetition buzzing around his brain: replaying every scene of their trip, every hand touch, every smile, every kiss…

'You must bring her to dinner. My wife Sireesha will be thrilled to have you both—'

'Tamara's in Goa.'

Dilip's black eyes widened at his snapped response. 'I see.'

'Glad someone does,' he muttered into his beer glass, grateful that Sunil had answered a call on his mobile and wasn't privy to this conversation.

Trying to present a professional front to an investor sure as hell didn't involve discussing his non-existent love life.

'You and your lady friend are having problems?'

'Nothing I can't handle.'

Yeah, right, which was why he was on the east coast of India and Tam was on the west.

Dilip shook his head, steepled his fingers on his

chest and wobbled his head from side to side in a gesture he'd seen many times in India.

'If you permit me to be so bold, I have a story for you, my friend.'

Darting a frantic glance in Sunil's direction in the hope his phone call had ended, his heart sank as the investor held up a finger at him, pushed away from the table and headed for the foyer to continue his conversation.

'Look, Dilip, I'd rather focus on business—'

'Patience, my friend, patience.' He squeezed his eyes shut, as if trying to recall the story, before his bulging eyes snapped open and fixed on him. 'When I met my Sireesha, I was a penniless student and she was engaged to the son of a prominent doctor. Our paths crossed at university one day, when she dropped her books and I helped pick them up, and from that moment I knew she was the one for me.'

'And you're telling me this because?'

Dilip frowned, waggled a finger at him. 'Because I never wavered from my pursuit of her, no matter how unlikely it was we would ever be a couple. I was determined to have her and all the obstacles in our way were inconsequential.'

Ethan rubbed the back of his neck, shook his head. 'That's great but we're different. There are complications—'

'Complications, pah!'

Dilip waved his hand like a magician waving a wand. If only he could make all his problems disappear.

'The only complication is up here.' He tapped his head like an overzealous woodpecker. 'You think too much, you overanalyse, you lose.'

He pointed to his heart. 'You need to think with this. Let your heart rule your head. I know you are a brilliant businessman, so this will be foreign to you, yes?'

Hell, yeah. He never let his heart rule his head, not any more.

His mum was the only woman who'd ever had a piece of his heart and she'd taken it with her the second she'd walked out of his life and left him to fend for himself, a bewildered five-year-old with no family, no money, no home.

'If you want her, this—' he tapped his heart '—needs to rule this.' He pointed to his head. 'Simple.'

Was it that simple?

Was he thinking too much, overanalysing everything, obstinately refusing to relinquish control despite the potentially incredible outcome?

What could be a greater incentive to lose control just a little than dating Tam?

Dilip snapped his fingers, jerked his head

towards the door. 'Sunil is returning. For now, we do business. But later, my friend, you remember what I've said.'

He'd remember. But would he do anything about it?

Tamara needed a walk.

Her mum's cooking had been amazing but the authentic Goan cuisine she consumed way too much of at every meal was sublime.

She was particularly partial to bibinca, a rich sweet made from flour, sugar, ghee, coconut milk and about twenty egg yolks, baked and flavoured with nutmeg and cardamom.

Rich, delicious, addictive.

Exactly like Ethan, though his sweetness had evaporated around the time he'd stolen her hard-fought trust in him and flung it into the Ganges.

Picking up the pace, she headed for the water's edge, where the ocean tickled the sand, the only sound being the waves breaking gently on the shore.

Colva Beach was tranquil, lazy, the type of place to hang out the 'do not disturb' sign and just chill out. Her mum had said it was special but she'd always attributed her partiality to the fact she'd met her dad here. But mum had been right. This place had an aura, a feeling, a sense that anything was possible, as she stared out over the endless ocean glowing turquoise in the descending dusk.

She slowed her pace, hitched up her peasant skirt and stepped into the waves, savouring the tepid water splashing about her ankles.

As a kid, she used to run through the shallows at St Kilda beach, jumping and splashing and frolicking, seeing how wet she could get, her folks strolling hand in hand alongside her, smiling indulgently.

They'd head to Acland Street afterwards, trawling the many cake shops, laughing as she'd pressed her face up to each and every window, trying to decide between melt-in-the-mouth chocolate éclairs or custard-oozing vanilla slices.

And later, much later, when her tummy was full and her feet dragging, she'd walk between them, each parent holding her hand, making her feel the luckiest little girl in the world.

A larger wave crashed into her legs, drenching the bottom half of her skirt and she laughed, the sound loud and startling in the silence.

How long since she'd laughed like that, truly laughed, totally spontaneous?

Ethan had made her laugh last week, several times… Shaking her head, she resisted the temptation to cover her ears with her hands.

Ethan, Ethan, Ethan—couldn't she focus on a new topic rather than the same old, same old?

With her skirt a dripping mess, she trudged up the beach, heading for her hut. Maybe a nice long soak in that killer tub filled with fragrant sandalwood oil would lull her into an Ethan-free zone?

As she scuffed her feet through the sand, a lone figure stepped onto the beach near her hut.

She wouldn't have paid much attention but for the breadth of his shoulders, the familiar tilt of his head… She squinted, her pulse breaking into a gallop as the figure headed straight for her, increasingly recognisable with every determined stride.

It couldn't be.

It was.

In that instant, she forgot every sane reason why she should keep her distance from Ethan and ran towards him, sprinting, her feet flying across the sand as she hurtled herself into his open arms.

CHAPTER TEN

'IS THIS real?'

Ethan smoothed back her hair, caressed her cheek, his other hand holding her tight against him. 'Very.'

'What are you doing here?'

Tamara touched his face, her fingertips skimming his cheek, his jaw peppered in stubble, savouring the rasping prickle, still not believing this was real.

'I came to be with you.' He brushed his lips across hers—soft, tender, the barest of kisses that had her breath catching, along with her heart. 'There's nowhere else I'd rather be.'

She couldn't comprehend this. One minute she'd been alone and confused, the next he was here. For her.

'But after what happened in Delhi—'

'I was a fool.'

He clasped her face between his hands, his

beseeching gaze imploring her to listen. 'I owe you an explanation.'

Her response of *you don't* died on her lips.

Considering the retreat and parry he'd been doing and the way they'd parted, he owed her that at least.

'Come on. I'm staying in that hut you just passed. We can talk there.'

She stepped out of his embrace but he swiftly pulled her back into his arms, hugged her so fiercely the breath whooshed out of her lungs.

'Tam, I missed you.'

'Me too,' she murmured against his chest, her cheek happily squashed against all that lovely hard muscle.

Stroking her hair, he held her, their breathing in sync with their beating hearts, and for that one brief moment in time she understood the incredible power of the emotion that had drawn her mum and dad together on this very beach all those years ago.

There was something magical about this place, something transcendental and, as the first stars of the evening flickered overhead and the faintest tune of a soulful sitar drifted on the night air, she wondered if it was time to take a chance on love again.

'Any chance this hut of yours has a fully stocked fridge?' He patted his rumbling tummy. 'Feels like I haven't eaten in days.'

'Better than that. The hut is part of a resort so

I put in an order for my meals first thing in the morning and they deliver.'

'Great. So what's for dinner?'

She laughed. 'You can take the boy out of the restaurant but you can't take the restaurant out of the boy.'

'Too right.' He slipped his hand in hers, squeezed. 'So, what's on for tonight?'

For an insane moment she could've sworn he wasn't talking about food as his steady blue-eyed gaze bored into hers, questioning, seeking, roguish. And, for the life of her, she couldn't remember what she'd ordered that morning.

Chuckling at her bemused expression, he fell into step beside her. 'Never mind, whatever it is I'll devour it.'

He paused, sent her a significant look. 'Happiness does that to a man. Gives him an appetite.'

'You're happy?'

He stopped, pulled her close again. 'Considering you didn't run the opposite way when you first saw me, you're still talking to me and you've invited me to dinner, I'm downright ecstatic.'

Joy fizzed in her veins, heady and tingling and making her feel punch-drunk. Sure, they needed to talk but, for now, she was happy too. Happier than she'd been in days. Heck, happier than she'd been in years.

This last week with Ethan, she'd found a surprising peace. She didn't have to pretend to be someone she wasn't, to fake a smile, to be poised and elegant and refined all in the name of appearances.

He saw her for who she was—a woman out to make a new start, a woman happiest with no make-up, no artifice and no platitudes.

'I've never seen you like this.'

He tucked a strand of hair behind her ear, twisting the end around his finger, brushing the delicate skin beneath her ear.

'What? With my hair frizzy from sea water and wearing a kaftan from a local market?'

His gaze searched her face, her eyes, focusing on her lips.

'I've never seen you so relaxed. You're truly happy here, aren't you?'

She nodded, filled with a sense of serenity she'd never had elsewhere.

'Maybe it's a mental thing, knowing my mum spent half her life here and I feel more connected to her here than anywhere.'

'It's more than that.'

He was right. It was the first time in a long time she'd been on her own, content in her own company.

She'd been alone in Melbourne since Richard's death but that had been different. There'd been the whirlwind of the funeral, countless trips to the solicitors, endless paperwork to tidy up and the personal fallout from Richard's little bombshell in the form of his girlfriend, Sonja.

Here, there was none of that. She could finally be true to herself, true to *her* needs.

She smiled. 'You've got to know me pretty well, huh?'

'Enough to know I've never seen you so at ease.'

'It's this place.'

She waved at the endless stretch of sand, the shimmering azure sea, the purple-streaked sky scattered with diamond-like stars.

'Not just the tranquillity, the pace of life, but everything about it. I can just be myself, you know.'

'I'm happy for you, Tam, I really am.'

He was, she could see he was genuine, which made her like him all the more.

'But a part of me can't help but wish I'd found you with unwashed hair and chewed-to-the-quick fingernails and pale and sallow from pining away for me, rather than the picture of glowing health.'

She'd pined all right. She'd struggled to sleep the first night, moped around while sightseeing, dragged her feet through this sand on more long walks than she'd ever taken.

Nothing had soothed the hollow ache in her heart, the anxiety gnawing at her belly that she'd lost her chance at exploring something new, something exciting, something that could potentially be the best thing to ever happen to her.

Yet here he was, in the flesh, wearing his trademark rakish pirate smile, khaki shorts and a white T-shirt setting off his newly acquired tan.

He was gorgeous, every tantalising, delectable inch of him, and by coming here, she was hoping he'd made the statement that he was ready to explore this spark between them.

'You're staring.'

She raised an eyebrow, fought a blush. 'Am I?'

'Uh-huh.' He ducked his head for a quick kiss. 'And I like it. That gleam in your beautiful eyes tells me I still have a chance.'

'Only if you're lucky.'

Laughing at his wounded expression, she slipped out of his grasp, hitched up her long skirt and sprinted across the sand with him in hot pursuit.

She'd never felt this carefree, this spontaneous, and while Colva Beach may have worked its magic on her, it had more to do with the man rugby-tackling her to the sand as they reached the hut.

'Hey! Don't go trying out for your Kangaroos footy team by practising on me.'

He rolled onto his back, taking her with him so she lay deliciously along the length of him. 'Wouldn't dream of it. Besides, those guys are way out of my league.'

'Am I?'

All too aware of their heated skin being separated by the sheer chiffon kaftan and cotton, she propped on his chest, the teasing smile dying on her lips as she registered the sudden shadows in his eyes.

'Maybe you are.'

'I was kidding, you great oaf.' She whacked him playfully on the chest, disappointed when he stood and hauled her to her feet.

'Yeah, well, my ego bruises easily. You need to take it easy on me.'

She didn't buy his rueful grin for a second, something akin to hurt still lingering in his eyes.

'I'll keep that in mind.'

Eager to restore the playful mood between them, she gestured to the hut. 'Maybe you won't be so sensitive once you get some food into that great bottomless pit of yours.'

He instantly perked up. 'Did you mention food?'

She laughed, opened the door. 'Kitchen's on the left. Dinner's ready to be heated. I'll just take a quick shower before we eat.'

While she preferred the au naturel look here, she felt distinctly grubby in the presence of his sexy casualness. That glow he'd mentioned probably had more to do with a day's worth of perspiration than any inner peace.

'Right. See you in ten.'

She held up one hand. 'Make that five. I'm starving too.'

Before she could move, he captured her hand, raised it to his lips and placed a hot, scorching kiss on her palm and curled her fingers over. 'I'm really glad I came.'

'Me too,' she murmured, his kiss burning her palm as she kept her hand clenched, backing slowly into the bathroom, not breaking eye contact for a second, waiting until she all but slammed the door before slumping against it in a quivering heap, her hormones leaping as high as her heart.

Ethan headed for the tiny kitchen, drawn by the faintest aroma of fish, onions and ginger.

For a guy who hadn't been able to face food in the last forty-eight hours, he was ravenous.

Not just for food.

The instant he'd laid eyes on Tam, the craving was back, so intense, so overwhelming, he wondered how he'd managed to let her walk away from him in the first place.

All his doubts had washed away on the evening tide as she'd run towards him, her incredible green eyes shining, her smile incandescent.

He wasn't a romantic kind of guy—dating arm-candy women who liked to be seen with rich guys took all the gloss off romance—but, if he were prone to it, he'd say their reunion had been picture perfect, the type of moment to relate to their kids, their grandkids.

Whoa!

He stopped dead, backing up a moment.

He'd gone from the possibility of dating to kids?

This hunger must be making him more light-headed than he'd first thought and, heading for the fridge, he dug out a casserole dish filled with fish curry, a bowl of steamed white rice and a raita made from yoghurt, cucumber, tomato and onion.

Food of the gods, he thought, smiling to himself as he heated the fish and rice, amazed he'd gone a whole day without thinking of his precious Ambrosia.

He spent all day every day in constant touch with the managers of each restaurant around the world, keeping abreast of the daily running, meeting with accountants, conference calling with staff.

Being in control of Ambrosia, seeing his business grow to international stardom status never failed to give him a kick, a solid reminder of how far he'd come.

From loitering around the back door of Ma Petite, hoping for food scraps, to being taken under the wing of the great Arnaud Fournier and given an apprenticeship in his world-class restaurant, to working eighty-hour weeks and scrounging every cent to invest in his first restaurant, to running one of the most famous restaurant chains in the world was heady stuff for a guy who could still remember the pinch of hunger in his belly and the dirt under his fingernails from scrabbling for the last stale bun out of a dumpster.

From bum to billionaire and he couldn't be prouder.

Then why hadn't he told Tam the truth?

They'd discussed her family, her career, but he'd neatly sidestepped any personal questions she'd aimed his way, reluctant to taint her image of him.

Why? Was he ashamed? Embarrassed? Afraid she'd see him as less of a man?

Hell, yeah. The less said about his sordid past the better. She was taking a huge step forward, both career-wise and personally, in letting him get close and he'd be a fool to risk it by giving her a glimpse into the real him.

'Something smells good.'

She stepped into the kitchen, her hair wet and slicked back into a low ponytail, her skin clear and glowing, wearing a simple red sundress with tiny white polka dots, and he slammed the hot rice dish onto the bench top before the whole thing slid onto the floor courtesy of his fumbling fingers.

She had that effect on him, could render him useless and floundering out of his depth with a smile, with a single glance from beneath those long dark lashes that accentuated the unique green of her eyes.

'Now who's staring?'

She sashayed across the kitchen, lifted the lid on the fish and waved the fragrant aroma towards her nose. 'Wait until you try this fish moilee. It's fabulous.'

Thankful she'd given him a chance to unglue his tongue from the roof of his mouth where it had stuck the moment he'd caught sight of her, he quickly set the table.

'How's moilee different from curry?'

'Different spices, different method of cooking.' She gathered a jug of mango lassi, a delicious yoghurt and fruit drink he loved, and glasses and placed them on the table. 'You add a little salt and lime juice to the fish, set it aside for a while. Then you fry mustard seeds, curry leaves, onion, ginger, garlic, green chillies and turmeric before adding the fish, covering the lot with coconut milk and letting it simmer.'

She inhaled again, closed her eyes, her expression ecstatic and he cleared his throat, imagining what else, apart from a tasty curry, could bring that look to her face.

'My mouth's watering. Let's eat.'

Her eyes snapped open at his abrupt response

and he busied himself with transporting the hot dishes to the table under her speculative stare rather than have to explain why he was losing his cool.

For a couple who'd chatted amicably during most meals on their Palace on Wheels journey, they were strangely silent as they devoured the delicious fish and rice, darting occasional glances at each other over the lassi, politely passing the raita, focusing on forking food into their mouths.

Tension stretched between them, taut and fraught, as he wished he could articulate half of what he was feeling. Overwhelmed. Out of control. And more attracted to anyone than he'd been in his entire life.

He'd dated many women, most had left him cold. He told himself he liked it that way; he chose fickle women because he didn't want to get emotionally involved.

So what was he doing here, now, hoping this incredible woman would let him into her heart when he knew that would be an irrevocable step down a very dangerous road, a road less travelled for him, a road peppered with emotions he'd rather ignore?

Tam had been grieving, had closed down emotionally, hadn't dated, let alone looked at a guy since Rich's death.

Yet here she was, opening her heart to him,

welcoming him back despite how he'd acted like a jerk, first on the train, then in Udaipur, lastly in Delhi. Which could only mean one thing.

She was already emotionally involved with him, was willing to gamble her heart on him.

He had no idea if he deserved it.

'That was delish.' She patted her mouth with a napkin, refolded it, before sitting back and rubbing her tummy. 'I don't think I could move for a week after that, which gives you plenty of time to start talking.'

So much for being let off the hook. She'd lulled him into a false sense of security, yet he'd known it would come to this.

He had to tell her the truth—some of it—if they were to have any chance of moving forward from here.

Wishing he hadn't eaten so much—it now sat like a lump of lead in his gut—he sat back, crossed his ankles, wondering if she'd buy his relaxed posture while inside he churned with trepidation.

Opening up to anyone, let alone the woman he cared about, didn't sit well with him and he'd be damned if he messed this up after what had happened in Delhi.

Folding his arms, he looked her straight in the eye. 'You want to know why I backed off at India Gate.'

'For starters.'

She didn't look angry—far from it if the gentle upturning of her lips was any indication. Yet she had every right to be, every right to kick his sorry butt out of here after the way he'd treated her.

'Did you ever want something so badly as a kid, something you wished for, something that consumed you yet, when you got it, you didn't know what to do with it?'

Understanding turned her eyes verdigris. 'I was a bit like that with my Baby Born doll. Really wanted one, then when I got it for Christmas, didn't know whether I should feed it or burp it or change its nappy first.'

'You're laughing at me.'

'I'm not.'

Her twitching mouth made a mockery of her last statement and he chuckled, shook his head.

'I'll be honest with you, Tam. I came on this trip because I wanted you. Then I started to get to know you—really know you—and it's like…'

How could he explain it? Like being hit over the head with a four-by-two? Like being struck by lightning? Like having the blinkers ripped from his eyes only to see the stunning, vibrant woman he desired was so much more than he could've possibly imagined?

'It's like…?'

Her soft prompt had him saying the first thing that popped into his head.

'It's like finding the person you want most in this world is holding the key to your heart as well.'

No way—had he really said that?

Inwardly cringing at his emotional explosion, he met her gaze, the shimmer of tears in her eyes slugging him harder than the realisation that this had already moved beyond caring for him, that he was already half in love with her.

'Look, that's too heavy—'

'Don't you dare apologise for saying that!' Her head snapped up, her gaze defiant as the tears spilled over and rolled down her cheeks. 'Do you have any idea how I feel, hearing you say that?'

'Like bolting?' he ventured, earning another wide-eyed stare.

'Like this.'

She stood so abruptly her chair slammed onto the floor and she traversed the tiny table in a second, flinging herself onto his lap and wrapping her arms tightly around his neck.

'Well, now, maybe I should blurt my innermost thoughts more often if this is the type of reaction I get.'

Her eyes gleamed with mischief. 'No, *this* is the type of reaction you get.'

She covered his mouth with hers in a desperate, frantic kiss filled with longing and passion and recklessness.

The type of kiss that filled his heart with hope, the type of kiss with the power to teach him this relinquishing control lark wasn't half as scary as he'd built it up to be.

She was warm and vibrant and responsive in his arms, her hunger matching his and, as she shifted in his lap, inflaming him further, he knew he had to put a stop to this before they jumped way ahead of themselves.

He wasn't a Boy Scout and he'd like nothing better than to carry her into the bedroom right this very second and make love to her all night long but he'd botched things with her once; he'd be damned if he made another mistake now.

And that was what sex would be, despite the blood pounding through his body and urging him to follow through—a mistake.

He wanted to take things slow this time. He'd rushed her on the train journey, had almost lost her because of it, and there was no way in Hades he'd make the same mistake twice.

'Tam?'

'Hmm?'

She nuzzled his neck, giving his good intentions a thorough hiding as she straddled him, her breasts pushing deliciously against his chest.

'I can't stay.'

She stilled, raised her head, her eyes glazed, confused. 'Why not?'

Cradling her face in his hands, he brushed a soft kiss across her swollen lips.

'Because I want to do this right.'

He didn't have to add *this time*.

He saw the respect in her eyes, the understanding, and knowing this incredible woman was on the same wavelength as him sent another flood of intense longing washing over him.

'Great, the playboy has morphed into a goody two shoes,' she said, sliding off his lap in a slow, deliberate movement designed to tease as he clenched his hands to stop himself from reaching out and yanking her back down.

'Oh, you'll see how good I really am.'

He stood, pulling her back into his arms, enjoying her squeal of pure delight. 'Soon—very soon.'

'I'll hold you to that.'

'I'm counting on it.'

This time their kiss was slower, exploratory, leisurely, and as he reluctantly slipped out of her arms and raised his hand in goodbye he feared there'd come a time in the not too distant future where he'd find it near on impossible to walk away from her.

CHAPTER ELEVEN

'I THOUGHT Goa was settled by the Portuguese?'

Tamara nodded, browsing the market stall's brightly coloured powders for the Holi festival tomorrow. 'It was. That's why you see so many Portuguese-inspired buildings and a lot of the population are Catholic. Apparently thousands of people make the pilgrimage to see Saint Francis Xavier's body at the basilica here every five years.'

Ethan trailed his fingers through a mound of sunshine-yellow powder and earned a frown from the vendor for his trouble.

'If it's predominantly Catholic, what's with this Holi festival? Isn't that Hindu?'

'Uh-huh. But, like most of India, there are so many different religions and castes living side by side that everyone's pretty tolerant of the different festivals.' She pointed to several piles of powder, smiling at the vendor, who began shovelling mini mountains of the stuff into clear plastic bags. 'I think it's fabulous everyone gets involved. It's such a joyous occasion that you can't help but get swept up in the fun. At least, that's what Mum told me.'

He nodded, pointing to the bags being thrust into her hands. 'So tell me about it. All I know is everyone goes berserk and throws colour on everyone else.'

Upon hearing this, the vendor frowned again and shook his head, while she handed him rupees and laughed. 'Come on, I'll enlighten you over a cup of masala chai.'

'Sounds good.'

He held out his hand for her carry-all and she gratefully gave it to him. Choosing every colour of the rainbow for Holi mightn't be such a great idea if she had to lug all those kilos back to the hut.

'Do the colours mean anything?'

She nodded, instantly transported back to the first time she'd heard about Holi, sitting on her mum's knee. She'd just learned to make her first chapatti that same day, and had had so much fun rolling the balls of dough into flat breads, standing on a stool next to the stove as her mum had fried them.

She'd been five at the time and her dad had come home after work, scoffed three with jam and pronounced them better than her mum's.

It'd been a magical day, one of those days where her mum was reminiscing about India, eager to tell stories, and she'd lapped it up. Yet another thing she missed.

'Green's for vitality, red is purity, blue is calmness and yellow is piety.'

He squinted through the bag. 'So what happens when you mix the lot together?'

'You'll find out.'

She could hardly wait. Ever since she'd first learned of the festival of colour, she'd been entranced. The freedom to play and dance and sing like a kid, flinging coloured powders and water balloons over anyone and everyone, visiting friends, exchanging gifts and sweets, all sounded like a good time.

'Let's have a cuppa here.'

They stopped at a roadside café, ordered masala chais and relaxed, watching the passing procession of people gearing up for Holi, each weighed down with vibrant magentas, daffodil-yellows, peacock-blues, dazzling emeralds and vivid crimsons.

Ethan gestured towards the passing parade. 'Looks like everyone gets in on the act.'

She nodded, delighting in the infectious excitement of the kids bouncing down the street, laden down with colour-filled bags.

'It's a time where age is irrelevant; everyone joins in. You can get wild and no one will blink.'

It was also a time for lovers, where the application of colour to each other was a sign of their love. Wisely, she kept that gem to herself. It was hard enough handling the swift shift in their relationship, and trying not to dwell on the erotic dreams of the last few nights, without adding to it.

He leaned forward, crooked his finger at her. 'How wild?'

She laughed. 'It's good clean fun. Well, if you discount getting dirty with colours, that is.'

His devilish grin sent heat sizzling through her. 'I'm all for getting dirty.'

'I bet.'

Her dry response had him chuckling as the waiter deposited two stainless-steel mugs filled to the brim with steaming chai in front of them.

'So what does it all mean?'

'There are loads of different legends surrounding it, centring on the ultimate victory of good over evil. Holi helps people believe in the virtue of being honest and banishing evil. It helps bring the country together and the tradition is that even enemies turn into friends during the festival.'

She sipped at her chai, sighing as the burst of cardamom-flavoured tea hit her taste buds. 'And there's no differentiation between rich and poor. Everyone gets in on the fun. It's about strengthening bonds between friends, revitalising relationships.'

'Wow, sounds like the world could do with a good Holi festival every now and then.'

She nodded. 'Wouldn't it be great? A sea of colour and a giant group hug.'

'I could do with a hug myself.' He stared at her over the rim of his mug, his blue eyes mischievous. 'Similar to that one you gave me at your kitchen table the night I arrived.'

She blushed, tried a frown and failed miserably when her lips curved into a secretive smile at the memory.

'Drink your chai. We have about half an hour to get changed before the fun starts.'

'Make that five minutes if we get back to the hut in time.'

She almost choked on her tea. He hadn't flirted so blatantly since he'd arrived, hadn't pushed, despite the increasingly heated kisses they'd shared the last few days.

He wanted to take things slow and while her head and heart were grateful for the fact, her body was way behind in the acceptance stakes.

Something had shifted today. Ever since he'd turned up on her doorstep this morning and all through their stroll around the market he'd been pushing the boundaries, flirting outrageously, hinting at something more than a quick, sizzling kiss at the end of the day.

She'd put it down to infectious Holi madness. Who knew—maybe, just maybe, there would be some revitalising of their relationship happening later tonight?

'This is insane!' Ethan shouted at the top of his lungs, dodging another kid pointing a super-sized water soaker at him, bright blue this time, only to be splattered in the middle of the back by a magenta water bomb from Tam.

'Yeah, isn't it great?' She flung her arms overhead, twirled around, did a defiant jig in front of him, taunting him now he'd used up his colour supplies.

He advanced towards her, pointing at the remaining bags in her hand. 'Give me some of that.'

'No.' She stood on tiptoe, jiggled the bags in front of him. 'Not my fault your aim is lousy.'

'That does it!' He grabbed her around the waist and she squealed, her laughter firing his blood as much as having her wriggling and warm and vibrant in his arms. 'Tam, I'm warning you—'

'You're in no position to warn me. I'm the one holding the ammunition.'

To reinforce the point, she swung one of the bags at his back, where it exploded, drenching him further.

'What colour was that?'

'Red, to match your face for letting a girl beat you at this.'

'That does it.' He hoisted her over his shoulder, growling when she emptied the last few bags on his back, then proceeded to pummel him with her fists.

'Put me down.'

He patted her butt in response. 'Nope, sorry, no can do. This is Holi, remember? Anything goes.'

'I take it back.'

'Too late.'

She stiffened as he slid a hand up her calf, reaching her thigh, all in the name of getting a better grip. That was his excuse and he was sticking to it.

'Are you copping a cheap feel?'

'No, just don't want to drop you and ruin your outfit.'

'But it's already ruined—'

'Gotcha!'

She pummelled harder, he laughed harder and he jogged the last few metres to her hut, deliberately sliding her down nice and slow, her body deliciously rubbing against his.

This was madness—pure and utter madness.

So much for taking things slow.

Every moment he spent in Tam's company, he found it harder to resist her, harder not to say caution be damned and sweep her into his arms and make slow, passionate love to her all night long.

He wanted her. Thoughts of her consumed him every waking moment and most sleeping ones too and now, with her standing less than a foot away, her tie-dyed kaftan plastered to her curvy body, he knew he couldn't hold out much longer.

He wanted to do the right thing, give her time to adjust to their new relationship but his knight in shining armour routine had taken a serious beating since he'd arrived on her doorstep earlier that week and she'd welcomed him with open arms.

'So?'

'So…' His gaze dipped, took in her orange, green and blue spattered face, her purple matted hair and the Technicolor kaftan.

Despite the mess, she'd never looked so beautiful and he clenched his hands to stop himself from reaching out to her and never letting go.

'Time to clean up.' She stepped back, as if sensing his urge. 'Though some of us need more cleaning up than others.'

She pointed to his irredeemable T-shirt. 'Not only can some of us not throw, we're none too crash hot at dodging too.'

'You're asking for it.'

He made a grab for her and they tumbled through the doorway, drenched to the skin and laughing uncontrollably.

'You look like a preschooler's finger-painting.'

'You look worse.'

They stared at each other and laughed again, as Tamara clutched her side. 'I'm sore.'

'From taking my direct hits full on?'

'More like from dodging your average throws.' He pointed to her powder-spattered kaftan. 'Then how do you explain all that colour?'

She shrugged, put a thumb up to her nose and waggled her fingers. 'Other people.'

He advanced towards her. 'Are you saying my aim is lousy?'

She smiled. 'Oh, yeah. Though you might've landed a few lucky shots. Beginner's luck and all that.'

'Beginner, huh?' He continued to advance, his mouth twitching, his eyes filled with devilry and she backed up, stumbling into the bathroom. 'You going to admit I'm good?'

He halted less than two feet in front of her, close enough to feel his radiant heat, not close enough according to her body, straining towards him.

Tilting her chin up, she tossed her bedraggled hair over a shoulder. 'Never.'

'Never's a long time, sweetheart.'

His hand shot out, captured her wrist, tugging her closer and she laughed when their bodies made a strange squelching sound as they came into contact.

'Ready to concede?'

'Nope.' She shook her head, spraying them with the finest purple droplets, like sparkling amethysts raining from a jewelled sky.

'Well, then, I might just have to make you.'

His eyes glittered with pure devilry as he lowered his head, brushed his mouth across hers in a slow, masterful kiss that had her clinging to his wet T-shirt, her knees wobbling.

'Concede?'

Her tongue darted out to moisten her lips, still tingling from his kiss. 'I think I need more convincing.'

He growled, swept her up in his arms and deposited her on the hand basin, the hard, cold enamel barely registering as he swooped in for another kiss, a fiery, passionate explosion of melding mouths that heated her from the inside out and would've dried her clothes if they'd continued.

But she stopped, uncurled her fingers from where they clung to his T-shirt, all too aware of where this would lead.

'What's wrong?'

How could she articulate half of what she was feeling?

Blinding anticipation at being touched by a man after so long?

Good old-fashioned lust that licked along her veins and made her throb with need?

Crippling uncertainty that she wouldn't live up to his expectations?

Or the mind-numbing fear that, once she took this irreversible step, there'd be no going back?

Making love with Ethan would be just that for her—making love—and it would cement what she'd known the last few days.

She'd fallen in love with him.

Enough to take a chance on love again, enough to want it all—with him.

'Tam?'

He tipped up her chin, leaving her no option but to stare into his glittering blue eyes, those eyes she'd seen clear and sincere, determined and focused at work, currently a smoky gentian with passion.

'I'm scared.'

He cupped her cheek, drawing comforting circles in the small of her back with his other hand. 'I'd never do anything to hurt you.'

'I know, but—'

'But?'

'What if—' *this doesn't work, this makes you pull back again, this makes me fall in love with you even more and you don't feel half as much for me as I feel for you?*

'What if you stop second-guessing this and let me love you?'

She knew he meant it as a physical expression

of love, but hearing him say the word out loud banished the last of her lingering doubts.

She'd spent every moment of her marriage carefully weighing and assessing—trying to say the right thing, do the right thing, wear the right thing. And she'd been miserable.

Now she had a second chance, a real chance at happiness and she'd be a fool to let it slip through her fingers.

Her hands slid up his chest, caressed his neck, cradled his face as she wrapped her legs around him. 'What if I show you how much I want this?'

His face creased into an instant smile, the heartrendingly familiar sexy smile that never failed to set her pulse racing.

'Sounds like a plan.'

He sent a pointed glance at their clothes. 'But we're filthy.'

Shocked at her bravado, she met his gaze head-on.

'Let's take a shower, then.'

His eyes, radiating enough heat to scorch her clothes right off her, never left hers as she reached out, her fingers grappling with the hem of his wet T-shirt before peeling it upwards with slow, exquisite deliberation, revealing inch by inch of spectacular hard, bronzed chest.

When she reached his shoulders, he helped

shrug it off, leaving his torso deliciously bare, beckoning her fingertips to explore.

And explore she did, smoothing her palms over every hard plane, skating her fingertips over every ridge, every delineation, her breath catching as his hands shot out and captured her wrists.

'My turn,' he gritted out, ducking for a searing kiss before almost tearing her kaftan off. 'I've waited too long for this to take it slow.'

'Fast is good,' she gasped as, with a deft flick of the clasp on her bra, he had her breasts spilling free into his waiting hands.

'Ethan…'

She whispered his name on a sigh, a long, drawn-out, blissful sigh as his mouth replaced his hands until she almost passed out from the blinding intensity.

'You're so beautiful, so responsive,' he murmured, kissing his way down her body as sensation after sensation slammed into her, rendering a simple task like standing impossible.

She sagged against the basin, braced her hands on it as his fingers hovered, toyed with the elastic of her panties.

'I want this to be beyond special for you,' he said, wrenching a low moan from deep within as he set about doing just that.

She'd never been loved like this, never had a

man want to please her first, please her so totally before taking his satisfaction and as Ethan brought her to the peak of ecstasy and she tumbled over the edge into an explosion of mind-numbing bliss, she finally came alive.

When he stood, she cradled his face, stared into his eyes, hoping he could read the depth of emotion there.

'Thank you,' she said, gasping as he pressed against her, her desire needing little to reignite.

'The pleasure's all mine.'

His roguish smile brought out the pirate in him and she gladly wrapped her arms around his waist, more than happy to be ravaged.

As the steam rose around them, she lost all sense of time. His shorts joined her discarded clothes, his body melded with hers and he made passionate love to her until she almost cried with the beauty of it.

Later, as he held her close, cocooned in the safety of his arms, the heat from their bodies drying them better than any towels, she knew without a doubt that this man was her destiny.

Ethan groaned, sat back and patted his stomach. 'Okay, now I'm done, are you going to tell me what's in that sorpotel?'

The corners of Tam's mouth twitched, the tiny movement slugging him as he recalled in vivid detail how those lips had explored his body last night. He'd dated widely but never had he felt so connected with a woman in the bedroom.

Though it was more than that and he knew it—knew it with every guarded cell in his body. What he felt for Tam defied description and had him jumpier than a mongoose around a cobra.

If she'd zapped his control before, he didn't stand a chance now; he wanted her more than ever. It was like sampling the finest Shiraz Grenache: one taste was never enough.

'You sure you want to know?'

He pointed to the empty bowl, where he'd mopped up every last bit of gravy with a paratha. 'Considering I've just devoured the richest curry I've ever had without leaving a drop, I think I can handle it.'

'It's made from pork, beef and pig's blood.'

Ignoring the smallest tumble of revolt his belly gave, he reached for his coconut milk and raised it to her.

'Nothing like those magic secret ingredients.'

She leaned across the table, giving him a delectable view of her cleavage and, to his credit, he managed to keep his gaze on her face.

'You don't have to pretend with me.'

His belly griped again but this time it had nothing to do with the thought of eating pig's blood.

He *was* pretending with her, living a fantasy—one he'd craved a long time. But fantasies didn't mesh with reality and if there was one thing he'd come to respect, it was reality.

He lived the reality every day—of trusting no one but himself, of staying on top in business, of never losing control.

Yet here, now, with Tam staring at him with a new sparkle in her eyes and a permanent smile on her face, he wasn't just in danger of losing control. He was in danger of losing his mind.

Seeing curiosity creep into her gaze, he clanked his coconut against hers. 'I couldn't come to a Goan institution like Souza Lobo's and not try the sorpotel. So, whatever's next, bring it on.'

Her eyes twinkled as she lowered her coconut. 'Brave words from a guy who got obliterated during Holi.'

He shrugged, thankful they'd safely navigated back to playful. 'I just wanted you to think you had the upper hand.'

'Didn't I?'

'I'll let you in on a little secret.'

He crooked his finger at her, laughing when she twisted it. 'I was lulling you into a false sense of security.'

The twinkle faded, replaced by a flicker of fear that had him cursing his poor choice of words.

Of course she'd be insecure with how fast things had developed between them. In effect, he was her rebound guy, the first guy she'd allowed near her after the love of her life, and having her questioning whether it was the right thing to do was a dumb move, however inadvertent.

Placing a finger under her chin, he tipped it up. 'I'm kidding.'

'I know.'

But he'd shattered the light-hearted mood and, considering he had no idea how to deal with emotion, was having a damn hard time getting it back.

'I know.' He snapped his fingers. 'Let's go haggle for some of those handmade Kashmiri scarves you were admiring on the way over here.'

Her mouth twisted in a wry grin. 'That's the second time this trip you've tried to distract me with the inducement of shopping.'

'Is it working?'

'I'll let you know when you've bought me a scarf or two.'

Happy to have the smile back on her face, he held out his hand. 'Me?'

'Yeah, don't you tycoons like flashing your cash around?'

'Only to impress.'

'Well, I'm ready to be impressed. Lead the way.'

As she slipped her hand into his, it hit him how truly lucky he was.

Despite her joking around, Tam wasn't remotely interested in his money. With the type of women he usually dated that meant a lot to him, but here, with the pungent aromas of frying spices and fresh seafood in the air, the hot sand squelching between his toes and the relentless sun beating down, it merely added to the unreality of the situation.

He was in a tropical hot spot with a gorgeous woman, they'd become lovers and grown closer than he'd dared imagine.

Was any of this real?

Would it evaporate as quickly as the steam off flavoursome mulligatawny when they returned to Melbourne? Did he want it to?

He liked Tam—a lot. But did he like her enough to give up the habits of a lifetime and relinquish control of his tightly held emotions?

'Come on, I see a flea market over there with my name written on a few dozen scarves.'

He groaned, delighting in her wide grin while trying to hide his inner turmoil.

Tamara leaned back against Ethan, secure in the circle of his arms. These days, there was no place she'd rather be.

'Comfortable?'

Turning her face up, her breath caught at the beauty of his face, shadows from the fire flickering over his cheekbones, highlighting his strong nose, the curve of his lips.

He was gorgeous and, for now, he was hers.

'Very.'

She wriggled back slightly, enjoying the sudden flare of heat in his eyes, the wickedly sexy smile.

'When you first mentioned a full moon party at Arjuna Beach, I envisaged a bunch of hippies drinking and having a full-on rave complete with bubbles. Nothing like this.'

He cuddled her closer, sweeping a kiss across her lips before resting his chin on her shoulder, content to just hold her as they stared at the bonfire one of the revellers had lit not far from the water's edge.

The stubble peppering his jaw brushed her cheek, the tiny prickles strangely comforting. Gone was the slick, smooth, clean-shaven corporate pirate; in his place was his laid-back, easy-going, constantly smiling counterpart.

And she liked this guy much better.

How had she ever thought him distant and ruthless and aloof? The Ethan she'd got to know the last two weeks, the Ethan she'd fallen for, was warm and spontaneous and generous. He made her laugh, made her forget every sane reason why she shouldn't be losing her heart to him.

But what if it was too late? For, no matter how attentive and carefree he was here, she knew once they returned to Melbourne he'd revert back to type and she'd be left with nothing but memories.

She'd known it from the start, had held him at bay because of it, but no amount of self-talk could withstand a barrage of Ethan at his best: charming, gregarious and able to make her feel one hundred per cent female.

That was most seductive of all, for she hadn't felt this way in a long, long time.

Not only had Richard sapped her identity, he'd battered her self-esteem and, thanks to Ethan, she'd rediscovered another part of herself she'd thought lost—she was still a desirable woman, capable of instilling passion in a man and, right now, that made her feel like a million dollars.

'You've heard pretty much anything goes at these full moon parties, right?'

'Yeah.' His soft breath caressed her ear, sending a shiver of delight through her. 'So what do you have in mind?'

Tilting her face up to see him, she said, 'Dance with me.'

'Here?'

His dubious glance flicked to the couples surrounding the fire, some of them entwined, some holding hands, some lying back and staring at the stars, and she laughed at his doubtful expression.

'I love dancing and haven't done it for ages.'

His reticence melted away at her wistful tone and he stood, tugging her to her feet in one fluid movement, pulling her close until her breasts were squashed against his chest and her pelvis snuggled in his.

'How's that?'

'Perfect.'

And it was, not just the way their bodies fitted but the way he held her, as if she was something precious, something he never wanted to let go.

While logic said she was kidding herself in thinking that even for a second, her heart was going with the flow, caught up in the magic of the moment with soft sand still warm from the day's sun under her feet, Ethan's sandalwood scent enveloping her and his body speaking to her on some subconscious level.

They didn't speak, her head resting on his shoulder as they swayed in time to the sultry strains of a sitar, the drugging beat of a tabla. Closing her eyes, everything faded: the other couples, the fire, the music, the waves lapping at the water's edge.

She wanted to remember every second of

tonight, imprint every incredible moment in her memory, for this was the night.

The night she admitted she'd fallen in love.

While she might not be ready to admit it to Ethan yet, the knowledge that she'd come so far—opening her heart again, learning to trust, taking a chance—was beyond empowering.

As the sitar faded, Ethan pulled away and she looked up, wondering if he could read the exultation in her eyes.

Cupping her cheek, he said, 'You're glowing.'

Smiling, she stood on tiptoe and kissed him. 'Thanks to you.'

'So I'm forgiven for muscling in on your holiday? And for deliberately making us miss the train in Udaipur?'

'Why, you—'

She whacked him on the chest and he laughed, swooping in for a quick kiss. 'I had this stupid notion you'd fall for me surrounded by all that romance.'

'I don't need all those trappings.'

Sliding her arms around his waist, she snuggled into him again. 'You've kind of grown on me.'

'Good. You know why?'

'Why?'

'Because we only have a few days left and I intend to spend every second by your side. Think you can handle that?'

Ignoring the flutter of panic at the thought of what they had ending in a few days, she nodded. 'Yeah.'

'Then what are we waiting for? Let's head back and start making the most of our time together.'

His mouth captured hers again, his kiss searing as she melted against him, powerless to do anything other than want him, no matter how much her inner voice warned her their time together would soon be coming to an end.

'You sure you don't want me to come with you? I can always postpone this meeting.'

Tamara waved Ethan away. 'Go take care of your business. I'll meet you back at the hut later.'

'Not too much later.'

He pulled her in for a swift scorching kiss that sizzled all the way to her toes, leaving her breathless as he winked and waved, heading for the nearest five star hotel.

She watched him until he was a tiny speck in the distance, a tall figure striding down the dusty road with the long, determined steps of a man with things to do, places to be.

But he wasn't running from her and that was a bonus—a big one.

Since they'd made love two nights ago, they'd spent every waking moment together. All the things she'd planned on doing, like eating at

Souza Lobo's and attending a full moon party, had been much more special with Ethan by her side, sharing the experience.

As for the nights…exploring each other's bodies, pleasuring each other…had surpassed any expectations she'd ever had.

Richard had been selfish so it figured he'd been a selfish lover too. But Ethan… Just thinking about the ways he gave her joy brought a blush to her cheeks.

Their time together had been beyond special. They were good together—really good. You couldn't fake what they had.

An unexpected chill ran down her spine as she remembered how she'd faked a lot during her marriage, how easy it was to act one way while feeling another.

Ethan may be a player but surely he didn't treat all his women this way? Surely his actions spoke louder than words in the way he'd cherished her in Goa?

While she hadn't gone into this expecting him to love her, now she'd fallen for him she couldn't help but wish they could explore this further.

He'd barrelled into her life when she'd least expected or wanted it but, now he was here, she hoped he'd stay.

She stopped in front of a sari shop, pressed her

hands to the dusty glass and peered inside. Her mum had always wanted her to wear a sari, just once, but she'd never had the occasion or the inclination. Besides, Richard would've had a fit if she'd paraded her ethnicity around in front of his posh friends.

She'd overheard him once, boasting about her royal heritage or some such guff, implying she descended from a line of exotic East Indian princesses. She'd confronted him later and in typical fashion he'd laughed off her concerns, saying he had standards to live up to in the public eye and people liked that sort of thing.

She hadn't, though. She'd hated it and, while she'd toed the line in the vain hope of making her marriage work, the lies he'd told had never sat well with her.

Lies far more poisonous and extending further than she'd ever thought possible, considering what had come to light after his death.

Making an impulsive decision to buy one more souvenir of her memorable time here, she pushed open the door and stepped into the welcome coolness of the shop.

'*Namaste*. Can I help you, madam?'

The older woman placed her palms together and gave a little bow, her sightless eyes honing in on Tamara with unerring accuracy as she wondered how a blind woman could assist customers in a shop filled with so much vibrant colour.

'Yes, thanks, I'm looking for a sari.'

Duh! Not unlikely, considering she'd entered a sari shop.

'Anything in particular?'

She shook her head, belatedly realising the woman couldn't see her. 'I've never worn a sari before.'

'But it is in your blood.'

Her eyebrows rose at that. How could the woman know her background? Even if she could see, her light olive skin, green eyes and black hair could be any nationality.

'You are after something like this.'

It was a statement rather than a question as the woman ran her hands along countless silk, chiffon saris until she hovered over one, in the palest of mint-greens.

Her breath caught as the woman held it up, the exquisite length of material catching the sunlight filtering through the front window, the sari shimmering like the iced peppermint milkshakes she'd loved as a kid.

It was perfect, something she'd never imagine wearing; yet, with the shop filled with so many dazzling combinations, she should have a look around rather than grab the first thing on offer.

Probably the most expensive sari in the shop and the woman thought she'd be foolish enough to pounce on it.

'Actually, I'm not sure what I want.'

The sari slid through the woman's fingers like quicksilver as she turned her head towards her.

'I think you do.'

A ripple of unease puckered her skin as she registered the woman wasn't talking about the sari.

She knew India was a country big on legends and myths and superstitions. Her mum had told her many stories of ghosts and ghoulies and mysterious happenings but, as far as she was concerned, her superstitious nature extended to a quick glance at the daily horoscope in the morning newspaper, and only then for a laugh.

But here, now, standing in this ancient shop, the heady fragrance of neroli and saffron in the air, surrounded by the soft swish of silk as the woman continued to run her hands over the saris, she could almost believe there was something 'otherworldly' at play.

'The sari is beautiful but—'

'You are searching. For many things. For love. For a home. For yourself.'

Another shiver ran through her. Okay, this was getting too spooky.

The woman was scarily accurate, though her

predictions had been pretty generic. What tourist wouldn't be on a quest, searching for something, if only a good time?

'You have love. But all is not as it seems.'

She'd got that right. Since when was anything in her life simple?

'You will face many obstacles on your path to true happiness.'

More generic stuff and she'd had enough.

'Actually, that sari's perfect.' Checking out the price tag, she sagged with relief. 'I'll take it.'

She thrust money towards the woman, somewhat chastened when she shook her head, sadness creasing her face.

Great, she'd offended the soothsayer. Who knew what fortune she'd get now?

'You will face trials, recross oceans, to find true happiness.'

Giving the woman money and all but yanking her purchase out of her hands hadn't stopped the predications so she'd better make a run for it.

'Thank you.'

She had her hand on the door handle, eager to leave, when the woman stopped her with a low groan that raised the hackles on her neck.

'Take care, my dear. You will need to be on the lookout for false happiness.'

Okay, enough was enough.

She bolted from the shop, wishing she could outrun her doubts as fast as the blind woman. As if she wasn't filled with qualms already, she had some crazy fortune-teller fuelling her insecurities.

This was why she didn't pay attention to superstitious nonsense. Yet, no matter how hard she tried to forget the woman's predictions on the walk back to the hut, she couldn't help but feel she'd voiced some of her own concerns.

Was her relationship with Ethan too good to be true?

Was it all just a mirage, a *false happiness* that would fall down around her ears once they returned to Melbourne?

She'd talked herself into believing what they had was real. She was good at that. Convincing herself to see things in a positive light, no matter how dire they were. She was an expert considering she'd done it for most of her marriage.

There was a huge difference between faking happiness and experiencing the real thing and, while this last week with Ethan had shown her the difference, she still couldn't banish her doubts.

She'd come so far. Over the past year she would've wallowed in them, let them drag her down. Not now. Taking this trip had not only boosted her esteem, fuelled her confidence and encouraged her to take risks she'd never thought possible, she'd also become an optimist. Looking on the bright side was much more liberating than brooding and, for now, she'd take each day as it came with Ethan.

As for what happened in Melbourne, she'd find out soon enough. They were due to fly back tomorrow.

Back to the real world. Back to a new life for her. She had a new job to find, apartment-hunting and a new beginning with Ethan.

Ethan, the man she'd fallen in love with against her will. Her friend, her lover, her soulmate.

Her mum had been right. Every person had a soulmate and she'd just taken a detour on the way to finding hers.

They could have a future together—a good one.

This time, she wouldn't settle for anything less.

CHAPTER TWELVE

'LET me guess. You have business to take care of.'

Ethan leaned over, brushed a kiss across her lips. 'You know me too well.'

'I do now.'

Tamara placed a possessive hand on his arm, scraped her fingernails lightly across the skin, enjoying his slight shudder before he clamped his hand over hers, blatant hunger in his eyes.

'I promise I'll make it the fastest investors meeting on record.' He glanced at his watch, grimaced. 'I have to run. How about I meet you at Ambrosia afterwards?'

'Only if you make me a hot chocolate.'

'Over your chai addiction already?'

'No, but I remember that fabulous hot chocolate you made the day you came back and have a real hankering for it.'

He paused, his expression inscrutable and for a

split second a finger of unease strummed her spine. 'So much has changed since that day.'

'For the better.'

He nodded, his tight-lipped expression not inspiring her with confidence. 'I've been doing a bit of thinking.'

The shiver increased. 'About?'

'About making up for lost time. About how much time I wasted not being around this last year, not seducing you earlier.'

That surprised her. She'd been anticipating many responses but not that one.

'Maybe I wasn't ready to be seduced?'

He smiled at her hand-on-out-thrust-hip defiance. 'Lucky for me you are now.'

'You think you've got me wrapped around your perfect little finger, huh?'

'Hey, I'm not perfect. Pretty tarnished, in fact.'

'Not to me.'

She wound her arms around his neck, snuggled close, breathing in his fresh, just-showered scent, wishing he didn't have to dash off.

They'd barely been back in the country six hours and it was business as usual for him. Not that it surprised her. His dynamic go-get-'em attitude was one of the things she loved about him.

While Richard had been good at his job—the best according to the experts—Ethan had a quiet confidence underlined by success.

She'd once been good at her job too, before she'd given it all up for Richard, and she couldn't wait to get back to it.

The restaurateur and the food critic.

People would talk, would say she'd moved on from the chef to the owner, but let them. She'd faced the media barrage after Richard died and, while she'd hated every minute at the time, she'd weathered the storm.

She'd never want to do it again, couldn't face it, but knew the man holding her close would protect her; she'd learned to trust him that much.

Pushing him away, she patted down his collar and smoothed the lapels of his suit jacket.

'Okay, off you go. Go do what you tycoons do.'

He smiled, ran a fingertip down her cheek before tapping her lightly on the nose. 'See you in two hours.'

'If you talk real fast, maybe one?'

'I'll try.'

As she watched him walk out of the door, utterly gorgeous in a charcoal pinstripe suit, she had to pinch herself to make sure this wasn't all a dream.

They'd landed back in Melbourne and the dream hadn't evaporated. Instead, he'd dropped her at the hotel suite she was staying in until she found a suitable apartment to buy, had raced home to get ready for his meeting and had paid a surprise visit back here on the way.

He must've thought she was a grub because he'd found her the way he'd left her—dishevelled and tired and still wearing the clothes she'd worn on the flight home. All his fault; after he'd dropped her off, she'd mooned about, flicking through travel brochures on India, lolling on the couch, lost in memories, remembering every magical moment of their journey.

The trip had exceeded all her expectations.

She'd discovered a part of her heritage that enthralled her, had finally released the last of her residual anger and had put the past—and Richard—behind her.

And she'd discovered a guy who had been on her periphery until now was in fact the love of her life.

Exceeded? Heck, her expectations had been blasted clean into orbit.

But, for now, she had a date with a shower. She wanted to get cleaned up before heading over to her favourite place in the world: Ambrosia, and right by Ethan's side.

Tamara pocketed her keys, grabbed her bag and was halfway out the door when the phone rang.

She paused, glanced at her watch and decided

to let the answering machine pick up in case Ethan had finished early and was waiting for her.

With one ear on the garbled voice coming through the machine, she tapped the side of her head, wondering if water from the shower had clogged her ears. She could've sworn the guy was a reporter from a prominent Melbourne newspaper, the same guy who had hounded her relentlessly after Richard's death. What could he want with her now?

Not interested in anything he had to say, especially on the day she'd landed back in the country, she slammed the door, took the lift to the ground floor, strode through the swank foyer and out into a perfect autumn day.

There was nothing like Melbourne in autumn: the frosty weather, the crisp brown leaves contrasting with the beautiful green in the city parks, the fashionable women striding down Collins Street in high boots and long coats.

She loved it all and as she took a left and headed for Ambrosia, she'd never felt so alive. With a spring in her step, she picked up the pace, eager for her hot chocolate fix—her Ethan fix, more precisely.

Smiling to herself, she passed the newsstand she occasionally bought the odd glossy food magazine from. She may not have worked for a while but she'd kept up with the trends, critically analysing her competitors' work, knowing she could do better if she ever got back to it. That time had come and she couldn't be happier.

However, as she slowed to scan the latest cover of her favourite magazine, her blood froze as her gaze fixed on the headlines advertising today's newspapers.

CELEBRITY CHEF'S MISTRESS HAS LOVE CHILD.

She inhaled a sharp breath, let it out, closed her eyes and opened them.

This was silly. That headline could be referring to any number of celebrity chefs around the world.

With legs suddenly jelly-like, she forced her feet to walk forward, past the newsstand. She'd almost made it when the truth hit her.

The reporter's phone call.

The headline.

No, it couldn't be…

With her lungs screaming for oxygen, she turned back and snatched the nearest newspaper with trembling hands.

'Haven't seen you around here for a while, love?'

She arranged her mouth into a smile for the old guy who'd been working here for ever, when all she wanted to do was flap open the paper and see if the horrible sense of impending doom hanging over her was true.

'Been away.'

She thrust a ten dollar bill at him. 'Here, keep the change.'

'But that's way too much—'

She waved over her shoulder and half ran, half wobbled to the nearest wrought-iron bench, where she collapsed, the newspaper rolled tight in her fist.

It's not about him…it's not about him…

However, no matter how many times she repeated the words, the second she opened the paper and saw Richard's face smiling at her, right next to Sonja's, adjacent to that of an adorable chubby baby with her husband's dimples, the life she'd worked so hard to reassemble crumbled before her very eyes.

She had no idea how she made it to Ambrosia, no recollection of the walk as she unlocked the restaurant and relocked the door before falling onto the nearest chair.

She stared blindly around the room, the place that had become a safe haven for her. The pale lemon walls, the honey oak floorboards, the open fireplace along one wall, the glittering bar along the other—she'd spent every Monday here for the last six months, drinking hot chocolate, honing her work skills, putting her life back together.

A life now laid bare for the public to see and scrutinise and judge.

It had been hard enough discovering Sonja's existence, the evidence that not only had Richard been cheating on her, but he'd done it in a house bought and paid for by him too while he'd imposed ridiculously tight budgets on her.

She'd been humiliated at the discovery of the other woman, had told no one, and now her degradation would be seen by everyone, her hopes for a new start dashed.

She fisted her hands, pushed them into her eyes in the vain hope to rub away the haunting image of that cherubic baby picture in the newspaper.

That should've been her baby, the baby she'd wanted but Richard had always vetoed, the baby he'd been too busy to have, the baby that would've given her the complete family she always wanted.

She'd pushed for a child, had been placated with lousy excuses and now she'd come face to face with yet more evidence of how much her husband hadn't loved her, how little he'd really thought of her.

Damn him for still having the power to annihilate the self- confidence she'd so carefully rebuilt.

She'd handled his infidelity but this…

Deep sobs racked her body as she bundled the paper into a ball and flung it across the room with an anguished scream.

'What the—' Ethan dropped his briefcase near

the back door, where he'd entered, and ran for the main restaurant, where he'd heard the most God-awful sound.

He burst through the swinging doors, his heart leaping to his mouth at the sight that greeted him.

Tam, slumped on a chair, her head buried in her arms while great sobs rent the air, her delicate shoulders heaving.

'Tam?'

He raced across the room, pulled up a chair next to her and reached out to touch her.

'Sweetheart, it's me.'

Her head snapped up and the raw pain radiating from her red-rimmed eyes slammed into him like a cast-iron skillet. He opened his arms to her, wanting to comfort her, desperate to slay whatever demon had driven her to this.

She shook her head, hiccuped. 'He had a baby.'

Who had a baby?

She wasn't making sense.

With tears coursing down her cheeks, she jerked her thumb towards the floor, where he spied a balled-up newspaper.

He reached it in two strides, smoothing it on the bar, the picture painting a shocking scenario before he sped-read the accompanying article.

Hell, no.

White-hot rage slammed through him, quickly

turning to blinding fury as he bunched the newspaper in his fist, searched Tam's face, seeing the truth in every devastated line.

That bastard.

That low-life, lying, cheating, no good, son of a— He sucked in a deep breath.

He needed to support Tam, not fuel his anger. An anger that continued to bubble and stew and threatened to spill over as he watched her swipe her eyes, her hand shaky, her lower lip trembling.

He'd never seen her so bleak, even when she'd lost Rich, the jerk he'd like to personally kill at this very moment if he weren't already dead.

'That baby should've been mine.'

He froze. Surely she didn't mean that?

After what he'd just learned about Rich, about their marriage, how could she have wanted a child by that monster?

'I wanted one, you know.'

She scrambled in her bag for a tissue, her fingers fumbling as she finally found one and used it to great effect. 'More than one. I hated being an only child.'

What could he say? That he thought she was crazy for wanting kids with Rich? That now, a year after his death, she shouldn't be reacting this way to proof that the guy was scum?

Then it hit him.

What he'd been trying to ignore all along.

She still loved him.

He'd kept his distance all these years, had only made a move now because he'd thought she was over him.

But she wasn't and, despite everything Richard had done, clearly stated in that paper for the world to see, she still wasn't over him.

His hands balled into instant fists, frustration making him want to pound the table.

It was the reason why he hadn't rushed her at the start, this fear that she still had feelings for Richard, the fear that he'd just be the rebound guy, no matter how long he waited.

He'd put it down to his own insecurities, had ignored the twinge of doubt, had taken a chance by letting his iron-clad control slip for the first time ever.

He'd made a monumental mistake, just as he'd feared. Losing control, allowing emotions to rule, only led to one thing: disaster.

'I don't believe this.'

Her red-rimmed eyes sought his, her expression bleak. But she didn't reach out to him and he wanted her to. Damn it, he wanted her to need him, to want him, to love him.

As much as he loved her.

The realisation sent him striding from the table

to behind the bar, desperate to put something concrete and solid between them.

He'd made enough of an idiot of himself over her without adding an inopportune declaration to the mix.

She didn't need his love. How could she, when she was still pining for Richard?

She wished her late husband's girlfriend's baby was hers.

He couldn't compete with that. He couldn't compete with the memory of a dead guy. He didn't want to.

'I'm sorry you're going through this.' He switched on the espresso machine, needing to keep busy, needing to obliterate the driving need to vault the bar and bundle her in his arms. 'Coffee? Or a hot chocolate?'

She stilled before his very eyes, her hands steadying as she pushed her chair back, her legs firm as she stood and crossed the restaurant to lean on the bar.

Confusion clouded her eyes. 'I thought you'd be more understanding about this.'

'Oh, I understand a lot more than you think.'

Silently cursing his hasty response, he turned away and busied himself with getting cups ready.

'What's that supposed to mean?'

Rubbing a hand across the back of his neck, he

swivelled to face her, trying not to slam the cups onto the bar.

'I've never seen you this upset, even after he died.'

He had time to swallow his words, clamp down on the urge to blurt out exactly what he was thinking. But nothing would be the same after this anyway, so why not tell her the truth? Go for broke?

'Yet here you are, wishing that child was yours.'

He shook his head, poured milk into a stainless-steel jug for frothing to avoid looking at her shattered expression.

'I don't get it. I've just learned the guy I thought I knew had a mistress he shacked up with whenever he could and he had a kid with her, yet here you are, still affected by him. Makes me wonder why.'

When she didn't respond, he glanced up, the emerald fire in her eyes surprising him. She'd gone from quivering victim to furious in a second.

'Why don't you go ahead and tell me what you think? You seem to have done a pretty good job until now.'

He didn't deserve her anger—Rich did, and somehow the fact that she'd turned on him when she should've turned to him lit a fuse to his own smouldering discontent.

'Fine. You want to know what I think?'

His palms slammed onto the bar as he leaned

towards her. 'I think Richard left a lasting legacy. I think you're so hung up on the guy you can't get past him, maybe you never will. And I think as long as you let your past affect you this way, you won't have the future you deserve.'

Derision curled her upper lip, her eyes blazing, but not before he'd seen the pain as he scored a direct hit.

'What future is that? With you?'

She made it sound as if she'd rather change that baby's diapers for a lifetime than be with him and he turned away, anguish stabbing him anew.

He had his answer.

She'd just confirmed every doubt he'd ever had— that he'd never live up to King Richard in her heart.

'You know, this place has been a safe haven for me lately. Not any more.'

Her heels clacked against the floorboards as she marched to the table, scooped up her bag and headed for the door.

He watched her in the back mirror, his heart fracturing, splintering, with every step she took.

He could've called out, stopped her, run after her.

Instead, he watched the woman he loved walk out of the door.

CHAPTER THIRTEEN

THE drive down the EastLink Freeway passed in a blur. It was as if she'd been on autopilot ever since she'd stormed out of Ambrosia, hell-bent on putting the past behind her, once and for all.

Ethan was wrong. Dead wrong. About everything.

Except one thing: she had no hope of moving forward unless she confronted her past and that was why she was here in the peaceful ocean retreat of Cape Schanck, clutching a crumpled piece of paper in her hand, staring at the address written in a woman's flowing script, her heart pounding as she slowly looked up at the beautiful beach house.

Richard had been careful to hide his infidelity from her while he'd been alive but she'd found this in an old wallet in the back of his wardrobe after he'd died.

She'd been clearing out his stuff, donating his

designer suits to charity and had come across it. At the time, she hadn't cared what it meant but later, when she'd discovered his private appointment diary detailing every sordid detail, along with a stack of emails complete with pictures, it had all made sense.

Cape Schanck. Haven for gold-digging mistresses. And their illegitimate babies.

She blinked several times, determined not to cry. This wasn't a time for tears. She had to do this, had to get on with her life before the bitterness and anger threatened to consume her again; there was no way she'd go back to living the way she had been before India.

Taking a steadying breath, she strode to the front door and knocked twice, loudly.

As she waited, she noticed the spotless cream-rendered walls, the duck egg blue trim, the soft grey shingles. The garden was immaculate, with tulips in vibrant pinks and yellows spilling over the borders, the lawn like a bowling green, and she swallowed the resentment clogging her throat at the thought of Richard tending this garden, on his hands and knees in the dirt, with *her*.

She knocked again, louder this time, feeling foolish. She'd driven the hour and a half down here, fuelled by anger and the driving need to forget, yet hadn't counted on Sonja not being here.

As she was about to turn away, she heard footsteps and braced herself, thrusting her hands into the pockets of her trench coat to stop herself from reaching out and wrapping them around the other woman's neck when she opened the door.

The door swung open and she came face to face with the woman who had stolen her life.

Sonja Van Dyke was stunning, a Dutch supermodel who had graced the catwalks for years in her late teens and, even now, couldn't be more than twenty-five.

She'd taken Australia by storm when she'd first arrived and was rumoured to be making her television debut on a reality show any day now.

Considering how she'd just splashed her sordid affair with Richard all over the tabloids with gay abandon, heaven help her, for who knew what gems she'd drop on live TV?

Even though they'd never met, instant recognition lit the redhead's extraordinary blue eyes as she took a step back, her hand already swinging the door shut.

'Wait.' Tamara stepped forward, wedged her foot in the doorjamb.

With a toss of her waist-length titian hair, Sonja straightened her shoulders as if preparing to do battle. 'I've got nothing to say to you.'

'Well, I've got plenty to say to you.'

Her eyes turned flinty as a smug smile curved the mouth that must've kissed her husband's. The thought should've made her physically ill but now she'd arrived, had seen this woman, all she felt was relief.

She'd done it. Confronted her demons. Now all she had to do was slay them and she could walk away, free.

'It's not a good time for me. Little Richie will be waking from his nap soon.'

Just like that, her relief blew away on the blustery ocean breeze, only to be replaced by the familiar fury that one man had stolen so much from her.

Her dignity, her identity, her pride, and she'd be damned if she stood here and let his mistress steal anything else from her.

'Tough. You need to hear what I have to say.'

She drew on every inner reserve of strength, determined to get this out and walk away head held high.

'By making this fiasco public, you've guaranteed a media frenzy for a month at least. Just keep me out of it. Richard owed me that much at least.'

Sonja drew herself up to an impressive five-eleven and glared down at her. 'Who the hell are you to tell me what I can and can't say? As for Richie owing you, you meant nothing to him.'

She ignored the deliberate provocation of the

last statement, needing to get through this and slam the door on her past once and for all.

'I don't give a damn what you say as long as I'm left out of it—'

'Did you know I was six weeks pregnant when Richie died? He was so happy. Thrilled he was going to be a daddy.'

Her blue eyes narrowed, glittering with malice. 'He was going to leave you, you know. Over, just like that.'

She snapped her fingers, her cold smile triumphant.

Tamara's resolution wavered as a fresh wave of pain swamped her. Richard had known about the baby, had continued to come home to her every night and play the dutiful husband while preparing to leave her.

Her belly rolled with nausea and she gulped in fresh air like a fish stranded on a dock, willing the spots dancing before her eyes to fade.

'As for little Richie, he's going to be just as famous as his mama and daddy. That's why I waited until now to sell my story and have him photographed.'

Her eyes gleamed with malice. 'He had terrible jaundice for the first eight weeks and would've looked awful. But now, at four months, he's absolutely gorgeous. Ready for stardom, like his parents.'

Just like that, she realised nothing she could say to this woman would get through to her. She'd been a fool to come here, to try and reason with her.

Being confronted by reports and pictures of Richard and herself in the newspapers and glossy magazines every day for a fortnight when he'd died had driven her mad and now the tabloids would have a field day. This could go on for months; she'd hoped by appealing to Sonja she might refrain from fuelling the story.

But she'd been an idiot. There was no reasoning with the woman. She wanted to relaunch her career and was planning on using her affair with Richard and their child to do it.

She'd never be free of them, free of the scandal, free of the whispers and pitying glances behind her back.

She had to get out of here, escape.

Like a welcome oasis for a thirsty desert traveller, the image of Colva Beach, the Taj Mahal, shimmered into her mind's eye.

There was a place she'd never be plagued by her past, continually reminded of her foolishness in trusting a man totally wrong for her.

A place linked to her heritage, a place filled with hope, a place she could dream and create the future she deserved.

A place she would return to as soon as possible.

'Richie trusted me implicitly. He'd back me one hundred per cent on this, as he always did. Nothing like the love of a good man to give a woman courage to face anything, wouldn't you say?'

Sonja's sickly sweet spite fell on deaf ears— until the implication of what she'd said hit her.

She had a guy who backed her one hundred per cent, who'd travelled all the way to India to do it.

A guy who'd given her courage to start afresh.

A guy who deserved to hear the truth, no matter how humiliating for her.

Walking out on Ethan had been a mistake. A rash, spur-of- the-moment action fuelled by that stupid newspaper article.

She'd been living a lie, had thought she'd put the past behind her, only to have it come crashing down around her and, rather than tell him everything, she'd run.

How ironic—it had taken a cheap tart like Sonja to point out what had been staring her in the face.

Without saying a word, she turned on her heel and headed down the garden path towards the car.

'You're just as spineless as Richie said you were.'

The parting barb bounced off her and she didn't break stride. Nothing Sonja could do or say could affect her now.

Coming here might've been stupid but it had been cathartic. She'd soon be free of her past.

And ready to face her future.

Ethan stepped out of the limo in front of Ambrosia and dropped his travel case at his feet.

He'd thrown himself back into business since Tam had walked out on him four days ago, making flying visits to Sydney, Brisbane and Cairns.

Facilitating meetings, presenting figures, convincing investors, he'd done it all in a nonstop back-to-back whirl of meetings but he was done, drained, running on empty.

Earlier that week he'd landed back in the country, had lost the woman he loved on the same day and buried his head in business as usual to cope; little wonder he could barely summon the energy to step inside.

He stood still for a moment, the slight chill of a brisk autumn evening momentarily clearing his head as he watched patrons pack his restaurant to the rafters.

Intimate tables for two where couples with secretive smiles held hands, tables filled with happy families squabbling over the biggest serving of sticky date pudding, tables where businessmen like himself absentmindedly forked the delicious crispy salt and pepper calamari into their mouths while shuffling papers and making annotations.

He loved this place, had always loved it. It was his baby, his home.

Then why the awful, hollow feeling that some of the gloss had worn off?

He should be punching the air. He'd had a lucky escape. Tam had made her true feelings clear before he was in too deep.

Though what could be deeper than falling in love with a woman he could never have?

With a shake of his head, he picked up his bag and headed in, the warmth from the open fire on the far side instantly hitting him as the fragrant aromas of garlic, bread fresh from the oven and wok-sizzled beef enveloped him.

He was home and the sooner he banished thoughts of his failed relationship with Tam the better.

'Hey, boss, how was the trip?'

He mustered a tired smile for Fritz, his enthusiastic barman. 'Busy.'

'I bet. Want a drink?'

'A double shot espresso would be great.' He patted his case. 'Help me get through these projections. I'll take it upstairs.'

Fritz saluted. 'No worries.'

As he turned away, Fritz called out, 'Almost

forgot. Tamara's popping in soon. She came in earlier, asked when you'd be back and I told her. Said she'd come back.'

His heart bucked and he carefully blanked his expression before nodding. 'Thanks. Give me a buzz when that coffee's ready. And throw in a hot chocolate for her.'

'Shall do, boss.'

He trudged up the stairs to his office, too weary for this confrontation. If it had happened a few days earlier, when he hadn't had time to mull over his foolishness, he might've been more receptive to hearing what she had to say.

But now? What could she say that would change any of this?

She was still in love with her dead husband.

He was in love with her.

A no-win situation, something he never dwelled on in business and he'd be damned if he wasted time wishing things were different now.

After flinging his bag down and bumping the door shut with his hip, he headed to his desk and sank into the chair, rubbing his temples.

They'd both been angry that day she'd walked out. They'd probably had a case of mild jet lag, but that didn't explain her reaction to that baby. Strange thing was, she'd been more upset by the baby than her husband's infidelity.

Unless… He sat bolt upright.

She must've known about the affair.

But for how long? Surely a woman of her calibre wouldn't put up with anything like that?

Something niggled at the edge of his thoughts, something she'd said in India… Another bolt of enlightenment struck as he remembered her saying something about wives putting up with their husbands to keep the peace or some such thing…

The ache behind his temples intensified as the impact of what he was contemplating hit him.

He'd thought he'd known Rich: capable, gregarious, master in the kitchen. But while Rich may have been a talented chef, it looked like he'd had another side to him, a side that made him want to knock his teeth in.

A tentative knock had him striding to the door and yanking it open, all his logical self-talk from the last few days fleeing as he stared at Tam, looking cool and composed in a simple black dress, her eyes wide and wary as they met his.

'I needed to see you.'

Stepping back, he gritted his teeth against the overpowering urge to sweep her into his arms. 'Come in.'

'How've you been?'

He gestured towards the stack of paperwork on his desk. 'Busy. Business as usual.'

She didn't glance at the desk, her wide-eyed gaze fixed on him instead. 'Yeah, Fritz told me you'd been away since the day we got back.'

Shrugging, he indicated she take a seat. 'Duty calls.'

'I admire that about you.'

He searched her face for an indication that she was anything but sincere and came up lacking. But there was something in her tone, as if she was judging him for his work ethic.

'Your ability to slot back into the groove as if nothing has happened.'

'Oh, plenty's happened. I just think I'm better suited to business than figuring out what happened with us.'

She winced and he clenched his hands into fists, thrust them into his pockets to stop from hitting himself in the head for letting that slip out.

His legendary control vanished around this woman, shot down, like his hopes of ever being anything more than a holiday romance for her.

'I overreacted the other day. I'm sorry.'

'Hey, you had every right to overreact.'

He paused, hating to dredge up pain for her but needing to know. 'Did you know Rich was cheating on you?'

Her slow nod had his fists bunching, as he wondered for the hundredth time in the last few days what sort of a jerk would screw around on an amazing woman like Tam.

'I had my suspicions and discovered the truth after he died, but I had no idea about the baby.'

'That must've hurt.'

To his surprise, she shrugged, as if it meant little. 'It did at the time. Made me crazy for a while but I'm over it now. I've moved on.'

She perched on the edge of his desk, so close, so temptingly close. 'Thanks to you.'

'Rebound guy.'

The words were out before he could stop them and she frowned, looking more formidable than he'd ever seen her.

'What?'

'You heard me.'

'You think you're my rebound guy?'

'Yeah.'

Her laughter shocked him as much as her quick swivel towards him, leaving her legs dangling precariously close to him, so close they brushed his arm.

'You're not rebound guy. You're *the* guy.'

He had no idea what she meant, was too confused by her nearness to ask.

Was she deliberately trying to provoke him?

Get him to touch her? His palms tingled with the urge to do just that and he kept his hands firmly lodged in his pockets.

'The guy I want to have a future with. The guy who has helped me learn to trust again. The guy I'm in love with.'

His gaze zeroed in on hers, searching for some signal that the stress of the last few days had sent her batty.

All he saw were clear green eyes locked on his, eyes brimming with sincerity and tears and love, the latter enough to catapult him out of the chair and reach for her before he could think twice.

'Say it again.'

She smiled, blinked several times. 'I love you. Can't believe I'm actually saying those words to a guy like you, but there you go.'

He gripped her arms, his initial elation dimming. 'A guy like me?'

'The ultimate playboy, remember? Serial dater? Guy voted most likely to break a woman's heart?'

'Who said that?'

Her lips twitched and he itched to cover them with his. 'Okay, so I made that last bit up. But I have to tell you, loving you is the ultimate risk for me.'

'Because of what Rich did to you?'

To her credit, she didn't flinch or react when he mentioned the jerk's name.

'Because I'd sworn never to trust another guy again.'

She cupped his cheek. 'But you're not just any guy, are you?'

She'd put her heart on the line for him. The least he could do was give her a healthy dose of honesty in return.

'No, I'm the guy who doesn't do emotion. I'm the guy who's a control freak, who's so damned scared of letting go that I almost messed up the best thing to ever happen to me.'

'What's that?'

'You.'

He crushed his mouth to hers, devouring her, hungering for this kiss like a starving man being offered a Michelin- starred buffet.

The kiss went on for ever, a fiery union of two people who couldn't get enough of each other.

How he wished that were true.

In reality, he was chary. For while Tam thought she loved him, he couldn't get the image of her reacting to Rich's baby out of his head; the same head that warned him to tread carefully, as always.

He'd had time to think, time to take back control of his uncharacteristically wavering emotions and, whatever happened, he knew he couldn't simply pick up where they'd left off.

As the kiss gentled, their lips reluctant to disengage, he hugged her, tight.

She'd fallen in love with him and, whether it was on the rebound or not, he knew what it must've cost her to come here and tell him.

'I've got something to tell you.'

He pulled back, searched her face for a clue to the sombre edge in her voice.

'I'm going back to India.'

Fear ricocheted through him, a fear he'd long conquered. Fear that no matter how badly he wanted something, when he could almost taste it, it was snatched out of his reach.

He'd battled the fear when on the streets, when first taken in by Arnaud, when he'd clawed his way to the top, expecting at every turn to have his goal taken away.

With success, he'd expected to lose the fear but here it was, rearing its ugly head and tormenting him anew.

'For another trip?'

She gnawed at her bottom lip, shook her head. 'I'll never be free of the past as long as I stay here. I want to make a fresh start and I can do that over there.'

The fear coalesced, consolidated, pounding in his ears, yelling that he'd lost her before they'd really started.

'I love you but I have to do this, for me.'

His shocked gaze collided with hers, the depth of her feeling evident in the way she looked at him with stars in her eyes.

She loved him.

She was leaving.

So much for being back in control. His wildly careening emotions swung between exaltation that she returned his love to despair that she'd snatched it out of reach before they'd really begun.

'Ethan? Say something.'

Releasing her, he turned away, needing breathing space, needing time to think.

What could he say?

That he loved her so much it'd kill him to see her walk away now?

That he loved her but couldn't contemplate following her for fear of losing ground with the one solid, reliable thing in his life—his business?

That, until recently, being the number one restaurateur in the world was his dream but, thanks to her, his dream had changed?

He could say any of those things. Instead, he had a sinking feeling that his lifelong need to control everything would eradicate his dream.

He'd fought long and hard to conquer the insecurities borne from being dumped by a mother who didn't love him, of enduring beatings from older step-siblings, from sleeping in doorways and foraging for scraps of food to fill the ache ravaging his empty belly.

Nothing intimidated him any more. In the business arena, he was king.

Yet right at this moment, with Tam's declaration echoing through his head, haunting him, taunting him, he was catapulted back to a time where he felt sick to his stomach with fear.

Fear he'd lose total control and there'd be no coming back.

Dragging a hand through his hair, he turned back to face her, met her eyes, saw his fear reflected there.

'Not very often I'm lost for words, huh?'

'Try never.'

Her bottom lip wobbled, slugging him to his soul, before she squared her shoulders.

'I'm not asking anything of you.' She waved around the office, pointed at the stack of paper-work on his desk. 'I know you've got a business to run but if you take another holiday, you know where to find me.'

'Where will you be?'

'Agra for the first month or two. I'll probably haunt the Taj for the first fortnight. There was so much more I wanted to see. Then back to Goa. I'll base myself there, start looking for a place to live and exploring job opportunities then.'

His heart almost burst with pride as he saw her standing there, confident in what she wanted, in stark contrast to the fragile woman of a few months ago. She'd come so far.

And she loved him.

It all came back to that. Considering what Rich had done to her, for her to trust him enough with her love let alone be honest about it, blew him away.

With her on another continent, damned if he knew what to do about it.

'You're amazing, you know that?'

He slid his arms around her, hugged her close, wishing he could hold her like this for ever.

'I do now.'

Her voice wavered and he cuddled her tighter, wishing he could throw caution to the wind and follow her to the ends of the earth.

She settled into his embrace for a moment before placing her palms against his chest and pushing away.

'I better go.'

He frowned, tipped her chin up, hating the hint of sadness, resignation, in her voice.

'Don't we have time to—'

'My flight leaves tonight.' She held her hand over his lips, pressed lightly, as if imprinting his lips on her palm. 'I have to go.'

He opened his mouth to respond, to tell her to

stay, to give them time, to explore the incredible, wondrous love they'd opened their hearts to.

But he couldn't do that to her, couldn't put his needs in front of hers. He'd be damned if he treated her in any way remotely like that bastard Richard.

This was *her* time.

He loved her enough to let her go.

'My Tam.'

He caressed her cheek, his fingertips skating across her skin, imprinting the feel of her into his memory to dredge up at the end of a long day.

Tipping her chin up, his gaze skimmed her face, memorising every detail and, when his gaze collided with hers, the pain in her shimmering eyes took his breath away.

'I'll miss you.'

Before he could move she plastered her lips to his, a swift, impassioned kiss filled with the yearning clamouring at his soul, breaking the kiss when he tried to hold on to her.

'Tam!'

'Maybe I'll see you at the Taj some time.'

With wooden legs rooted to the spot, he watched her hurried yet dignified exit, stifling the urge to chase and beg her to stay, the dull ache in his chest spreading, gutting him.

He rubbed at his chest, pacing his office like one of the tigers they'd seen at a National Park.

The ache gnawed at him, eating away a large hole that soon flooded with a sickening mix of regret and frustration and fear. Fear that he'd lost her—for good.

Maybe with distance, time apart, he could figure out what to do. The thought alone made a mockery of his need for time.

Time for what? Time to second-guess himself at every turn? Time to dredge up every reason why he couldn't do this? Time to dissociate from the crazy, wild, out-of-control feeling loving Tam fostered?

The way he saw it, he was all out of time.

She'd had the guts to lay it all on the line for him. So what was he going to do about it?

Real life was far from rosy and happy endings usually required a hell of a lot of hard work and compromise. He knew that better than anyone else.

But he wanted that happy ending, craved it with every ravenous cell in his body.

His gaze lighted on the phone. He had the resources and the contacts worldwide to make anything happen.

How hard could it be to organise his life for the next month or so in order to follow the woman he loved?

Snatching up the phone, he punched in numbers. Only one way to find out.

CHAPTER FOURTEEN

TAMARA lay back on the wooden massage table, wriggling around to get comfortable while latching onto the skimpy towel in an effort to cover her breasts.

Her mum had extolled the virtues of Ayurvedic therapies at length, a firm believer that all aspects of life, from people to animals to diseases, were combinations of the three energy elements: air, fire and water.

Apparently, her *dosha*—constitution—was predominantly air, which explained why she was prone to worry, anxiety and the occasional bout of nerves.

Right now, she was all three as the therapist, a woman of indeterminate age dressed in a simple white sari, positioned a pot of hot oil directly over her head.

'Relax. This will help rebalance you.'

Easy for her to say. She wasn't the one about to get hot oil dripped onto her forehead.

However, as the first trickle flowed gently onto her forehead, she exhaled in relief and closed her eyes, filled with a serenity she'd been craving for a week.

Coming back to India was supposed to centre her, help her feel safe, and while she'd been more grounded in the last seven days than she had in a while, a strange restlessness still gripped her.

She'd expected an instant fix coming back here. Crazy, considering what she'd been through, but at least she could relax here without fear of opening a newspaper or turning on a television to find evidence of Richard's disregard leering at her.

The oil stream stopped as she squinted through one eye, watching the woman straightening the oil pot before she delved bony fingers through her hair to her scalp.

'Too tense, too tense.' She tut-tutted, digging her fingers deeper until Tamara sighed, determined to ignore her negative thoughts and luxuriate under the expert tutelage of massaging fingers.

'Breathe. Let the oils help you.'

Great, she'd stumbled across another wannabe fortune-teller.

Though, from the tension in her muscles, it didn't take a psychic to figure out she was anxious about something.

'Sandalwood is good for stress, frankincense

for fear, gardenia for anger. Breathe, let the oils work for you.'

Yeah, she was stressed. Discovering your husband was a lying, cheating hound and his mistress had just told the world about it led to loads of stress. Not to mention the baby bonus.

And she was scared—scared she'd made the wrong decision in leaving behind the one man who'd brought joy to her life in a very long time.

As for anger, she'd thought she'd left all that behind when she'd walked away from Sonja and all she stood for.

'Your *dosha* needs soothing, many treatments. Abhyanga and aromatherapy today, meditation tomorrow, colour and gem therapy the day after. Yes?'

She could handle abhyanga—this massage really was to die for—and the oils and meditation at a pinch, but she had the feeling that this wise woman was giving her a sales pitch along with the amateur psychobabble.

Mumbling a noncommittal response, she concentrated on relaxing her muscles, blanking her mind.

It didn't work.

Her thoughts zoomed straight back to Ethan.

What was he thinking? Doing? Feeling?

It had taken all her limited supply of courage to see him again after she'd stormed out of

Ambrosia the day she'd discovered Richard had a love child by his mistress.

But she'd had to—had to tell him the truth. She loved him, trusted him and, while he hadn't said the words back, she now knew he was a man of action rather than words.

His admission, ripped from somewhere deep within, spoke volumes. He was a control freak and, for someone like him, this powerful yet nebulous emotion gripping her would be terrifying.

She understood. But it didn't make the ache gripping her heart any easier, or eradicate the fruitless wish that he could've come with her. She hadn't expected him to, would've argued if he'd suggested it, but that didn't stop the constant yearning she had.

'No good, no good.'

The woman pummelled her thigh muscles, lifted a leg and dropped it. 'Too tense. You go, come back tomorrow.'

She opened her eyes, sat up, clutching the towel to her chest. 'But I paid for an hour.'

The woman waved her away. 'I will give you two hours tomorrow but today—useless. Your muscles—' she banged the wooden table with a fist '—hard as this. Abhyanga not work for you today.'

She opened her mouth to protest again but the woman floated out of the room on a whirl of sari, leaving her cold and semi-naked and ruing her decision to have a massage to unwind.

Maybe she would come back tomorrow.

Then again, she had a feeling that nothing could help release the pent-up tension twisting her muscles into ropes of steel.

Nothing, apart from having Ethan arrive on her doorstep. And that just wasn't going to happen.

He'd been here since daybreak every day for a week, watching the pale dawn bathe the marble monument in translucent light, staying until dusk when the purple streaks turned the Taj luminescent, grateful the law only allowed electric vehicles within ten kilometres of this stunning monument to avoid pollution staining it.

He'd traversed the place from end to end, lingering around the main gateway, oblivious to the beauty of the entwined red lotus flowers, leaves and vines motifs inlaid in semi-precious stones around the niche, always on the lookout.

He'd drifted past the red sandstone mosque on the western side of the Taj and the Taj Mahal Naggar Khana—Rest House—to the east, buoyed by hope.

He'd sat by the tranquil River Yamuna snacking on tiffin packed by the hotel, he'd strolled through the gardens, scanning the crowds for a glimpse of Tam.

Nothing.

An endless week where he'd scoured the Taj Mahal, a shadow to its greatness, drifting to every corner of the magnificent monument with the hope in his heart lending speed to his feet.

He'd walked. And walked. And walked.

Always on the lookout, his gaze darting every which way, following the hordes, desperate for a glimpse of long black hair and sparkling green eyes.

Still nothing.

While the flight details he'd obtained said she'd landed in Delhi, then hopped a train to Agra and hadn't left again, Tam could be anywhere.

Maybe she'd changed her mind about haunting this place, had taken a train, a bus, to goodness knows where. Or she could be holed up in some ashram seeking higher guidance. Or planning a trek up Everest. Or back in Goa already.

Wherever she was, she wasn't here.

He rubbed his eyes, refocused on the crowd heading towards the Taj. This was crazy. A waste of time.

He could spend a lifetime here and she still wouldn't turn up.

This was the last hour.

Come tomorrow, he'd instigate phase two of his plan to track her down. In the meantime, he had one more lap of the grounds to complete.

* * *

Tamara's breath caught at her first glimpse of the Taj Mahal, as it did every day she'd come here.

As the sun set the faintest pink blush stole across the marble, the highest dome a breathtaking silhouette against the dusk sky.

Despite the tourists milling around, snapping away, an instant sense of peace infused her and she headed for the back where the river flowed quietly on a familiar path as old as time.

That had been their favourite spot—hers and Ethan's—and, while it may seem foolish, she knew she'd feel closer to him there.

Rounding the corner, she was almost mown down by a pair of rambunctious six-year-olds and, once they'd disentangled themselves, she brushed off her dusty trousers and set off for the river.

A lone figure stood on the banks. A man, dressed in khaki chinos and a white T-shirt. A man whose breadth of shoulders she'd recognise anywhere, whose casual stance, with hands thrust into pockets, heartrendingly familiar and, as the figure sensed her presence, turned, her belly clenched and tumbled with the overwhelming rush of recognition.

A surge of adrenaline urged her to run towards him but she'd done that before and he, despite her declaration, still hadn't said he loved her.

He could be here for any number of reasons:

scoping out another restaurant site, poaching another master chef, a business meeting.

However, as he strode towards her, long, hungry strides rapidly closing the distance between them, she knew he was here for none of those reasons.

The expression on his face told her why he'd come.

And the realisation took her breath away.

CHAPTER FIFTEEN

THEY stopped less than a foot apart, enveloped in uncharacteristic awkwardness.

Tamara didn't know whether to hug him or strangle him—for making her love him, crave him, unable to forget him.

'What are you doing here?'

Ethan smiled, his casual shrug pulling his cotton T-shirt across his shoulders in delicious detail. 'Haunting this place in the hope of finding you.'

He'd come for her and her spirit soared.

'Exactly how long have you been here?'

'About a week.'

'You've been here every day for a week? Are you nuts?'

'Yeah.' He stepped closer, swamping her in warmth and charisma and magic. 'About you.'

Her heart swelled, filled to overflowing with love for this man. But it wasn't that easy. Nothing ever was and she couldn't get carried away because he'd arrived on her doorstep.

He was here but did he love her?

She needed to hear him say it, craved the words more than her next chai fix.

Trying to hide the cobra's nest of nerves twisting and coiling in her belly, she took a step forward, slid her hand into his.

'The feeling's mutual.' She squeezed his hand, knowing his presence here spoke louder than words ever could but needing to have everything out in the open for them to really move forward. 'Do you know why I chose here to start my new life?'

His fingertips skated over her cheek, lingered on her jaw, before dropping to her shoulder, his touch firm and comforting, as always.

'Because, when we were here, you said it made you feel safe. I get that now, your need for security.'

'Do you? Do you really?' Her gaze searched his, needing reassurance, desperate for it. She wanted to believe him, wanted to believe in him. 'Because I really needed to feel safe when I discovered the baby and you weren't there for me.'

Shadows drifted across his eyes, turning them from startling blue to murky midnight. 'I'm sorry.'

She accepted his apology but it didn't cut it. Not now, after they'd shared so much, been through so much together.

'Why did you shut me out?'

He squeezed her shoulder before releasing it, turning away and dragging a hand through his hair, but not before she'd seen something shocking on his face.

Shame.

Ethan Brooks, the man who had it all, was ashamed.

He dragged in a deep breath, another, before turning back to face her.

'I didn't want to have to tell you this—any of it.'

He was struggling, she could see it in the muscle twitching in his jaw, in his thinly compressed lips. Looked as if she wasn't the only one with enough baggage to bring India's railway system to a screeching halt.

'Tell me. If nothing else, we're still friends.'

His head reared up. 'I want to be more than friends, damn it. I want—'

'Then give us a chance.' She softened her tone, touched his cheek. 'Tell me.'

He raked his hand through his hair again, looking decidedly ruffled and adorable. 'I've never told anyone this.'

She waited, wondering what could rattle him this badly.

'I was jealous that day at Ambrosia, furious you were still hung up over Rich—'

'But I'm not—'

'If you are or aren't doesn't really excuse how I treated you. What really pushed my buttons was not being in control of the situation. And that's something I don't like, not being in control.'

'You've told me. You're a businessman, a successful one, it figures.'

He shook his head. 'That's not the reason.'

He paused and she knew by the bleakness in his eyes that he was leading up to something big.

'I used to be a street kid. Dumped by my mum when I was five, shoved from foster family to family, scrounged on the streets from the age of thirteen.'

Sorrow gripped her heart. 'I had no idea, I'm so sorry.'

A wry smile twisted his mouth. 'We're doing a lot of that—apologising. Not real romantic, is it?'

'This is about honesty.'

As for romance, it would come. Having him open up to her, knowing how much it cost him, told her they had a future—a great one.

'And us.' He scanned her face, searching for reassurance. 'This has always been about us, Tam. I'm not telling you all this for any other reason than to give us a second chance.'

He cupped her chin, tipped it up. 'Do you believe in second chances?'

'You have to ask me that?'

Heck, she was the queen of second chances. She'd given Richard enough of them: after he'd stood her up the first time, after he'd blown her off for a restaurant opening, after she'd caught him groping a waitress within six months of their marriage.

Yet here was this incredibly honest man standing in front of her, his feelings shining bright in his eyes, asking her for a second chance? How loud could she scream yes without getting arrested?

Holding out her hand to him, she said, 'Come on, let's take a walk.'

'That's not exactly the answer I was hoping for.'

She smiled, recognising the instant he glimpsed the love in her eyes—for his eyes widened, all that dazzling blue focused on her.

'I have so much I want to say to you but let's go somewhere quieter.'

He glanced around, puzzlement creasing his brow. 'You can't get much quieter than this. The closest couple is twenty metres away.'

She tapped the side of her nose. 'Trust me, I know somewhere quieter.'

Sliding his hand into hers, she sighed as his fingers intertwined with hers. This felt right, had always felt right from the first moment he'd held her hand at Colva Beach.

Leading him to the furthest corner of the garden, she pointed to a young cypress tree.

'I've come here a few times over the last week. Seems I do my best thinking here.'

His eyebrows shot up. 'You've been here for a week too?'

'I told you I would be. I just didn't expect in my wildest dreams you'd be here too.'

He brushed the barest of kisses across her lips, her eyes welling at his tenderness, but she had to say this, had to make sure he knew where she was coming from.

She slipped her hand out of his, sank down and patted the ground next to her. 'I also came here to think, to figure out some stuff. Seems like every second person in this country is intent on predicting my fortune. I can't even get a massage these days without the therapist giving me a free glimpse into the future.'

He chuckled, sat next to her. 'So what's in the cards?'

She opened her mouth to respond and he held up both hands and waved them in front of her. 'On second thoughts, I don't want to know if they predicted some tall, dark and handsome stranger sweeping you off your feet.'

He winked, his rakish smile so heartrendingly familiar she leaned towards him without realising. 'Unless they mentioned me by name, that is.'

Hugging her knees close, she rested her chin on

them, staring at the Taj Mahal, a translucent ivory in the dusk.

'Honestly? I've done so much thinking this last week, I think I can predict my own future pretty accurately.'

She'd sat in this very spot for hours on end, analysing her life, pondering the choices she'd made, knowing she should learn from mistakes of the past in building a better, brighter future.

While she felt safe here, she hadn't quite achieved the peace she'd hoped for, gripped by a relentless restlessness, no matter how many hours she tried meditating.

She knew why.

The reason was staring her in the face with concern in his blue eyes.

'So go ahead. Give it to me straight. What does the future hold for Tamara Rayne?'

Now that the moment of truth had arrived, she balked.

He'd surprised her, turning up when she'd been contemplating some vague, pie-in-the-sky dream, a nebulous idea she'd pondered at great length, debating the logistics of a long-distance relationship, wondering if they could really make it work.

But she couldn't shake off the fear that still dogged her, the fear she'd finally recognised as undermining her relationship with Ethan right from the very beginning.

She shrugged, hugged her knees tighter. 'My future is here. I've put feelers out and loads of the big newspapers are after food critics. Plus I can free-lance for some of the glossy magazines and—'

'While it's great your career is back on track, I'm more interested in you. What does the future hold for you?'

Us, was what he really meant.

The unsaid word hovered between them, tempt-ingly within reach if she had the guts to reach out there and grab it.

She took a deep breath and shuffled her bottom around to face him. In the fading light, with the low-hanging branches casting shadows over his face, she couldn't read his expression. And she wanted to, needed to.

He'd come but there'd been no declaration, no emotional reunion, just two people dancing around each other, throwing out the odd bit of truthful information.

Should she put her heart on the line, once and for all? Confront her fear, at the risk of losing the love of her life?

'I guess some of my future depends on you.'

He didn't move a muscle, not the slightest flicker.

'I've done a lot of soul-searching this last week

and the only thing I regret in leaving Melbourne is not being completely honest with you.'

'I'm listening.'

She released her arms, shook them out, stretched out her legs, which were cramping as badly as her belly.

'When I ran out of Ambrosia that day, I didn't correct your wrong assumptions. I was too disappointed, too caught up in the moment. I wasn't thinking straight. It wasn't until later, much later, I realised how it must've looked.'

'You still love Richard, I know—'

Her gaze snapped to his, beseeching him to understand. 'No, you don't. I don't love him, I probably never really loved him.'

She bit her bottom lip, knowing she'd sound callous but needing to get this out of her system.

'I'd barely dated before I met him, then suddenly this brash, famous guy is all over me. I was flattered, just a little bit in love and the next thing I know we're married.'

'I always thought you were happy.'

She nodded, slowly. 'We were, for the first few months. I loved being married, loved how safe I felt having a husband who adored me. But then his lies started. And the rest.'

Her heart twisted at the memories of what she'd endured, all in the name of 'for better or worse'.

'He made my life hell. If I wore black, he said I looked too thin. If I wore white, too fat. He be-littled my job, saying no one ever read the crap I wrote. He rifled through my handbag and diary to keep tabs on me. He hated what I cooked, threw a chicken Kiev at the wall once.'

'Hell, Tam—'

'He called me a useless bitch too many times to count, used subtle put-downs in front of his friends, demeaned the way I decorated our place, rubbished my friends, disparaged my mum.'

He swore, shook his head but she had to continue now she'd started, had to get this out of her system once and for all.

'Did you know he was a classic passive-aggressive? I started walking around on egg-shells, doing the right things, saying the right things, in an effort to avoid the inevitable explo-sion if things didn't go his way.'

Ethan reached out to her, placed his hand over hers lying on the grass. 'I had no idea.'

'No one did.'

She blinked back tears, swallowed the bitter-ness. 'How could you, when Richard Downey, Australia's favourite celebrity chef, was all smiles, the life of every party?'

He squeezed her hand. 'Why did you stay?'

She'd asked herself the same question a million times, had come up with different answers.

How could she verbalise her craving for love, for security, for the perfect happily-ever-after scenario her parents had until her dad died?

It sounded so soppy, so stupid, especially after she'd realised Richard could never be that man for her.

'I stayed because I wanted the family I never had after my dad died. I craved it, which is probably half the reason I married him in the first place. As misguided as it sounds, at the time I thought if I could be a good wife, our marriage would stand a fighting chance.'

She wriggled her hand out from under his on the pretext of retwisting her hair into a loose chignon, his touch too painful, too poignant with what she had to say next.

'I became invisible. I lost my identity, my dignity and my self-respect for a man who didn't care about me, no matter what I did. I got caught up in a vicious cycle, trying to convince him I wasn't worthless in order to regain some semblance of self-respect in order to leave him. Round and round I went, trying my guts out, never being good enough, totally helpless. And I'll never forgive myself for that.'

He swore under his breath, bundled her into his arms and she slowly relaxed as he stroked her back in long, comforting caresses. 'It's finished. Over. You're not that person any more.'

But she was the same person, with the same fears dogging her.

Drawing back, he cradled her face in his hands. 'Tam, it's going to be okay.'

'Is it?'

In response, he lowered his head and kissed her, a slow, tender kiss on her lips, a kiss of affirmation and optimism and faith, a kiss filled with promise and hope.

The hope was the clincher.

She had to tell him—all of it.

Reaching up, she trailed her fingertips down his cheek, the familiar rasp of stubble sending a shiver up her arm.

'I know you care about me and you're nothing like Richard. But I've finally found myself again, I'm finally comfortable in my own skin and I don't want to risk losing that. For anyone.'

Wariness crept across his face. 'What are you trying to say?'

'I'm scared to get involved in a relationship again.'

She dropped her hand, wriggled back to put some distance between them. 'I'm willing to date but I can't make any promises.'

'You're wrong.'

Confused, she stared at him.

'I don't just care about you. I love you.'

Her sharp indrawn gasp sounded harsh in the silence and his hand shot out and latched onto her wrist as if he expected her to bolt.

'And I get it. You're scared. Scared to take a chance on a relationship for fear of losing your identity again. But hell, Tam, this is me. Not Richard. Surely you know I'd never hurt you?'

Hot, scalding tears burned the back of her eyes—tears of hope, tears of fear.

If loving Richard and losing herself had been painful, loving Ethan and losing him would be a hundred times worse.

But the fear was still there, still undermining her new-found confidence, whispering insidious warnings that her inner strength could vanish in a second if she made the wrong decision again.

'I know. You just being here is proof enough but I guess the fear has been a part of me so long, it's hard to shake.'

He shook his head, his grip unrelenting. 'Do you think this is easy for me? I've never loved anyone, let alone admitted it. I don't trust easily—'

'Which is why you date those airheads,' she finished for him, the realisation flooring her.

After what he'd told her today—being abandoned by his mum, dumped from family to family—everything suddenly slid into place.

He was just as frightened as her: frightened to love, frightened to get emotionally involved, frightened to lose control.

Yet he'd confronted his fear, overcome it, for her.

'You're as scared as me,' she said in a hushed tone, scrabbling on her knees to get closer to him.

'That's it, isn't it? Why you closed off that day at Ambrosia? You thought I still cared about Richard, about having his baby and you loved me then. You were just hiding your fear, weren't you?'

His slow, reluctant nod had her launching onto his lap and wrapping her arms around his neck. 'Jeez, we're a fine pair. We can read each other's minds, we just don't want to delve into our own.'

He nuzzled her neck, sending a delightful shiver skating across her skin. 'So I take it this means you want to take a risk on an old scaredy-cat like me?'

Laughing, she pulled back, planted a loud, resounding kiss on his mouth.

'You bet.'

She kissed him again—slower this time, much slower—and they came up dragging in great lungfuls of air several long moments later.

'I love you too. The for ever kind of love.'

He smiled, his arms locked firmly around her

waist, every ounce of devotion and adoration and love blazing from his guileless blue eyes.

'Is that your prediction?'

'Oh, yeah.'

He jerked his head towards the Taj Mahal, the majestic monument standing tall and strong, a silent observer of yet another romantic drama playing out in its honour.

'You know, they say this place is mystical. The ultimate dedication to love. So what do you say we live up to its romantic promise?'

She held her breath, her heart racing with anticipation as her mind took a flying leap into the future.

Maybe her predictive powers were developing, for she had a sneaking suspicion Ethan was about to—

'Tam, will you marry me? I promise to love you, cherish you, let you be your own person and do whatever you want.'

His wide smile had her grinning right back at him with elation filling her soul and joy expanding her heart.

'How can a girl refuse a proposal like that?'

'You can't.'

He stole a kiss and she poured all her love for him into it.

'You once asked me if I believed in love at first sight.'

His eyes crinkled adorably, the roguish pirate smile back in place. 'And do you?'

'Whether first sight, short sight or long sight, I believe in loving you.'

As their lips met, the moon rose, casting an enchanting glow over the Taj Mahal and its latest pair of lovers bound by destiny.

INVITATION TO
THE BOSS'S BALL

BY

FIONA HARPER

MILLS & BOON

For my grandmother, Alice Johnson,
who always encouraged me to daydream,
and helped make some of my early ones became reality.

First published in Great Britain 2009
Harlequin Mills & Boon Limited,
Eton House, 18-24 Paradise Road, Richmond, Surrey TW9 1SR

© Fiona Harper 2009

ISBN: 978 0 263 86965 1

Set in Times Roman 13 on 14½ pt
02-0909-53058

Printed and bound in Spain
by Litografia Rosés, S.A., Barcelona

Dear Reader

I've always loved fairytales. I used to act them out with my grandma and my younger sister when I was a child. Granny was always the wicked witch or the woodcutter. My poor younger sister was only ever allowed to be a dwarf or an ugly relation of some sort. As older sibling, I claimed the right to be the heroine, the princess. (Sorry, sis!) Cinderella was one of my favourites. Rags to riches, living the dream, falling in love with a handsome prince—what's not to like?

And that's why we like reading romance, isn't it? We like to identify with the heroines and fall in love with tall, dark and handsome strangers. We want to walk in the heroine's shoes for a few hours and live the fantasy.

Alice, in INVITATION TO THE BOSS'S BALL, has the most fabulous pair of shoes. I would literally love to strut around in them for a while. What a pity she doesn't believe she's princessy enough to wear them—that is until she meets the yummy Cameron! In fact, I wouldn't mind stealing *him* for a few hours myself too…

This book is my modern-day take on the classic Cinderella story. It has a downtrodden heroine, a suitably remote and regal prince, and it even has versions of the ugly sisters and the fairy godmother—who actually waves a wand at one point. See if you can spot it!

Love and hugs

Fiona Harper

As a child, **Fiona Harper** was constantly teased for either having her nose in a book or living in a dream world. Things haven't changed much since then, but at least in writing she's found a use for her runaway imagination. After studying dance at university, Fiona worked as a dancer, teacher and choreographer, before trading in that career for video-editing and production. When she became a mother she cut back on her working hours to spend time with her children, and when her littlest one started pre-school she found a few spare moments to rediscover an old but not forgotten love—writing.

Fiona lives in London, but her other favourite places to be are the Highlands of Scotland, and the Kent countryside on a summer's afternoon. She loves cooking good food, and anything cinnamon-flavoured. Of course she still can't keep away from a good book, or a good movie—especially romances—but only if she's stocked up with tissues. Because she knows she will need them by the end, be it happy or sad. Her favourite things in the world are her wonderful husband, who has learned to decipher her incoherent ramblings, and her two daughters.

CHAPTER ONE

THE old oyster-coloured satin had the most wonderful texture—smooth, but not slippery like modern imitations, stiff and reassuringly heavy. Anyone who saw the cocktail dress would just itch to touch it—and that was what Alice did, letting her fingertips explore it fully, lingering on the crease of the sash as it folded into a bow just under the bustline. This wasn't just a dress. It was a piece of history—a work of art.

She placed it carefully on a padded floral hanger, then hooked the hanger on a rickety clothing rail at the side of the market stall. The next item she took out of the crate was totally different but just as fabulous: a black seventies maxi skirt—a good label—with velvet pile deep and soft enough to get lost in and just not care.

'We're never going to get the stall set up if you don't get a move on.'

She looked up at her best friend and soon-to-be business partner Coreen.

Today Coreen looked as if she'd stepped right out of the pages of a nineteen-fifties ad for washing machines or toasters. She wore a red and white polka-dot dress with a full skirt, her dark hair was coiled into a quiff at the front, and a bouncy ponytail swished at the back as she carefully arranged gloves, little beaded evening bags and shoes on the velvet-draped trestle table that made up the main part of Coreen's Closet— vintage clothing stall *par excellence*.

In comparison, Alice looked positively ordinary. Like many of the other market traders, she'd gone for warmth and comfort over style. Her legs, as always, were covered in denim, and an old, battered pair of trainers graced her feet. Coreen had already made fun of the oversized bottle-green fleece she'd stolen from one of her older brothers. Okay, so she wasn't the epitome of style, but she didn't stand out either. She *was* ordinary. Completely average. No point trying to kid anyone any different.

'Hey, Gingernut!'

Alice sighed and looked up to find the man that everyone at Greenwich market knew only as 'Dodgy Dave' grinning at her.

'Cheer up, love. It might never happen!' he said in his usual jolly manner.

Too late. It already had. Exactly six weeks and two days ago. Not that she was going to tell Dodgy Dave all about her broken heart.

'I wasn't… I was just…'

She waved a hand. Ugh—who cared? It was easier to play along than to explain. She beamed back at Dave, and he gave her a thumbs up sign and carried on wheeling his stash of 'antiques' to his stall.

Okay, there was one thing about her that wasn't ordinary—her hair. And though that sounded as if it was a good thing, it really wasn't. Some people were kind and called it red. The more imaginative of her acquaintances had even tried to say Titian or auburn with a straight face. The fact was it was just plain ginger.

Coreen snapped her fingers in front of Alice's face, and when Alice had focused on her properly she realised Coreen was giving her one of her looks.

'You're not still mooning around over that useless Paul, are you?'

Thanks, Coreen.

Just for a few moments she'd lost herself in the texture and colours of these wonderful old clothes, but Coreen's blunt reminder had brought her back to earth with a bump. 'We only broke up just over a month ago. A girl is allowed to lick her wounds, you know.'

Coreen just snorted. 'I can't believe you didn't dump him first, after the whole kebab incident. I would have done.'

Alice sighed, regretting the fact she'd ever told Coreen about the disastrous evening when she'd got all dressed up to go out to dinner—she'd actually worn a *dress*—only to discover that Paul's idea of a treat was a new computer game and a greasy doner kebab. He'd flung the paper-wrapped kebab in her direction as he'd helped her nerdy flatmates set up the games console. It had landed in her lap and left an unsightly grease stain on the brand-new dress. And he hadn't even noticed when she'd disappeared into the bathroom for twenty minutes, cross with herself for welling up over something so stupid.

At least Paul had *tried*. How could he have known that she'd been hoping for a romantic dinner rather than a boys' night in? She'd never complained before.

But, still….

Okay, she hadn't expected him to roll up in a limo and give her the princess treatment. But being treated like a *girl* for once might have been nice.

'No wonder your luck with men is so awful,' Coreen said as she pulled on a suede coat with a fur collar. 'You should have "welcome" tattooed on your stomach, because you practically lie down and invite guys to walk all over you.'

Alice didn't look at Coreen. She craned her neck to look at one of the entrances to the market. It was just short of eleven on a Thursday morning—not their busiest day of the week, but someone had to stop and browse soon, surely? Hopefully, that would take Coreen's mind off lecturing her.

'I do not invite men to walk all over me,' Alice said in a quiet but surprisingly defiant tone, well aware that Coreen would have no trouble kicking just about any man into line with her pillar-box red patent peep-toes wedges. Vintage, of course.

Coreen cocked her head to one side. Her curls bounced. 'You *so* do.'

It was no good. Coreen would never get it. She was vivacious and sassy with a glint in her eye and a wiggle in her walk that could stop traffic. Alice knew that for a fact, because she'd once witnessed that same wiggle cause a minor collision down Greenwich High Street. Coreen didn't know what it was like to be as interesting to men as last year's wallpaper.

And, while Paul had not been Coreen's cup of tea, Alice had thought he was lovely. A little bit too into his computer games, and not one for grand gestures, granted, but she'd really liked him. She'd even thought she might have been on the verge of falling in love with him. How stupid. All the time he'd been pining for his ex-girlfriend, and had ended up going back to her. All Alice had fallen into was moping around at home, eating chocolate and feeling rejected and foolish.

'Sometimes when you're in a relationship you have to be prepared to compromise,' she said, hoping desperately that one of the other regular stallholders would wander over for a chat now they were all set up.

No, Alice was a realist. Men weren't even going to press slightly harder on their brake pedals when she walked down the street, let alone swear undying love or promise to bring her all her dreams on a silver platter. But maybe she'd find a nice guy to settle down with eventually.

She frowned. No, 'settle' wasn't the right word. It made it seem as if she *wanted* to settle—which she didn't. She still had dreams. But maybe they weren't as glitzy as the next girl's. Prince Charming could keep his castle and his fairy kingdom. Alice would be happy with an average Joe who just wanted an average Jill to share his life with.

But how did she explain all of that to quirky Coreen, who not only expected but demanded all-out devotion from the men in her life?

'Hey.' An arm came round her shoulders and she smelled Coreen's lavender perfume. 'Just don't forget that even though relationships need compromise, it shouldn't be just *you* doing all the compromising—okay?'

That sounded fine in theory, but no man was ever going to be bowled over by her looks. And if you didn't have looks, you needed a great personality to make a good first impression. Alice didn't think she did too badly in that department, but she was a little shy, and it took her time to relax around people she didn't know and let them get to know her properly. And not many of the guys she met were willing to sit around and hang on a girl's every word unless she had the *looks*. Basically it was a vicious circle Alice had no part in.

But she had discovered one weapon in her arsenal when it came to interacting with members of the opposite sex. One she'd stumbled upon quite by accident…

Somewhere around her fourteenth birthday she'd discovered she'd suddenly become invisible to the male species. They'd all been too busy being at the mercy of their hormones and drooling after girls who had more, should she say, *obvious* appeal. But Alice had worked out a way to be around guys. She'd become one of them. Almost.

It hadn't been hard. Somehow she'd never got the hang of doing all those unfathomable, girly things that tied teenage boys' brains in knots and drove them insane. So, while she was busy being their buddy, boys got to know her. And when the divas dumped them, they asked her out instead. I hadn't really been a grand plan. Just a pattern she'd noticed and hadn't done anything to discourage.

All her ex-boyfriends had said they liked her calm, straightforward nature. 'You're so easy to be with,' they'd said, and had laughed about how they'd raced around like headless chickens trying to live up to their previous girlfriends' whims and finally exhausted themselves.

Men didn't have to walk on eggshells around her. She could be friends with them. And friendship was a solid base for something more permanent. The 'obvious' girls might be good for the short term, but when it came to the long haul Alice knew other qualities came into play. Qualities she had in spades—loyalty, honesty, supportiveness.

She turned to look at Coreen. Okay, Paul maybe hadn't been The One after all, and it probably *was* time to look forward to the future, concentrate on her work instead of her love life.

'Believe me, Corrie, I'm not mooning around about anything other than these clothes.'

Coreen grinned and clapped her on the back 'That's the spirit! But you can't daydream about every piece you hang up, you know.' She took the skirt from Alice and slung it on a hanger. 'And it's a good idea not to fall too much in love with the stock. Yes, it's fabulous, but when someone comes and pays cold hard cash for it I'll be waving each piece bye-bye with a smile on my face.'

Alice nodded. She knew Coreen was right. This was a business—a business she was on the verge of buying into. But falling in love with the clothes was what it was all about, surely? It couldn't hurt to just…*flirt* with them a little, could it?

'We've got a business to run,' Coreen said, her eyes narrowing slightly.

Alice shrugged. 'Technically—until we get the money together for a lease on a shop—*you've* got a business to run. Until then I'm not your partner. I'm just moonlighting from my "proper" job, as my dad calls it.'

Coreen made a dismissive little snort and Alice smiled. That was what she loved about her one-of-a-kind friend. Only Coreen would consider hauling second-hand clothes around the markets of south-east London a proper job, and Alice's home-grown IT consultancy a waste of time.

Actually, Alice's 'proper' job was coming in rather handy at present. Not only was she able to set her own hours, leaving her free to help Coreen out and learn the vintage clothing business, but some of the small companies she did computer troubleshooting for paid her nicely for being at their beck and call. All her spare cash was going

into the start-up fund for their dream—Coreen's
Closet in bricks and mortar, with a stockroom and
a small office. A place where Gladys and Glynis,
the two battered mannequins that Coreen had
rescued from a skip, could stand in the warm and
dry, safe from the danger of being toppled by
blustery autumn winds.

At that moment, another gust blew through the
market. Although they were in a courtyard with a
corrugated roof, surrounded by small shops,
Greenwich market was basically an open-air
affair, and the wind still whistled through the
access alleyways and pillared entrances. Alice
pulled her scarf tighter around her neck, and
Coreen pulled her coat around her and stamped
her feet. Braving the elements was part of the life
of a market trader, even if you dealt in old furs and
satins, so all in all it was a very ordinary day—
and Alice was totally unprepared for what
happened next.

Coreen had been to an estate clearance the day
before, and had brought back some truly amazing
pieces, obviously hoarded by a woman whose
children didn't see the designer labels she'd
tucked away in the back of her wardrobe as a
useful part of their legacy. Some people were like
that. They could only think of vintage fashion as
wearing other people's clothes, and would never

see the inherent beauty of the pieces they were on the verge of throwing away or cutting up for rags.

The satin cocktail dress and the velvet skirt were only part of that haul. Alice carefully lifted a peacock-blue taffeta evening cape out of the box, and when she saw what was underneath it she froze. There they were, just sitting there—the perfect pair of shoes.

She'd been on a steep learning curve about the history of fashion since she'd first met Coreen, but she knew enough to date this pair of evening sandals somewhere in the early fifties. They were the softest black suede and hardly worn. They were elegant, plain—apart from a small diamanté buckle on one side—with a slingback strap. But it was the heels that made the shoes unique. They were totally transparent. Not dull, cheap plastic, though. They were hard and solid, and reflected the light like glass.

Alice hardly dared touch them, they were so beautiful, but she picked one up gingerly and showed it to Coreen.

Her friend nodded in agreement. 'Fabulous, aren't they? I swear, if I was a smaller size, I'd have swiped them for myself.'

Alice peeked at the label. 'But they say they're a five and a half—you're only a smidge bigger than that. Are you sure you don't want them?'

Coreen shook her head. 'American sizing. That's a size four to you and me.'

Size four? Really?

That was it, then. This was destiny.

They were the sort of thing a twenty-eight-year-old *should* be wearing on a regular basis—not canvas sneakers and the big, clumpy things that made Coreen tut.

'They're mine,' she whispered.

Coreen was looking at her again, this time with an understanding light in her eyes.

'How much?' Alice asked.

The ponytail bounced violently as Coreen shook her head. 'I only paid fifty quid for the whole box, and I can sell the rest of the contents for five times that. You have them.'

'Really?'

Coreen winked. 'Really. I know that look. That's the look of a girl who's fallen completely in love and is never going to fall out again. Go on—try them on.'

Even though the stall was only half set up, Alice couldn't wait. She sat on the collapsible chair behind the main table and pulled off her ratty old trainers and thick woolly socks. She didn't even notice the cold on her toes as she took a deep breath and slid her foot into the right shoe, praying fervently that Coreen was correct about the sizing.

Oh, my.

Her first instinct had been right. They were perfect. The shoe moulded to her foot as if it'd been crafted especially for her, and when she slipped the other one on and pulled up the legs of her jeans to get a better look, she gasped. Somehow the shoes made her skinny little ankles and feet look all curvy and shapely and sexy.

She looked up at Coreen. 'The heels? What are they made of?'

Coreen bent forward as Alice twisted her foot to give her a better look. 'Lucite. It's a type of perspex. Really fashionable in the fifties—and not just for shoes. I think I might have a pair of gold-coloured Lucite earrings in my treasure trove.' She indicated the glass-topped wooden display box full of costume jewellery on the other end of the stall. 'But the things to look out for are the handbags.'

'Handbags?' Alice looked shocked. 'Made out of *this* stuff?'

Coreen nodded. 'Cute little boxy things with hinged handles. They come in all shapes and colours and they are really collectible—mainly because a lot of them haven't survived undamaged. In good condition, they can go for hundreds of pounds.'

'Wow!'

'Yes, so keep your eyes peeled.'

Coreen went back to setting up the stall, and Alice looked down at her feet and twisted her ankles this way and that. She wasn't a girly girl, and she didn't normally get excited about something as frivolous as shoes, but it was almost a wrench to slip her feet out of the sandals and return them to her hiking socks and trainers.

'That settles it, then,' Coreen said, bustling Alice to her feet and snatching the shoes away so she could pack them up in a box. 'They're yours.'

Cameron Hunter stood facing the plate glass window that filled one side of his office. From seven hundred feet above sea level, this was one of the most spectacular views in London. It was as if the whole city had prostrated itself at his feet.

Although the day had started crisp and bright, pollution had turned the autumn sky hazy, and now the cityscape below was all pale colours, smudged greys and browns. He stared at the silvery water glinting in the docks below.

He should feel like a king.

Most days he did. Head of his own software company before the age of thirty-five. A company he'd started with nothing but a loan he couldn't afford and an idea that had woken him up in the middle of the night.

And now look at him. This building in the heart of Canary Wharf—and his office within it—could be seen all over London. Further, even. Now every day in the south London suburb where he'd grown up the boys who'd bullied him, the ones who'd taunted him mercilessly, could see the proof of how spectacularly they'd been wrong about him when they walked down the street.

Even better, when they got to work and switched on their computers, it was probably *his* innovative software they were running. Not that he'd leased these offices because of that—it had just been a pleasing perk. When Orion Solutions had first moved in here he'd smiled every time he'd glanced out of the window.

But now… Sometimes he felt…

He shook his head. This was nonsense.

The intercom on his desk crackled.

'Mr Hunter?'

He didn't move, not even to twist in the direction of the speaker. His eyes were fixed on a blue patch of sky on the horizon.

'Yes?' He didn't speak loudly. He never spoke loudly. Somehow there was something in the timbre of his voice that just carried. He had no doubt that Stephanie heard every syllable.

'I know you asked not to be disturbed, Mr Hunter, but something urgent has come up.'

Now he turned and stared at the speaker. 'Come and fill me in.'

He stayed where he was and transferred his gaze to the door. He was not a man accustomed to being kept waiting. Not that he was impatient—far from it—but when you were Cameron Hunter people tended to ask how high it would be convenient for them to jump before he'd even thought of demanding anything of the sort.

There was a timid knock at the door and Stephanie peered round it. He motioned for her to come inside, and she stopped as close to the threshold as she could without actually being outside the room. He'd been having trouble finding a new PA since Aimee had left to have babies and devote herself to full-time mothering. He'd offered to double Aimee's salary if she'd stay. He needed her organisational skills here at Orion. But she'd turned him down, damn her.

Aimee wouldn't have crept into the office as if she was scared of him. But Stephanie, just like her three predecessors, jumped every time he spoke. He didn't mind the fact that his staff respected him—were in awe of him, even. In fact it had been something he'd cultivated when his business had grown beyond a handful of employees. It didn't bother him that people thought him remote. He wasn't the kind of boss who chatted about pets and children, and people didn't expect that of him. They expected him to be in charge, to keep their wages and bonuses coming. His staff knew he was dedicated to them and the company, that he was hard-working and that he rewarded loyalty richly. That should be enough. His personal life was out of bounds. He respected his staff enough not to pry into their business, and they in turn afforded him the same courtesy.

Stephanie clasped her hands together in front of her, looking as if she'd really like to bolt but was attempting to anchor herself. Cameron sighed inwardly.

'The Japanese party have rung ahead to say they've been delayed at the airport. They've asked if we could push the meeting back to three o'clock.'

He nodded. 'Fine. Make the arrangements, would you?'

She gave a hasty nod and sidled round the half-open door.

He walked back to his desk. Before he sat down, he ran his fingertips over the flat, square and now empty jewellery box sitting next to the phone. Until very recently there'd been at least one woman in his life who hadn't quivered with fear when he'd walked into the room. Far from it.

Jessica Fernly-Jones. High society darling and professional butterfly.

She was the woman every red-blooded male in London was dying to have on his arm. And for a while she'd been his. His triumph, his coup.

She'd made him dance through hoops before she'd consented to date him regularly. Not that he'd cared. It had all been part of the game—part of the sacrifice to win the prize. And there was always a sacrifice if something was worth having. When she'd finally relented and agreed to go out to dinner with him, he'd relished the looks of envy and awe on other men's faces as he'd walked through the restaurant with her. It had been even better than when he'd dated a supermodel.

But after two months the hoop-jumping and game-playing hadn't relented, as he'd expected. And he'd started to wonder whether one woman really was worth all the aggravation.

His answer had come the night he'd given her the jewellery box. Lesser women would have squealed and gone all dewy-eyed when they saw the logo of a rather exclusive jewellers on the box. But, give Jessica credit, she'd merely raised an eyebrow and given him a sexy smile. A smile that said she'd knew she'd deserved it, that she was worth every carat the box contained—probably more.

She'd prised open the lid and her eyes had roved the contents of the box.

It had been a diamond pendant. Simple. Elegant. Outrageously expensive.

A small pout had squeezed Jessica's lips together. 'It's lovely, Cameron,' she'd said. 'But don't you remember? It was the *pink* diamond I wanted—not a boring old white one. You *will* be a darling about this, won't you?'

At that moment Cameron had known suddenly and unequivocally that he wouldn't be a darling about anything for Jessica any more. Still, there had been no need to make a scene. They'd gone out to dinner, and he'd explained it all quite carefully before Jessica had flounced off.

Now he had his own little empire he supposed he would need a woman to stand by his side, someone to share all this bounty with. On the climb up he'd always imagined she'd be someone exactly like Jessica. Now, though…

Instead of sitting down he turned round and walked back to the window.

The view was starting to bore him. Just as well he'd be changing it soon.

'Alice? Alice Morton?'

Alice's hand closed around a pound coin in her money belt. She hadn't heard that voice in years. She looked up to find a stylishly dressed woman with a wavy blonde bob smiling at her.

'Jennie? I can't believe it!'

It looked as if Jennie's trademark stripy leg-warmers of a decade ago had finally been declared a fashion no-no, because the woman in front of her oozed sophistication. However, there was no mistaking Jennie's bright smile and the aura of excitement she carried with her wherever she went. In a flash Alice had scooted round the velvet-draped stall and the two women launched themselves into a rib-crushing hug.

A polite cough from Alice's left reminded her of what she'd been doing just seconds before Jennie had arrived. She handed the customer she'd been serving her change.

'I'm so sorry! Here you go.'

The woman shrugged and wandered off, with a genuine 'Choose Life' T-shirt in her shopping bag.

Coreen braced her hands on the stall and leaned forward, her eyes practically out on stalks. 'Who's this? Long-lost sister?'

'Almost,' Jennie said, as she and Alice smiled at each other. 'I was engaged to Alice's brother for a couple of years. The fact I didn't get to be Alice's sister-in-law was the thing that made me the saddest when we broke up,' she said.

'Anyway, what are you doing selling vintage lace and platform shoes? The last I heard your IT consultancy was just getting off the ground.'

'Oh, I'm still doing that. It helps pay the bills. In fact, that's how I met Coreen…' She paused briefly to introduce the two women properly. 'When Coreen started selling her stock online a few years ago, she decided to upgrade her system. I sorted her out with what she needed.'

'That doesn't explain how you've ended up selling Wham! T-shirts on a chilly Thursday morning rather than hooking up cables to PCs,' Jennie said to Alice.

Just at that moment another customer walked up and asked Coreen something in-depth about alligator handbags. As she talked to the woman, Coreen made shooing motions with her hands. Bless Coreen! Alice mouthed her a silent thank-you and guided Jennie away from the stall, so they could walk and talk, browsing the clothing and arts and crafts stalls and catching up on over ten years' worth of gossip. She filled Jennie in on what the family were doing now, and she seemed genuinely interested in what Alice had been up to since she'd known her as a shy sixth-former. Alice gave her a potted history—there really wasn't that much to tell— and finished up with how she'd fallen in love with vintage clothes herself after getting friendly with Coreen.

'We're saving hard so we can open up our

own vintage clothes boutique,' she said as she finished off.

Jennie smiled at her. 'That'll be just fabulous,' she said, nodding her head, and then she pressed her lips together and looked skywards. 'Tell you what, when you finally open your shop give me a call—I'll organise a launch party that will put you firmly on the map.'

'A party?'

Jennie reached into a soft leather handbag the colour of clotted cream—the stitching on it was fantastic, and screamed quality. She pulled out an elegant business card and handed it to Alice.

'You're an event planner?'

Alice couldn't have thought up a better job for Jennie if she'd tried.

Jennie nodded. 'Isn't it a scream? I get paid to have fun!' She sighed. 'Actually, sometimes the "planning" bit of event planning is a bit of a drag. That's why I'm down here at the market this morning—hunting for inspiration.' She gazed at a stall filled with home-knitted baby cardigans. 'Did you ever meet my stepbrother?'

Alice blinked. Okay—swift change of subject, but she could keep up. She'd heard a lot about the stepbrother during the years Jennie had gone out with Patrick, but he'd been away at university for much of the time they'd been together.

'Tall?' She resisted adding *skinny*, mainly because she hated being described that way herself. 'With glasses?'

Jennie laughed. 'Yes! That was Cam back then. He hasn't shrunk any, but he's lost the specs.'

A flood of memories entered Alice's head and she smiled gently. She'd met Cam—Cameron— just once or twice, the most memorable occasion being at a Christmas do at Jennie's parents' house. She'd been living in fear that she'd get picked next for charades, and had sneaked into Jennie's father's study to hide. She'd almost jumped out of her skin when she'd found a tall, lanky young man sitting in an armchair with a book. He hadn't said anything—just raised an eyebrow and nodded at the other chair.

They'd spent a couple of hours like that, reading quietly, chatting occasionally, until Jennie had discovered them and dragged them out again to join the 'fun'. They'd both pulled a face at the same time. Then he'd smiled at her, and she'd smiled back, and just like that they'd become co-conspirators.

The details of their conversation that evening were fuzzy in her memory, but she hadn't forgotten his smile—or his eyes. Dark brown, streaked with warm toffee, like the tiger's eye stones in a bracelet she'd inherited from her grandmother. What a pity those eyes, with all that warmth and intelligence, had been hidden behind a pair of rather thick, ugly glasses.

'I remember him,' she said quietly. 'He was nice.'

More than nice. But he'd been older. And she'd been sixteen, and still a little terrified of boys she wasn't best buddies with. But that hadn't stopped her wishing it had been New Year's Eve instead of Christmas Eve, just in case he'd been in need of an available pair of lips when midnight struck.

'Well, he's driving me nuts at the moment, because his company is doing up some old building and he wants—and I quote—a "*different*" opening bash. Something distinctive, he says.' Jennie gave a little huff, as if she were offended that anyone would think she would do anything less.

They'd come full circle, and were now standing next to Coreen's stall again. Jennie reached out and lightly touched the bow on the front of the sixties cocktail dress. 'This really is exquisite,' she murmured.

'Try it on,' Coreen said brightly. 'I've got a deal going with Annabel, who runs the posh children's clothes shop over there. She lets me send customers across to use her changing cubicles as long as I give her first dibs on any gold lamé that comes in.'

Jennie bit her lip.

'Go on—you know you want to,' Alice said. 'The dress is lovely, but you need to see if it works for you. Things that look great on the hanger can suddenly look all wrong once you get them on.'

'And sometimes,' butted in Coreen, 'you find something that's—oh, I don't know—more than the sum of its parts. Like somehow you and the dress combine through some kind of synergy to create… well, a *vision*…'

Alice smiled, glad to see that Coreen wasn't as oblivious to the magic of her stock as she claimed to be. Jennie disappeared with the dress into the ultra-white, minimalist decor of Annabel's emporium.

'Just you wait!' Coreen punched Alice lightly on the arm. 'One day you'll put a dress on and it will happen to you. You'll see!'

Alice imitated one of Coreen's little snorts. 'Yeah, right. Like *that's* ever going to happen.'

Coreen shook her head. 'You'll see…'

There was only one way to deal with Coreen when she got like this: agree, in a roundabout way, and then change the subject quickly. Alice started off gently. 'You're right about some dresses looking magical…'

Pretty soon she'd managed to steer the conversation on to the fashion shows the vintage clothessellers staged each year, to advertise their spring and autumn 'collections'. They were always a huge success, and Coreen had heaps of tales about amateur models, slippery-soled shoes and fragile vintage stitching. It wasn't long before they were giggling away like a pair of schoolgirls.

All laughter stopped when they realised Jennie had emerged from Annabel's shop and was staring at herself in the full-length mirror Coreen always placed next to her stall.

'Wow!' both Alice and Coreen said in unison.

It was stunning. The pale colour complemented Jennie's skin tone perfectly, and the skilful tailoring accentuated all her curves. Somehow the dress made her look positively translucent.

An elbow made contact with Alice's ribs. 'Told you,' Coreen said. 'That's *her* dress.'

Okay, perhaps Coreen had a point. But it wasn't hard to look fabulous if you had a figure like Jennie's. She was tall and slim, and she swelled and curved in all the right places. Finding a dress that did that for someone who had more angles than curves, and no chest to speak of at all, would be nothing short of a miracle.

Jennie twirled in front of the mirror. 'I don't care how much it is,' she said, striking pose after pose and never once taking her eyes off her reflection. 'I *have* to have it.'

Coreen grinned and high-fived Alice as Jennie

glided away to get changed. When she arrived back at the stall she had a thoughtful look on her face.

'I couldn't help overhearing what you were saying earlier—about the fashion shows, that is.' She looked from Alice to Coreen and back again. 'I've got a proposition for the both of you. And, if I am right about this, this idea could put you well on the way to owning that shop you're after.'

CHAPTER TWO

ALICE sat on the edge of her bed and gazed at the one good photo she had of her and Paul together. One word echoed round her head.

Why?

Why hadn't she been good enough for him? Why had he gone back to Felicity when by all accounts the old trout had made his life a misery by being the ultimate high-maintenance girlfriend?

'Alice,' he'd said, 'you're such a relief after her.'

Relief.

At the time she'd been too caught up in the first flush of a new relationship to be anything but flattered. Now his words just stung.

Her nose was running badly enough for her to give in and sniff. She had promised herself she wouldn't cry any more. She was made of sterner stuff than that.

A phone started to ring. Probably the one in the hall. It rang on.

Alice blew her nose.

It still rang.

'Al-lice!' It was one of her housemates. She shared a house with the two biggest geeks on the planet. The untidiest geeks too. Roy and Matthew were no doubt on their brand new games console, occupied with slaying aliens and zombies and saving the universe. There was no way they would shift themselves unless their thumbs had locked up and they'd gone cross-eyed. She swiped her eyes with the backs of her hands, then ran down the stairs into the hall and grabbed at the phone before this very persistent person hung up.

'Hello?' she said, not a little breathless.

'Can I speak with Alice Morton?' a male voice said.

Alice's heart began to hammer a little. That was one sexy voice. Deep and warm.

'Hello?' he said again.

'Hi…yes…sorry. This is Alice.' She winced. Compared to The Voice, she sounded all silly and schoolgirlish.

There was a brief pause, and then he spoke again. 'It's been a long time, Alice.'

Was it her imagination, or had his voice got just a little bit softer and warmer—almost as if he were smiling?

'Erm…who is this?'

Please don't let it be a prank caller. Just for a few seconds she'd had the giddy feeling that a man was actually interested in talking to her, in hearing what she had to say. And if this turned out to be a huge joke it would make her life unbearably pathetic. Which was actually quite an accomplishment at this present moment.

'It's Cameron Hunter.'

Cameron? She didn't know anyone called—oh.

'Jennie's step-brother…' he added. 'Didn't she tell you to expect my call?'

Realisation hit Alice like a bolt of forked lightning. Of *course*! The voice was deeper, and more mature, but all of a sudden she recognised the quiet precision, the slight edge of dry humour.

'Oh, of course. Erm…hi, Cameron.'

Blast. Jennie *had* warned her that Cameron would be calling some time soon. According to his stepsister, he was a bit of a control freak, and if they wanted him to agree to the idea that they'd hatched with Jennie for this new building launch party of his, either Alice or Coreen would have to pitch it to him. Alice had begged Coreen to do it—after all, she had all the experience—but Coreen had refused, saying Alice and Cameron had prior history. Alice had argued that reading books on the opposite side of a room from each other while their tipsy families had embarrassed themselves could hardly constitute a 'history', but Coreen would not be budged.

'You're right,' she said, finding her voice had gone all soft and girly. 'It *has* been a long time.'

'Almost twelve years.'

Wow. He hadn't even taken a few seconds to work it out—he'd just remembered. Not many people remembered things about her. Mostly because she kept her head down and kept herself to herself. If it wasn't for her hair she'd be instantly forgettable.

Alice had been staring at the textured glass on the front door while she'd been listening to Cameron. Now she turned around and wandered off in the direction of the kitchen.

Jennie had obviously pitched her idea to him, and now *she* was going to have to convince him to agree to it. The plan had all seemed so stunningly brilliant when she and Coreen and Jennie had hashed it out over drinks last Thursday. The three of them had bounced ideas around, waved their hands in the air, and generally talked over the top of each other for most of the evening.

But now she was on her own, without the benefit of a couple of cocktails inside her, she suddenly realised there were gaping holes in her knowledge of the project. Like what Cameron Hunter's company actually *did*.

There was no point trying to blag her way through this. The Cameron she remembered was too sharp for that, and besides, blagging was a foreign language to her. Maybe when all this was over she'd have to get Coreen to give her lessons. She had a feeling it might come in handy in her future career.

'Jennie said your company is computer-related?' Might as well get the facts straight before she dug herself an even bigger hole. And she might find some common ground.

'Trust my darling stepsister to be a little sketchy with the details. She's normally very efficient, but recently…well, she's been somewhat distracted. Just so you know, my company produces software.'

'And how's it going? I know myself that starting up your own business can be hard. Are you doing okay with it?'

She *heard* him smile. 'Yes, I'd say I'm making ends meet.'

'Good for you!' she said brightly. Oh, dear. That had sounded all fake and patronizing, and she hadn't meant it to be that way at all. She entered the large kitchen she shared with the boys and flicked on the light, hoping that Cameron would take the comment in the spirit it had been meant.

It was time to turn the conversation to something more solid—something she couldn't put her foot in. 'What exactly has Jennie told you so far?' she said.

'Not much. I don't know what's got into her lately—she's been disappearing for hours at a time and being very mysterious. It's more than I can manage to get any sense out of her.'

There was a gentle huff and Alice smiled, knowing how infuriating her own siblings could be.

'She phoned me up and yabbered away at me about a ball and jazz bands and a show-stopping highlight to the evening.' Cameron said in a dry tone. 'I got the impression that bit had something to do with you. Jennie tells me you're some kind of fashion guru these days?'

She'd just been about to perch herself on one of the high stools by the breakfast bar, and she almost burst out laughing and very nearly missed plonking her bottom on the seat of the stool. Alice Morton a fashion guru? Hah!

She almost said as much, but an image of a scowling Coreen flashed across her mind and she quickly changed tack. She was supposed to be inspiring confidence in her abilities as a vintage fashion retailer, not ridiculing her new choice of career. The PR this job would generate for Coreen's Closet could be priceless.

'I see what you mean about Jennie being sketchy with the details,' she said, and then proceeded to give him a potted history of Coreen's Closet. When she'd finished he didn't say anything for a few seconds.

His voice held a hint of surprise when he answered. 'I would never have guessed you would have chosen that as a profession.'

Alice opened her mouth to tell him about the IT work, then closed it again. She kind of liked the fact she'd surprised him, and she decided she wasn't about to kill the first little hint of mystery anyone had ever held about her. She was going to enjoy this while it lasted.

'Well, I think if you love something you should pursue it, no matter the cost.'

That was her new motto. Starting right now. No more distractions. She was going to stop moping about Paul and throw herself into her work. At least with the vintage clothes business it was work she actually liked.

'My thoughts exactly.'

Just for a split second Alice sensed a common bond, a feeling she and Cameron were both wired the same way. The sensation was so strong she wondered if he felt it too. This was how it had been when they'd been younger. Even though he'd been nearly six years older than her, they'd just clicked.

'So, this is what we envisage for the launch party…'

Alice had been folding and unfolding the corner of a takeaway menu, and now she flattened it with her free hand and tucked it between the salt and pepper shakers, removing the distraction.

Jennie had told Coreen of her plans for a lavish ball to celebrate the opening of Cameron's new premises—the fact that the building was 'old' and 'a bit different' was all Alice had been able to get out of her. Jennie had been struggling to come up with something to set the evening apart, something that encapsulated the idea of new and old coming together, and then she'd overheard Coreen and Alice's conversation about the market fashion shows and she'd made a connection.

Cameron wanted something that spoke of class, success, elegance. And what could pull all these things together better than a unique charity fashion show, full of the glamour and romance of a bygone age, but showing how vintage clothes could add individuality and style to a twenty-first century wardrobe? And if they sold the idea to Cameron, Coreen's Closet were going to supply and source the clothes. Alice explained all of this to him, and as she talked she forgot she was selling a business idea and just rambled on about the glorious clothes, the icons of yesteryear, and how everyone who attended it would feel as if they'd stepped back into a magical time.

Cameron listened. He said 'mmm-hmm' and 'okay' quite a few times as she outlined the plan to auction the clothes off as the show progressed. But she knew that they weren't the normal noises of a man who was pretending he was listening when he was really thinking about last night's game. She knew he was taking it all in, capturing every detail with his quick mind and mentally sorting it all.

'I presume, from what you've told me about the history of your new business venture, that you and your partner aren't just going to be giving the clothes away? How does the charity angle work?'

'I wish we *could* give them away. However, we've worked out a plan with Jennie. We'd set very reasonable reserve prices on all the pieces—similar to what we'd get if we were selling them one-by-one on the stall. As each piece is auctioned off we'll keep the reserve price, and anything that is bid over that will go to charity.'

'What if the reserve isn't met—or all the clothes only just reach the set figure?'

'Jennie suggested my business partner, Coreen, should be the auctioneer. She's extremely knowledgeable, and believe me, she could sell mink coats to…well, minks.'

A loud and unexpected snort of a laugh erupted from the earpiece of the phone.

'Alice,' he said, his tone still full of warm

laughter, 'you always did have a very singular way of looking at things.'

Was that a good thing or a bad thing? Had she just blown it?

'With Coreen doing the talking you'll have more than enough to donate to charity, I promise.'

'If this Coreen is anything like you say she is, I don't doubt it.'

'And Jennie said you'd put in a hefty donation yourself.'

'Did she, now?'

Alice winced. 'Yes.'

Coreen's Closet could handle giving the extra money to one of the local children's charities because they'd be shifting a whole lot of stock in one go—and, even better, they'd be attracting the attention of a lot of well-to-do potential customers. The free publicity would be fantastic. With the extra money in their account, and the press coverage, she and Coreen might just be able to twist the arm of their business manager at the bank to give them a loan for the rest of the capital needed to lease and outfit a small shop.

'If we do this right, this won't just be another party—same drinks, same faces, same canapés. It will be something truly memorable. Each piece of vintage clothing we sell is unique, one of a kind. For those that buy at the auction, every time they wear that jacket or carry that handbag they'll remember your company and *think* one of a kind. Even those that don't buy anything will have their memories jogged when they turn on the TV and catch an old movie, or see a poster in a shop display. They'll be instantly transported back to the elegant and original night when you opened your new offices and your company started a new chapter in its history. And that's what you want, isn't it? For the event to be distinctive, because then it will be remembered.'

Alice had now run out of words, and she had the sense that adding to them with empty silence-fillers would just be a mistake. So she closed her mouth and stared out of the kitchen window into the dark evening sky, waiting for Cameron's response.

Suddenly his good opinion—of her, of her hopes and dreams—mattered. She held her breath.

'Okay, Alice. You've got a deal. I like the idea.'

Alice was very glad Cameron didn't have a video phone, because she took that moment to do a silent victory dance around the kitchen.

'I understand you're going to liaise with Jennie about the party, and she's going to keep me in the loop. Do you really think you can pull this off in four weeks?'

Alice was tempted to hyperventilate. She was

so far out of her depth it wasn't funny. 'Of course,' she said.

'I look forward to seeing you then. Sorry to have interrupted your evening, but I was intrigued by what Jennie had told me and I wanted to find out more immediately. I've always found it helps to put the brakes on before she gets too carried away. Sometimes her ideas just don't pan out. Anyway, I'll let you get back to…whatever you were doing.'

'It's fine. I wasn't really…'

She knew she should just say goodbye gracefully and put the phone down, but she didn't.

'You know, Alice, I always thought you had it in you to surprise everyone.'

That was possibly the nicest thing anyone had ever said to her.

Oh, her clients gushed occasionally about her, but, to be honest, they'd have sainted anyone who could have got their e-mail going again when an IT disaster struck. And not only was Cameron saying nice things, he was saying them in his lovely voice. She could have listened to it all evening.

'Thank you, Cam.'

He chuckled. 'Cam… I don't think anyone but Jennie calls me that any more.'

'Sorry…Cameron.' She frowned. 'What *do* people call you, then?'

'Oh, *Your Highness* pretty much works for me.'

Now it was Alice's turn to laugh.

'See you in four weeks, Alice.'

And then he was gone.

She pulled the phone away from her ear and stared at it. This evening was getting progressively more surreal.

She cradled the phone to her chest as she slipped off the kitchen stool and wandered down the hallway to replace it on its base.

She made her way upstairs and pulled a book off her shelf, intending to read at least five chapters while soaking herself in a very hot bath. And as she threw her clothes onto the bed and pulled on her comfy old dressing gown, the slightly crumpled photo that had been lying face-down on the duvet fluttered to the floor and hid itself under the bed.

'Moon River' chimed from Alice's pocket as her mobile vibrated. In an effort to contort herself into a position whereby she could reach it, she whacked her head on the underside of the desk she'd been crawling under. There was a muffled snicker from somewhere else in the office.

Finally she got her phone to her ear. 'Hello?'

'Hello.'

That one simple word, said in a calm, deep,

velvety voice, set Alice's heart-rate rocketing. Why did his voice make her think of log fires and thick hot chocolate?

'Cameron?' Oh, flip. Did that nauseating little squeak of a voice belong to *her*? She cleared her throat.

'Alice, we have a problem.'

We? Had he just said *we*?

'We do?'

She heard a muffled shuffling sound, as if he was pacing around. 'My ridiculous stepsister has decided to…decided to…*elope*! I knew she was acting strangely, but…'

Did modern-day women still elope? Alice wasn't sure. Didn't that only happen to corset-wearing heroines in historical novels? Either way, it was wildly romantic. She drifted off into a little daydream about carriages, hooded velvet capes and moonlight.

However, Cameron's voice sliced through her fantasy. 'No Jennie means no ball. Which means no fashion show.'

That's right. Break it to me gently, Cameron.

Was she mistaken, or was there a hint of imperious displeasure in his tone?

Anyway, the fashion show *couldn't* be off. She and Coreen had already planned what to do with the money. They'd set their hearts on being in a

shop by February. Without the income and publicity from the show, they might have to wait until
the following year.

Alice thought of the market fashion shows, how
all the traders pulled together and made it happen.

'*I* can do it. I can organise the fashion show.'

Had she really just said that? A market fashion
show, with people's sisters and cousins as models,
was a bit different from the kind of upmarket
affair Jennie had been planning.

There was a split-second pause before Cameron
said, 'I like your fighting spirit, Alice.'

She didn't have much of a choice, did she?

'We both need this event to be a success,' he said.
'And I agree that bailing out now isn't an option.'

That wasn't *exactly* what she'd meant…

'You'll just have to take over,' he added, almost
to himself.

Alice blinked. For a while she'd forgotten
where she was. She'd stopped noticing the faded
blue carpet and the tangle of wires in every direction. But now she was back in the real world,
staring at a bare patch somebody's feet had worn
under the desk.

'I beg your pardon?'

'You'll just have to help me. You said you could
organise the fashion show part. Couldn't you do
the rest too? I'll pay you Jennie's fee.'

He mentioned a figure that made Alice's eyes water. With that sort of capital behind them Coreen's Closet could have its own premises by Christmas, never mind February. It almost made her forget that he hadn't exactly asked nicely.

'But I have no experience of—'

'Neither do I. But I'm prepared to give it a go if you are. We've only got three weeks now, and it's too late to start from scratch with another event planner.' His voice softened. 'Come on, Alice. For our own reasons, we both need to pull this off.'

It didn't matter if Cameron had asked nicely or not. He was right.

'Okay,' she said slowly. 'I'll think about it.'

Cameron obviously decided to take that as a yes, because he started to reel off instructions and bark at her about couriering Jennie's files over.

'Slow down a minute!'

Cameron broke off in mid-flow, seemingly flummoxed by the concept that someone might have something better to do with their time than fulfil his every whim. Alice took advantage of the silence.

'You can't send stuff round right this minute. I'm not at home. I'm at work. I won't be there to sign for it.'

'Oh. Sorry. I should have… But Jennie said you weren't at the market today. I haven't interrupted you on a house visit, in the middle of rifling through someone's wardrobe, have I?'

'No—ouch!' Alice had turned to sit cross-legged on the floor and her head had made contact with the desk once more. 'Actually, I'm rifling through someone's network.'

There was a pause. 'Did you say *network*?'

Alice nodded to herself. 'Jennie really is sketchy on the details, isn't she? I'm an IT consultant by day and a vintage fashion retailer by night. Think of it as my alter ego—my secret identity.'

'Not so secret any more...now that you've told me.'

She grinned. He had a point there. Somehow she knew Cameron was grinning back on the other end of the line. For a few moments neither of them said anything, then Alice shook herself—literally—and decided to get back to business. Perhaps that would stop this slightly light-headed feeling that seemed to be sweeping over her.

'I need to get an idea of what your new offices are like—to make sure what we're planning matches the surroundings. The building is what we'll be there to celebrate, after all, isn't it?'

Just as she'd been able to 'hear' him smile, she now sensed him...what? Gloating?

'You should see it. It's something else—totally unique. An old nineteen-thirties factory on the

Isle of Dogs. Classic Art Deco style. All the plant and machinery is gone, but we've done as much as possible to preserve the original features.'

A picture formed in Alice's mind as he talked: geometrical shapes, cool white plaster, long horizontal windows. 'It sounds fascinating. And what about the space for the party? Is there enough room? How big is it? Over how many levels?'

His voice was full of dry humour when he answered. 'And you told me to slow down. One question at a time, Morton.'

But he didn't sound displeased in the slightest. In fact, he addressed her queries one by one in detail, and she could tell from the tone of his voice he was enjoying the chance to talk about his current pet project.

'I mean it. You need to see it, Alice. What are you doing tomorrow?'

Why don't you get to the point, Cameron? Stop beating around the bush.

She frowned. 'I was supposed to be sorting out a—'

'Cancel it.'

Alice spluttered. 'I can't do that! My clients are relying on me.'

'Give me the address and I'll send a team from my own IT department. I'll see to it you won't lose any business because of this.'

It was all very well for Cameron to wave his magic wand and make all her objections disappear, but she wasn't at all sure she wanted a bunch of strangers doing her work for her. But it was that or give up on the whole fashion show idea. And that meant delaying her launch into her new career, which she really wasn't prepared to contemplate now it was almost within her grasp.

And by the way, Mr Hunter…See that mountain over there? You couldn't just tell it to up and jump into the Thames, could you? It's spoiling my view.

She was starting to realise that the focussed, determined young man she'd met all those years ago had matured into a formidable force. And something was bothering her. Something on the fringes of her consciousness.

'Cameron?'

He stopped mid-flow, in the middle of giving her more potted history of his new building. 'Yes?'

'What did you say your company was called?' Now she thought about it, she didn't remember getting down to specifics—she'd been too busy pitching her idea.

'Orion.' He sounded puzzled. 'Didn't Jennie tell you that?'

Alice almost dropped her phone. 'Orion?' she whispered. 'As in *Orion Solutions*?'

'Yes. That's it.'

Very clever.

Hunter…Orion…It all fitted now.

She'd booted up the computer on the desk above her only a couple of minutes ago. Full of Orion software. Like almost every other computer on the planet. Suddenly the air in her office had grown a little sparse. She wanted to open a window and stick her face outside into the cold air, but she had a feeling they were welded shut.

Had she just agreed to organise a party for the head of Orion Solutions—one of the fastest growing software enterprises in the world? Boy, she was way out of her league. Way, *way* out of her league.

But this was *Cameron*. The young man she'd hidden out at a Christmas party with.

No, it wasn't working. She couldn't marry the two ideas together in her head, even though she knew deep down he must have changed since then. Just talking to him, she sensed subtle changes. Now it all made sense. He'd always been reserved and precise. But now when he talked there was an unmistakable undercurrent of confidence and inner strength she'd always sensed had been there which now had risen to the surface. Would he have changed on the outside too? Twelve years was a long time.

The mental image that thought conjured up was

appealing. She could see a tall, slim man—not gangly and awkward any more—with the same unruly dark hair that curled past his collar. His eyes would be the same warm brown, but there would be more lines round his mouth and at the corners of his eyes.

There was a meaningful cough from beyond the desk. Alice noticed a pair of pinstriped legs move a few steps closer. Mr Rogers. She'd forgotten all about him.

'I better go,' she mumbled. 'I'll see you tomorrow.'

'I'll meet you at noon.' He reeled off the address of his new headquarters.

As he spoke, she was vacantly staring at a web of cables off to her left. Something drew her attention—some instinct told her to take a closer look. And then she spotted it—the source of all of the solicitors' problems. It was going to be a nasty job to sort out but, hey, 'nasty' normally meant 'time-consuming', and that translated into more cash. Something she was only too glad of.

'Alice? Is that okay?' The deep, rich voice made her jump.

'No…yes…that sounds fine. I'll see you then.'

Cameron rang off with his normal brevity, and Alice crawled over to the knot of cables she'd been inspecting. There was a murmur and a shuffle and the pinstriped legs moved even closer.

'Anything I can do?' a thin voice enquired.

Mr Rogers wasn't being helpful—far from it; he had the air of someone trying to hurry someone else along. Fair enough, since he paid for her services by the hour.

'No, I'm fine,' she said, running her thumb and forefinger along a stretch of wire to check where it disappeared to. 'But I'd love a cup of tea—if you're making one, that is.'

There was a quiet huff, and the legs disappeared out of the office door.

Alice didn't feel guilty about that in the slightest. She'd get much more work done if someone wasn't hovering over her all the time. And she didn't feel guilty about stopping for five minutes to take Cameron's call. If she hadn't been sitting here under the desk, staring at the wires, it would have taken her hours longer to find the source of the problem. She backed out from under the desk, stood up and brushed herself down, pleased to be off her knees and standing tall.

Cameron arrived at the construction site early, keen to meet with the foreman and get an update before he showed Alice around. Although he was required to wear a hard hat, it was hardly necessary as all the major work had been done. Only the finishing touches were being seen to—doors were being hung, sockets were being fixed to the walls and flooring was being laid.

He checked his watch. She'd be here in an hour. He brightened unexpectedly at the thought. Alice had been a nice kid. A little unsure of herself, as teenage girls often were, but kind and intelligent. He was glad to know she'd lost none of that warmth in the intervening years. And she'd certainly seemed full of fire when he'd talked with her on the phone. It was nice to actually converse with someone for a change rather than just give orders.

What was she to him, then? A friend?

He didn't really have many friends. Hadn't really had time for them while he'd worked himself stupid getting where he was today. Most of the men he socialised with fell into one of two categories. They were either colleagues or competitors, and both were apt to put on a false front because they either wanted to impress the boss or they were hoping to get close to him and learn something to their advantage.

And women… Well, women *never* wanted to be just friends with him. They also fell into two camps: tigers and jellyfish. The tigers, like Jessica, were blatant about their attraction to him—and his money. And he obliged them by taking them out to the best spots in London, treating them like royalty... As long as they understood he wasn't looking for anything permanent, wasn't looking for someone to share his throne at present. They were all just *temporary* princesses.

The jellyfish—the second type of woman, like his current PA—trembled and stuttered in his presence. But he saw the glint of attraction in their eyes too—they were just too scared to act on it. Both responses were starting to get on his nerves.

He couldn't pigeonhole Alice into either of these groups, and that made her an unknown species. Intriguing.

She'd been pretty too, in her own way. Beautiful eyes—a fascinating hazel that were one moment green and the next nutty brown. She'd been like an ugly duckling, just on the cusp of becoming a swan. Sometimes, when she'd moved a certain way or changed her expression, he'd had the strangest sense that a glorious, transformed Alice was about to burst through the meek outer shell.

He shook his head.

This was his problem with women. He let his imagination run away with him and started thinking all sorts of ridiculous things. He became dazzled by the *idea* of the woman, and always ended up being disappointed when they didn't live up to the dream. But he'd dated enough gold-diggers now that he could spot them at thirty paces. It didn't stop him taking them out, though. In fact, it suited his whole 'temporary princess' idea. He didn't expect much from the Jessica-types, and therefore he was rarely disappointed. And there was no danger of them leaving a scar when the relationship ended.

When people got too close, they judged. They found all the bits of your psyche you didn't want to acknowledge and held them up in front of your face to see, along with a few more faults you didn't realise you'd had. No, he'd had enough of being judged.

But that really was a moot point these days. He was top dog. *He* did the judging. And if anyone was foolish enough to put him under the microscope they'd only come away with the verdict that he was the best and that he had the best of everything. And that was just what he'd been aiming for all these years.

A tall fence of chipboard panels painted roughly in forest green surrounded the new headquarters to Orion Solutions. The gate was covered with brightly coloured signs warning of all sorts of dire consequences to those who dared step inside. The boundary fence was at least twelve feet high, and this close to it, Alice could see nothing of the building beyond.

Being fairly local, she now realised she remembered the factory in its previous incarnation as a bakery. It had been left almost derelict for more than a decade, and the only details she could recall were broken panes in the wide horizontal windows and a dirty concrete façade.

Now she was actually here, ready to see the site and show her ideas to Cameron, her stomach was churning. Coreen really should have come. She was good at the talking and schmoozing. Alice was good at the practicalities—the behind-the-scenes stuff.

But you didn't need to *schmooze* Cameron on the phone, a little voice inside her head whispered. You talked, he listened. It'll be the same now.

But her stomach didn't seem to believe her head. It was still rolling around as if it was being battered by one of the old kneading machines that had lived in the old bakery.

And Coreen hadn't helped this morning. She'd insisted Alice go round, so she could make sure she was dressed 'fittingly' for a representative of Coreen's Closet. Coreen had taken a single look at Alice's one good trouser suit, tutted, and then dragged Alice into her bedroom. In no time she'd bullied Alice into stripping down to her underwear. Alice had stood there like a shop dummy, being prodded and poked and pinched, and when Coreen had pronounced her ready she'd taken one look in the mirror and flipped out.

She'd looked like Coreen's freaky twin sister, with her hair quiffed and pinned. The floral fifties dress was undoubtedly gorgeous, but Alice's chest didn't fill the darted bodice and the large circular skirt just swamped her. The icing on the cake had been the bright red lipstick.

She'd looked ridiculous. She wasn't that girl— that frilly, sexy, pouting girl. She was Alice. And Alice looked like a big fat fake in that get-up. This time Coreen hadn't been going to get her way. Alice had told her friend so in no uncertain terms, and then she'd reached for a tissue and wiped the lipstick off, leaving a wide red smudge on her cheek.

Once Coreen had got over the shock of being contradicted, she'd set to work again, agreeing that the full-on retro look maybe wasn't for Alice, but a touch of vintage might add a little pizzazz to an otherwise dull department store outfit.

So here Alice stood, the result of makeover number two. Coreen had let her keep the loose-legged chocolate trousers, as she'd said they flattered Alice's shape and made her look like Katherine Hepburn, but she'd replaced the suit jacket with a collarless forties one in deep crimson tweed. Even Alice liked the fake fabric bunch of grapes in autumn colours that adorned the breast. She's brushed out the ridiculous hairstyle and opted for a low, sleek ponytail, and had let Coreen add some lipstick in a berry shade that complemented both the jacket and her colouring.

It would have been madness to tell Coreen—it would only have made her even more incorrigible—but Alice *did feel* smart and stylish, in a way that was uniquely *her*. At least she did until she reached the tall chipboard gates that barred her entrance to Cameron's building. Now she was tempted to turn and run away on her chunky-heeled boots. She looked back down the road to where she'd parked her car.

'Alice Morton?'

She spun round to find a gruff-looking builder eyeing her up and down through a gap in the gate.

'Yes,' she said, finding her voice unusually croaky.

He nodded towards the construction site. 'This way,' he said, and cracked the gate wider so she could pass through it. 'The boss and some of the architects are inside. I've been told to take you to them. Oh—and you'll need this.'

He jammed a bright yellow helmet on her head. Alice was relieved for the second time this

morning that the quiff hadn't stayed. She'd have
been digging hair pins out of her scalp for weeks
if it had still been there.

She clutched the old school satchel that held her
drawings and ideas—Coreen had sworn it would
make a funky alternative to a boring old briefcase—and followed the man along a path towards
the new Orion building.

And then she looked up and her feet forgot to
walk.

Wow.

CHAPTER THREE

CAMERON had said he wanted a 'distinctive' opening celebration, and now she saw why. These types of buildings had been considered ugly and out of fashion until relatively recently—left to crumble or bulldozed and replaced with yet another chrome and glass structure.

The building was a low rectangle, with maybe only three or four storeys—it was difficult to tell where the divisions lay, because the whole width of the building was filled with tall windows with horizontal panes, punctuated by plain white pillars and, in the centre, a fabulously ornate doorway that made her think of Greta Gabo films and Egyptian tombs all at the same time.

Alice seemed to remember the door and its stone and glass surround having been painted a sickly green in days gone by, but now the giant sunburst design that reached to the flat roof was highlighted in glossy black and gold.

She started walking again, trying to take it all in.

The stock of Coreen's Closet had always seemed so glamorous and high-quality to Alice, but in the face of such opulence it suddenly seemed a little…second-hand. Could they *really* pull this off? How did you live up to a building like this?

However, as she got closer, she reminded herself that this building had once been old and tired, and it had only taken someone with a little vision to see past the grimy exterior to the potential underneath. It too was second-hand. And didn't it look fabulous? With this thought in mind, she steeled herself and followed the builder to the main doors.

At least she'd find a friendly face inside—someone she knew she'd be totally comfortable with.

Her guide left her, and she took a moment to smooth down her jacket before she pushed at the door with diagonal glass panels. The entrance hall was dirty and dusty, but clues to its splendour were there if one looked hard enough. The floor was white marble, and she could see a contrasting interwoven border in black at the edges of the space. And, underneath a dust cloth, the corner of what must be the original wooden reception desk was visible—all sleek lines and curves.

Two men in suits—the architects, probably—

were standing near a second set of double doors that were reached by three low steps spanning the width of the reception area. The men were deep in conversation, pointing things out to each other on a set of plans. Alice stood in the centre of the space, her feet together, her satchel clasped in both hands in front of her, and looked around to see if she could spot Cameron.

'Alice?'

Her pulse did an odd little leap at the unmistakable rumble of that voice. She twisted round, first to the right and then to the left, to see where it was coming from. The acoustics in this bare space must be a little weird—because it sounded as if he was close by, but he was nowhere to be seen.

She turned to face front again, and noticed one of the architects looking at her. Her pulse did another little syncopated skip, and this time it had nothing to do with nerves at seeing an old acquaintance again or putting her business on the line.

Time stopped and sped up all at the same time. A wave of awareness hit her so hard it was as if she'd run full pelt into a brick wall.

She hadn't paid much attention to the two men when she'd first entered, too intent on locating Cameron, but now the taller of the two had fixed her with a very intense gaze and she was feeling oddly breathless.

And then his mouth moved, and she heard her name on his lips, and everything slowed down even more and became all far away and echoey. She tried to decipher what her senses were telling her, but they were making no sense at all. The log fire and chocolate voice was coming from *that* mouth, from *those* lips…

She began to shake as he walked towards her. But not from fear; this was something totally new—a reflex she'd never known she'd possessed. She'd found men physically attractive before—of course she had—but never this…this…whatever it was.

She wanted to sit down. Or lean against something. Preferably him.

It couldn't be…could it?

As he moved towards her, his hand beginning to reach forward for hers, she studied him, and in the odd little bubble of time she found herself in there was plenty of opportunity to do so. He was still tall, but now he was broad—without being bulky. Gone was the slightly shaggy hair, replaced by a short, neat cut that did wonders for his cheekbones. Was it illegal for a man to have cheekbones that gorgeous? And even though his mouth was hard, and every line in his face an angle, she wanted to reach out and touch him—just to feel the skin, explore the planes and creases. And his eyes…tiger's eyes. Cameron's eyes.

This was Cameron.

Finally her tongue unknotted itself. 'H—Hi.'

She extended her hand to meet his and instantly regretted it. She could feel the trembling all the way up to her shoulders. He took her hand, but instead of shaking it, he merely clasped it and leaned forward—and down, of course—to place a feather-soft kiss on her right cheek.

Alice dropped her satchel.

The bag landed on his rather expensive Italian shoes and Cameron reached down and picked it up. He offered it to Alice. She fumbled with it and finally anchored it in her grasp. A horrible sense of disappointment settled in the pit of his stomach. He'd felt the quivering in her small hand and it meant only one thing. Jellyfish.

Still, he smiled as he gestured for her to follow him. No matter what he felt on the inside, he never let a glimmer of it reach the surface. He'd learned long ago that being that weak cost dearly.

She'd surprised him once again. But this time it hadn't been a nice surprise.

Where was the Alice he'd spoken to on the phone—the woman who was full of bright ideas, enthusiasm and humour?

He gave her the grand tour, showed her the sweeping white staircases with the original black cast iron railings, pointed out the boxy ceiling lamps in opaque glass, the door furniture, the floor-to-ceiling windows. Alice said nothing. Just trotted around after him, taking the odd snap with a slim digital camera. In the end he got sick of the sound of his own voice so he summoned Jeremy, the chief architect, to come and spout facts.

Alice blinked at Jeremy, with those large, changeable eyes of hers, and pulled a small black notebook out of her pocket, occasionally scribbling something in it.

The last stop on the tour was the atrium—the chosen venue for the launch party. In days gone by the factory had had a large courtyard in the centre of the building. Jeremy's firm had suggested changing nothing about the exterior walls, save a little cosmetic work, and had proposed enclosing the long rectangular area with a glass roof, carefully constructed not to ruin the line of the building.

But they didn't enter it at ground level. Cameron wanted her to have the best view, so he led the silent Alice and the chattering architect up to his suite of offices on the top floor. He'd chosen this section of the building as his domain. Soon, instead of looking out of his window and seeing the rest of the world that had yet to be conquered, he would walk out onto a balcony that ran the entire width of his office and see his kingdom:

people scurrying this way and that, talking, networking, making plans and creating ideas.

From up on the balcony, overlooking the entire atrium, she'd get a sense of the vastness of the space. If *that* didn't elicit a sentence from her, he didn't know what would.

They entered his office, almost complete now, and Jeremy, who was starting to seriously get on Cameron's nerves, wittered on about the original dark wood panelling and plans for the décor. Cameron silenced him with a look, and led Alice to the double doors in the wall of glass and steel windows and opened them wide.

She gave him a quizzical look, and he stood there on the threshold and watched her walk across the balcony, which was a good twenty feet deep, until she reached the polished brass rail that topped the parapet. For a few seconds she didn't do anything—not even breathe, it seemed to Cameron. Then her ribcage heaved and she turned to face him, her eyes sparkling. Slowly a smile blossomed, stretching her lips wider and wider until she was beaming at him.

Suddenly he realised she hadn't needed to say anything at all. Foolish of him to have required it of her.

He found himself walking to join her, an unplanned smile changing his own features. Silently, they both stared at the empty courtyard, a multi-layered geometric fountain its only feature. It was bone dry at present, but by the night of the ball, it would be bubbling joyously.

She turned to face him. 'This is it?' she asked, her face suddenly alive. 'Is this where the ball is going to be held?'

He nodded.

After a few seconds she returned to staring at the atrium. 'It's perfect,' she whispered, and then she fell silent again, her eyes roving over the long horizontal windows of the offices, the simple elegant lines of the building, the white plaster-work with contrasting black paintwork that somehow seemed anything but stark, with all the light and warmth radiating from the glass roof above, creating shadows and depth.

As Alice studied his building he studied her, discarding his first impressions and looking more carefully.

He could see her mind working, and she ran the fingers of her left hand over the top of her ear in an unconscious gesture, almost as if she was smoothing down her hair under the yellow plastic hat. But her hair was in a ponytail and didn't need tidying. He was glad to see she hadn't hidden her hair colour with dye. He'd never seen anyone with a shade of red hair to match it—not that he'd been aware he'd been making comparisons all these years. It was almost *impossibly* red. So bright he couldn't do anything but stare at it as she concentrated on the view.

Alice wasn't pretty—not in the traditional sense. She didn't have dimples and a cute little nose, big blue eyes or fluttery lashes. But there was an elegance about her, a fragility that was understatedly feminine. Every tiny movement, even the redundant motion of her fingers in her hair, was full of a quiet grace that even the dusting of pale freckles across her nose and cheeks could do nothing to dispel.

No, she wasn't pretty. But she might well be beautiful one day—if she ever chose to grow into it.

'Can we go down? Take a look around?'

There was no trace of timidity in her voice now. Her eyes were full of determination, and he could see the glint of ideas firing in their depths. He led her downstairs, saying nothing, letting her thoughts have room to grow and develop. He didn't like people who chattered uselessly. A fact that Jeremy, who was trailing after them, would do well to remember. As they reached the entrance hall, with its doors onto the courtyard, the architect opened his mouth—probably to say something about the construction of the glass roof—but Cameron waved him away. He wasn't needed any more.

Alice stepped into the atrium and was suddenly energized—almost as if she'd been hit by a bolt of lightning. She walked briskly this way and that, talking nineteen to the dozen, pulling sketches and notes out of her funny little bag, then stuffing them back in again before he'd had a chance to even glance at them.

Inwardly, he grinned. Yes, *this* was what he'd expected from her. This vision. This unbridled enthusiasm. This…passion. Working with Alice Morton wouldn't be a problem—far from it. In fact he had a hunch it might be a real pleasure.

And before he'd even realised quite how it had happened he'd joined her—talking and gesticulating and smiling.

Jeremy, the discarded architect, was standing in the entrance hall watching them—watching Cameron. His eyebrows were halfway up his forehead and he shook his head in total wonderment. If he hadn't seen the transformation in Mr Hunter himself, he'd have never believed it.

There was a large package waiting for Alice when she got home the next evening. She ripped open the plastic bag and discovered a folder stuffed with notes and sketches about the ball.

There was a note in black ink, written on heavy paper in a precise hand. With typical Cameronness, he hadn't bothered with pleasantries and got straight to the point:

Alice, here are all of Jennie's notes on the ball. I sent my PA over to Jennie's offices to pack the stuff up and she couldn't make head nor tail of it. Good luck.
Cameron.

He'd sent his PA? Alice was tempted to laugh. What would it be like to have people snap to attention when you walked into a room, rather than tread on your toes because they hadn't noticed you standing there? Believe it or not, the latter happened to her a lot more than most people realised.

Thankfully, Jennie had obviously been a lot more together on this project than Cameron had thought. There were lists of caterers, with different ones ticked or crossed off, a note of the band that had been booked, the addresses of a number of florists. All in all, it seemed she'd been planning a wonderfully glamorous event, but…

Something was missing. Something to tie everything together.

That was why she and Coreen had been struggling to come up with a collection of outfits that would work for the show. Over the weekend they'd inspected all their stock thoroughly, teaming up accessories with clothes, putting aside those they knew they wanted for the show. But the outfits they'd earmarked seemed to have no common thread. Seeing them individually would be great, but if they were to go down a catwalk together it would seem like a total mish-mash.

In short, they needed a theme.

There were pages of scribbles, where Jennie had obviously brainstormed ideas with herself, but she'd come up with nothing solid. In fact there seemed to be an awful lot of doodles of love hearts, wedding rings, and the details of a flight to Las Vegas. Not Alice's dream wedding venue— but each to their own… In recent days, it was obvious Jennie's mind had not been on the job.

Thinking of bright lights and big names, an idea popped into Alice's mind.

Old Hollywood glamour.

A mix of old and new, extravagance and elegance—just like Cameron's wonderful building. And it fitted Jennie's plans for a thirties feel for the evening—she'd already booked a big band and some swing dancers before disappearing over the Atlantic in a haze of true love. Oh, yes. This was *perfect*. She got on the phone to Coreen straight away, and they spent the whole evening in Coreen's lounge sorting through stock. Now they had an over-arching idea it would be easy to hunt for outfits and place them in collections. Each mini-collection would then make a smaller section of the fashion show. They hatched a plan to show each collection and then auction those pieces off before carrying on with the next one.

Once they started thinking evening wear, day wear, and different eras, Alice's love of old movies came in handy and she suggested film title themes for each part of the show. As she and Coreen drank wine and sorted through clothes, they settled on a shortlist of five: *Roman Holiday* would be all printed fifties cottons, full skirts and summer wear. *Some Like It Hot* would show off evening dresses, sequins, tight skirts and high heels. *Pillow Talk* would contain vintage lingerie—corsets, babydoll nightdresses and silk slips that these days many women bought to wear as cocktail dresses. *Casablanca* would be boxy jackets and high-waisted trousers, wool knits and kid gloves. And, last but not least, Coreen's favourite: *Rebel Without a Cause*. She was practically salivating at the thought of male models in soft blue jeans and leather jackets.

And it was precisely as they began discussing models that they realised they'd hit a bit of a brick wall. The market fashion shows were really a bit of fun to help sell the clothes, using people's relatives and a few of the more eager wannabes from one of the local performing arts schools. Now they'd seen Jennie's plans and Cameron's atrium, they knew they needed professionals.

Alice scurried home and checked out Jennie's files again. Booking models wasn't a problem; Jennie had made a shortlist of agencies. But as Alice picked up the phone to ring them on Wednesday morning, she froze mid-way through dialling the first number.

Just *where* was she going to hold a 'go-see' for these models? In the last two days her tiny rented bedroom had become a makeshift office, and was now mostly buried under bits of paper, hanging rails and boxes of clothes. Now when she fell into bed at night she had to scoop a whole load of mess off of her bed and dump it on her desk. The next morning she scooped it right up again and threw it back on the bed. She could hardly phone up the modelling agencies and ask them to send a steady stream of girls and boys to 27b Laburnham Terrace, so they could tramp up the narrow stairs and parade around in her boxroom. What sort of impression would *that* create?

She put her mobile on the only titchy free bit of space on her desk and stared at it. There was only one thing she could think of doing. Phoning Cameron. And she really, really didn't want to do that.

How could she face him again after the site meeting? Thank goodness she'd recovered a little when she'd seen the building and realised all the possibilities for the ball. She'd been able to block all the stupidity out for a while and talk sense. A shudder rippled through her as she remembered how she'd suddenly got all clumsy and wordless. She'd practically been drooling, for heaven's sake! No wonder she had no desire to repeat the humiliation.

Yes, okay, she knew they'd see each other again on the fourteenth—the night of the ball—but until then she'd hoped to keep things completely to e-mail. She'd already sent him a few lengthy updates, keeping him abreast of everything, pre-empting any more unexpected phone calls.

Why?

There was no point hiding from it. She'd got the hots for Cameron Hunter, and she'd got them bad. Which was a disastrous idea. She needed to be cool and professional to make a success of this project. Being so far out of her comfort zone, she was practically on a different planet.

She rested her elbows unevenly on top of some notebooks strewn across her desk and put her head in her hands. It was probably just some subconscious reaction to being recently dumped. Something to do with feeling on the shelf and un-attractive. Just a subconscious thing.

And a physical thing. Definitely a physical thing.

Which was why she was aiming to keep being in the same room as him to a minimum. Perhaps then she'd have time to gather herself together. By the time the fashion show and the ball came around she'd be over it, and far too busy organising things on the night to even speak to him. And he'd be too busy mixing with the great and good on the guest list to want to talk to her. No, if she kept her distance, it would all work out fine.

But then there was the voice…

Log fires were so yesterday. Today's trend was *furnaces*. Every time he'd opened his mouth on their tour of the building she'd felt a fire lick the soles of her feet, and it had travelled up and up and up until her ears had burned and she'd been sure he'd notice the heightened colour in her cheeks.

Hence the e-mails. E-mails were good. E-mails didn't require her to stop listening to the actual words and just drift away on the warm, earthy sound of his voice…

Alice's eyes had slid shut and she snapped them open. *Stop it!* She picked up a bright yellow folder from her desk and fanned herself down with it. Was twenty-eight too young to be having hot flushes?

Now she thought about it there *was* a problem with the e-mails—the replies. When they arrived, and she read Cameron's sharp, concise verdict on her notes, she couldn't help picturing him standing on that balcony, standing so close to her that she'd been able to smell his clean, unfussy aftershave, close enough to see those warm flecks in his dark eyes. And that led to thinking about his rare, show-stopping smiles, and then her pulse would start to get all silly.

So, whichever way she looked at it, she was in big trouble. In which case she might as well just stop sitting here daydreaming, pick up the phone and get it over and done with.

In a minute, anyway. She'd just look at her notes first.

She booted up her laptop. Her fingers were hovering over the keyboard when her phone rang. Her heart did a sickening lurch, as if it had tripped over its toes and gone tumbling down the stairs. She stared at it.

It was a number she didn't recognise.

Answer it, you fool!

What? Oh, right.

'Hello?'

'Hello, Alice.'

Whoomp. The furnace rushed into life.

'Hi, Cameron! I got the stuff you sent over.' Great. She'd been aiming to sound like a calm, professional woman and instead she'd got closer to Minnie Mouse.

'Were those files any help?' he asked, a slight tinge of desperation in his voice.

She spread the sheets out on her desk and frowned. 'I've only been able to leaf through so far, but Jennie seems to have a lot of the details covered. I suspect she may have booked musicians and caterers already, but I'll have to ring and check.'

Cameron made a noise that sounded suspiciously like a relieved sigh. 'Good. I'm glad it's not a complete disaster. Is there anything I can do to help?' he asked, and she took a deep breath and told herself to behave.

She explained about the models—the casting session, the lack of a suitable venue.

'We'll do it here,' he said, before she'd finished her last sentence. 'In fact I should have thought of the fact that you'd need space, an office…'

'But I've got—'

'You can have space here. There's a spare office in my suite, and you can use the meeting room for casting the models.'

Alice's face crumpled into a look of utter despair. 'Really, there's no need for an office. Just the meeting room would be fine. I can do the rest from—'

'It makes sense for you to be on hand. That way I can answer any queries immediately, approve things quickly, and you can stop flooding my inbox with charts and pages of notes.' It was only the faint edge of humour in that last comment that stopped her flinging the phone down on him.

What was it about this man that made it impossible to say no to him? It was like having an argument with a steamroller. One minute you were standing your ground, pleading your case, and the next you were flat on the floor, agreeing to everything he said and wondering what had hit you. If she was going to manage to work with him on this party—this *extravaganza*, as she was now beginning to think of it—she was going to have to start giving as good as she got, even if no one else seemed to do it.

She'd seen the way everyone at the building site had behaved around him. It was, *Yes, Mr Hunter... No, Mr Hunter*. Well, maybe not *no*. She hadn't actually heard anyone be brave enough to utter that word in his presence.

But she had an advantage his employees didn't have.

None of his staff had seen him playing ridiculous party games. That Christmas, after they'd escaped from the party, they'd eventually been discovered and told off for not joining in. His staff hadn't seen him trying to pass an orange to Aunty Barb with the thick foundation. It had been cringeworthy and hilarious all at the same time. Cameron had screwed up his face and desperately tried not to get smudged with make-up that was almost as bright as the fruit under his chin. He had failed miserably.

She'd just have to keep that image in mind every time he decided to get all high and mighty on her. Yep. That ought to do the trick.

Alice moved into a little office at Orion Solutions the following morning. It was a small space near the lifts, and nowhere as huge as some of the other rooms nearby, but that suited Alice just fine. She didn't want big and expansive. She wanted a little hole she could hide in until all this was over and done. Even though Cameron's office was on the same floor, her new office was as far away from his as it was possible to be without falling off the edge of the building. Hopefully that kind of geography would help her concentration.

Cameron had been as good as his word. He'd arranged for all of Alice's IT bookings for the next three weeks to be covered by a team of experts from Orion Solutions, and now she had a chance to live her dream and get a taste of what it was like to live and breathe vintage fashion without all that pesky computer stuff getting in her way.

At least, she'd be able to live and breathe

vintage fashion once she got a few other annoying things off her mind. Yesterday evening she'd got an e-mail from Cameron's PA, letting her know he had arranged for them to have lunch together the following day to discuss preparations for the ball. There had only been his voicemail to talk to by the time she'd found the message. This morning she'd tried to ring him again, to cancel, but had been told he was out and would be meeting her at the restaurant. She should just make her way to the lobby at twelve-thirty, where somebody would meet her and let her know where to go.

She didn't even get a chance to explain that she'd rather *not* have lunch with the boss. The fact that someone might deviate from his instructions was obviously an unknown concept around here. So, while she should have been getting down to business—making calls, crossing things off her ever-expanding list—she spent most of her time worrying about seeing Cameron in the flesh again, and whether her wardrobe today was going to be up to anywhere he was going to take her.

The chocolate trousers had had to make a reappearance. Alice discovered a burning need to go shopping for new work clothes. Her usual jeans and boots, more suited to crawling around on the floor looking at cables, just weren't going to cut it here at the rather upmarket Orion Solutions. All the men wore really nice suits, and the women looked sharp and smart, as if their feet didn't protest at all when they marched round the office all day in heels.

Alice's feet had protested at just being prised out of her comfy trainers and forced into a pair of low-heeled pumps.

Still, however scarily smart the Orion bunch seemed to be, they were all very friendly, and there seemed to be a lot of good-natured banter going on. Cameron's PA got her a coffee and chatted away so incessantly about him that Alice's eyes started to glaze over. It seemed she felt she'd found a kindred spirit.

At twelve-twenty-five Alice stepped into the lift and felt her stomach float and churn in a disturbing way as the doors closed and she started the downward journey. It seemed to go on for ever, and she was heartily relieved when they reached the lobby.

As soon as she stepped from the lift, a serious dark-suited young man who introduced himself as just 'Henderson' approached her, and indicated she should follow him. Alice trotted after him, wondering which sandwich bar they were headed for. But instead of leading her to a little café, with pictures of coffee cups on the windows, Henderson stopped in front of a long black limo and opened the door.

Alice just stared at him.

'We're eating in there?' she said, confusion written all over her face.

Henderson, bless him, didn't even crack a smile.

'No, madam. Mr Hunter would like you to join him up in town, and has asked me to drive you to the restaurant.'

Oh.

Work lunches to self-employed Alice meant a Thermos of soup or a ham salad bap and a packet of crisps. They obviously meant something totally different to Cameron Hunter.

Not wanting to seem even more gauche than she already had, she slid into the back seat of the limo, and didn't dare squeak another word until they arrived at their destination.

The drive out of Docklands into the West End seemed to fly past. Perhaps it was Alice's imagination, but the traffic seemed to melt away, deferring to the powerful, sleek black car. The other drivers probably imagined somebody famous or important was inside. That made her smile. It was like having a secret joke, seeing all the other traffic let them pass and knowing it was only ordinary old her on the other side of the tinted glass.

Henderson finally drew up outside an imposing hotel on the edge of Hyde Park, and before Alice could even thank him she was being ushered out

of the car and into the foyer by a liveried doorman.
From there she was escorted towards the restaurant, which was hidden behind a screen of glass
shelves stacked with hundreds of bottles of wine.
Even before she saw the restaurant she knew it
was going to be somewhere scarily minimalist
and trendy, and that she probably wouldn't recognise half the ingredients on the menu.

She smoothed down the hem of her soft heather-
coloured polo neck as she followed the waiter to
a table near the windows overlooking the park.
There was no sign of Cameron, and she had no
idea what time the table had been booked for, so
she sat as still as she could and tried not to look
too out of place.

A different waiter appeared and asked her if
she'd like some wine. She desperately wanted to
say yes, but decided she needed a clear head and
asked for water instead.

Where, oh, where was Cameron? Far from
wanting to avoid meeting him, she was now desperate to see something—someone—who wasn't
totally alien to her.

Two women in extremely expensive coats
walked past her table.

'Did you see who was in the lobby?' the one in
the camel coat asked the other one.

'No,' the other woman, who had bumped Alice

with her massive shoulder bag as she passed, replied. 'Anyone we know?'

'Cameron Hunter,' Camel Coat muttered under her breath as she sat down at a table only a few feet away. 'I don't actually know him personally, but he used to go out with my sister.'

'Really? I think my cousin dated him once too.'

Alice's ears tingled. She didn't want to listen to this conversation, but she didn't have much choice. Apart from sticking her fingers in her ears and going *la-la-la*, there wasn't much she could do.

'Silly girl,' Large Shoulder Bag said with a sigh. 'I don't think there's a heart in London he hasn't broken. But she thought she was going to be the one to succeed where all the others had failed. Of course he ended it.'

Alice's urge to ram her index fingers in her ears was almost irresistible.

'Of course,' Camel Coat said sagely. 'He always does.'

'She should have known the score from the start—silly girl.'

CHAPTER FOUR

ALICE had her fingers ready, and was just about to lift them from under the tablecloth when she saw Cameron striding across the room. Something odd happened. An invisible ripple emanated from him, and everyone it touched straightened their spines, looked his way, then hurried on about their business. Even the two women in the coats stopped gossiping, thank goodness.

'Sorry I'm a little late,' he said, as he leaned over to kiss her cheek.

Alice burbled something noncommittal in reply. Stringing words into sentences was suddenly beyond her.

Immediately two—not one, but two—waiters snapped to attention at their table. Cameron ordered off-menu, and Alice let him pick for her too. She wasn't even sure she knew what 'ballotine of rabbit' or 'celeriac remoulade' were, anyway. And that was only from the list of starters!

But Cameron seemed completely at home with the waiters bobbing up and down, almost sprinting off to get him anything he desired, and Alice realised with astonishment that he was just as comfortable here as *she* would have been in that little café with the coffee cups on the window. This was *his* world. Somehow she hadn't really believed all the millionaire software entrepreneur stuff up until now. Being slapped in the face with it was somewhat of a shock.

Thankfully, after they'd demolished their starters, they got on with discussing the ball, and she filled him in on the details of what Jennie had already booked and how the plans were progressing. Cameron seemed happy with everything she said, but somehow, Alice just couldn't seem to relax with him as she had the other day. It was as if she was seeing him with a completely fresh pair of eyes.

Was there even a hint of the sensitive, serious young man she'd known all those years ago? If there was, she was struggling hard to see it in him today. He was all quiet charm and confidence, understated power. There was something compelling and magnetic about him, and he drew every female eye in the busy restaurant, but Alice couldn't help feeling that she was sitting opposite a stranger.

Well, perhaps that was for the best. The past

was the past, and she needed concentrate on the future—the next few weeks in particular. For that time period he would effectively be her boss. She was just another one of his paid minions.

He was all business during lunch, treating her as such. And that started to rankle with Alice. Even the divine food couldn't take her mind off her irritation. *She* was doing *him* a favour, actually, not the other way around. A smile now and then wouldn't go amiss. But he was so totally focussed on the project in hand it seemed he'd forgotten how to be…well, human.

Things didn't improve much when they headed back to the office. Alice returned to her own little room, and there she stayed, glued to the phone, frantically taking notes and generally filling the space with an ever-expanding mess that she wasn't quite sure Cameron would approve of.

Every time she thought of him, even when she remembered lunch with the cold, emotionless business tycoon, her whole body buzzed and she flushed hot and cold—just as she had that day at the building site. Time and distance didn't seem to dilute the effect he had on her, unfortunately. And neither did being in a slight strop with him.

She was starting to understand Jennie's multitude of doodles, because she'd caught herself in the act too. Nothing incriminating, like initials or love hearts, but it was the fact she was doodling at all that bothered her. She was supposed to be concentrating.

At the end of the day, when she'd made her last phone call and her to-do list had started to go all blurry, she headed for the lift. Just as the doors were about to close, a large hand sliced between them and pulled them open again. Alice didn't need to see the rest of the body to know who it was. All at once the blood in her veins started to hum.

Stop it! she told herself. *Stop it at once!*

Cameron merely nodded at her and stood silently beside her. And as they rode down in the lift together, preparing to go their separate ways to their separate homes, Alice held her breath and tried to anchor her stomach yet again.

Cameron turned to her.

'Thank you, Alice, for all you're doing.'

Alice struggled hard not to let her surprise at his words show on her face.

'I really enjoyed our lunch,' he added.

Had he? Had she been the only one feeling as if she was teetering on a tightrope the whole time, then?

And then he did something even more unexpected. He smiled at her. 'It reminded me of that Christmas party. Do you remember?'

He shuddered. And she knew as surely as she

knew her own name that he was remembering Aunty Barb's orange foundation. The very same thought that had popped into her own mind.

The grin widened, suddenly taking years off him, changing his face from granite into something softer, warmer, and infinitely more alive, more appealing. Breathing suddenly became something less than automatic.

Oh, yes. She remembered.

With his unheralded smile Cameron had brought all those warm feelings rushing back. Alice couldn't help but smile back. Something clicked into place, and once again they were partners in crime.

Cameron knocked on the office door, but didn't wait for an answer before he pushed it open. Alice was on the phone. She glanced up at him, but almost too quickly her eyes flitted back to the large spiral-bound pad in front of her. As he stepped closer he saw that she wasn't taking notes, but filling in the detail of an elaborate doodle.

By the sounds of it she was talking to someone who hired out staging, and she was busy telling them, in her soft, understated voice, that what they were proposing to build for the fashion show catwalk just wasn't good enough, and could they please pass her on to someone who knew what they were talking about or she'd take her business elsewhere.

Alice might seem meek in person, but in the week she'd been based in the spare office on his floor he'd realised that underneath she was a woman who had very clear ideas about what she wanted and how she wanted it done. Once she'd set her mind on something, she wasn't easily shaken.

When she put the phone down she was almost smiling, and he surmised that she had indeed once again got her own way. Not by shouting or manipulating, but through quiet determination.

'You wanted to see me?'

She flushed an attractive shade of pale pink. A shade that matched the simple embroidered blouse she was wearing. While other women in the office either power-dressed or wore bland outfits he hardly even noticed, Alice always wore something that caught his attention. Not that what she wore wasn't suitable for the office—just that somehow he stopped and looked. Perhaps it was the vintage fashion angle. If so, that boded well for the ball and the fashion show. It certainly would be memorable if every outfit had this effect on every guest.

Alice looked apologetic. 'Oh… no. I mean—I didn't mean you had to drop what you were doing. It could have waited.'

Yes, it could have. He had calls to make, reports

to read, marketing meetings to attend. But somehow wandering into Alice's temporary office had seemed much more appealing.

The room had been bare less than a week ago, only a desk and a dead pot plant occupying the space. Now there were clothing rails, sketches stuck haphazardly to the walls, and two dilapidated mannequins staring at him, rather as if they were keeping guard. The one on the right only had one good eye, and the effect of her bright green stare was rather unnerving. He moved his gaze away from the bald-headed figure to look back at Alice.

'Here I am,' he said. 'Ready to do your bidding.'

She seemed to find that funny, because her eyes shone and she pressed her lips together, squashing a smile away. He couldn't help smiling back. Not his nice-to-do-business-with-you smile, but a real one—a lazy one that gently lifted the corners of his mouth. That seemed to have an odd effect on Alice, because she stopped being all cheeky and started tidying things on her desk, squaring her notepad, dropping paperclips in a pot.

He couldn't make this woman out.

Sometimes she reminded him of the quiet, shy girl he'd known years ago. Sometimes she was a confident, strong-minded professional. But then she'd get all absent-minded and start knocking things over, spoiling the polished picture. It didn't matter, though, that he couldn't solve the riddle that was Alice. He just enjoyed watching her slip from one persona to another, wondering what she would do next.

And in that respect their relationship seemed to be a two-way street. It was refreshing to be in the company of someone who didn't label him as just one thing—a software tycoon, a hard-nosed businessman. Or a meal ticket.

She stood up and walked round to the front of the desk, leaned back against it. 'We need to find you something to wear for the party,' she said, looking him up and down.

Now, hang on a minute. There was no *way* he was wearing second-hand clothes to the biggest event of his career. Not when he'd invited specific people just so he could rub their noses in his success. He'd been there, done that, worn the T-shirt—literally—and he'd promised himself he'd never do it again.

He gave her a steely look and shook his head. Alice didn't bat an eyelid. Most of his employees would have bowed and backed out of the room if they'd been on the receiving end of that look.

'Everyone else on your senior management team has agreed to wear something vintage—even if it's only a waistcoat or a hat.'

'I am *not* wearing a hat.'

The little smile was back. 'All right. Don't get your knickers in a twist.' She rolled her eyes and walked over to the clothing rails, where she started moving things around. Beneath the sound of scraping hangers he could have sworn he'd heard her mutter something along the lines of, 'Obviously it's a crown or nothing, then.'

A few moments later she held up an ensemble. 'Everyone else has agreed to be a little adventurous. How about this?'

Jeans and a leather jacket? She had to be joking.

'Try it on,' she said. 'We put a screen in the corner so the models could get changed for the casting session the other day.'

She thrust the hanger at his chest and let go, and he didn't have much choice but to grab onto it to stop it all landing in a heap at his feet. See? Quiet determination. Alice liked having her own way just as much as he did.

Leather jackets were so not him. He'd never been a rebel—had always had a clear vision of where he wanted to go in life. Messing around hadn't ever been on the timetable. But the faded denim was soft between his fingers, and the smell of the leather made him think of motorbikes and open roads.

'Okay,' he mumbled. 'I'll try it on. But I'm

telling you this: I'm *not* wearing it to the party.' His staff would all fall about laughing.

He marched behind the screen and started to undress, wondering as he did so just how he'd ended up stripping down to his boxers in the middle of a Thursday afternoon. He was taller than the screen, and as he pulled on the clothes Alice had given him he kept catching glimpses of her as she shuffled papers on her desk and generally ignored him. He couldn't remember the last time a woman had been so clearly unaffected by the thought of him being semi-naked in the same room as her. It was probably good for his ego. It didn't mean he liked it, though.

Finally he was done. The jeans were a perfect fit—felt as if he'd owned them for years, had *lived* in them. The white T-shirt was brand-new, thankfully. It was crisp and clean and still had the sales tag attached. As he rounded the screen he shoved his arms into the leather jacket and pulled it over his shoulders.

Alice seemed to be doing that silent, unimpressed-but-rooted-to-the-spot thing she did, but her eyes were round and she was staring at him.

'Happy?' he said, in a voice that was a tad gruffer than he'd intended it to be.

Alice just nodded.

'Very,' she whispered, when she finally got her voice. 'You've got it... Um...it's caught...'

She walked over to him, not looking him in the eye, and sorted out the lapel of the jacket, which had somehow got tucked under itself, smoothing it into place. He stared at her small, long-fingered hand as it came to rest on his chest, on the white T-shirt.

'You're right,' she said, and then gave a little cough to clear her throat. 'It looks…g-good…but it's not right for the party.'

'Uh-huh,' he heard himself say. He'd been staring at her cheekbones and had got distracted by the translucent quality of her skin. Like most redheads she was pale—almost white—but she seemed to glow. How did she do that? He ran his tongue across his dry bottom lip, all at once overtaken by the urge to find out what a *glow* like that might taste like.

'No,' she said.

No to what? To glowing? To *tasting*…?

'I'll find you something else.'

And before he'd had a chance to say James Dean she'd darted away and hidden herself between the racks of clothes.

Nothing else worked. Cameron tried not to think about who might have been the last person to wear each of the five suits he tried on, tried not to think about mothballs and funerals and caskets. Just as well that none of them fitted. Either the trouser legs flapped above his ankles or the shoulders were way too tight.

'I happen to have some really nice suits of my own,' he yelled over the top of the screen as he finally clambered back into his own clothes. 'The one I was intending to wear—to *my* party, remember?—is being made for me by a man on Savile Row.'

She looked impressed when he mentioned the name, clearly knowing that the man in question never needed to advertise and that being admitted into the inner sanctum of his fitting rooms was rather like gaining entry to an exclusive gentlemen's club.

'Sizing with vintage clothes is often a problem for someone as tall and… Well, with all those… with all that—with your physique,' she finished in a hurry. 'We could search for months and not find anything suitable. A few *distinctive* vintage accessories may be the way to go. I'll see what I can find.'

He shrugged his suit jacket back on and straightened his tie. 'In other words, the last forty-five minutes were a complete waste of time?'

She pulled an apologetic face.

'My time is valuable,' he said, trying not to smile. 'I should charge you.'

Suddenly she looked extremely serious and thoughtful. 'It'd be worth every penny,' she said, glancing at the leather jacket and jeans hanging innocently on the other side of the room, a decidedly naughty twinkle in her eye.

Wait a minute. Was Alice…*flirting* with him? In a totally *Alice* way, of course. She'd just hinted at it with that look, done something almost undetectable with her voice. It was all so subtle he started to doubt it had been there in the first place.

When he looked again she was hanging the last of the suits up, all brisk efficiency, and he decided he must have imagined it after all.

His forehead crinkled into a slight frown.

The thought he might have imagined it disappointed him, and the realisation he was disappointed surprised him. Did he *want* Alice to flirt with him? She was just a kid he'd once been kind to at a Christmas party a very, very long time ago. As she walked back to her desk she did the hair-behind-the-ear gesture. The gentle, unselfconsciously feminine movement made his stomach knot, even though she wasn't paying him the slightest bit of attention. All at once surprise gave way to irritation. Another thing he didn't like. This feeling of being at a disadvantage, of not being the one to hold all the cards.

'Am I dismissed, then?' he asked, as she tucked herself behind the desk and got back to work.

She looked up at him, bit her lip and released it slowly, emphasising its fullness. Somehow that just made him crosser.

'Yes.' The cool, restrained tone was back, but there was something—an undercurrent—that made him eye her suspiciously. 'I've finished dressing you up. You can go now.'

Well, he didn't know how to respond to that. Nobody ever dismissed him. He didn't like that much, either.

'Fine. I will, then.'

And he crashed out of the door and down the hallway without looking back.

Alice stared after him. Was she going crazy? She certainly seemed to be behaving strangely today. She swung round on her chair and looked out of the window. First of all she'd made Cameron get dressed up in an outfit she'd known he would never consent to wear to the party— just on a whim.

She sighed. It had been *so* worth it.

And just now, only a few seconds ago, had she actually been *flirting*?

Well, it hadn't done her much good, had it? He'd gone all prickly and she'd just got worse, goading a reaction out of him. Well done, Alice. You just sent Cameron Hunter packing when he's the key to your whole future. Very professional. But it was just… Well, when Cameron pushed, she had the stupidest urge to push back twice as hard.

What was wrong with her? She was doormat girl—voted by everyone she knew as most likely to just lie down and take rubbish from the men in her life—and she'd decided to lock horns with Cameron Hunter? Great time to grow a backbone, Alice.

Aw, shut up. You've always had a spine and you know it. You just chose to put it out to pasture because it suited your plan of being the perfect low-stress girlfriend no man could resist.

And look how well *that* had turned out. Yet another well-thought-out plan.

She let out a deep breath and rubbed her eyes. It must be the long hours, being flung into the deep end of her new career—and Jennie's—without really knowing what she was doing.

A sudden blush crept up her cheeks.

Keeping her tongue under control hadn't been the only problem, had it? Her hands seemed to have developed a will of their own too. But that white T-shirt had smelled of warm, clean man and had looked all soft and fresh and…touchable. She'd been feeling the heat of his chest beneath her palm before she'd even registered a decision to put it there.

This was bad. The party and the fashion show were in another nine days, and then she'd be back in the real world—not stuck up here in this impossibly high tower where the altitude must be getting to her brain cells. She couldn't let this ill-timed crush grow any further.

I mean, get real, Alice. It's all just a fairy tale, a daydream. He dates the likes of social-ites and supermodels. If you can't hold on to the likes of geeky Paul, how in hell have you got a chance of keeping a man like Cameron Hunter interested?

Two hours later, Alice was knocking on Coreen's door. Coreen answered, resplendent in an embroidered black silk kimono and a bright green face pack. Alice pushed past her, marched into the kitchen, grabbed two wine glasses out of the cupboard and started pouring cheap Cabernet from the screwtop bottle she'd brought with her.

Coreen skidded into the kitchen behind her. 'Whoa!' she said, her eyes widening as Alice filled the oversized glasses nearly to the brim. Her voice sounded funny, escaping through clenched teeth as she tried not to crack her face mask. 'What happened?'

Alice picked the glasses up and handed one to Coreen. Her hand was shaking and she sloshed wine all over her fingers. Shaking her head, she slammed the glass down, spilling more.

'Me. *I* happened. I've had an epiphany! I'm the anti-girlfriend.'

Coreen's face mask crumbled, and large chunks rained down on her kimono. She shook her head. 'This is all about Paul, isn't it?' she said. 'You're going through the five stages of grief…I thought you were in denial; now you've obviously moved on to anger.' She stared at Alice. 'What happened to bargaining? You should be bargaining now.'

Alice took another swig of wine and held it in her mouth for a second before swallowing it. She nodded at the bottle and headed out of the kitchen. 'How's this for bargaining? You keep the red stuff coming and I'll tell you all about it!'

Coreen had no choice but to follow her into the sitting room, where Alice not so much sat down as crumpled onto the couch.

'Now, what's all this about you being an anti-girlfriend? Is it like being an anti-hero? I'm not sure I quite get it.'

'More like being an antidote,' Alice said gloomily. 'And not in a good way.' She sank back into the sofa and stared into space. 'I know what Paul meant when he said I was "a relief" now. Men *love* those girly girls.' She narrowed her eyes and looked at Coreen. 'Girls like you. Pretty girls, who run them a merry dance and keep them on their toes. Girls who torture them and treat 'em mean to keep 'em keen. But after a while either she gets tired of him not being up to scratch, or he gets tired of all the game-playing and one of them ends it. And that's when the guys come looking for me—the perfect antidote to a demanding diva.'

'That's good news, surely?' Coreen said. She thought a while, then pouted. 'Not for girls like me, of course. But for girls like you it is.' She grinned, destroying the rest of the face pack completely, and held her hand up for a high five.

'What do all my exes have in common?' Alice asked in a wistful voice.

'Erm…bad hair?'

Alice shook her head, and kept on staring at the paisley curtains.

'Anoraks?' Coreen ventured, and got a scowl for her efforts.

'I figured it out on the way over here.'

'Figured *what* out?'

'All of them said how lovely I was—how *easy* I was to be around. Easy to dump when something better turned up, more like it.' Alice turned to look at her. 'I am—and will only ever be—a *transition* girlfriend.'

'I thought you said you were an antidote…'

'They all say they are fed up with the high-maintenance women in their lives, but they all eventually find a new siren to trot around after—or, in Paul's case, trot back to.' Her face fell. 'I'm just a…a…*stopgap* until that happens!'

Coreen flung her arms round Alice and squeezed. 'You are so much more than a stopgap!'

'Then why don't the guys I go out with get that?' she wailed. 'Why am I always the one they go out with just *before* they find the love of their lives? Why can't somebody think *I'm* the most wonderful thing to happen to them for a change?'

Coreen hugged her tighter. 'You want the truth?'

Alice nodded. If her friend had some advice on how she should keep men interested, she might as well hear it. She was tired of being discarded like an old shoe.

'I think that until *you* believe you're more than a stopgap, you're going to keep attracting men like Paul. He was too much of an idiot to see what he had.' Coreen swivelled to face her. 'Where's all this coming from anyway? I don't think this is all about Pathetic Paul after all.'

Alice avoided her gaze. 'Nonsense. Of course it is. I've been so busy recently, when have I had time to meet any other men?'

A naughty smile quirked Coreen's lips. 'There *is* one rather yummy specimen you've come into contact with on a daily basis recently.' She paused and looked a little sheepish. 'I Googled him, you know.'

'Who?' Alice said, fearing she already knew the answer.

'Mr Orion Solutions, of course.' Her eyes brightened. 'Did you know he went out with—?' She took one look at Alice's face and closed her mouth. 'Never mind…'

Alice sighed. 'Yes, I know he went out with Sierra Collins last year. Suddenly I keep seeing her face everywhere. On bus shelters, batting her eyelashes at me…in my bathtime magazine, showing off her perfect bikini body…I think I hate her.'

Coreen sighed too, and flumped back onto the sofa next to Alice. 'She's a supermodel. What's not to hate?'

They sat in silence for a few minutes.

'You like him, don't you?' Coreen finally said, so quietly it was almost a whisper.

'I do *not*!' Alice said with venom, and then buried her face in a cushion. Coreen tapped her on the shoulder, and Alice looked up. 'Oh, Corrie…I really do. I really do like him. A lot. It's like a bad joke, really.'

A soppy smile spread across Coreen's face. 'Aww, I can see it now—childhood sweethearts, and then he whisks you off your feet and takes you away from all this…'

Alice burst out laughing. 'I hardly think so! He was lovely back then, you know. Sensitive, thoughtful, kind…I'm sure he's still that way underneath, but he's changed, Corrie. He's used to the finest things in life, to having the best of everything. Somehow he's harder, pushier. It wouldn't be a good idea to get involved with him. It really wouldn't.'

'Not even a teensy bit?' Coreen replied, her incorrigible smile back on her face.

Alice laughed again, but this time it was more with gallows humour than hysteria. She walked over to Coreen's stack of fashion magazines and flicked through one, then another. Finally she found what she was looking for. She folded the magazine back on itself and held the picture up next to her face.

On one side the glossy picture of Sierra Collins—flawless skin, sparkling blue eyes, a cleavage…

On the other, plain old Alice Morton. So used to being 'one of the lads' she was almost androgynous, with her face flushed pink and a figure like an ironing board.

Coreen looked at both Alice and the magazine picture, her eyes sombre.

'I rest my case,' said Alice, and threw herself back down on the sofa.

Coreen silently handed her back her glass of wine, patting her on the hand.

'And you know why?' Alice went on. 'I learned my lessons from *Anne of Green Gables*.'

Coreen blinked. 'What on earth are you talking about?'

Alice hugged her wine glass to her chest and let it warm her fingers as she gazed off into the distance. 'Anne went searching everywhere to find her Mr Right—looking for dashing strangers, full of adventure—and where did she find him?'

Coreen opened her mouth, but Alice didn't give her the chance to provide her with a smart answer.

'She found him right underneath her nose! Gilbert!'

A blank look crossed Coreen's face.

'The boy next door that she'd always been in love with but never realised until it was almost too late. Well, I'm not going to be that stupid. There are plenty of ordinary, lovely guys right under our noses—I just have to find which one's mine.'

Coreen snorted. 'Well, you go on looking under rocks, or whatever, but you can count me out.' Then she went very still. 'Anne of Green Gables? Wasn't she the one who said she'd die if she didn't get a pair of puff sleeves?'

Alice bit her lip and nodded.

Coreen took a large slurp of wine. 'Now, *there's* a sentiment I can agree with,' she said, as she waved her glass at Alice.

CHAPTER FIVE

A WEEK later Alice was starting to think that nothing else existed but the inside of Cameron's spare office and this blasted *extravaganza* she was planning. There had never been anything else. There never would be anything else. Eternity would be full of to-do lists, phone calls and an inbox that clogged up faster than she could unclog it. She ought to keep a plunger under her desk for the very purpose.

The ball to celebrate the opening of Cameron's new building was in two days, and she was fantasising about slipping into a coma when it was all over and done with.

Thankfully, Jennie was obviously marvellous at her job, and it hadn't been as hard as she'd expected to pick up the reins; it had just made life very, very busy. All of Jennie's suppliers and contacts had been wonderful when she'd phoned them and explained that Jennie was on her honeymoon and she was the new girl filling in. But with a job this size it was inevitable that there would be a multitude of last-minute hitches. It was eating up all her time.

And somehow, at some point in the next forty-eight hours, she had to find herself a dress to wear.

She pushed her swivel chair away from the desk and let it slide backwards. Her shoulders were all bunched up, and she rolled them a couple of times in an attempt to release them. They complained loudly. There was a headrest on her chair, and she let her head fall against it…

'No napping on the job, Morton!'

Alice easily resisted the urge to jump to attention, and lifted one eyelid. 'Hi, Coreen. What are you doing here? Shouldn't you be at the market?'

Coreen shook her head. 'Dawn looked after the stall for me today—and besides, the market closed an hour and a half ago.'

Already? Now the evenings were drawing in, and it was dark by five, it was easy to lose track of time. She raised her arms above her head and stretched.

Coreen started bouncing on her rather spectacular platforms. 'Anyway, I have something utterly *fabulous* to show you!'

Alice eyed the garment carrier Coreen was clutching with interest.

'I've found *your* dress.'

'*My* dress?'

Coreen's grin was a little scary as she unzipped the bag and pulled out the most amazing—

Alice was dumbstruck. In a flash, she was out of her chair and across the room.

'That can't be mine,' she said, her hands over her mouth. 'It's too… It's too…'

'Nonsense. It's nothing of the sort. It's fabulous.'

Of course it was fabulous. It was a gorgeous deep emerald satin—a floor-length bias-cut evening gown. The most beautiful thing she'd ever seen.

But it would look stupid on her. What about her hair? She opened her mouth to say so.

'Na-huh!' Coreen held up a finger and wagged it at her. 'Don't you *dare* say it. This is a genuine Elsa Schiaparelli and it's going to look stunning on you—I have a gut instinct about these things and you know it.'

Alice had to reach out and touch the fabric, feel its glossy weight, run the thick satin between her fingertips.

'Where did you get this?' she whispered.

Coreen's smile buckled a little. 'At an auction.'

'An auction!' They *never* bought clothes at specialist auctions. The clothes there were normally designer labels, exceptional quality, and way out of their price range. They'd never make back what they spent on clothes like that on a poky little market stall. 'How much did it cost?'

'I paid a quarter of what it's worth,' Coreen said. 'If you're worried about the money, you don't have to keep it. We can auction it off at the party. Along with all the rest…'

Alice's eyelid began to twitch, and she looked at Coreen.

'What exactly do you mean by "the rest"?'

Something was different. Cameron had just been heading for the lifts, at the end of a long day, but halfway down the corridor he stopped. He didn't know what it was, but something was definitely…not *wrong*, but different. He just had to work out what it was.

There was an extra light on somewhere. And then he noticed a fuzzy yellow slash on the carpet at the far end of the hall, emanating from the office he'd given Alice.

He stood in the semi-dark, looking at it.

He'd tried not to go into that office too much in the last week, but somehow he kept finding himself in there, even though he had plenty of reasons to be busy—plenty of reasons to keep him tied up for hours. With his normal workload, plus all the extra stuff involved with moving premises in the next few weeks, he'd been up at the crack of dawn and sliding into bed in the small hours of the morning. Perhaps it was tiredness, then. Maybe that explained the strange tug he felt towards that particular room.

And it didn't just stop at the doorway. Once he was inside, other strange things happened.

He'd spent years crafting a persona to fit his ambitions, and even more years shaping himself to make it all real, but when he was in Alice's office he found he forgot to be himself. He did uncharacteristic things—laughing, teasing, even talking about things that weren't business related. And the atmosphere in there heightened his senses. He noticed little things he was sure he normally missed: the delicate curve of an ear, a faint scent of floral perfume, the way her fingers curled around her pencil. Yes, something odd was definitely going on in that room. He made a mental note to get the air-conditioning checked out.

While he was standing in the half-light of the corridor, a noise came from the direction of Alice's office. It was a shout of frustration, immediately followed by the sound of rustling paper, as if a folder had been hurled across the room. Suddenly he was running, and when he rounded the office door loose leaf pages were still fluttering towards the floor.

Alice was sitting at the desk, her head in her hands, muttering to herself.

'Alice? Is everything okay?'

She started, and a further pile of papers ended up on the floor as she jumped up and jogged them with her elbow. 'Sorry…I'm having a bit of a tantrum.'

He shook his head. Alice didn't do tantrums. She did calm and collected—just like him.

'Do you need me to fetch someone?'

She looked thoughtful for a moment, then leaned forward over the desk. 'Know any hit men?' She seemed to droop. 'The only way to cope at times like this is to descend into humour. Very dark humour, it seems.'

'Problems?'

She nodded. 'Coreen got a little carried away today. You remember Coreen, don't you?'

How could he forget? When she visited Alice at the office here she looked him up and down as if he were a prime piece of beef. He had half an idea she'd once been on the verge of chasing him down the corridor and pinning him to his desk. Yes, he remembered Coreen. She was definitely a young lady with the capability to get more than a little carried away.

He walked over to the desk and perched on the edge. Alice looked up at him. She was wearing a soft cream cardigan with woolly embroidery and little pearls dotted all over it. Was it cashmere? Must be. That would explain his urge to reach out and touch it—touch her. His fingers tingled with the need to do just that.

'Coreen went to a vintage clothing auction today, because she wanted to pick up a couple of dresses for the finale of the fashion show. She lucked out. A rather famous heiress had recently died, after reaching the grand old age of ninety-two, and all her wardrobe was up for sale.'

'Surely that's a good thing?'

Alice twirled a pencil on the desk, and Cameron's eyes followed the motion of her fingers.

'It would have been if she'd stuck at one or two of the smaller pieces. But she went a little loco and bought the lot.' She looked up at him and placed a reassuring hand on his arm—before whipping it away again. 'Don't worry. It won't affect the party or the fashion show.'

He looked at her hand, now back on the edge of the desk. 'It sounds like there's more to it than that.' He made a point of peering at the collection of papers littered all over the office floor.

She sighed. 'We'd been saving. For our own shop. Coreen's dipped into our start-up fund and almost wiped it out. If we don't get back what we paid for them… Well, let's just say we're taking a bit of a risk.'

She met his gaze, and he felt an odd little surge of something deep inside. They weren't the most stunning eyes he'd ever seen—not if you only counted shape and structure—but they were possibly the most unusual. They had...depth.

Tonight they'd lost some of their sparkle. Tonight they looked weary.

She must be exhausted.

Exhausted working for *him*, bailing him out of the hole Jennie had left for him. And he hadn't heard a murmur of complaint until her outburst this evening—and even that wasn't directed at him. He should have realised, done more... But he'd been too busy enjoying her company to think about making her go home earlier or insisting she take a day off. *You're selfish, Cameron.*

He stood in front of her and held out a hand. 'Come on.'

She raised her eyebrows and looked at him suspiciously. 'I was kidding about the hit man thing. You know that, don't you?'

There it was. The room was working its magic. He realised he was smiling.

'I know,' he said softly.

She blinked and looked away. But her pale fingers met his and she slid her hand into his waiting palm.

Alice felt like a firework inside—a firework whose fuse had been lit and which was jittering, waiting, until it fizzed and then shot into the sky. Cameron had led her back to his office and motioned for her to sit on the ridiculously long leather sofa while he headed for the phone. But she didn't seem to be feeling very obedient this evening, and she ignored the deep cushions in favour of the vast window that spanned the entire width of Cameron's office.

Her little office had a fantastic view too, but it was just round the corner of the building, and partially blocked by another skyscraper. Cameron's view was unobstructed and faced towards the heart of the city. They were so high up, and the window so clean, it was kind of like being suspended in mid-air, far away from the blinking lights, the red steaks of tail lights, the flashing aircraft. It was a beautiful view—the best—but she couldn't help feeling it was a little lonely up here too.

He was behind her. Suddenly she just knew it. The soft hair behind her ears lifted.

'It's beautiful,' she said. The silence needed to be broken, and stating the obvious was as good a way as any.

'Yes.' His voice was low and slightly husky.

She closed her eyes and placed a palm on the glass. *Think of Aunty Barb and oranges...*

Control yourself, Alice. It's just a little crush.

It'll pass. And you know why? Just open your eyes, look at where you are, and you'll remember that you're from different worlds. You're a mere mortal, while he's...he's... Cameron Hunter.

She made herself do just that. But instead of seeing the lights, the dark indigo clouds edged with silver, all she could see was Cameron's reflection—and he was watching her.

Time skipped. She caught her breath and held it.

No, she must be mistaken. He wouldn't— *couldn't*—be looking at her that way. It must be a trick of the light as it bounced off this tinted glass.

Maybe it had been only wishful thinking, because when she turned around to look at him he was the same old Cameron, his eyes unreadable, almost blank.

'You must be hungry,' he said, and everything she'd been feeling crashed back down to earth. Practicalities. Reality. Yes, let's talk about those things for a while. Perhaps they'd get these daft notions out of her head.

'I've ordered a takeaway,' he added, still staring at her. 'I don't think either of us is in the mood for polite chit-chat in a restaurant.'

She began to protest, but he held up a hand.

'It's the least I can do to say thank you. You've worked your socks off to get me out of a nasty jam.'

Alice should have known that Cameron's definition of a takeaway would be vastly different from her own. No greasy paper-wrapped parcels for Mr Cameron Hunter—oh, no. Their meal was delivered from one of the local 'happening' restaurants. When the bags had been handed over and the delivery driver tipped—very generously, by the looks of it—Cameron walked to his desk and began moving stuff aside.

'What are you doing?' she asked.

Cameron paused, looking puzzled. 'Clearing a space. I always eat at my desk. You can have my chair, and I can pull up—'

Alice shook her head, effectively cutting him off. 'You can't eat takeaway sitting at your desk—like you're pretending you're at a fancy restaurant.'

'But this *is* restaurant food.'

Alice walked to a space in the centre of the vast royal-blue carpet, dropped onto her bottom and crossed her legs. 'To really appreciate the flavours and textures of a takeaway you have to picnic. Honestly, it makes the food taste better.'

Cameron looked as if he was going to choke. 'You want me to eat my dinner off the *floor*?'

'No.' She made a quick gesture with her hand, indicating that he should just stop making a fuss and pass the food over. She was starving, for goodness' sake! 'I'm saying we should *sit* on the floor and eat off the plates they've provided.'

For the first time since she'd known him she witnessed Cameron in a state of bemusement. It was quite funny, actually. He obediently picked up the bags of food, crossed the room, and awkwardly lowered himself down so he was sitting beside her. His trouser legs had ridden up and she could see his socks. Somehow that made him seem more human, less dangerous.

So from now on, Alice, if you get thoughts above your station, you can think about Aunty Barb, bruised oranges and *socks*. Okay?

The food was gorgeous, and Alice discovered she wasn't just starving, she was ravenous. As they made a dent in the multitude of cartons Cameron had ordered, he began to lose some of the hard angles from his posture, began to relax, and they chatted about work and the plans for the ball before changing the subject to books they'd read but hated. And from there they moved onto family news. Alice realised she knew a lot about Jennie, but knew hardly anything about Cameron. Since he seemed as laid back as she'd ever seen him, she decided to satisfy her curiosity.

'So, how old were you when your mum married Jennie's dad?'

There was a slight pause before he answered,

as if she'd caught him off guard and he was re-grouping.

'Seventeen.'

Cameron spent an inordinate amount of time staring at his food.

Twin urges, equal in force, took hold of her. Half of her wanted to heed the 'keep out' warnings he was radiating—his stiff posture, the failure to meet her eyes. He wanted her to leave this subject well alone, which was odd, because his and Jennie's blended family seemed so happy. The other half of her wanted to say *What the hell* to the warning signs and poke around a bit.

Tonight was a night for strange alliances—her and Cameron, five-star food and a carpet picnic—and Alice embraced the part of herself she'd usually tell to shut up.

'And before that? You never mention your own father.'

The atmosphere around them thickened. Cameron looked at her. 'Okay, technically the man had a minor part to play in my existence—' he looked vaguely disgusted at the thought '—but to earn the title of "father" one needs to care about one's offspring. To me, that man is nothing but an unfortunate biological connection.'

She wanted to reach for his hand, but sensed he'd shrug it off, was feeling too raw to let anyone touch him. She'd hit a nerve. A big one. Her instincts had been right. Despite his reluctance, Cameron needed to talk about this. It was burning a hole deep inside of him.

She kept her next question simple. 'When did he leave?'

He stared blankly at the wall. 'Fifteen days before my twelfth birthday.'

Tiny pieces of expressions he was trying desperately to hide flitted across his face. She guessed he was watching the memories play out in his mind. Maybe if she gave him space, just sat back and waited, he'd open up and—

'He was tired of us.'

Cameron blinked. Almost as if he was surprised at his own outburst. She held her breath, waiting to see if the rest would come.

He started off quietly, slowly, and then the words began to flow. 'He didn't like the domestic routine, our ordinary lives. Thought he was too good for it—that he deserved better.' He tore his gaze from the blank patch of wall and looked her in the eye. 'My mother and I weren't enough for him, so he jacked it all in to move to the Costa Brava with a barmaid from the local pub. Haven't seen him since.'

Alice inhaled. That was possibly the longest speech about personal matters she'd ever heard Cameron make.

'I'm so sorry,' she said, feeling completely inadequate to do or say anything to make it all better.

He shrugged. The mask was back.

'I don't care about knowing him. I haven't lost anything with his departure. What made me cross was the mess he left my mother in. My father had been a head teacher, on a very good salary, and suddenly all that was gone. Struggling along as a one-parent family was hard for her. We had to sell the house… She went from being a housewife to working two jobs just to keep food on the table and a roof over our heads.'

Alice pushed a container of spiced rice in his direction, trying to keep things as light and normal as possible, afraid she would spook him if she showed any emotion whatsoever.

'I didn't know that,' she said. 'I knew you went to St Michael's College, so I just…assumed.'

The exclusive boys' school just outside Greenwich had a stellar reputation and even higher fees. She'd never have guessed Cameron and his mother had had it so hard before she'd remarried.

He dug his fork into his rice and left it there. 'Scholarship. I was in my second term when Dad left and the money dried up, but I took the test and they let me stay on.'

'You must have been really grateful for that.'

Cameron let out a dry laugh. 'When I think of

my school days, *grateful* is not the word that comes to mind—believe me.'

He stood up and walked to the window, leaving his half-eaten meal behind. Alice got the impression that he'd reached his limit, and she decided to turn the conversation in another direction and hopefully cheer him up in the meantime. She uncurled herself and got up.

'I'll just be a second,' she said, and raced down the hallway to her little office. When she returned, Cameron was still staring out of the window, but she doubted he was actually noticing anything.

Here goes.

'You know you said you'd wear something vintage to the party?'

He looked at her over his shoulder. 'Nice try, but I don't think I actually agreed to anything.'

Technically, he was right. But she wasn't going to let that stop her. 'But you didn't disagree—so by default you agreed.'

A sudden laugh burst from him, surprising both of them.

'You're a very persistent woman, Alice.'

She gave him a sheepish smile. 'Sorry.'

'Don't be,' he said as he walked towards her. 'I like it.'

In an effort to hide the horrible giddiness that had just overcome her, she pulled out the first of the items in the bag she'd had stashed under her desk for a few days, opened the little box, and held it out for him to see.

'Cufflinks?'

His eyebrows rose but he didn't lose his smile, which had to be a good sign. Alice reminded herself to breathe out.

'They're very…unusual,' he said.

The cufflinks were a simple Art Deco octagon—she had passed over many more intricate designs, knowing Cameron would prefer something simple, understated and elegant.

He picked one of the cufflinks out of its cushion with a thumb and forefinger. 'What's the stone in the centre?'

She swallowed. 'Tiger's eye.'

They reminded me of you. But I can't tell you that.

Another gift was in the bag, and she made a show of rummaging for it to hide the blush that was about to give her away. When she looked up again, he was removing the cufflinks from his midnight-blue shirt cuffs and placing them on the edge of the desk, where they rolled to and fro slightly. Platinum, no doubt. With diamonds.

See, Alice? *There's* your proof of why you can say nothing, why you should rob this silly crush of oxygen until it suffocates. You give him old silver and semi-precious stones when he has the ability to buy the most exquisite jewellery from the world's top designers. Why would he want anything you have to give him?

She almost pushed her second gift back into the bag, suddenly horribly afraid it would miss the mark, like a prank gone wrong, but Cameron was busy admiring his new cufflinks. He stopped to look at her. 'I like them. They're diff…' He paused, and then a small smile curved his lips. 'They're *distinctive.*'

She couldn't help but smile softly back at him.

'If you think *they're* different, wait till you see what I've got in here.' And she shoved the bag towards him and took a swift step back once it was in his grasp.

Cameron took a moment to study the small black gift bag with gold ribbons for handles. *Coreen's Closet* was stamped over the front, in blocky letters that reminded him of old movie posters. He gathered up his courage and peeked into the bag.

'It's a tie,' he said, feeling relief wash through him. And for something old, once discarded, it was a rather nice tie—deep green silk, so dark it was very nearly black. The perfect match for the charcoal suit he'd be wearing. He looked up at Alice without bothering to hide his surprise.

'Thank you,' he said. 'I'll make sure I return these in good condition after the party.'

Alice flushed a deep pink—at least that was the way it seemed in the subdued light from his desk lamp. She shook her head. 'They're a gift.'

Cameron didn't know what to say—he didn't do *gushing*. He'd had many gifts from women in the last few years, much more expensive than this, but he knew that he could probably search the world over and never find duplicates of these things. And no one had ever given him something that summed him up in a way he couldn't even verbalise. Alice *knew* him. That should have worried him, had him running for the fire escape, but it didn't. Instead he just felt something akin to relief—as if he could breathe out for once.

'So you'll wear them for the party?'

Her question caught him by surprise. Did she honestly think he'd be that rude? He'd have worn them even if he'd hated them, but as it was he was warming up to the idea of joining in with the theme of the evening, rather than standing alone, marked out as different.

'Of course I will.'

'It's just that…' She made a glum little face. 'I got the feeling that you weren't very keen on the idea.'

The fact he'd almost hurt her feelings bothered him. She'd gone to so much trouble that he felt he owed her something. The sofa was only feet away, and he sat down on it, requesting she join him with merely a look. She frowned slightly, but sat down next to him, twisting a little to face him by tucking her right leg under herself.

'I can talk to you, Alice. You're so easy to be with.'

She didn't say anything to that—just gave him an odd look. He took a moment to look back at her and then let his gaze wander. He'd never be able to tell her this if he saw sympathy in her eyes. In fact her eyes in general seemed to be bothering him this evening. Over and over in the back of his mind he kept imagining her lids sliding closed, a small sigh escaping from her mouth. Although he'd asked her to sit next to him, he had the feeling now that it had been a bad idea. She was too close, too distracting.

His desk lamp was an obvious object to focus on—the sole source of light apart from the backdrop of the city—and he made himself focus on it as he prepared to talk.

For what seemed like hours he didn't say anything at all. Then, 'People think that going to a school like St Michael's is a blessing, a privilege. But that's only the case if you fit in.'

'And you didn't?' The soft concern in her voice almost made him falter.

He let out a little huff of a laugh. 'No. I didn't.'

He'd only just been tolerated in his first couple

of terms. The fact that he was the class swot had earned him a few dirty looks. But he hadn't been about to dumb down for anyone—no matter what Daniel Fitzroy and his chums whispered about in their exclusive little huddle.

'Word that I was a charity case on a scholarship soon got around. There was a group of boys—a pack, really. You know how boys are.'

Out of the corner of his eye he saw her nod gently.

'Once they knew I had free school dinners too, they made my life a misery.'

He wasn't about to tell her how. But boys in smart public schools tended to go further than just words, and Fitzroy had been unusually creative in his approach.

'It all came to a head one day when one of the gang realised I was wearing one of his cast-off school blazers. My mum had been so chuffed to find it in a local charity shop because it was in such good condition.'

A wave of cold nausea swept over him and he clamped his mouth shut. He could still hear the taunts…

Charity case. Loser. Nobody.

So that time, instead of shrugging it off and ignoring their childish name-calling, instead of just picking himself up and refusing to lower himself to their level, he'd fought back.

It had been worth the weeks in detention and the lecture he'd endured from the headmaster—which, funnily enough, hadn't bothered him at all. Because the man had reminded him of his father. In a perverse kind of way he'd enjoyed it—as if it had been a rude gesture to dear old Dad by proxy.

Although Fitzroy and his buddies hadn't touched him again after that, the name-calling had continued. But after that day he hadn't cared. As for the blazer, he'd refused to put it on again—no matter how many further detentions he'd chalked up for not having the correct school uniform. He'd gone out and got himself a paper round, saved up and bought his own damn blazer. And he'd worn it with pride. Not that it had mattered to the bullies. They'd already labelled him. They'd already passed their verdict. He knew they would never change their minds about him, no matter what he did.

He didn't tell Alice any of this, but when he finally turned to look at her he knew that she knew. Not the details. But she knew about his sheer bloody humiliation. It made him unexpectedly angry to think the reason she understood was because she might have been through anything even vaguely similar herself. He just knew she understood it all—about not being able to live up to other people's expectations…everything.

When he spoke again, he aimed for levity. 'So—no—my memories of wearing other people's clothes are not good.'

She reached out and touched his hand. Such a simple gesture—nothing, really—but he felt his throat clog.

'Quality endures,' she said, looking deep into his eyes. 'It outlasts everything—fashion, prejudice, wrong opinions. In the end it proves itself, even if no one could see it for what it was at the time.'

He got the oddest feeling when she looked at him like that, her eyes all big and round, welling with moisture. He lifted a hand and wiped the underside of each eye with his thumb.

No, she mustn't cry for him.

Even though he was touched beyond belief by her honest reaction, he couldn't let her tears fall. He was scared of what he might do, what he might feel, if they did. So, instead of concentrating on her glittering eyes, he diverted his gaze to her mouth. The lips weren't overripe, but they were beautifully sculpted. Suddenly, he had the urge to *taste* again. And this time he didn't bother to ignore it.

CHAPTER SIX

ALICE felt a shiver run through her. Cameron was looking at her with his tiger's eyes and the warm glints seemed to glow brighter. Her heart began to pump faster than was strictly necessary.

Think oranges…

She started well. Aunty Barb was there in her mind, scrunching up her face and huffing with the effort of keeping the orange in place, but that image morphed into one of Cameron, his eyes dark and intense, concentrating on not dropping the darn fruit. And then he wasn't passing it to Aunty Barb any more, but passing it to her, coming towards her, his face getting close, lifting his jaw to meet hers so they could make the switch. And then the orange was gone, and it only took a minor adjustment in angles before lips were on lips and no one was trying to pass anything anywhere.

A tiny sigh escaped from her lips…

And then a jolt like a thousand volts shot through her.

It was real. Cameron's lips were on hers—kissing, teasing, coaxing. She was stunned at first, too overwhelmed to respond in any way, but then she couldn't help but kiss back, meet his lips and tongue with equal sweetness.

This was a kiss of fairy tales. Perfect in every way. It was warm and skilful and doing crazy, crazy things to her insides. Then suddenly it changed, deepened. Far off she heard something she could only think of as a growl, and a firm pair of hands closed around her torso and lifted her onto his lap.

And then—oh, wow—the hands didn't stop, but skimmed over the top of her cardigan, stroking, feeling. His lips moved away from her mouth, travelling along her jaw, down the side of her neck. She clung to him, ran her hands up his back and through his hair. What was he doing to her? What was *Cameron* doing to her?

Cameron.

The waves of tingles started to subside and cold reality crashed in, sweeping everything else away. This was Cameron Hunter. Software tycoon. The man who had to have not just everything but the *best* of everything. And while the kiss had been as near perfection as she could imagine it wasn't real—it was just a knee-jerk response at an emotional moment. She was Alice and he was Cameron. This was never going to be anything other than a moment of madness. A mistake.

Slowly she tried to extricate herself from his hold, but she was starting to discover he was pretty darn persistent himself. But it wasn't *her* he was kissing, not really. He'd just been feeling vulnerable…

'Cameron,' she managed to whisper between kisses, and pulled away enough to rest her forehead against his, her breath coming in short gasps.

She sensed rather than felt him smile, being too close to focus properly. 'Alice,' he breathed, and she just wanted to close her eyes and forget she had to stop this now—stop it before they did something monumentally stupid. He moved in to kiss her again but she managed to pull back enough to stop him reaching his target.

'Cameron… I have to…'

She didn't finish her sentence, too caught up in using his bewilderment to free herself and stand up. He looked totally dishevelled—and totally adorable, with a look of sheer confusion on his face. She'd bet not many people had seen *that* expression on Cameron Hunter.

She wobbled on her left foot, finding she'd put her weight on it awkwardly, but the momentum

was enough to get her going—to get her backing
away and heading for the door.

He jumped to his feet. 'Don't go.'

She bit her lip and shook her head, still
backing towards the exit. 'I have to… You know
that, don't you?'

And then she was running down the corridor to
the lifts, leaving her handbag, her coat—everything—in her office. The lift door glided open and
she bolted inside, pressed herself against the
brushed steel interior. It seemed an age before the
doors closed again, but no one came. No hand
suddenly appeared on the edge to stop its progress.

Easy to be with? Easy to let go, more like.

He hadn't followed her.

He'd understood, damn him.

The opening ball for the new Orion Solutions
headquarters was only hours away, and Cameron
was in a foul mood. His PA had disappeared some
time ago, squeaking something about an urgent
errand, and hadn't returned yet.

Alice was also nowhere to be seen.

Why had he kissed her?

Alice had been nowhere to be seen since
Thursday evening. And while his head told him
she was probably at the new building—oversee-
ing stage construction, briefing caterers—some

other, more stubborn part of himself was taking it personally.

Even Jessica and Sierra had known the score. Nothing serious, no strings. When it was over, it was over. Women didn't just kiss him and then run. Basically women stayed, until he was ready to dismiss them.

Hah! That sounded so…so…pompous! He told himself he was being monumentally unbearable. So full of himself he'd really like to have given himself a slap. Had he really got that bad? Why had nobody told him?

Alice told you. When she looked at you with shock and horror and ran away. She knew what she'd done—what you'd become.

And, stupidly, all he could think about was that kiss. When he kissed other women it was all about playing a part, playing games—a subtle shifting of power back and forth, testing each other, seeing who had the most control.

He hadn't thought about any of that when he'd kissed Alice; he'd just *been*. Caught in the moment, thinking of nothing but how soft and right she felt pressed up against him, feeling nothing but a sense of completeness.

There was such an honesty about Alice. She didn't pretend to be something she wasn't. She wore what she wanted to wear, said what she wanted to say. She hadn't constructed some larger-than-life persona that she now had to live up to. So why had he?

It was as if he'd been forging ahead in one direction, never looking back, consuming everything in his wake, and Alice had made him stop and take a look over his shoulder at where he'd come from, who he'd once been. It had been a shock to see how much he'd changed. And now he couldn't switch off that knowledge. His other, truer self was like a ghost at his shoulder, whispering things in his ear, making him second-guess everything he now had and everything he'd attained.

Even this blasted ball tonight.

It now seemed like a three-ring circus rather than a stupendously elegant affair. The only reason he hadn't pulled the plug on the whole thing was that he knew he'd see Alice again there. Exactly why he wanted to and what he was going to say he wasn't sure; he just knew he had to see her.

Fighting a rather over-enthusiastic Coreen about hair and make-up was something Alice just wasn't up to at the moment. For the last forty-eight hours she'd been able to block out the memories of Cameron's lips on hers, of her flight headlong into the night, by working herself to a standstill.

But now everything was done, and the only remaining job was to get herself ready for the ball. Ready to be a knowledgeable, outgoing representative of Coreen's Closet. Meanwhile, her head felt like fudge.

It didn't help matters that she was standing in the middle of Cameron's office—his *new* office— now gloriously furnished. It was his personal space, and although he hadn't actually inhabited it yet, the rich intense colours—the midnight-blue carpet, the dark glossy wood of the desk and paneling, even a brass desk lamp identical to the one he had in his other office—made it impossible for her to ignore that the space belonged to him. She was in *his* territory.

Since Coreen and Alice would be on site all day, dealing with last-minute preparations, it had been agreed some weeks ago that they could get ready for the ball here. Because, tucked away behind a door in the panelling, there was a spacious bathroom and even a small dressing room.

Thankfully, even though she was on his territory, there was no sight of Cameron.

Thankfully?

What a lie! Every cell in her body was aching to see him again. Her brain was doing its best to argue back, but she thought it might be outnumbered.

So she let Coreen powder and brush and pluck and tease. That only made things worse. With nothing to keep her distracted, the rational side of her was overpowered by the side of her she'd tried to ignore. In her mind she started to regurgitate the events of that night in Cameron's *other* office.

Why had Cameron kissed her? Really?

She had theories, but no solid facts. Sympathy? Because they'd connected on some level? Had she finally got her wish and merely been the nearest available pair of lips?

She sighed, and Coreen, who was busy applying foundation, ticked her off for moving.

There was no future between a man like Cameron—he was probably a multimillionaire, for goodness' sake—and an ordinary girl like her. She was a second-hand girlfriend. And she knew for a fact that Cameron didn't do second-hand.

'Will you stop with the incessant sighing, please?' Coreen snapped. 'I almost took your eye out with the mascara brush.'

Alice blinked and came back to the real world. 'Sorry.'

Coreen was standing in front of her in a little black dress that was fifties restraint and pure sin all at the same time. It had a medium-length full skirt, a tiny, tiny waist, and a halter-necked bodice covered with sequin-studded chiffon. The four-inch red stilettos that finished off the look would make grown men weep.

She made a last little flourish of the mascara wand and stepped back to survey her handiwork.

'Fabulous. Even if I do say so myself.'

The only difference Alice could see was that her eyelids seemed to be weighed down with more gunk than usual.

'Next—the dress!'

Coreen was like a runaway train tonight. She suddenly dashed into the dressing room and Alice heard a rustling sound, then Coreen reappeared, looking smug.

'I've put my coat over the full-length mirror. No peeking until both the dress *and* shoes are on. You'll want to get the full effect.'

Alice just nodded, and trotted obediently into the little room. Her dress was hanging up in there, and she took it out of its protective cover and slid it on over the insanely expensive underwear Coreen had practically *made* her buy. Not that she'd actually needed to be forced that hard. Not when most of her bras were a little less than pristine white and held together with safety pins. She'd needed something to do this dress justice.

The dress went on easily, zipping up at her side, and then she reached for her shoes. Her Lucite-heeled shoes. The emerald of her dress reflected in the clear heels as she held them, making them seemed enchanted. It was the first time she'd felt

worthy of wearing them—at least was wearing a
dress that was worthy of them. She slipped them
on and stood tall.

'You can come in now,' she said, staring at the
fluffy collar of Coreen's coat draped over the full
length mirror.

She turned slightly as Coreen entered, expecting to see a self-satisfied look on her friend's
face—Coreen liked to think she was queen of the
makeover—but found her looking slack-jawed.

'Wow. I mean…*wow*.'

Alice made a face. Coreen was such a drama
queen. It was just the fact that for once she was
wearing a dress and had a bit of…

Coreen whipped the coat off the mirror.

…make-up on.

Now it was Alice's turn to feel her jaw hit the
floor.

'Told you!' Coreen had obviously got over her
shock and was practically jigging from foot to
foot. 'Told you it was *your* dress!'

The dress had *felt* exquisite as she'd put it on,
but she'd been too busy stressing about the whole
Cameron thing to think about how it would *look*.
This was it. What Coreen had been talking
about—the sum being greater than its parts. This
was her dress.

The bias-cut satin floated over curves she

hadn't even realised she had—maybe because she spent all her time hiding them rather than accentuating them with scary underwear. The colour was… It made her skin look like porcelain. And her hair… It was still as bright and fiery as ever, but it was parted on one side, falling in soft waves over her face, her long fringe almost covering one eye. Coreen had been mumbling about Rita Hayworth and Veronica Lake when she'd been doing it, but Alice hadn't really been paying attention. In this dress her hair…*worked*! She loved it. All of it. The hair, the dress, the shoes—especially the shoes.

'Thank you,' she whispered to Coreen's reflection in the mirror, suddenly finding herself all emotional.

Coreen came up behind her and gave her a quick squeeze. 'Don't you dare!' she warned. 'The ball starts in twenty minutes and I don't have time to do our eyes again. Come on—it's time to go downstairs and discover what last-minute snags have cropped up.'

They left the dressing room, and Alice went over to an abstract-looking chair to retrieve her handbag.

'Leave it,' Coreen said. 'We'll need both hands once we get downstairs.'

Good idea. She hadn't been quite sure how she was going to manage a clutch bag without looking as if she was clutching *onto* it. And, compared to the dress, it looked a little—well, downmarket.

'Showtime!' Coreen grinned at her, her bright red lips making her look like a Varga girl.

Showtime. Cameron's show. And, after all the work she'd done, hers too.

There was the last-minute snag—right there. It was her show, and it was time to step up and become the leading lady rather than just the understudy.

The exterior of the new Orion Solutions building was floodlit—the stark white lights throwing the carved stonework into relief, making it seem as if the columns rose into the sky and just kept going. Low box hedges framed the clipped squares of grass where only recently mere rubble had been, and as they arrived the guests marvelled at the transformation the indomitable Cameron Hunter had wrought. It was truly magical, they said. How amazing that this wonderful building had been under their noses all this time and nobody had ever paid it the slightest bit of attention.

They milled inside, continuing to exclaim at every little thing: the wonderful black and white marble floors, those darling Art Deco glass lights on the ceiling, and oh, *look* at that original dark wood!

Old Hollywood glamour.

The theme had been whole-heartedly embraced by those lucky enough to get an invite. Fabrics shimmered and swished, jewels sparkled, and everyone had an air of quiet self-importance. Some of the men had top hats and canes like Fred Astaire. One man had even gone to the trouble of putting on spats—although the general consensus was that they made him look more like a mobster than anything else.

The chatter increased as the guests wandered through the entrance hall into the atrium, and there everyone took a breath, a moment, and fell silent for a few seconds. Then they all started talking again, this time louder and more emphatically.

The lighting was deliberately low, and tiny white spotlights glinted in the glass roof like stars that had swooped down to see what all the excitement was about. Creamy white flowers were everywhere. At one end of the long rectangular courtyard was a wide stage, with chairs arranged in rows in front of it, and at the other end a large space for dancing and a forty-piece jazz band complete with a singer in a long white dress and an orchid tucked behind one ear.

But no one was dancing yet. That would come later—after the fashion show. For now an army of waiters offered trays full of colourful cocktails, and the topic of discussion became whether it really *was* better to have a martini 'shaken' and what exactly was *in* a Sidecar.

In the centre of the atrium was the fountain, flowing with water that fizzed and bubbled like champagne. It was surrounded by a thick black border in the marble tiles, marking out a square, and at each corner of the square stood a towering potted tree, leaves delicately draping themselves downwards as if reaching for the spray of the fountain. And there, standing under one of those trees, was Cameron Hunter, as calm and poised as everyone expected him to be. The perfect host. He greeted his guests warmly, remembering all their names, making them all feel welcome as he ushered them in to his little corner of the universe.

Cameron, however, was feeling far from calm or poised, but he was—as always—doing an excessively good job of hiding the fact lest anyone suspect, lest anyone *judge*.

He turned, a smooth smile on his face, at the sound of his name. Only a microscopic twitch of an eyelid gave him away as he saw who had spoken.

'Daniel Fitzroy.' He omitted to say how pleased he was to see the man who'd made his schooldays a living nightmare, because it really wasn't true.

'Cameron.' The man grabbed his hand and shook it warmly. 'Thank you so much for inviting me—us.' He flicked a glance at the woman standing next to him, a small brunette with sharp eyes and an obvious bump under her stretchy black dress. 'We're really thrilled to be here.'

This was what he'd wanted—to see and hear Daniel Fitzroy bowing down before him, smiling like a weasel and pretending the past hadn't happened because he was so desperate to impress him. Cameron had always known that when this day finally came he'd have won. The memory of all those beatings would be erased and he'd be free.

And then, as if the universe had decided that granting his every desire tonight wasn't enough, and it was going to go ahead and grant his every thought as well, there she was.

Jessica.

Strolling towards him, resplendent in a long, deep pink dress with a bow that reminded him of a scene in a Marilyn Monroe movie—the one where she sang about diamonds. And Jessica hadn't scrimped on *those* either.

Why was she here? How had she got in? He definitely hadn't added her name to the guest list. But, then again, she was Jessica Fernly-Jones, and she never needed an invite to turn up to anything.

Despite the fact he hadn't seen her in weeks, and she'd not been happy when he'd left her standing in her swish apartment with a scowl on her face and an 'ordinary' white diamond in her hand, she seemed perfectly at ease. She sauntered up to him and placed a soft kiss on his cheek before turning to smile at Fitzroy and his wife.

Cameron made the introductions. Everyone smiled at each other.

But, to his credit, Fitzroy's tongue stayed in his mouth, and he gave his little wife an affectionate squeeze. Bizarrely, that pleased Cameron. The small, serious woman at his side didn't deserve to be made to feel second-class, whatever he thought of her husband.

'Actually,' Fitzroy said in a low voice, pulling him to one side, 'could I have a word with you?' And he drew Cameron a few feet away, behind the potted tree and out of view of the guests spilling in through the doors.

The fashion show was due to start in fifteen minutes, and backstage was bedlam. Models were running around in their underwear, clothing rails filled every available space, and the clouds of hairspray necessary for some of the elaborate retro styles were starting to make Alice cough.

Even with all their friends from the market to help dress everyone and take care of the clothes it was madness. Alice took a moment to rest against a table and wonder why—for the thousandth time—she'd ever got suckered into doing all of this. She hadn't even managed to get out from backstage to see how the rest of the party was going. She was having to rely on reports from Stephanie, Cameron's PA, who actually seemed to be thriving in all the high-stress excitement.

Suddenly a hand clapped on her shoulder, and she jerked to a standing position.

'We've got an emergency,' Coreen said, a deathly serious look on her face.

It had to be at least the fifth time she'd made such an announcement this evening.

Coreen must have read her thoughts, because she added, 'No—this time it's a real emergency! One of the models, Amber—you know, the one with the hair?'

As far as Alice was aware none of their models was bald, but she let it slide.

'Well, she's throwing up in the toilets. Blaming it on a rice salad she ate at lunchtime. Boy, she does *not* look good! There's no way she can do the runway.'

Alice frowned. 'Can we give her dresses to some of the other models—share them out?'

Coreen shook her head. 'The changes are too quick. We'll have gaps in the show if we wait for them, and that will look unprofessional.'

Alice frowned even harder and put her thinking cap on. Everything was silent for a few seconds.

Hang on a minute. Coreen *lived* for drama. Why wasn't she relishing the moment, wringing her hands and gnashing her teeth? She turned to Coreen, who was still standing patiently next to her.

'You've got a plan, haven't you?'

A bright smile lit Coreen's face. 'I *have* got a plan!'

'And the plan is…?'

A manicured finger poked her in the chest. 'You. My plan is *you.*'

Cameron had followed Fitzroy behind the potted tree, too taken aback by the thought of Fitzroy wanting something from him to say anything. Now they were effectively in private Fitzroy shuffled a little, and couldn't meet Cameron's eyes.

'Actually, I wanted to apologise to you.' He glanced up, then returned to looking at the floor. 'I should have done it sooner, but…well, I just didn't. Perhaps I'm a coward.'

Yep. Pretty much what Cameron had always thought.

But Fitzroy suddenly squared his shoulders and looked Cameron in the eye—something Cameron didn't think he'd ever done before, not even when he'd been punching seven bells out of him.

'I want to apologise for the way I treated you at school. Back then…let's just say I had issues at home, and I dealt with it by taking it out on people like you—easy targets.' A genuine look of remorse clouded his features. 'Not that you were ever the soft touch I'd taken you for. You just refused to cower, no matter how hard I tried. In the end it just made me all the more determined to try. Not the right way to handle it, I know. But I'm afraid I just wasn't brought up to know any better. It was the only example I had.'

Cameron had come across Mr Fitzroy Senior over the last couple of years. He was a big cheese in banking, and Cameron wouldn't have liked even to work for the old goat, let alone be related to him. He bullied everyone he came into contact with. Being his son had to be a nightmare. From what he'd witnessed, nothing was ever good enough for that man.

He was suddenly reminded of his laser eye surgery—how everything had gradually come into focus, how he'd felt he was seeing every-thing in a new light afterwards. He looked at Daniel Fitzroy now and no longer saw an arrogant enemy too powerful to prevail against. Now he just saw the remnants of a boy who hadn't had the inner strength to cope with a vindictive father. How had he never seen how weak, how deserv-ing of pity Daniel Fitzroy had always been?

And how had he never realised how similar he

and the other man had been on the inside? How they'd both been damaged by their fathers' low opinions of them, even if they'd worn that pain very differently on the outside.

'I'm not that person any more, Cameron. I've changed.' He stole a look at his wife, who was deep in conversation with Jessica. 'And I want you to know that I am truly sorry.'

Cameron stood there, blinking at the man, the hot coals of the anger he'd been stoking for almost twenty years now smoking and hissing. He couldn't pretend he hadn't heard what the man had said, although part of him wished he could. Then he'd be able to go on hating, letting the furnace drive him forward. But Daniel Fitzroy had just made a genuine apology, and Cameron was not a man to ignore courage and integrity—even when it appeared in the most unlikely of places.

He reached out and shook Daniel's hand.

The other man breathed out a long sigh of relief and signalled with a quick glance at his wife that the deed was done. Silent communication. Unfortunately it gave Jessica an excuse to walk over with the woman, and she looped her arm in his and leaned into him, her large blue eyes wide and blinking—a little trick he knew she thought men found appealing, and once upon a time he had.

He honestly didn't object to talking to Daniel

and his wife for the next ten minutes or so. The only drawback was that Jessica seemed to be attached to his arm as if she had octopus suckers, and he couldn't shake her loose without creating a scene.

Daniel's wife was obviously very much in love with him. She looked adoringly at him as he spoke, her arm in his, her free hand rubbing the top of her bump almost constantly.

Cameron got the oddest feeling. He looked at the man Daniel had become and, while he wasn't sure they would ever be friends, he acknowledged how much he'd grown. He might not be the power-player his father was, but in Cameron's eyes it took guts to humble yourself before your greatest enemy.

In comparison, Cameron felt a little two-dimensional.

Where was his *own* adoring wife? His *own* promise of new life for the future? Nowhere. Because he'd dedicated his life to proving to the Daniel Fitzroys of this world that he was every bit their equal. And, for some totally unfathomable reason, he'd decided the best way to go about it was to amass as much money as he could and gallivant about town with useless creatures like the one currently affixed to his left arm.

Fitzroy hadn't let the past define him as Cameron had done. All these years he'd been

fighting ghosts, fighting the shadows of bullies
who had moved on with their lives, become men
with lives and families. And now the anger was
gone he realised there was a huge gaping hole in
his life. The abscess had been drained, removing
the fiery pain, and now there was nothing left but
an ugly-looking hole. What was more, he had no
idea how he was going to fill it.

Alice brushed Coreen's sharp little fingernail
away. 'What do you mean *me*…? Oh, no! No
way! Absolutely *no way*!'

Now the dramatics kicked in. Coreen threw her
hands in the air and her voice boomed. 'Look
around! Although we've booked models of different shapes and sizes, lots of these girls have
exactly the same build as you. Poor old sick-as-
a-dog Amber is virtually your body double.'

That might be true—sort of. But Alice knew for
a fact that just because she'd been labelled a stick
insect since her first day at school, just because
she might *look* the part, it didn't mean she could
actually model!

'Coreen, you must be out of your mind. You've
obviously got me confused with someone who
can walk more than five steps in heels without
tripping over. And there are *stairs*…'

She ran to the back of the stage and peered

through a gap in the scenery. The stage was flat enough—a wide rectangle, long side facing the audience, but they'd decided against the traditional T-shape of a catwalk, reasoning that if more space was needed for dancing later it would be better to have the models walk down a short flight of steps and parade along the marble floor before turning back and doing the process in reverse.

'Nonsense,' Coreen said, shoving her to the side to get a look herself. 'You'll be fine.'

Alice put her hands on her hips. Her future business was on the line here, and she wasn't going to muck it up with her clompy walk and complete lack of gracefulness. She couldn't go out there and have everyone looking at her—the whole room looking at her. Especially when *someone* would be looking at her, making her stomach flutter, her pulse race. There was a huge probability she would fall at his feet—literally.

She grabbed Coreen from where she was gawking at the other guests and made her look at her. 'This isn't a fairy story or a Broadway musical. The poor little insignificant nobody isn't going to step into the star's shoes and save the day! I can't do it.'

She waited for the fireworks, for Coreen to beg and plead and manipulate, but Coreen's eye was back at the crack in the scenery, and she was eyeing up the runway again. It didn't even look as if her fuse was lit.

'Hold that thought,' she said, and ran back to the dressing rooms.

The lights everywhere but on the stage dimmed, and a rustle of excitement went through the crowd. Gentle music—a little bit fifties, a little bit Italian—filtered through hidden speakers. The two banks of chairs with a central aisle weren't arranged to face the stage but each other, leaving a wide channel for the models to walk down, allowing the onlookers to get the best view of the outfits on display.

A lone figure stepped out onto the stage, and there was a collective gasp from the crowd. Cameron, seated in the front row, smiled. This wasn't usually his thing, but somehow this was different. He knew all the hard planning that had gone into it—every minute detail.

He knew, for example, that this wasn't really Audrey Hepburn, in a full skirt, flat shoes, prim white shirt and a scarf knotted round her slender neck, but a professional lookalike—one of a handful Alice had hired to make the fashion show a little more dramatic. By the looks of the people on either side of him, it had worked. 'Audrey' made her way down the short flight of four or five steps from the stage to the floor of the atrium and stayed in character as she walked, looking every inch the Hollywood star. A spontaneous round of applause rippled round the room. And then, as Audrey passed him, another model appeared— this one in a white dress with big red roses on it. A white scarf covered her hair and she was wearing sunglasses.

There was something familiar about that woman. *Coreen?*

What was *she* doing modelling the clothes? That wasn't supposed to be her job—although, by the reaction of a couple of men sitting opposite him, it really ought to be. It looked as if they were ready to leap off their seats and follow her wherever she went.

He was still puzzling as the *Roman Holiday* section ended and a small spotlight came up on a lectern at one side of the stage. A woman stepped into the pool of light and coughed slightly, before leaning a little too close to the microphone so it squealed back at her.

'Sorry,' a gentle voice said through the speakers, and every hair on every inch of Cameron's body stood on end.

He thought he was going to have a heart attack right then and there in the middle of his own party. It was Alice. And she was… Alice was… All he could think of. All he could look at. All he'd ever thought she could be and more.

The little vintage outfits she'd worn to the office had been cute, but this… Rich, dark green, swelling and curving and flowing around her. And her hair—her eyes! Dark, liquid, smoky make-up, and the deep crimson lips of a goddess. She turned round to ask someone behind the scenes something, and he really did think his heart had stopped for a second or so.

If the front of the dress had been spectacular, the back was…

He'd run out of words.

Two wide satin straps crossed over between her shoulder blades and travelled down, down, down until they reached the low back, just where the top of her bottom rounded away. Someone across the room wolf-whistled, and Cameron almost jumped out of his seat and started searching for him so he could knock his teeth out. But he managed to contain himself. Just.

She turned back again and tested the micro-phone, which was now behaving itself.

What was Alice doing there, staring at the audience, her eyes large and round?

CHAPTER SEVEN

OH, LORD, thought Alice. What I am I doing here?

Every eye in the room was on her. Every ear straining to hear what she was going to say. The only problem was she didn't *know* what she was going to say. They were expecting something witty and engaging. All she had in her head was garbled phrases.

Why, oh, why had she refused to model? What was so hard about strutting about a bit? At least that would only have involved being *looked at*. But with Coreen stepping in for Amber she'd been forced into the role of auctioneer. Now she had be looked at *and* say stuff.

The plan was to auction off the pieces straight after their section of the show, so they were fresh in people's minds. The first model—Annie, the Audrey lookalike—stepped out onto the stage and struck a relaxed pose, her hands clasped behind her back in a girlish manner, and it instantly reminded Alice of stills she'd seen from *Roman Holiday*. She could almost hear the music—almost see St. Peter's Square and the Colosseum, feel her own heart beating with the first love of a shy girl escaping from her life of duty for a few precious days.

And then the words were there, inside her head. She took a deep breath and leaned into the microphone.

'Ladies and gentlemen, imagine yourselves in Rome at the height of summer, zipping through the crowded streets on a Vespa, the wind in your hair, the swell of freedom in your heart…'

If anyone had asked Cameron what each piece of clothing had sold for, he wouldn't have been able to tell them. He hadn't been paying attention to the numbers, only to the soft clarity of Alice's words, the way she moved her hands when she described a piece, the smile she bestowed on the winning bidders. Cameron wasn't a man who took his time deciding what he wanted, and he knew what he wanted right now—one of those smiles.

The final section of the auction was progressing—the one with the Marilyn lookalike. Evening dresses in all colours of the rainbow, made out of all kinds of fabrics: lace, satin, taffeta, organza…

Not that Cameron knew anything about fabrics,

but he retained the information because it had been delivered in Alice's voice.

She was amazing. The whole audience was eating out of her hand, leaning forward to catch every syllable she uttered. Coreen would have been a great auctioneer, parting the punters from their money with her outrageous curves and cheeky banter, but Alice… Alice was something else. Totally different.

A unique way of looking at things, he'd said. And now she was putting that gift to work with marvellous effect.

She didn't sell the clothes, she sold the *dream*— the very essence of all those classic movies. She didn't just describe each item of the sale, but she put it in context, creating a little story about each blouse, each handbag, each dress, until the guests were desperate to outbid each other for just a little bit of that fantasy. He wasn't sure, but he thought some of the pieces had gone for ridiculously high sums.

He'd been so busy caught up in her spell he realised that he'd forgotten to bid for anything— had forgotten to earn one of her smiles. Not that he'd have known what to bid for. Whatever would he do with a stole or a pill-box hat? It wasn't as if he had a woman in his life to shop for any more. And now the last bid had been made, for a metallic embroidered sheer dress similar to the one

Marilyn had worn in *Some Like It Hot*. That dress he remembered all on his own. What red-blooded male wouldn't?

But it wouldn't have done. He wouldn't have bought it anyway, because it would have looked so wrong on her...

Oh.

Mentally he'd been looking for something for Alice, and he hadn't even known it.

He frowned and berated himself. He should have known, should have made more of an effort, because now everything had been sold and his chance to surprise her with a gift, to say thank you for the wonderful job she had done, was gone. A little voice in his ear urged him to stand up, *make* one of the happy bidders give something up for him. He could do it. It was his ball, his building, his night, and he knew he could make any outrageous demand he wanted and people would scurry round to make it a reality.

But he didn't.

In his imagination he could see the look of disapproval on Alice's face. She wouldn't accept anything he obtained for her by those means anyway. So, although it was almost painful, he kept his mouth shut and his bottom in his seat.

Silence fell, and Alice removed the microphone from its stand and walked to the centre of the stage.

'We have one last piece of vintage clothing to auction off this evening…' She did a little twirl and Cameron felt his stomach clench, the blood pound in his ears. 'This Elsa Schiaparelli dress.'

A murmur of excitement rumbled around the room.

'It's a deep emerald satin evening gown, designed in 1938 for…'

The details blurred in Cameron's ears. He didn't need to know them. This was Alice's dress. No one else should ever be allowed to wear it— and he was going to make sure they wouldn't.

He was going to buy it for her.

And, in the process, he was going to earn himself one of those smiles.

It had been a spur-of-the-moment decision. Coreen had said she could auction this dress if she wanted to, and while it was the most beautiful thing she had ever worn and was ever likely to wear, when would she *really* ever have the chance to wear it again? After tonight she'd be back to blue jeans and T-shirts, bashed-up old trainers and her brother's fleeces.

The amount the auction had managed to raise for the local charity so far this evening was truly amazing, much more than she'd ever imagined possible, and she'd rather that this exquisite dress put an extra couple of hundred pounds in the kitty rather than sit in the darkness at the back of her wardrobe doing nobody any good.

'I'm going to start the bidding at one hundred pounds.' The reserve was five hundred. Surely it would go for much more than that. 'Do I have one hundred pounds?'

Instantly a hand shot up, the woman half rising out of her seat.

'One hundred pounds to the lady over there. Do I hear—?'

'Two hundred.'

Alice stopped mid-flow and turned in the direction of the voice. Not just *a* voice, but *the* voice. Her eyes met Cameron's. He was looking straight at her, his expression completely open. What on earth would Cameron want with a dress like this?

She couldn't look away as she said, 'Do I hear—?'

'Three hundred.'

This was a new bidder. She acknowledged a woman in a mink stole with a nod, but before she could open her mouth that deep, sexy log fire kind of voice said, 'Five hundred.'

And that was how it carried on. Every time someone else bid, Cameron topped it. She stopped looking at the other bidders and felt a gentle heat rise to her cheeks as she kept her focus on him.

Only on him. He was smiling too. A secret smile. A shared smile. One that connected them in such a way that the rest of the room melted away, became like background music.

She really must remember to breathe. It was interfering with the whole auctioneer thing. But the way that Cameron was looking at her—as if she was the only thing in his field of vision— seemed to be having an effect on her ribcage, making it squeeze tight around her lungs.

He's bidding for your dress. For you.

Don't be so stupid, she told herself. That would mean…Well, it would mean all sorts of things it was impossible for it to mean.

But that warmth in his eyes, his smile…

She knew it was true even as she accepted a bid of a thousand pounds from the original bidder and the whole room gasped. Cameron just smiled, and Alice knew his lips would open again, that he would add another hundred.

And he kept doing it. But Cameron was not a patient man, even though his nonchalant expression all through the auction almost fooled her. Hard lines of irritation at being constantly trumped started to show around his jaw. When the bid reached one thousand eight hundred, he snapped and stood up.

'Ten thousand,' he said, in his low, controlled voice, daring anyone to go higher.

Nobody did. They were all too shocked, busy whispering about his outburst, and before anyone with enough capital behind them had enough thought to bid against him it had gone. It belonged to him.

She belonged to him.

And, while the crowd dispersed in a collective hunt for another champagne cocktail before the ball proper began, she stayed centre stage and he stayed in his seat. They were grinning at each other.

She would wear this dress again. One day soon. She didn't know when or where, but she knew one thing for sure: Cameron would be at her side.

Cameron found himself in the midst of a group of businessmen, all congratulating themselves on their foresight in investing in his company and haw-hawing over each other's off-colour jokes. He listened with only half an ear while he scanned the vast atrium for any hint of a green dress.

He hadn't seen her since right after the fashion show, when he'd been but a few steps away from her and then Coreen had bustled her off backstage to do something urgent. She'd smiled at him, raised her eyebrows in apology, and since then he hadn't even had a glimpse of her.

When he was able, he excused himself from the group of men and went in search of her. That was the problem with being the man of the moment. Everybody wanted to shake his hand, or have a word, or slap him on the back and remark on his ten-thousand-pound bid.

He started at the edge of the dance floor, which was packed, all the time looking, his eyes searching out a particular shade of emerald. And then he saw her, talking to some of the guests who'd been unlucky in the auction. He recognized the woman in the fur who'd bid for Alice's dress. She wasn't looking very pleased, and she was trying to press something into Alice's hand.

Cameron tried to get to her, but he kept having to dodge people as they circled the fringes of the dance floor. It seemed whichever way he decided to go people deliberately stepped in his path, causing him to zig-zag. Once he'd cleared a particularly obstinate clump of left-footed dancers he looked to the space where Alice had been standing—but she was gone.

Damn.

The fashion show had finished almost an hour ago and it was nearing eleven o'clock. He needed to find her before the party ended.

Something rather round and rather solid barrelled into him, almost sending him flying—and that was no mean feat. He twisted round to find a portly man in a white dinner jacket mouthing apologies at him.

He'd just planted his feet solidly on the ground again when he became aware of someone standing behind him, waiting for him. Some unknown instinct told him it was a woman. Slowly, very slowly, he turned to face her.

Alice stopped dead, and her skirt swirled round her ankles then fell into perfectly spaced folds.

There he was, maybe only twenty feet away, and she watched as he turned without seeing her and faced the most stunning woman she'd ever seen outside the pages of the fashion magazines. If she'd needed a definition of glamour, this woman was it. Blonde. Tall. An eye-popping figure. In other words she was everything Alice was not. And she couldn't even fault her for her carriage or her dress sense. She held herself as if she was entitled to get everything her heart desired, especially the man she had set her sights on, and there was nothing cheap or nasty about her recreation of Marilyn's pink dress from *How To Marry a Millionaire*. Even from this distance Alice could tell it was beautifully made.

The blonde snaked her hand around Cameron's arm and reached down to twine her fingers with his, then leaned in close to whisper something in his ear. His back was to Alice, so she couldn't see his expression, but he leaned forward and whispered something back. Just the thought of his lips being that close to another woman, so she'd feel his breath tickle her ear, made Alice's stomach instantly freeze with jealousy.

The way was open now. A clear path between her and Cameron. She could just walk up to him, tap him on the shoulder, smile and cut in…

But she didn't

She watched her moment slide away, watched the crush of the crowd push Cameron and the blonde further away from her until they had disappeared. Stupid, she knew. But she didn't want to have to stand next to the vision in pink. She didn't want Cameron to make comparisons. Alice never did well in that kind of situation. She had never been anyone's first choice.

Later. When he was alone. When he wouldn't be distracted, dazzled… Maybe then she'd have the chance to see if that warm smile was still in his eyes for her. She turned and walked in the other direction, her sense of euphoria deflating as quickly as an old wrinkled party balloon.

Later seemed as if it would never happen. Alice found herself at the beck and call of all sorts of people for the next half an hour. The bar was running out of ice, someone had twisted their ankle trying to foxtrot and needed the first-aid kit, the clothes sold at the auction needed to be hung properly and labeled, so they could be claimed by the right owner. As organiser of the evening Alice had to deal with all of these things, and although she managed to delegate, something else often popped up to suck away her time.

The large, square white-faced clock above the main entrance to the atrium showed that it was twenty to twelve, and she hadn't been able to find Cameron anywhere since she'd dealt with her latest emergency. Alice had the horrible feeling that if she didn't find him tonight that warm smile for her would disappear from his eyes and never come again.

All around her people were dancing. Some twirled expertly, like Fred and Ginger, some merely held onto each other and attempted to match the beat of the music. Alice's brisk walk slowed as she took in the sights and sounds around her.

She watched as a couple near her swayed. They were so taken up with each other that they weren't even really dancing any more. They weren't moving in time with the music, just moving in time with one another. His hand held her firmly round her waist; one of her hands was cupped at the back of his neck, claiming him. Their free hands were knotted together and laid against his chest, and they were just staring into each other's eyes. After a few moments, he kissed her nose.

She sighed and rested her forehead against his and they shuffled away.

One dance, thought Alice. That's all I want. Once dance.

Surely that can't be too much to ask for—not after all the hard work I've put in?

As if on cue, she saw him. The undulating sea of dancing couples parted long enough for her to catch a glimpse of Cameron. He was dancing with someone. Slowly. Gently.

Her heart stopped.

But then he turned his partner and her pulse kicked into life again. It was an older lady he was with, her silver hair festooned with a long black feather tucked into a twenties headband, and Cameron was smiling indulgently at her.

Once again Alice made her way towards him, picking up speed now, but just before she was close enough for him to hear her call his name the blonde materialised, cutting in and leaving the older woman to smile politely and then look daggers at her back as she steered Cameron away.

But Cameron looked up over the blonde's shoulder and his eyes locked onto Alice's. He gave her the barest of smiles—one that said *Sorry. I'll be with you soon...*

Alice exhaled as he disappeared out of sight again. The warmth had been there—the smile—and she knew without a doubt that when the song ended he would make his excuses and come and find her.

Suddenly, for the first time in her life, Alice had the burning urge to go and check her lipstick.

Being quite familiar with the ground floor layout by now, she knew that a ladies' room was just outside the side door nearby—one that other people might not know about. It would be cool and quiet, and she could check her make-up and gather herself together before Cameron found her. She slipped out through the door and hurried down a short corridor.

When she actually got in front of a mirror, she realised that she couldn't have done anything about a lipstick disaster anyway. The little tube of deep berry-red Coreen had lent her was in her bag. And her bag was in Cameron's office. But it turned out she needn't have worried. The lipstick had lived up to the advertising campaign and was still virtually tattooed on. By the looks of it she'd still be trying to scrub it off next Tues—

The door creaked and Alice instinctively straightened. It seemed a bit vain to be caught nose to mirror, examining her reflection. She ran her fingers through the long wave of bright hair that half covered her face before glancing in the direction of the person—the woman—now hovering just beyond her field of peripheral vision.

Oh. It was *her*.

She turned to leave, not really wanting to share a confined space with the blonde—Cameron's blonde—but found her blocking the exit, one hand on a curvaceous hip. The other woman looked her up and down, the tiniest of sneers twitching her lips into an ugly shape.

'Excuse me,' Alice said, and moved to pass her.

But Blondie didn't budge. She licked her glossy lips and gave Alice a slow, predatory smile. 'I think we need to have a chat, darling.'

Dah-ling. On her lips, the word sounded positively vicious, despite the fact that her voice matched her appearance—cool, cultured. Expensive. Alice felt her hackles rise, but she wasn't about to give this woman the advantage by letting her irritation show.

'A chat about…? And who are you, anyway?'

She laughed—a soft, husky sound. 'Oh, I think you know the subject we both have in common. And I'm *Jessica*.' She raised her eyebrows, clearly waiting for a response.

Alice didn't have one to give her. She had no idea who *Jessica* was—other than that she'd been wrapped around—

'Jessica Fernly-Jones,' she added, as if it should mean something.

Alice just stared back at her, and waited for her

to get whatever it was she wanted to say off her ample chest.

'Cameron and I…we've been seeing each other for months. We're very…*close*, if you know what I mean?'

Alice's stomach began to churn, but she pulled her abdominal muscles in tight. 'And what has this got to do with me?'

That laugh again. It probably drove men wild, but it was as soothing to Alice as nails down a blackboard.

'Now, now. Don't be coy with me, darling. We're both women…' Her gaze fluttered down to Alice's chest and back up again. 'We can be frank with one another.'

Jessica Fernly-Jones could be as frank as she liked. It didn't mean Alice would return the favour.

'He's a very attractive man, as I'm sure you've noticed…'

Alice flushed, then a rush of anger at her own involuntary response compounded the problem. Jessica gave her a long, knowing look.

'He uses it to his advantage, you know—to get what he wants. Whether that be sealing a deal, crushing his competitors…' a split-second glance in the direction of the atrium was all it took to add a little venom to her next words '…to see a project finished to his high standards. But he never gets involved. He always moves on, looking for that elusive perfect woman. You *do* know that, don't you?'

Alice forced her lungs to expand, even though her rib cage felt horribly tight. The action helped her keep a lid on her anger.

Jessica gave her a look of mock-sympathy. 'Oh, poor girl…'

Girl? From the looks of it Miss Fernly-Jones was only a year or so older than she was. That was it. She wasn't listening to any more of this.

She could hardly believe that Cameron could get involved with someone like this. But she knew just from the body language she'd witnessed on the dance floor that Jessica was telling the truth—she had a history with Cameron. Whether it was anything more than ancient history remained to be seen.

Once Dawn from the market had learned who Coreen's Closet was working with, she'd tried to inveigle her way into the project by being useful. She'd sent Alice e-mail after e-mail with information about Cameron she'd found on the internet. There'd been articles from the business pages, but also snippets from the gossip columns—and in every entry he was pictured with a different woman, each one more stunning than the last. That was obviously what appealed to him, and even in her current state of fancy dress Alice knew she just didn't qualify. Cameron liked eye-candy.

She didn't want to believe he was that shallow, but she couldn't ignore it. He was driven, but damaged. After his revelations the other night, she knew that he was capable of all the things Jessica had just accused him of—but she understood why. How pathetic was it that the knowledge just made her ache for him more, made her want to soothe his pain? Why couldn't she just harden herself and walk away?

Jessica had been watching her face, and now a look of self-satisfaction spread a smile across her lips.

Alice pulled herself tall. 'Well, thanks for the tip, Jessica. Now, if you don't mind, I'll be on my way…'

This time Jessica shifted position to let her pass, and Alice celebrated a very minor victory in these horrible few moments of her life. She hadn't let Jessica win. The woman had thrown all her ammunition at her and she hadn't let Jessica Fernly-Jones see her crumble. Alice felt Jessica's eyes drilling holes into her back as she headed for the door. Her fingers had just closed round the handle when Jessica released her parting shot.

'It's a beautiful dress.'

Alice just pulled the door open. This conversation was over.

'I'm looking forward to wearing it.'

Just go. Don't react. Walk away.

The tug of curiosity was too strong—like the morbid fascination that caused drivers to slow down and rubberneck on a motorway when there'd been a pile-up, even though they knew what they saw might disturb them. She looked over her shoulder. Jessica was walking towards her, her mask of civility discarded, half hanging off.

'That's right, darling. He bought it for *me*. Didn't you see me sitting next to him, egging him on?'

Alice gasped. At the time she'd been too busy looking at Cameron and running the auction to process the other details her eyes had been sending to her brain, but now the information arrived, breathless and apologising for its lateness.

Jessica with her hand on Cameron's forearm. Jessica whispering into Cameron's ear...

Jessica ran a hand carelessly through her platinum waves. 'Cam's always said he likes me in green.' Her eyes narrowed as she came to stand virtually nose to nose with Alice. 'Or should I say he likes it so much he prefers to see me *out* of it?'

Alice felt sick. She didn't know what kind of game this woman was playing, but even the thought of her naked with Cameron turned her stomach to ice. And she couldn't even dismiss the images rushing through her brain as nonsense, because at some point recently they probably had been reality. She yanked the door open and left Jessica standing alone in the ladies'.

There was only one way she could respond to all of this information. Alice did what she did best.

Alice ran.

CHAPTER EIGHT

THE cold air hit her hard. The heavy glazed door swung closed behind her and she dragged in a breath and folded her arms around herself, trying to rub flat the goosebumps that appeared instantly on her upper arms. The imposing building towered above her, the lines of the giant sunburst above the door harsh and foreboding in the floodlights.

Blast. Her coat. It was upstairs in Cameron's office.

Even though it was bitterly cold she wouldn't have thought twice about leaving it there, but it wasn't just her coat she needed. Her bag was up there too, and without it she had no phone to call a cab, let alone the means to pay for it.

She sighed and headed back indoors. At least she wouldn't have to pass through the atrium to get her things. She could just nip up the winding stairs and be out again before anyone saw her. Not that anybody was likely to be looking for her but Coreen, and the last Alice had seen of her she'd been chatting up one of the saxophone players on his break.

It seemed to take for ever to clomp up the three flights of stairs in her shoes, her Lucite heels announcing her presence to anyone who cared to listen. So much for 'nipping' anywhere. But there was no other noise in the echoing stairwell. She was pretty sure she was alone.

Finally her telltale shoes were silenced by the thick dark carpet of Cameron's office. Alice realised from the soft glow coming from the open doorway that, although she'd turned the office lights off when they'd left earlier, she'd forgotten the one in the dressing room. Not wanting to announce her presence in the office to all the partygoers in the atrium, who would be able to see the light in the windows if they looked up, she decided not to hit the main switch. She only needed to find her bag, and her eyes were becoming accustomed to the dark already. The light from the dressing room would be enough.

Now, where had she left it?

Oh, yes…by that funny-looking chair with the chrome frame and wide leather straps. It looked very stylish, but it had to be the most uncomfortable thing she'd ever sat on. Obviously Cameron didn't want any of his visitors getting too relaxed.

Cameron.

Just the thought of him made her sigh.

She shook her head and went in search of her bag. But it wasn't on the chair. Where had it gone? Alice squinted in the dark and thought she made out a shape on the floor. It must have dropped through the leather straps. She crouched down and reached for the dark lump. Her fingers met velvet, and she picked up the slightly tired clutch bag. She was just straightening her legs when she heard a door graze the carpet.

Someone was coming. Please let it be Coreen. Please don't let it be…

The world started to spin faster and faster. He was silhouetted in the doorway by the bright lights of the hallway, and then he stepped into the shadows and the door swung closed behind him.

Even though purple blobs were filling her vision, multiple imprints of Cameron's outline in negative, she knew he was looking at her.

'You can't leave yet, Alice.'

What was it Jessica had said? Oh, she couldn't remember the exact words, but the truth had hit home, and the squeeze of her heart at the thought brought the stinging sentiment behind them rushing back. Something about Cameron being very charming when he needed to be—when he wanted something from you.

The ball was almost over. What on earth did he need from her now? Couldn't he just let her go before she made a fool of herself? She hugged her bag to her midriff. Her heart and her head were telling her completely different stories, and she needed time to work out which one was fibbing.

'I—I have to.'

I must.

She had to leave now, before he guessed. Before he took pity on her.

Cameron stepped forward. 'No.'

Such a firm word, in such a firm voice, but with such an undercurrent of gentleness. His voice had always affected her, and now it called tears forth from her eyes. Let him be gruff, let him be impatient and bossy. Please, please, don't let him be kind.

He started to walk towards her, and Alice wanted to scurry away and grab her coat, but she stayed rooted to the spot. It was as if he was holding her there just by the sheer weight of his stare.

She broke eye contact.

That was better. Shakily, she started in the direction of the dressing room, where her coat was hanging. She'd be fine as long as she focussed on the little diamanté buckles on her shoes, if she didn't look him in the eye.

'Alice.'

A soft command.

He reached for her. His fingers brushed the bare skin of her arm, and it was as effective at stopping her in her tracks as a rugby tackle. Her chest rose and fell as she concentrated on each little rhinestone on her buckles in turn. But it couldn't shut out the awareness of him, of how he was circling her, how he'd come to stand in front of her.

'Don't leave. Not yet.'

She made her first fatal error. But with fatal errors one was all that was needed. She looked up at him. His eyes were dark, holding a riddle.

He took the bag from her hands and dropped it on the desk.

'Come.'

Cameron's voice was low and soft. When he got assertive it reminded her of the big crackling flames of a log fire, but right now it was more like the little tiny flickering ones. They were the dangerous flames. Their little licks fairly *seduced* the logs into ash.

He didn't take hold of her hand, but she followed him as if he had, tugged along by him as he led her to the balcony. They ended up at the railing, staring down at the party still in progress below them.

'Look,' he said.

And she did look. From up here, suspended above the dance floor, the view was magical. The lights… The colours… Gold and silver, red and purple, turquoise…jade. All those beautiful ball-gowns set against the stark black of hundreds of dinner jackets, all spinning and turning. It almost seemed as if it wasn't just individual couples moving, but that every person, every pair, moved in harmony, creating shifting kaleidoscopic patterns on the wonderful mosaic marble floor.

She'd been so frantically busy tonight, so caught up with a thousand little details that she'd forgotten to step back and look at what she'd managed to achieve. The atrium looked amazing—everything she'd pictured when she'd scribbled all those notes and made all those phone calls had come to life. It was real—happening. As if she'd conjured it up by dreaming it.

She'd done it.

The evening was a success.

The soft sounds of the big band—saxophones, lazy trombones and the husky voice of the singer—floated up above the heads of the guests and drifted into the great glass roof, from where they echoed back again, just enough to make the sound seem distant, other-worldly.

'I asked you for "distinctive". You gave me more than that. *Much* more than that.'

Ah, that was what this was. A thank-you speech. Well done, little Alice. Big pat on the back. You finally did something that made people sit up and take notice. Good luck for the future. See you again some time…

But if that was all this was, why was his mere presence having such an intoxicating effect on her? Why was her heart pounding, her breath coming in shallow gasps? And why had his hand covered hers, his thumb now circling the back of her hand?

'I haven't seen you dance once this evening. Will you dance with *me*, Alice?'

This couldn't be real. It had to be something to do with this evening, this strange sense of…*fairy tale*…that just refused to leave her alone. But she let him pull her to him, too weak-willed to walk away. Too weak-willed to run this time.

Didn't he know why she hadn't danced all evening?

It had to be him. No one else. And all evening he'd been so distant, always just beyond her fingertips and out of reach.

He's still out of reach, she told herself. *Don't kid yourself that just because his arm is around your waist, pulling you close, because his chin is only inches from your forehead, because you can smell the fresh cotton of his shirt mixed with aftershave, that he will ever be truly yours. This is just now. This is just for tonight.*

I won't be a fool, she told herself back. I won't

forget. But I'm not stupid enough to rob myself of this memory either.

He'd been wrong when he'd listed all the things she'd given him. She'd given him *everything*. More than just a great party, a good idea, value for money. He had her heart, her soul, her very last breath.

The band started to play 'The Very Thought of You', and gently, almost so she didn't notice, he began to lead her, dance with her, moving with his signature efficient grace. Her heart was reaching out for him with a persistence that became a bittersweet ache. It was too late now. She might have been able to walk away with her pride intact if he hadn't come up here, if he hadn't offered her a taste of what life might be like if fairy tales happened every day.

She'd fallen in love with him. Just like that. Even though her brain told her it was all a spell woven by the magic of the night—magic she'd manufactured herself.

Thank goodness he wasn't ostentatious with his dance moves—dipping her, twirling her out and in again. Thank goodness he kept her pressed close against him, where she could feel his breath in the roots of her hair, where she could stare at his lapel and avoid his gaze.

Maybe it hadn't been *just like that*. Maybe, like

Lewis Carroll's Alice, she'd been falling for such a long time she could hardly remember when the downward journey had begun. All that had happened now was that she'd finally had the shock of hitting the bottom.

She loved Cameron.

She loved his quiet integrity, his single-minded focus. She loved the way he surprised himself sometimes by laughing out loud.

The song changed to something even mellower, and Cameron's circling movements became smaller and smaller—until they were no longer dancing, just holding each other.

It was almost too beautiful to be true up here amid the echoes of love songs, her face now against his shoulder, just the remnant of a sway keeping them from stillness. But it had to end soon. The knowledge settled in her like a stone sinking to the bottom of a pool. He'd pull away, look into her eyes and say goodnight. Goodbye. She was easy to say goodbye to.

But he was kind. He spun the moment out for her, and instead of releasing her his arms came around her completely, and she felt the soft pressure of his lips against her forehead.

She'd wanted a magical memory, but this was almost too intense. It wouldn't warm her in the future when she thought back to it; it wouldn't comfort her. It would burn, leaving her raw for ever, leaving her wanting relief, with none to be had.

'Alice? Look at me.'

She tasted salt on her lips. Quite how the tears had fallen there she wasn't sure.

'I…' She didn't get any further, but gulped the words away.

This time he didn't say *no*. His gravity didn't pull her. She knew she could keep her eyes on her feet and run out of there if she wanted to and he wouldn't stop her. After a few moments she tilted her chin up, but kept her gaze fixed on his chest, then slowly she raised her eyes to meet his.

He didn't look hard tonight, all angles and planes. He looked torn, almost sad. There was a softness in his eyes she'd never seen before. That feeling of *connection* hummed between them. It grew and grew until it pounded in her ears—until the only way to drown it out was to lean closer and closer and closer…

The first kiss was nothing more than the merest touching of lips, a promise. There was such purity in it, such sweetness, that Alice forgot all her stern words to herself about holding back. She ran her hands up his arms, around his neck, and dragged Cameron closer. She kissed him as if her life depended on it.

Maybe it did.

She'd never felt this overwhelming need to touch and taste a man before. She couldn't have stopped herself even if she'd tried. And Cameron…

His lips wandered down her neck, across her collarbone. His hands settled around her waist, his fingers brushing against the smooth fabric of her dress, creating a slow, sliding friction that drove her even crazier than she already was.

It had never been like this with anyone else. With Cameron she forgot to plan each move of her hands, her lips. She forgot to think about what she could be doing better, or to worry about not being sexy or experienced enough. With Cameron she just dissolved into the moment, losing her sense of self completely and then finding it again, reflected back to her in each brush of his lips, each caress of his hands.

This man in her arms was always so sure of himself, so sure his every move, every decision was the right one, and to feel him pull her tighter against him, murmur her name, to sense that he was just as lost in this as she was made her soar. Cameron desired her. He wanted her. With an intensity that was so strong it almost scared her.

And she loved this man. This was everything she'd ever dreamed of. Except…

Except in the dream he didn't just desire her, he hadn't just got caught up in the heat of the moment. In the dream he loved her back.

One miracle in an evening was enough to expect. She'd never realised Cameron *really* shared the intense attraction she felt for him until tonight. That should be enough. Asking him to love her too… Well, that was just being silly.

She put her hands on his upper arms, bracing herself slightly, and pulled away. Not enough to look into his eyes, but enough to be able to talk without just giving in to his magnetic pull and kissing him again.

'Cameron, what is this? What are we doing?'

Cameron, as always, was more comfortable with actions than words, and he ran both hands down her back. The feel of them through the satin of her dress was even more delicious. He let them come to rest on the curve of her hips. Alice was very tempted to just shut up, close her eyes and stop asking difficult questions. Questions she wasn't even sure she wanted the answers to—because that would only break the spell once and for all.

Oh, she knew he wasn't about to go back to Jessica Fernly-Whatsit. Cameron might be fickle with his women, but there was no way he would be up here with her on the balcony, kissing her the way he'd kissed her, if he still had anything going with Jessica. He just wasn't that kind of man.

But she wasn't sure he was the kind of man who could give her all she wanted either. He kept himself locked up so tight, used his anger to power him forward. She didn't even know if he'd be brave enough to let that shield down and give all of himself to someone. And, even though this was Cameron she was thinking about, Cameron who could so easily be the one she trotted around after for ever, she wasn't prepared to accept anything less than the full package from him.

It was high time she was somebody's first choice rather than just being second best.

Something was bothering Alice. He could tell. If only he had some of that intuition women were famous for, then he'd be able to work out *what* was making her brows pinch and her mouth set itself in a firm little line. He didn't like it when her mouth did that. It made her look very determined. And he'd much rather she was using her lips to kiss him again rather than produce an expression that put a niggle in his gut. He didn't know why, but he had the oddest feeling he wasn't going to like what she had to say next.

Maybe he could convince her to soften that line, to put the curves and arches of her lips to a much more pleasurable use. Maybe, just maybe, he could wangle it so they didn't need to talk at all. He was pretty sure he could convince her to sink against him again, to run her small fingers over his skin, to breathe tiny sighs of desire into his ears. And he didn't think he'd have to say a word to do it.

He moved his hands upwards from where they were still resting on the swell of her hips and circled her waist. She was so slender his large hands almost met in the middle, and somehow that made him feel even bigger and stronger. She seemed such a tiny, delicate thing in his hands, yet he knew that her response to him had been anything but delicate. In fact, it had completely blown him away.

Other women *tried* to be sexy when they were with him. They tried to live up to the idea of going out with an eligible millionaire bachelor as if they had to impress him to keep him interested. And, to be honest, he required that of them. Wanted them to be the fantasy women they both pretended they were. Even women like Jessica.

He hadn't wanted to know and be known. He hadn't wanted to get close enough to anyone to let them see who he really was, to expose himself and make himself vulnerable. The temporary nature of his relationships had been the perfect solution. Move on to the next one, promising himself he was looking for the pot of gold at the end of the rainbow, when really he was just running, running…

But with Alice it was different. She didn't do any of that with him. And that was what made her so wonderful and so confusing at the same time. She was sensuous and sexy because he knew every touch and every kiss was real, true, honest— as if she was undressing her soul for him.

Being a red-blooded man, the twin thoughts of 'undressing' and 'Alice' in close proximity made his core temperature rise. And thoughts of undressing led to thoughts of that dress, of sliding the wide straps off her shoulders and watching the heavy fabric sink to the floor.

She was looking at him, and underneath the film of caution in her eyes he saw matching heat, matching need. It was all the encouragement he needed to bend his head and deliver a kiss that was hot and sweet and hungry. Alice was still for a split second, and then she joined him, as if she'd been resisting but just couldn't hold back any longer. The knowledge just drove him even further overboard, made him want her even more.

What is this? What are we doing?

He knew exactly what they were doing. He knew exactly what he wanted and how he pictured this ending. And in his head the scenario involved that long leather sofa, him and Alice stretched along the length of it, and the sexiest dress he'd ever seen— his dress now, as he hadn't officially given it to her yet—in an emerald heap on the floor.

He continued to kiss her, continued to blot out

that concerned look in her eyes, and his hands skimmed her torso until they found their way under those silky straps. And then he was gently walking her backwards off the balcony and into the office.

After the third step Alice froze.

He wasn't a man to push in situations like this. In reality he'd never needed to. But that *something* that was bothering her, that he'd tried to wish away—it had just stamped its foot down hard, and it wasn't going anywhere until it had been dealt with.

Slowly he eased his hands from under the straps, careful to leave them in place, and dragged his lips from Alice's. But he was unable to resist returning for one last brush, one last taste, before he pulled away fully.

Just to keep his itchy fingers out of temptation's way, he ran his hands up her neck until he was cradling her head and just waited. This had to be about what Alice wanted.

This had to be about what Alice wanted.

The phrase repeated in his head.

How shallow, how *horribly* shallow, had he been up until now? All his relationships with women up until this moment in time had been about what *he'd* wanted. Not in the sense that he'd bullied or domineered—far from it. He'd always treated the women in his life well. But only because it had suited him to do so. Because he'd gone out with those women to boost his status, to prove to the rest of the male population that he could have what they could only dream about. This evening had turned all of that on its head.

First Fitzroy, showing that Cameron didn't have the best relationship by far, that he only had a poor imitation of the real bond Daniel had with his wife. And now Alice—sweet, lovely Alice—turning him inside out with her honesty, with her fragile power.

So, instead of persuading her any further, he stepped back, gave her space.

'Alice? Tell me.'

He knew he had to be the one to speak first, because he had been the one who had cut off the talking earlier. How he knew this he wasn't quite sure. This being real, being open, was all a bit new to him. He was just going to have to feel his way.

The pain he saw in her eyes made him wince.

The fear must have shown on his face, because her expression hardened.

'I can't have a fling with you, Cameron. You know you can make me stay if you want to, but I'm begging you—let me go. Let me walk away. I'm not one of your perfect women.' She gave a dry little laugh and shook her head. 'I wouldn't even know where to start!'

Then she surprised him by walking towards him and running her slim fingers down the length of his tie. When she reached the point at the bottom she flipped it over and parted the seam a little, revealing a brightly coloured lining.

'Here she is,' Alice said quietly. 'The other night I forgot…'

The blobs of colour all at once started to make sense. It wasn't just a swirling abstract pattern but a picture in the lining of his tie—a pin-up, to be exact. Betty Grable-style, with rolled hair, bright red lips and a skimpy white halter top. She was winking at him.

'This is the kind of woman you need. Always ready, always glamorous, never having an off day. Who cares if she isn't real? She'll never ask anything of you, never ask you for a piece of your soul. In short, she'll always be your perfect woman.'

She let the tie go and patted it back into place.

'They're very collectible, you know. Ties like these. If you ever decide you don't want it you should be able to get a nice price for it.' She smiled brightly at him even as her eyes brimmed over. 'Coreen's Closet would give you a really good deal.'

Despite his promise to himself to give her the space she wanted, he found himself reaching for one of her hands. 'I don't want you to be like—'

She pulled her hand away. '*Please*, Cameron!'

Tears shimmered on her lashes, ran down her cheeks.

He hated himself for being responsible for them, for not being enough of a man for her to stay for.

'I need to go home,' she said in a flat voice.

'You can have my car. It's—'

She shook her head. 'All I need is my bag and my coat.'

He fetched her coat for her while she got her bag, and then she walked out through the door. But before she left she turned slightly and whispered one last thing. 'Thank you…for not making me stay.'

For the longest time Cameron just stared at the back of the door. He wanted to go and drag her back, explain. But that would be the worst thing he could do. Instead he flipped his tie over and took a look at the hidden woman inside. That wasn't what he wanted at all!

He was through with fake two-dimensional women. He wanted someone who made him feel alive—someone who made him *feel*, full-stop. Someone like Alice. Someone exactly like Alice.

But he couldn't blame her for not realising he'd changed—not when he'd only just cottoned onto the fact himself. But he had to try and make her see…

He thought of Alice making her way home alone, tears in her eyes. He thought about the limo parked outside, ready to whisk him anywhere he wanted to go, anywhere he commanded. She'd asked him not to stop her leaving, but he hadn't said he couldn't follow her, had she? He had to give this one last chance.

He had a lot to offer a woman. And he was going to offer it all to Alice.

By the time Alice emerged from Cameron's office she discovered the ball was drifting to a close. Music still played, but it came from speakers. The band had been booked to play until midnight and they were now packing up. Only a few dozen people were left in the atrium. Some were still dancing, most were chatting, and every few seconds another small group peeled off and headed for the exit.

She deliberately didn't look up as she scurried across the vast space, past the stage and beyond, into the mayhem of the backstage area. It was all quiet now. Clothing racks stood empty, everything having been packed away by an army of helpers, and the only noise was a scuffling coming from one of the corners.

It was Coreen, sitting on one of the vintage suitcases—battered sky-blue leather with a chrome trim—that she'd brought some of their stock in. She was trying to persuade it to close, with the help of her curves and a little gravity. She looked up and saw Alice.

'Give us a hand, will you? I can't get the blasted thing shut.'

Alice dropped onto the suitcase next to her, too soul-weary to do it gracefully. It did the job, though, because Coreen leaned forward and clicked the fasteners into place. She grinned at Alice.

'Now, as long as it doesn't decide to spring open before I get in the cab, I'm all set.'

Alice sighed. 'Is that offer of sharing a cab still open?'

One of Coreen's eyebrows twitched upwards. 'Course it is.'

An even bigger sigh escaped from her lips and Coreen slung an arm round her and squeezed.

'Hey, come on. We did great! You're just having the slump after the adrenaline high. Get home, have a hot chocolate to pump up your blood sugar, and you'll be fine.'

Post-adrenaline slump. That was what this was, was it? Nothing to do with having just walked away from the man she was in love with? Good. She'd be fine by morning, then.

Only she wouldn't.

Love wasn't the comfortable armchair she'd always imagined it to be. It wasn't safe and warm and fluffy. It was scary and painful and heart-stoppingly exciting. Nothing like the sanitised version she'd inflicted on the men in her life.

Was this what Paul felt when he looked at Felicity? This heart-thumping, brain-frying, all-body tremor-inducing thing? She understood it now. Why he'd left. Why he'd had to follow it wherever it took him if he had a chance of finding someone who could make him feel like this, who felt the same way about him. Good luck to him. And she really meant that.

Coreen stood up, grabbed her hand and tugged her upright. 'Cab's due in five. We'd better get outside.'

Alice just nodded. Then she looked at the suitcase. 'Shouldn't that have gone in the back of Dodgy Dave's van with everything else?'

'Are you nuts? I've got all the costume jewellery in here, padded out with a few scarves and a mink cape. I'm not letting dear old Dave get his mitts on this!'

It made sense.

She let Coreen yabber away as they walked to the front of the building and climbed into the waiting cab. Alice sat numbly in the back as they nipped through the quiet backstreets to her house.

She'd done the right thing. She'd had to run when she had.

If she'd been weaker, had given in to Cameron's pull, then she'd have ended up in a terrible mess—her heart squished beyond recognition and no good to anyone, not even second-hand. That didn't mean that it didn't hurt like hell, but it did mean that one day, when she found someone who thought she was everything a woman should be, she'd have something to love him back with. She just hoped her poor heart had recovered by then—because it seemed to have a terminal case of something at the moment, despite all the sensible things she'd done to protect it.

At least she'd have her new business to concentrate on. From what Coreen had said they had been inundated with requests for more of the same kind of merchandise from some very wealthy potential clients. She was even talking about finding a shop to lease in a better neighbourhood than they'd looked at before—something a little more upmarket.

Coreen lived closer, so it made sense for the taxi to drop her off first. And, horrible as it might sound, Alice was quite relieved when she and her blue suitcase were gone. She was able to drop the fake smile, stop all the nodding, and just slump in the back seat of the cab.

Back to real life now, Alice. Pull yourself together. The ball was a success. Coreen's Closet is going to take off. You've got the whole world at your feet.

Thinking of feet, she looked down at her Lucite shoes. They were still as fabulous as ever, but they were both still accounted for. Cinderella she was not—even if she'd seemed to track of that for a while back there. No, it had all been smoke and mirrors, spotlights and glitter balls. Now it was time to get back to the real world. Time to turn back into a pumpkin.

CHAPTER NINE

THE limo didn't have any problem trailing Alice's taxi. Cameron drummed his fingers on the arm rest as he watched the cab stop and let her out. He paid careful attention to which path she went up in the narrow car-lined street filled with redbrick terraced houses. As soon as he'd pinpointed the right front door he was out of the car and knocking on it.

But it wasn't Alice who answered, but a short guy in a curry-dribbled T-shirt. He didn't even bat an eyelid when Cameron asked for Alice, even though it was half past one in the morning.

'You'd better come in,' he said, opening the door wide. 'We're not quite sure what to do with her.'

We? And what was the matter with Alice?

Cameron followed the man into a living room dominated by a large flat-screen TV and enough high-spec audio visual equipment to make any geek's heart soar. A battle game of some description was paused on the TV—a large, sharp-toothed monster frozen in mid-air, about to land on a blood-smeared dragon. The remains of a takeaway were littered across the carpet, along with a couple of empty cans of cheap beer. And in the middle of all this clutter and stale-smelling furniture was Alice, in her dark green ballgown, looking as beautiful as ever and sobbing her heart out.

He walked over to her, crouched down and took her hands. She didn't even flinch, too miserable even to be surprised to see him. She held up a shoe and gulped.

'I broke my shoe,' she said and just started crying all the harder. 'My beautiful shoe…'

Cameron was a bit wrong-footed by that. Maybe his male ego was bigger than it should have been, because he'd thought—had maybe even hoped in a warped kind of way—that she'd been crying about *him*.

He took the shoe from her. The clear glass-like heel was hanging off.

Puzzled, he looked at Alice again. He knew girls liked shoes, but *this* much…? And he hadn't ever suspected *Alice* was one of those girls. But until a couple of weeks ago there had been a lot of things he hadn't suspected about Alice. How funny and strong-willed she could be. How resourceful and determined.

'They're just shoes,' he said, sitting down next to her. 'You can get another pair.'

Alice looked at him as if he'd just insulted her mother. 'I don't *want* another pair! I want this pair. But it's broken and I don't know how to fix it and I'll probably never be able to wear them again.' She paused to take a deep gurgling sniff. 'And I'll never find another pair like them. I might never find another pair *at all*! And then I'll be *shoeless* for the rest of my life. Old and lonely and…and…shoeless!'

Cameron looked at Alice. He hated seeing her like this. If he could, he would hunt down her heart's desire and give it to her on a silver platter. Gently he prised the other shoe from her grip and put the pair down on the floor beside him, avoiding a foil curry container with an oily slick in the bottom.

If Alice wanted these shoes, and these shoes only, then he would have them repaired—whatever the cost. And if they couldn't be repaired he'd scour the globe for replacements.

He took a deep breath and hoped the universe was still in the mood for granting wishes tonight. Because he really wanted to convince Alice to give him a chance, to let them explore whatever this thing between them was.

'Alice, I'll take care of the shoes. Whatever you want, I'll get it for you.'

She looked up at him, her gaze flicking between his eyes, searching for the truth of his statement.

'What I want is to know what *you* want, Cameron. Why are you here?'

Such a simple question. So hard to answer. Partly because he wasn't sure how to put it all into words, and partly because he didn't know if he was brave enough to do it if he could. He settled on asking for something concrete.

'I would like to spend more time with you. I don't want...*this*...to be over.'

He'd had it with *temporary*.

A strange combination of suspicion and surprise clouded her eyes.

'Why? Why me?'

Because I can't stop thinking about you. Because I love being with you. Because I have a feeling that if I don't see you again something inside me will shrivel up and dry out.

Those words sounded so lame inside his head— like bad dialogue from a cheesy chick-flick. He couldn't say them, even if it was true. He reached out and took one of her hands in his.

'Because you deserve to be treated like a princess.'

There—that was much better. Women always liked to hear things like that.

So why did Alice swiftly pull her hand out of his? Why did her chin jut forward just a little?

'I'm not a princess and I never will be. Don't kid yourself.'

Frustration started to form a cloud in Cameron's head. Why was she being so stubborn? She was being ridiculous. Didn't she know how sweet and funny and clever she was? Who had been telling her otherwise? He'd like to find that person and make them eat their words—swiftly followed by their teeth.

She got up and walked away from him, and when she could go no further, when she had reached the corner of the room, she turned and faced him, one hand on her hip.

'Did you love Jessica?'

Cameron stiffened. Where the heck had *that* come from? And what did Jessica have to do with him and Alice? Had she been whispering in Alice's ear? Knowing *dah-ling* Jessica, she'd have had her claws out if she'd had the opportunity. He needed to put this right—make Alice see sense.

'No, I didn't love her.' Sometimes, towards the end, he hadn't even liked her—despite the fact she could be very charming company when she wanted to be. It struck him that even after four months of on-and-off dating he hadn't really known Jessica at all. She too put up a front—a bulletproof sensuality that deflected everything. And it had never bothered him. Maybe she was as much a coward as he was. He wondered what she was really like behind her fun-loving party-girl persona. Not because he was interested in her in a romantic sense any more, but because he was suddenly certain there was more under the surface than he had ever seen, had ever bothered to look for. 'I'm not sure I even knew her very well.'

He'd hoped it would put Alice's mind at rest, but somehow his response had just made her frown all the harder.

'Then what was it that made you want to go out with her in the first place? If that isn't a really obvious question…'

He tore his eyes from hers and looked across the room to the TV screen. The monster was still frozen; the dragon was still blood-smeared. He didn't want to open up and tell her this. Now he looked at his behaviour it all seemed so pathetic. Alice would think badly of him if he told her the truth—that he'd been afraid, that underneath all the hype he was still a quivering coward. He almost laughed out loud. Oh, God, the bullies had been right after all.

But she'd send him away if he didn't say *something*, so he'd just have to try and make it sound not too awful. He couldn't bear it if she looked at him in disgust, if he saw her opinion of him change.

'It's hard to explain…' He tried to tell her that it hadn't been as heartless and cynical as it sounded. Even though he hadn't been in love, he'd honestly been *infatuated* with the string of women he'd dated. It was just that the shimmer of perfection that had attracted him to them in the beginning hadn't seem to last. And just as he was starting to lose interest he'd spot someone else and he'd be off again, the whole cycle repeating itself.

As the words poured forth he felt himself hollow out. It was a horrible feeling because the space wasn't left empty. A cold wind of fear rushed in to fill the void.

'It wasn't a calculated thing. It's just…'

'It's just that you were living up to your name.'

He turned to look at her. 'What?'

'Hunter. You obviously love the thrill of the chase.' She looked at the floor. 'Not so keen on the *keeping* of what you've won, though. Always on to the next thing—bigger and better…'

Up until now that part of his character had always seemed a positive thing—it was how he'd achieved so much success so quickly—but the way Alice said it… She sounded so blank, so hopeless.

He got up and walked over to where she was standing.

'None of that matters now.' Inside, his stomach

began to pitch. 'I don't want Jessica. I don't even want someone else like her. I want you.'

'This isn't real,' she said. 'It's the evening, an adrenaline rush, a *moment*…'

Wasn't real? How could she say that? The very air around them was pulsing with authenticity. Couldn't she feel it? For the first time in his life he was seeing things clearly.

'And I can't do this if all it is going to be is a moment.' She fixed him with a serious look—one that made his pulse stutter. 'You know what I'm talking about, don't you?'

He nodded.

He didn't want just a *moment* either. But the implications of that were making his head spin, filling his stomach with a fear he just didn't want to name. The opposite of *temporary* was *permanent,* and he'd never really planned on 'for ever' with anyone. He didn't know if he could do it even if he wanted to.

'I think…I think there's something there between us, Cameron. But I'm not sure there's any mileage in it.' She nodded, more to herself than to him. 'And I'm ready for mileage—for long distance.'

He wanted to say he was too, but after what he'd said about his previous relationships the words sounded a bit empty as they echoed round his head. Now he was getting desperate. And when

Cameron got stuck in difficult situations he fell back on tried and tested methods.

He wanted to tell her about the life they could have together, the life she deserved. All the best restaurants. And she wouldn't have to wear anything second-hand ever again. He'd buy her *haute couture*—the sort of thing other people would be bidding for at auctions in fifty years time. She would be the first person to wear the clothes that would be *tomorrow's* vintage. But he didn't say any of this, knowing he would be digging his own grave.

She looked very glum, resigned.

'One evening—that's all I'm asking for.' For starters. Once he'd dazzled her, in true Cameron Hunter style, she would change her mind. She *had* to.

'I don't want just one evening, Cameron.'

Her chest rose and fell, and she stayed silent for the longest time—as if she was inwardly struggling with herself. In the end she walked over and opened the living room door.

Once again he found himself in the position of wanting to argue back but not really having a leg to stand on. He didn't know if he was ready either, but he *wanted* to be ready. Surely that had to count for something?

'Wait there,' she said, and disappeared upstairs.

She returned a few moments later. But now she was in stripy flannel pyjamas and she was holding the green dress in her arms. She held it out to him. The tears were gone—along with most of her make-up—and she looked pink, puffy, and slightly soggy. Cameron wanted to kiss her.

'Before you go,' she said, 'I thought I ought to give you this. It's *your* dress really.'

'But I bought it for you.'

She took a moment to think. He could tell she was doing that, because her forehead did a very characteristic crinkle and she looked at the floor. After a few moments she raised her head and looked at him, seemingly having reached some kind of decision.

'I know you did.' She held it out to him. 'But this isn't me. Not really. The woman who wore this dress tonight isn't the real Alice. This—' she indicated the flannel pyjamas '—is the real Alice. And she doesn't fit into your world. You'll see that in the morning,' she added. 'You'll be thinking more clearly then.'

He knew that anything he said would just make her resist him even harder. He'd definitely under-estimated this quiet determination of hers. It was as hard as diamonds. He took the dress from her, and she gathered up the shoes and placed them on top of it in his arms.

'Please go, Cameron.' Her voice was barely a whisper as she stood there, not looking at him, holding the door wide. 'I'm begging you. Just go.'

He couldn't bear the fact he was doing this to her, so he just had to do as she asked. But he felt as if he'd left a piece of himself behind when he walked out through the door. He was halfway down the street before he remembered his limo, parked across from Alice's house. His driver was fast asleep and he decided not to wake him. He'd give him an extra bonus to compensate for the ridiculous hours tonight. So, while Henderson snored softly, Cameron sat in the back of the car and watched as the lights went out one by one in Alice's house. He wondered which was hers.

She'd said he'd see sense in the morning, and maybe he would. Until then there was nowhere else he wanted to go. Not even with the whole city at his feet.

Alice had had a thoroughly disgusting night's sleep. When she'd finally been able to drop off she'd spent the whole night terrorised by images of random things waltzing through her subconscious—jewel-coloured dresses, doner kebabs, and shoes. Lots and lots of shoes.

Cameron had pushed her too much last night. Too much too soon. And the only thing she'd been able to do to give herself some time and space to sort all this out was to push back. She knew he thought he meant what he was saying, and she so wanted to believe him, but…

The street lamp across the road flickered off now dawn was breaking. The orange strip of light she'd been staring at on her wall disappeared.

Cameron was not a good bet. He was a relationship magpie, and she wanted a future—with a man who wasn't always going to be scanning the horizon for something better. She didn't need a high-flying playboy who got bored easily.

No.

She was being unfair to Cameron, thinking about him like that. He wasn't heartless. But she didn't think he was ready for love and commitment. When she'd said she didn't want just 'a moment', she'd seen the doubt written all over his face. Not that he'd ever say so; he'd rather die than admit he was deficient in any way. His pride wouldn't let him. And while he kept feeding that pride, while he *needed* to be Cameron Hunter, software developer and millionaire bachelor, while he needed to keep proving himself, he'd never be ready. She'd never be enough for him.

She breathed out and stared at the ceiling. No woman could *ever* be the perfect being he was hunting for. The knowledge gave her an odd sense of relief, and she rolled over and hugged her pillow, wondering if she'd be able to doze off now she seemed to have settled a few things in her own mind.

Her room was directly over the front door, and slowly she became aware of a gentle but very persistent knocking.

There was no hope Matthew or Roy would answer it. They never emerged from their rat holes until well after midday on a Sunday. But Alice was fed up with being the only one who did anything in this house, and she decided she wasn't going to haul herself downstairs to answer the door, but would open her window and just yell down at whoever it was to clear the hell off. It was eight o'clock on a Sunday morning, for goodness' sake. All civilised people were asleep or at the very least indoors at this time of day.

She lifted the catch on the window and shoved the sash upwards, ignoring the drips of condensation landing on her head.

'Why don't you just—?'

Another drop of water hit her just behind her left ear as she stared into Cameron's upturned face. He didn't smile at her, just indicated the large paper bag he was holding with a nod of his head.

'It's morning. I'm seeing things more clearly. Can I come in, please?'

Alice just continued to gawp at him. Had he

really taken what she'd said so literally? She was too surprised to argue with him, and discovered, despite her earlier rebelliousness, that she wasn't about to have a shouted conversation with him from her window so all the neighbours could hear. She'd seen a few curtains twitch already.

She shut the window, tiptoed downstairs and opened the front door. Cameron pushed the package in her direction.

'I brought you breakfast,' he said.

It smelled heavenly. Without looking inside she knew it was warm buttery croissants and strong coffee. Just what she'd have fetched for herself if she'd thought about it. She didn't say anything— just led the way to the kitchen.

He was still wearing the same clothes as last night. That dark suit… But the tie with the hidden pin-up was missing, and the top button of his shirt was open, making him look even more devastatingly sexy because now he had a slightly dishevelled un-Cameron-like appearance.

But he smelled the same. Of aftershave and fresh cotton. Possibly the most intoxicating scent ever.

All the memories of being pressed up against him on the balcony came flooding back, and when Cameron placed the package on the counter and pulled her close for a kiss she didn't have it in her to push him away.

It was even better than she remembered. Better because now it didn't just feel as if it was something she'd dreamed. He was here, in her kitchen, and he still wanted to kiss her. She wanted to hope, she really did, but the thought of him looking at her as Paul had done the night he'd dumped her squashed any lingering optimism flat.

She ended the kiss and stepped away from him, clasping her hands behind her back lest they get any funny ideas.

'I don't see how anything's changed since last night,' she said. 'It was only a few hours ago.'

He set about unpacking the croissants and coffee, getting plates and knives. He'd even brought butter—real, unsalted French butter.

'I've been thinking,' he said. 'About what you said. But you can't just push me away without giving me a chance. I won't let you.'

He stopped what he was doing and looked at her, *really* looked at her. All of a sudden it wasn't Cameron the big-shot businessman looking at her, but an unsure boy, full of fire and doubt and insecurity.

Not fair.

She could resist the armour-plated persona, but not this…

The backs of her eyes stung. He had her heart already. What more did he want from her? To play with it for a while? To try it on for size to see if it fitted? No way.

The 'old' Alice, the Alice who had let Paul use her as his personal doormat, would have gone along with whatever the man in her life said in an effort to please him. And there was no doubt that pleasing Cameron at this present moment would reap some very rich rewards for herself too. It would be so tempting to just fall into step with him, to live a charmed life for a while, but 'new and improved' Alice—the Alice who had appeared in the last couple of weeks since she'd started working with him—who liked to push back against him, just wasn't ready to lie down and surrender.

Maybe because more was riding on this. She'd never felt this way about anyone else before, not even when she'd been running around after the men in her life, doing everything in her power to convince them she was worth staying around for.

Why had she never thought to ask herself if *they* had been worth the effort? She'd foolishly just pursued her dream of finding someone to love her without asking if they were capable of it.

This time she needed to know.

Because if she was just going to be Cameron's 'stopgap', until somebody better came along, she couldn't bear it. If she watched his interest fade while she ran herself into the ground trying to convince him otherwise, if he appeared one day with a sheepish expression and told her there was *someone else*, she would never recover. She couldn't stand thinking about him with someone else after he'd been with her. For the rest of her life she'd torture herself with images, thoughts of Cameron looking deep into some other woman's eyes as he had hers last night, of Cameron's hands on the curves of someone else's body. She had to protect herself.

She drew in a breath to steady herself, and was surprised at the way her body shuddered as she did so.

'Cameron…we just can't be together. We're from different worlds.'

He had it in him to dig his heels in hard, and she prepared herself. He was going to fling objections at her, and she was going to have to bounce them right back.

'Don't be daft. Your brother almost married Jennie. We were almost related once. Your parents are still on my mum's Christmas card list, for goodness' sake.'

Alice's shoulders sagged. She was just going to have to try another tack. But he just mowed down every roadblock she erected against him until she felt desperate, trapped. After half an hour of fending him off, both of them still firmly entrenched in their positions, Alice was exhausted and Cameron was rapidly losing his cool. Just as she thought she only had enough energy left to flop onto a stool and cry into the kitchen counter, an adrenaline surge hit her and she came out fighting.

Cameron watched her march to the back door and then march straight back again. Her breathing was fast and shallow, and he suddenly realised she was right on the edge of coping with this whole situation. To be honest, he wasn't far behind her. They were getting nowhere.

He'd never really seen Alice angry before—worked up, exasperated, but never shimmering with rage as she was now as she paced around her poky little kitchen. This wasn't going to plan at all. He'd been hoping to placate her, to make her see sense, but with every word that came out of his mouth she'd just hardened herself further and further.

'Give it to me straight,' he said, running his hand through his hair. He could take it—he hoped. 'Tell me why you won't agree to even one date. I just don't understand.'

She gave a dry laugh. 'I bet you don't. But I've got news for you, Cameron Hunter. There are some things you can't buy, and I'm one of them.'

'I don't want to—'

She flung her hand wide, sweeping past the

bag full of breakfast things that neither of them had touched. 'What's all this, then? And how about the dress? You think that you can click your fingers and everything will fall into your lap. But I'm not going to be yours just because you've made some spur-of-the-moment decision that I should be.'

Where was she getting all this stuff? Was that really how she saw him? Or was this just desperation talking?

Alice's pacing had brought her close to him, and he reached out and gently pulled her into his arms. For the longest time he just held her there, feeling her warm breath against his shoulder. And then, when he felt some of the tension released from her shoulders, he pulled back to look at her.

'I thought you knew me, Alice,' he said softly.

The stillness that followed, the sadness, was worse than her pacing and heated words had been. She reached up and touched his face, her eyes wet. 'I *do* know you.'

The last of Cameron's defences slowly slid into a jellified heap. Standing before her now, looking into her eyes, he felt as raw and unprotected as he had the first day the bullies had jumped on him.

His voice was patchy and low when he finally managed to speak. 'This is all new to me. I don't *do* this. I don't do begging. Why do you think I'm

here on your doorstep on a November morning?
I'm begging you to give me a chance.'

She looked so horribly torn he wanted to pull
her back into his arms and pretend he'd never let
the words out of his mouth. Her eyelashes swept
downwards and back up again, and one slow tear
rolled down her cheek.

'You don't know how hard it is for me to say
this…' She bit her lip and took a moment to regain
her composure, pressing her mouth into a crinkly
line and crumpling her chin. 'I'm an ordinary girl
and I belong with an ordinary guy. You…you
always need the best—of everything. And I'm
really not sure I can ever be that for you. Oh, maybe
you'd think that for a couple of months, but…'

He opened his mouth to deny it, but she pressed
a finger to his lips.

'Even if by some miracle I could be that for
you, I've come to the conclusion that maybe—'
Her voice cracked and she went very still. 'Maybe
you're not the best thing for me. I don't think
you're ready, Cameron. I don't think you've got
it in you to give me what I need.'

The tears were slipping down her face now.

'I so want to be wrong, but I don't think I am.'

He started to speak, but she silenced him again.

'I know you're growing, learning, but I've been
hurt too. I can't take the risk. It's all or nothing

with me, and I'm sticking to my guns this time. I won't settle for anything less. I won't settle for second best.'

He felt his jaw clench under her touch.

'You're calling me second best?'

He'd thought he had a lot to offer a woman, and he'd offered Alice even more than he'd realised he had, and she was still telling him it wasn't enough—*he* wasn't enough.

She hung her head. 'I'm calling it how I see it, Cameron. I'm just telling you the truth.'

He felt his anger like a physical heat. Even Alice must feel it radiating towards her. And then he turned and left. It was the only thing he could do to stop himself losing it completely. The front door banged so hard behind him it bounced open again.

He was livid. Maybe because it was easier to be rip-roaring angry than feel the rawness her words had caused.

Alice didn't think he was good enough.

She'd declared herself judge and jury and sentenced him. Completely unfair. He hated this feeling—had *always* hated this feeling—the sense that he'd been held up to some invisible measuring stick that he could never quite catch a glimpse of and been found wanting.

For years he'd managed to evade this sensation. He'd made sure everything he did and everything he built was designed to eradicate it. And now Alice was telling him he was *wrong* for having done that.

Even though it was Sunday he went to the new offices and stomped around a bit, made some phone calls and barked at people. Not that there were many people around to bark at. He had to go hunting, and then he found only cleaners and people from the staging company removing the last of the evidence of last night's festivities. It was all very unsatisfying. But slowly his anger cooled, leaving him with only a dragging feeling that made him think unaccountably of the tree at the edge of the cricket pitch at his old school—the one he'd climbed up to hide in when Fitzroy and his gang had been on the prowl.

Alice had delivered her verdict. He had to deal with that.

That afternoon and most of that evening he pondered what she'd said. And in the end, no matter how painful the admission, he'd had to admit she'd been right—partially.

He'd been so busy creating a perfect front to present to the world he'd forgotten it was just that—a front. And in his stupidity he hadn't paid nearly as much attention to the man inside the iron shell. Nobody else questioned it. Everyone else saw the hype he'd created about himself and was deluded by it. But not Alice.

The man she'd met again a few weeks ago hadn't been ready for a real relationship. He'd been proud, arrogant, completely up his own backside. But she'd changed all that. He wasn't that same man any more. Why was that? What had she done to him?

The answer popped into his consciousness like a random fact suddenly remembered—like when you racked your brains for an answer to a general knowledge question that you knew you knew but just couldn't recall. Then, days later, it would come out of the blue, while you were doing something mundane and totally unrelated, and you'd wonder how you could have forgotten it when the answer had been obvious all along.

He loved her.

He loved Alice. Every molecule of his being vibrated with it and he knew it was true—just the way he knew the earth was round, the battle of Hastings had taken place in 1066, and the tallest mountain in the United Kingdom was Ben Nevis.

And now he *knew* that he knew he loved Alice, he also knew that he was ready to stand by her side for the rest of his life. This was gut knowledge, not a flimsy scientific theory that would be disproved by the next bit of research. The certainty of it was like a rock inside him.

Ironically, he wasn't sure Alice was ready to hear it.

He wasn't the only one who was battling with a pursuing fear.

I've been hurt too...

Her words came back to him. Who had hurt Alice? Who could possibly hurt her?

Alice was sure what he felt for her wasn't going to last, so he was going to have to show her. And the only way he could do that was by being patient, by letting time drift on and gently showing her he hadn't changed his mind, that he still felt the same way. And if it took a hundred years, so be it.

The next morning Alice went to bring the milk in and found a large paper bag on the front step. A large bag that smelled of warm, buttery croissants and fresh coffee. She picked it up carefully and looked around. There was no sign of Cameron, just a black car driving away, almost out of view at the corner of the road.

There was a note inside. Short, to the point. Very Cameron.

Your verdict was correct. But I'm going to appeal...
In the meantime, please enjoy your breakfast.
When you're ready, I'll be waiting.
Cameron
x

Also very cryptic. He was going to *appeal*? What did that mean?

An identical bag was on the step the next day, and the next… Alice began to dread going to bring the milk in. On the sixth day she just got angry and left it sitting outside. What was he trying to do to her? Wear her down? Drive her insane?

If that was the plan, it was clearly working.

And she was angry with him. Very, *very* angry with him.

How dared he make her love him even more when she was so desperately trying to get him out of her system? It just wasn't right.

After three more days of the bag sitting on the step—and Alice giving very strict warnings to a hopeful-looking pair of housemates that they were dead meat if they touched it—there were no more deliveries. No more notes. No phone calls. Not even a text message. No more Cameron.

He'd given up. Just as she'd thought he would.

Now she hated him for proving her right.

Really hated him.

CHAPTER TEN

JENNIE breezed into her stepbrother's office and blew him a kiss. 'The place looks fab,' she said, then perched on the end of his desk.

Cameron dropped the folder he was holding and stood up. 'Where on earth have you been for the last month?' he bellowed.

She waved an elegant hand. 'Vegas… Here and there…'

Here and there? Give him strength! She'd abandoned him when she was supposed to be helping him with a key point in his career, and now she just wafted back in here as if nothing had happened? And what about this whole *eloping* thing? He'd been so worried about her he'd even toyed with the idea of hiring private detectives to find her. But she seemed fine to him—sitting on the edge of his desk, squashing a report from the marketing department. More than fine. He wasn't sure if he wanted to drag her into a bear hug or wring her neck.

Brotherly concern triumphed over outrage. He circled the desk and came to stand in front of her, looked her over for any sign that something was wrong.

'You're okay? Nothing's the matter?'

She gave him a bright smile. 'Absolutely fine. Haven't you noticed the wonderful tan? Got it in Acapulco.'

That was so Jennie. He'd been worried about her emotional well-being and she thought a great tan was evidence enough that things were all right. He gave her a rough squeeze and found he couldn't let go. She might drive him insane, but he was really glad to have her back.

She laughed into his ear. 'Hey! Are you okay, Cam? You're on the verge of turning python here...'

'Sorry,' he mumbled, and loosened his grasp. After giving her a gruff kiss on the top of her head, he stepped away.

Jennie narrowed her eyes and looked at him. Despite her flighty nature, she could be horribly perceptive sometimes. He decided to sidetrack her, as he didn't want a whole barrage of questions about the ball. Questions about the ball might lead to questions about Alice, and he wasn't sure he wouldn't give himself away.

After more than a week of coffee and croissants he'd realised that even that had been *pushing*, and he'd stopped. But doing nothing was killing him—even though Alice had made it clear she needed space. He was fed up with spending all day thinking about her, so when a thought popped into his head, providing a distraction, he latched onto it and looked his step-sister in the eye.

'So…where's this guy, then?'

She blinked innocently at him. 'What guy?'

He could still rethink the whole neck-wringing idea…

'The one you married?' he said, with just a tiny trace of impatience in his voice.

For a second Jennie looked bleak, and then the bright smile was back in place. She made a dismissive noise and gave him a delicate shove in the chest.

'Don't tell me you bought *that* old chestnut!' Then she started to laugh—right about the same time as Cameron's blood pressure began to rise. 'Really, Cam, you take things so literally sometimes!'

'Jen,' he said through clenched teeth, 'a message on my voicemail saying, "Sorry, hon. I'm off to Vegas to get married", combined with your sudden disappearance, would tend to make a man think that way.'

'Something's up with you, Cameron Hunter, and I want to know what it is.' It seemed he wasn't the only one who was good at using distraction techniques. She hopped off the desk and eyed him suspiciously. 'You've gone all soft and mushy.'

Hah! Soft and mushy? Try telling that to Stephanie. He'd been so unbearable in the last week that he almost expected to find her hiding under her desk every time he walked past it.

'It's Alice, isn't it?'

What…? When…? How did she *do* that? How did she see into his brain and know the things nobody else could see? He could have understood it if they'd been twins, or something, but they weren't even blood relations!

'I hear she did a good job in my stead—that you worked very closely together.'

The smile was sweet as honey. It was the one she used when she thought she might be pushing things just a little bit too far.

'I always thought she'd be much better for you than the likes of Jessica Fairly-Loves-Herself, or whatever her name is. So…' She leant forward and her voice dropped to a whisper. 'How are things going between you and the lovely Alice?'

Cameron flexed his knuckles.

'That well, huh?' she said in a dry tone. 'What did you do?'

He walked round his desk and dropped into his chair. 'I didn't do anything. I'm still not doing anything…' He launched into a bullet-pointed rundown of the whole sorry affair while Jen pulled up a chair and for once looked sympathetic, instead of like Little Miss Know-It-All.

'She says she wants to be someone's first choice,' he said finally.

Jennie reached across and stroked his arm. 'Nice cufflinks,' she said, looking down at where his sleeves protruded from his jacket. 'Unusual stones.'

He just nodded. He hadn't worn anything else since the night of the ball.

Jennie's voice was low and soft. '*Is* she your first choice?'

Cameron clamped his jaw together and nodded one more time.

'Oh, Cam,' she whispered, and came round behind him to give him a hug over the top of his office chair.

He stared into space and tried not to let the pain show in his voice. 'Seems I'm not hers, though.'

Jennie's arms squeezed a little tighter. 'I bet you are. In fact I've become a bit of a gambler since my break in Vegas, and I'd lay good money on it. You just need to prove it to her.'

He rolled his eyes. 'I've tried that.'

Jennie let go and gave him a soft clip round the head.

'Ow!'

'Not *your* way, you daft man! I could have told

you *that* wouldn't work.' She walked over to the window and stared out into the atrium. 'Hmm. I might just have an idea, though—although it'll take a little setting up…'

Cameron put his head in his hands.

God help him.

Three weeks after the fashion show Alice and Coreen signed a lease for the first ever Coreen's Closet boutique. Initially they'd been interested in one of the tiny shops that fringed Greenwich Market, and one had become available. It seemed that thirty pounds apiece for frilly white baby clothes that would ultimately get covered in pureed carrot had not been Annabel's best business idea. Her children's clothes shop had closed down a few days after the Orion ball.

The success of the auction that night had been astounding. Coreen and Alice had been inundated with e-mails and phone calls, asking when and where they were going to be selling their merchandise. People seemed happy to part with obscene amounts of money if the label or the fabric was right.

They were now going to open their shop on College Approach, one of the roads in central Greenwich that surrounded the market and was full of chic little boutiques. The plan was to still keep a section of the shop that appealed to their loyal market customers—funky retro clothes for good prices—but to expand the high-end section of the business, stocking designer labels from yesteryear and becoming a place serious collectors and fashionistas would seek out.

After they'd signed all the paperwork, Coreen convinced Alice to go for a drink in one of the local cafés. 'Who cares if it's only one o'clock in the afternoon?' she said. They'd done it! Gladys and Glynis need never fear the elements again!

Alice smiled and nodded, even though she didn't really feel like it.

All her dreams had come true. She'd left her IT business behind, passing it on to a friend of a friend who was happy to pick up new clients, and she was starting a new chapter in her life. One where she was her own boss, where every day would be filled with fabulous clothes, glitz and glamour. That was what she told herself every hour on the hour, anyway. Sooner or later it would work, and she would cheer up and remember how happy she was.

The café was busy—a favourite with local office workers on a Friday lunchtime—but under the hum of conversation there was a tone, a hint of a voice she recognised. She turned from where she was sitting on a stool at the bar, waiting for her table, and scanned the room. Just as she found the face she recognised, he turned to look at her.

She hadn't seen Paul in months, and despite the fact she'd been really sore that he'd dumped her she'd hardly even thought about him during the last few weeks. He gave her a nervous smile. Alice's gaze drifted a little to the right and she saw why. The dark-haired girl he was sitting with must be Felicity. It was hardly an easy situation.

But, to be honest, she really wasn't bothered.

Paul leaned towards his new girlfriend—well, his *old* girlfriend, really—and said something in a hushed voice. She glanced up at Alice, then nodded at Paul, and kept a sharp eye on him as he got up and headed for where she was sitting at the bar.

'Hi, Al.'

She smiled at him and discovered she didn't even have to fake it. 'Hi, Paul. How are you doing?'

He shot a nervous glance back at his table. 'Oh, you know. Fine.'

Alice looked him up and down. Nope. She couldn't remember what she'd seen in him. Not that he wasn't okay-looking, in a very ordinary sort of way.

'You look different,' he said. 'Nice.'

Did he *have* to have that faint edge of surprise in his voice? She did look nice today. Ever since she'd had to think about nicer clothes to wear to

Cameron's office she seemed to have discovered her own style—the old, comfortable clothes she loved mixed with a bit of vintage. Today she was even smarter than that, having had official business to attend to. She wore a forest-green jacket and a full knee-length skirt with a large funky floral print. Coreen had even produced a pair of green shoes from her famous wardrobe to match the jacket.

Paul squinted and rubbed the bridge of his nose. She'd found that quite endearing once.

'I…uh…just wanted to check there were no… uh…hard feelings.'

Something struck Alice, and she decided she did want one last thing from Paul after all. 'Paul?'

'Uh-huh?'

'Do you mind if I ask you something?'

He looked at her suspiciously. 'Depends what it is.'

How did she put this without sounding too nosey—or scary?

'Why did you decide to go back to Felicity? Really?'

Paul shuffled a little, and she could tell he was just about to say something very neutral to placate her.

'Come on, Paul. You owe me at least this.'

He pulled a face and looked over his shoulder at Felicity. 'I suppose I do.'

When he looked back at Alice she sensed he'd lost all notion of palming her off with a platitude.

'Well…I don't quite know how to say this without feeling a bit mean.'

She waved a hand. 'Honestly, I don't mind. Just spit it out.'

He blinked. 'It's not just your clothes you've changed, is it? Well, okay… You're a great girl, Al, really nice and everything. But you never once looked at me the way *she* looks at me.'

'Oh.' That wasn't what she'd been expecting at all. 'How *does* she look at you?'

Paul looked over at his girlfriend again. He caught her eye, and instantly Alice saw her whole face soften and come alive.

'Like she means it,' he said, without looking back.

Like she means it.

Alice couldn't get Paul's words out of her head. Late that night she lay awake in bed and tried to make sense of them. She thought of the way Felicity had looked at Paul. Had she never even once shone like that when *she'd* looked at him?

No. No, she hadn't.

Because she'd never felt that deeply for Paul, never felt he was her sun, moon and stars the way Felicity obviously did. She'd never felt that way about any of the men she'd been out with, not even with Tim, her first real serious relationship. She'd been devastated when he'd gone off with one of her friends without so much as an apology. But when she thought back on it now it seemed more that the rejection had stung rather than losing the man himself. After Tim she'd lowered her expectations, decided to play in her own league.

But that hadn't helped either. They'd still left. And for the first time Alice considered that maybe she'd had something to do with that.

What if all of them, like Paul, had sensed that she'd *settled* for them? Because she had. She'd only been fooling herself when she'd pretended she hadn't. They hadn't been the fantasy, but they'd been attainable—or so she'd thought. She'd kidded herself that it had been good enough, close enough to love to last. Only she hadn't fooled anyone but herself. Without exception her ex-boyfriends had moved on to girls who thought they were 'the one'. Some of them were even married with kids now.

At the time she'd just thought they were rats who'd gone where the grass was greener, but perhaps she'd been uncharitable. At least all but Tim had been decent enough to break up with her *before* they'd started something with the new women in their lives. Maybe they'd just fallen in love and then realised that their undemanding, safe relationship with Alice wasn't all it had been cracked up to be.

She didn't grieve for the loss of any of them. Not any more.

But Cameron was a different matter.

She'd loved him. Still did. He was the one man who, when she looked at him, she meant it. And she'd sent him away. Too scared to see if maybe he meant it too.

While she'd stayed in her safe little bubble, being baggy-jumpered Alice who nobody ever looked at twice, she'd had hope. Hope that maybe she had the potential to be more, the potential to be really loved. But if she'd tried—stripped off all her defences and really tried—and Cameron had still moved on, then she'd have been crushed, knowing that if it didn't happen with him it wouldn't happen with anyone.

Had she hardened herself too much? Pushed him away too hard?

If he'd kept on sending her breakfast she might have had had the courage to ring him up right now, no matter what time it was. But the croissants and warm coffee had stopped coming, and she had no idea what he felt or what he was doing now. If she really wanted to find out she was going to have to dig up some strength from somewhere.

I'll be waiting…

The line from Cameron's note replaced Paul's words on the loop in her head.

Was it too late? Was he still waiting? Suddenly she really needed to know.

Coreen's voice was so loud that Alice had to hold her mobile phone away from her ear.

'You need to get your butt up to the V&A, pronto. They've got a new exhibit in the fashion collection. It's fabulous—right up your street— and there's a little drinks thing and a private showing tonight, before it goes on public display tomorrow. Just give your name at the side entrance and they'll let you in.'

Alice had wondered where Coreen had been all afternoon, and now it was all starting to make sense. Until the shop opened just after Christmas they were continuing to run Coreen's Closet as an open-air enterprise. Monday was their day off after all the weekend markets. Personally, she'd already spent a long afternoon doing ab-solutely nothing, and could really use a distrac-tion from staring out of the window and thinking about Cameron.

She'd composed an e-mail to him ten times. She'd deleted it ten times.

Perhaps these things needed to be said in person. In that case she'd have to wait until tomorrow and see if she could wangle an appointment out of Stephanie.

Her heart went into overdrive at the thought. What if she'd been right? What if Cameron had moved on to someone else? Someone even more elegant and stunning than Jessica—if that were possible.

'Erm…*hello*? Earth to Alice!'

Alice jumped. 'Sorry! Just drifted off for a bit. Thinking about this V&A thing…'

'Of *course* that's what you were thinking about.' Coreen didn't sound convinced.

Alice decided to ignore the sarcasm and talk clothes. They'd rehashed the whole Cameron thing so many times now that even Alice was getting sick of hearing herself talk about it.

'What will people be wearing?'

'Pff! People…Who cares what anyone else is wearing? But vintage would be a good choice, given the opportunity to mingle with like-minded people.'

Alice picked up a stack of the business cards they'd had printed for the new shop. At least her professional life was going right; it was only her love life that had disappeared down the drain.

'I know,' Coreen said. 'The little blue mini-dress. The one with the matching jacket.'

It was a good choice, but Alice had something else in mind. It was high time she listened to her instincts and learned to choose outfits without

Coreen's input. Coreen might sulk about that for a bit, but she had known this day would come. In the end she'd be pleased to see her protégé had spread her wings and learned to fly.

The Christmas lights were twinkling as Alice stepped out of South Kensington tube station. There was a Victorian tiled underpass that led to the cluster of museums situated on and around Cromwell Road, but she'd decided on fresh air instead. It was seven o'clock on a clear night. Alice hadn't needed to check opening times or consult a map. Her grandmother had brought her to the Victoria and Albert museum many times as a child, and she'd loved to see all the fabulous jewellery, the things from far-flung places around the globe and the massive sculptures.

The fashion collection, specialising in *haute couture* down the decades, had always been a draw. Maybe that was why she'd fallen in love with the whole vintage clothing scene when she'd stumbled across it. She and Gran had spent ages inspecting each dress carefully, picking out which ones were their favourites and settling on the one that they'd wear to a ball, if they ever got the chance.

Alice sighed.

Would her dress be all right? Suddenly she was second-guessing her choice of a cute little short-sleeved dress, with its wide panels of black satin dotted with pink roses at the waist and hem. Was it a little too much? Well, too late now to run home and hide away in a baggy fleece. She'd just have to brave it out.

She ignored the grand entrance and made her way to a smaller one at the side of the building in Exhibition Road. A security guard merely smiled at her and waved her on as she walked through the revolving doors and told him why she was there.

Her destination was only a short distance from the entrance, down a flight of marble stairs, just off a long hall full of sculptures. Her heels clipped on the mosaic floor as she passed headless and armless statues, all male torsos, rippling with muscles and leashed strength. That made her sigh too. Why did everything remind her of Cameron? And she hadn't even seen him without his shirt off.

The only thing visible at the wide entrance to the fashion exhibit was a long, horizontal display case filled with shoes—embroidered seventeenth-century court shoes, buttoned boots in deep red leather, and sequined platforms all stood proudly side by side.

As she climbed the few steps to the entrance she slowed down. If this was a preview, with cocktails and canapés, where were all the people? Why couldn't she hear them talking or glasses clinking? Perhaps Coreen had got the time wrong. Perhaps she was early.

Her hunch was borne out by the fact that, apart from the lone guard she could still see on duty by the entrance there wasn't a soul in the place. She glanced at him, wondering if it was really all right to enter the room and go exploring, but he just nodded and gave her a little wink.

Although the vintage clothes were all housed in a vast domed room, it always felt very close, very intimate, because the lighting was kept deliberately low to preserve the wonderful fabrics. The central part of the room was closed off, only used for special exhibitions, but the main collection could be seen by walking the perimeter—long glass cases on each side of the walkway, displaying clothes of all kinds on headless white mannequins.

She'd never been here at night before, but far from being creepy, the added depth to the darkness only made the exhibits seem even brighter and more wonderful, each one illuminated by a soft spotlight. It was almost too good to be true to be here on her own, with no one to crowd her view, no one to hurry her along.

Well, okay, then. If she was early, she was going to make the most of it and take her time. She'd probably never have this opportunity again. Keeping an ear out for anyone else arriving, she started to circle the room, stopping every now and then to pay special attention to some of her favourite pieces—a shocking pink fifties ballgown with a stiff skirt, a 'flapper' dress in swirling silk with sequins and jewels and a court mantua, all creamy satin and exquisite embroidery.

At each 'corner' of the circular room there was a curved alcove where the display cases made a C-shape. A large octagonal glass case stood in the extra space. The first she'd passed had housed an embroidered Regency wedding dress. She approached the second octagonal case with curiosity. This must be it—the new exhibit. Only she couldn't see what was inside properly because the lights were out. She walked towards it, trying to make out what it was…

A dress of some kind, in a dark shiny fabric.

When she was just a few steps away the small spotlights in the ceiling of the case started to glow, shining brighter and brighter until there was no doubt as to what it contained.

Her dress. Her dark green bias-cut Elsa Schiaparelli dress. It said so on the card—even mentioned her name as the person who had donated it.

And her shoes.

Beside the dress, at the bottom of the case on a specially created stand, lit so the Lucite heels sparkled and glimmered, were her shoes. She crouched down and inspected the heel of the left shoe. She would never have known it had been snapped off if she hadn't been the one to do the snapping.

But…

The silence in the darkened gallery thickened. Alice held her breath and slowly straightened. Someone was here with her. But she didn't turn round yet; her brain was working overtime. The only person it could be—the only way to explain all of this was if it was…

Suddenly her eyes adjusted. The dress and the shoes blurred away and a reflection in the glass came into focus.

Cameron. Standing behind her.

Looking at her as if he meant it.

She spun around, still unable to breathe. He didn't move, just continued to let his eyes wander over her. Somehow he didn't look a bit like the Cameron she'd come to know again in recent weeks, but more as she recalled him from the past. He wasn't even wearing a suit. Just jeans and a long-sleeved T-shirt.

The clothes were just a symptom. As she stared back at him, remembering to squeeze and release her lungs, forcing air into them, she saw the real transformation. All the layers had been peeled away and he seemed younger, more vulnerable. His eyes, far from being blank and unreadable, were telling her all kinds of things. Things she could hardly dare to believe.

'You said you wanted an ordinary guy…' He shrugged. 'I think I've found you one.'

She shook her head. He would never be ordinary, and she didn't want him to be. He was Cameron. *Her* Cameron. A perfect fit.

But in another way what he'd said wasn't too far off the mark. He wasn't an untouchable god or an out-of-reach prince. He was just a man, with all his faults and flaws and fears.

And how she loved him.

He must have seen something of that in her eyes, because he stepped forward, more determined now, and ran his hands down her bare arms. After weeks of being deprived of his touch it was all that was needed to blast any remaining defences away.

'You're not perfect,' he stated slowly, a smile starting at the corners of his mouth.

'Not being very romantic here, Cameron…'

He laughed softly and pressed a kiss to her forehead. 'I don't want you to be perfect. I just want you to be you.' His lips didn't stop there, and he placed tiny kisses along her temple, across her cheekbone. 'Because I'm not perfect either, and I'm finally okay with that concept. I don't need to prove myself to anyone who will take notice any more.'

She wound her arms around his waist and pulled him closer. He didn't need to explain—she got it. They were both incomplete, stupid, and very, very human. And thank heaven for that, she thought, as he slid his hands around her waist and held her tighter still.

'I don't care if you're perfect or not,' she said. 'You're my Gilbert after all.'

His lips had been poised to place a kiss at the edge of her jaw and he paused for a fraction of a second. 'Your *what*?'

'Never mind,' she whispered back. 'Just shut up and kiss me.'

She decided she liked it very much when control-hungry Cameron stopped being habitually stubborn and did as he was told. She liked it very much.

It was such a relief, such a joy to be here with him, that she felt tears collect in her lashes. 'I'm sorry I pushed you away,' she said, her voice scratchy. 'I couldn't understand why you of all people would decide to keep me—the second-hand girl that everyone else had discarded.'

He kept her pressed up against him, but leaned back a little so he could focus on her face.

'Oh, I'm planning on keeping you for a long

time—as long as you promise to keep me back. You're the best thing in my lousy life, Alice, because you challenge me to be the best man I can be. Because you demand it of me. And up until now I've been too afraid to be that man.'

'Shh,' she said, pressing her fingertips to his lips, feeling her tears fall.

He shook his head gently to dislodge her fingers and they fell away. 'No, it's true.' His gaze softened and her breath caught. It was as if he'd just reached out and dived inside her. 'I'm going to keep you because you love me, Alice Morton…'

That was also true. And no amount of running away was ever going to change that.

'You love me the way I love you,' he said. 'With everything I can give—good, bad and in between. You've got it all.'

And he bent forward to deliver the sweetest kiss yet, one that made the room spin and her feet tingle. Alice kissed him right back, sensing in some way that they were marking each other as the other one's property. Finally she could let herself pour everything into her kiss, with no fear barring her from giving everything she had in return.

As always, they managed to say a lot of what they wanted to say, resolve a lot of things, without the need for words at all. Alice gave a deep, heartfelt, happy sigh and steadied herself against the glass display case. She was feeling decidedly wobbly.

'I'm glad you rescued my shoes,' she said, glancing away from him for only a second. 'They look happy here. I don't think they would have stood up to twenty-first-century abuse. I'd have hated to see them ruined.'

He smiled. 'And the dress? Do you want it back? I'll get it for you if—'

She shook her head and kissed his neck, right where his pulse was beating, and felt a surge of power at the shuddering response it produced in him.

'I'm glad about that too.' She smiled up at him. 'Anyway, I don't think I need it any more.'

His smile grew into a wide grin.

'I was hoping you'd say that, because I have another dress in mind. I don't care what style it is, whether it's new or old, but I do have one stipulation…'

She chuckled. 'You're not going to go all *Cameron* on me again now you've got what you want, are you?'

A flash of the old arrogance returned. 'Of course I am. You wouldn't have me any other way.'

He was right. Who would want anything but this wonderful, determined, romantic, *thick-headed* man? He was definitely a keeper. She lifted onto her tiptoes and kissed him. She seemed to be doing a lot of that tonight. Oh, well…

Then she realised she'd been sidetracked and pulled away. 'What sort of stipulation?'

She'd expected him to laugh, but he pulled her close and breathed into her ear in a rough voice. 'Like I said… I don't mind if it's long or short, fancy or plain, old or new. Just as long as it's white. And I have to warn you, it comes with matching jewellery.' Suddenly he got all serious, took a few deep breaths. 'That means I'm asking you to marry me, if you hadn't worked that out yet.'

Alice threw her head back and laughed. He didn't do *subtle*, did he, this man of hers? When she stopped laughing, he was looking puzzled.

'That's a *yes*, if you hadn't worked it out yet.' She smoothed his forehead flat with the pads of her thumbs. 'But I have a stipulation too.'

A flash of fear glittered in his eyes and she kissed it away.

'Don't make that face, Cameron. Can't you see this look?' She paused and let her eyes do the talking. 'This is the look of a girl who's fallen in love and isn't about to fall out again.'

Cameron answered her with a delicious kiss, and as he pulled her closer still she whispered in his ear. 'I love you, Cameron Hunter. But about this jewellery… Let's be clear about one thing—I'm not wearing a tiara for anybody. Not even you.'

He just laughed, picked her up, and waltzed her round the empty gallery.

ROMANCE 2-in-1

Coming next month

BETROTHED: TO THE PEOPLE'S PRINCE
by Marion Lennox

Marrying His Majesty continues. Nikos is the people's prince, but the crown belongs to reluctant Princess Athena, whom he was forbidden to marry. He must convince her to come home…

HIS HOUSEKEEPER BRIDE
by Melissa James

Falling for the boss wasn't part of Sylvie's job description. Yet Mark's sad eyes intrigue her and his smile makes her melt…before she knows it this unassuming housekeeper's in over her head!

THE GREEK'S LONG-LOST SON
by Rebecca Winters

Self-made millionaire Theo can have anything his heart desires. There's just one thing he wants – his first love Stella and their long-lost son.

THE BRIDESMAID'S BABY
by Barbara Hannay

Baby Steps to Marriage… concludes. Unresolved feelings resurface as old friends Will and Lucy are thrown together as best man and bridesmaid. But a baby is the last thing they expect.

On sale 2nd October 2009

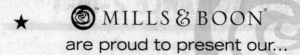

MILLS & BOON®

are proud to present our...

Book of the Month

★ Expecting Miracle Twins
by Barbara Hannay

Mattie Carey has put her dreams of finding
Mr. Right aside to be her best friend's surrogate.
Then the gorgeous Jake Devlin steps into her life…

Enjoy double the Mills & Boon® Romance
in this great value 2-in-1!

Expecting Miracle Twins by Barbara Hannay and
Claimed: Secret Son by Marion Lennox

Available 4th September 2009

*Tell us what you think about
Expecting Miracle Twins
at millsandboon.co.uk/community*

millsandboon.co.uk Community

Join Us!

The Community is the perfect place to meet and chat to kindred spirits who love books and reading as much as you do, but it's also the place to:

- **Get the inside scoop from authors about their latest books**
- **Learn how to write a romance book with advice from our editors**
- **Help us to continue publishing the best in women's fiction**
- **Share your thoughts on the books we publish**
- **Befriend other users**

Forums: Interact with each other as well as authors, editors and a whole host of other users worldwide.

Blogs: Every registered community member has their own blog to tell the world what they're up to and what's on their mind.

Book Challenge: We're aiming to read 5,000 books and have joined forces with The Reading Agency in our inaugural Book Challenge.

Profile Page: Showcase yourself and keep a record of your recent community activity.

Social Networking: We've added buttons at the end of every post to share via digg, Facebook, Google, Yahoo, technorati and de.licio.us.

www.millsandboon.co.uk

2 FREE BOOKS
AND A SURPRISE GIFT

We would like to take this opportunity to thank you for reading this Mills & Boon® book by offering you the chance to take TWO more specially selected books from the Romance series absolutely FREE! We're also making this offer to introduce you to the benefits of the Mills & Boon® Book Club™—

- **FREE home delivery**
- **FREE gifts and competitions**
- **FREE monthly Newsletter**
- **Exclusive Mills & Boon Book Club offers**
- **Books available before they're in the shops**

Accepting these FREE books and gift places you under no obligation to buy, you may cancel at any time, even after receiving your free shipment. Simply complete your details below and return the entire page to the address below. You don't even need a stamp!

YES Please send me 2 free Romance books and a surprise gift. I understand that unless you hear from me, I will receive 5 superb new stories every month including two 2-in-1 books priced at £4.99 each and a single book priced at £3.19, postage and packing free. I am under no obligation to purchase any books and may cancel my subscription at any time. The free books and gift will be mine to keep in any case.

Ms/Mrs/Miss/Mr_____ Initials _____

Surname _____

Address _____

_____

_____ Postcode _____

Send this whole page to: Mills & Boon Book Club, Free Book Offer, FREEPOST NAT 10298, Richmond, TW9 1BR